THE DESERT WALL

Raf Morgan

Book one of The Divided World Series

Books by
Raf Morgan

The Red Fortress (coming soon)

Writing as
R. Morgan

A Case of Plague (coming soon)
The Adventures of Roció Díaz Rossi and Hala Haddad Sosa (coming soon)

THE DESERT WALL

Raf Morgan

To my family.

1

Malenie was hiding. The sun burned hot and brilliant on the white plaster and dull adobe houses, banishing the shadows from even so narrow an alley. Sweat prickled along her hairline. She leaned against the wall, its grit rubbing off on her back, and tried to stop panting. Fear and humiliation made a hard fist of her stomach, urging her to run again. Only two streets over, the market hummed with activity, promising safety.

"I hate them," she whispered, though she wanted to shout. After almost a moon without trouble she had been careless, and now here she was, with at least one bully somewhere behind her. But a cactus never has just one spine, and bullies never travel alone. She tucked her black hair behind her ears, pressed closer to the house and crept forward. She peeked around the corner, thinking, *Please.*

The boy was so close she smelled fennel and anise on his breath as they both recoiled. "Told you," said the tall girl with him, stepping forward, forcing Malenie back into the alley. Malenie's heartbeat seemed to shake her whole body, demanding that she fight or run. Run or fight. The boy followed, straightening his shoulders, trying to look bigger, and glanced at the older girl for approval, but she didn't notice. Pursing her lips, she looked Malenie up and down. "Where you going, Orphan?"

The insult stung. "I don't want to fight," Malenie said, knowing it was the wrong thing to say even as she said it.

"She doesn't want to fight," mimicked the boy.

Malenie took a deep breath, letting the anger build up and push everything else aside, and screamed, "Rot you!" in the girl's face, using the noise as a weapon. The girl flinched back, and Malenie whirled, catching a glimpse of the boy's shocked expression, and pelted back the way she had come. She burst out of the alleyway, almost colliding with the skinny rooster of a boy who was the worst of the bullies. He flinched back and she dodged around him, rage flaming up at the sight of his four friends. Cowards. He shouted in wordless triumph and they closed in on her. Head down, she charged, as the camels did in the races, hoping they would scatter. They didn't. Her heart pounded in her ears. The bullies' jeers were still louder.

At the last moment she swerved, intending to slide through the gap between Rooster Boy and a house. She almost made it, but he grabbed her long, straight hair, jerking her head back. Pain seared her scalp. He stuck his foot between her ankles and tripped her. She fell, scraping palms and knees, and her attacker landed on top of her, knocking the wind out of her lungs, his grunting breath loud in her ear. The others hooted, urging him on.

Malenie elbowed him under the ribs as Nes had taught her and he rolled to avoid her. Tears burned her eyes as she wrenched her hair free and jumped to her feet, but she blinked them back. She'd never cry in front of them.

Rooster Boy and his friends crowded Malenie against the house. The boy and the girl from the alley jostled for space in the tight circle around her, but otherwise the street was empty. As usual, adults were never around when she needed them.

She glared at Rooster Boy, hoping he saw only her anger. His tightly curled hair, sculpted into a crest, bobbed each time he moved. "Where you going, Red?" he sneered, without getting too close, yet. She had taught him that caution in past fights, but that had been one on one, or two or three, never seven.

To cover her fear, she showed him the back of her hand, fingers pointing up, an obscene gesture that said exactly what she thought of him. Rooster Boy cursed her, fists clenched, looked at his friends to see if they were laughing at him and caught sight of one of the half-wild dogs that scavenged for food in Trader Town. He narrowed his eyes and Malenie's stomach flipped over. She knew that look.

"Hey, you ever notice Red here is the same color as the dogs?" His friends nodded energetically. Their skin was brown-brown, black-brown or gold-brown; in Trader Town only Malenie and her papa had an undertone of red to their brown skin. Enough travelers passed through that Malenie knew she wasn't a freak because of the color of her skin, but that didn't matter to them. She was different, and that was enough.

"Are you a dog, Red?"

"Do you eat trash, Red?"

"Hey, when are the slave takers coming for you?"

"Is that what happened to your Ma, doggie?"

"Shut up!" She jumped at Rooster Boy, fists swinging, and clocked him in the mouth. He fell back, howling, and she darted through the opening he gave her, stretching into a run, her knuckles stinging.

"Get that little dog!" Rooster Boy yelled. "I'm going to grind her face in the dirt."

Malenie ran faster. They'd done it before, but they weren't going to catch her again today. She raced down two more deserted streets and across the dusty north-south road, jumped over the empty irrigation ditch and startled a flock of chickens scratching in the long grass under the fruit trees. The Wall that bordered the eastern edge of Trader Town beckoned. Malenie didn't slow until its shadow touched her, and she smacked into it with enough force to rock her head back and bruise her forearms. It didn't matter. She was safe.

Since her friend Nes had started ignoring her, the Wall was Malenie's only refuge. The mica studding its surface flashed in the sunlight and drew her eyes, but no one else's. The townspeople never went close or touched it. Although it was only the height of two men, no one climbed it to find what lay on the other side. Whenever Malenie had tried, dizziness loosened her fingers and she fell.

Propped against the massive, rough blocks a shade paler than the gravelly dun desert, she waited for her heart to slow. The bullies ran past on the road in a cloud of dust, still shouting "little dog, little doggie!" They sounded muffled and far away even though she could have pitched a rock and hit them easily. Their eyes slid away from the Wall and Malenie in its shadow, looking anywhere but directly at it. She patted the stones as she would a friend and heaved a breath of relief as the bullies turned back into town and their shouts grew fainter.

"You're the dogs, except that's an insult to dogs everywhere," she muttered. "Go fight each other and leave me alone for a while." She pressed the back of her neck against the cool stones and the sick tension of the chase drained away, though a different anxiety replaced it. She pulled her cuffs past her wrists, inspected her indigo sleeves for rips, straightened her collar and twitched the legs of her trousers into place.

It was bad enough she was motherless, friendless and a Parthavian, with a physician for a father in a town full of Thessem guards and bandits, but if anyone ever saw Malenie's real secret, she'd never, ever have a hope of fitting in or having any friends.

Last she squeezed the bag at her throat. Meant to hold small coins, it also protected a gold chain that had belonged to her mama. Moons ago Malenie had slipped it out of the cedar box that held Papa's keepsakes and sewn it into the seam. It was the one thing she couldn't lose, the one thing neither Papa nor she herself would forgive losing. Especially since he didn't know she had it. Malenie wiped the sweat from her forehead, wishing she could wipe the bullies' insults away as easily. *At least I didn't have to fight this time.* Thinking about it didn't change anything and she still had to buy lunch for Papa.

Trailing her hand over the uneven stone and the fuzzy green vines clinging to it in places, Malenie followed the Wall to the market. Papa said the the north-south trade route and the western road met here because of the wide pools of fresh water spreading out from beneath the Wall. Eventually the meeting place had become a market and then Trader Town.

Malenie crouched to slurp water cold enough to make her teeth ache and then reluctantly turned to the marketplace. Travelers and residents thronged the narrow paths, carefully not stepping on the wares displayed on the sun-bleached squares of fabric on the ground. Malenie's slow scan didn't pick out any lurking bullies, so with a last pat to the Wall, she stepped out of its shadow. Suddenly she was noticed again; a neighbor shouted a greeting, a peddler shoved a packet of bone needles under her nose and a dog sniffed at her shins. She ducked under the edge of an orange awning that was flapping loose and found Steph, a big dark woman with dozens of thin braids wrapped around her head.

Steph relieved her two almost-grown sons of their trays of fresh pies and sent them for more with an affectionate swat. "Don't dally, now," Steph called after them.

Malenie's stomach rumbled at the smell of bread, pork sausage and cumin. "Steph, two, please," Malenie said to her back. "And good afternoon," she tacked on for politeness.

"As always." Steph's usual smile turned into a frown when she looked at Malenie. "You're late. And dusty." She dropped a pie, which broke on the counter, pulled out a wet rag and swiped at Melenie's face. Malenie ducked but took the rag. It was warm on her face and smelled slightly of lemons.

"If those were my kids, I'd give them a beating they'd not forget. No," she said over Malenie's stutters, "don't lie and say they weren't chasing you again today. Just because some people prefer to close their eyes and pretend they don't see, doesn't mean I do. Your pa is a sun-addled fool, even if his healing is the best thing to happen to this town. I don't know what he's thinking."

"I don't want him to worry." Avoiding Steph's eyes, Malenie folded the rag and put it on the counter.

"It's his job to worry." She shook a callused finger in Malenie's face. "No more 'Please, Steph, I'll handle it.' You need to learn how to ask for help sometimes. Everyone does. But since you won't, I'm talking to your pa tonight. Now that Nes isn't..." Steph pressed her lips together angrily. "Filthy slavers," she muttered. "Anyways, I owe your pa for saving my littlest. Not telling him what I see is no way to pay him back."

"Yes'm." Malenie shut her mouth on her protests. There was no stopping Steph once she dragged in her baby's health and the debt she felt she owed Papa, never mind she had paid in good coin. Dread churned Malenie's stomach and she hunted for a topic to distract both of them. "So, uh, what's new?"

Steph fixed Malenie with a stern glare. "This is not the end of it. But, since you asked, and it might cheer us both up, Salla's goat birthed twins and a few doomsayers proclaimed it an omen. Salla just laughed and said she got two for the price of one, and didn't she deserve some luck?" Her voice lightened as she rattled on and started to enjoy her gossip. "Remember how that boy broke the tannery's spell stone?"

Malenie wasn't likely to forget since it was Rooster Boy. The others had mostly left her alone while he worked off the cost. All of her muscles tightened at the thought of evading him day after day while delivering Papa's medicines.

Steph was saying, "The stone shaper still hasn't figured out how that boy broke the spell stone. But the shaper fixed up a new one to sniff up the fumes finally, and that's a blessing for all of us on the north side." She pushed aside the broken pie and rested her elbows on her counter to impart the last bit of news. "A runner came in last night. No matter what else you say of that Gravin, he always lets me know when my husband is coming home from a job. The caravan's expected to arrive late this afternoon. Eight moons Jak's been gone, past Pashtin, all the way to the Outer Cities." She deftly slid two hot pies into a basket Malenie was expected to return and tapped her on the hand. "You wait for my oldest to walk you home. He'll be back quicker than a goat can eat a burlap bag, and then you and your Papa can enjoy your lunch."

◊◊◊

Papa looked up absently as Malenie walked through the doorway and blocked the main source of light in their little house. He had a smudge of soot across one cheekbone, but his white turban was elegantly wrapped and pristine, a sure sign he hadn't had any emergencies today. "Lunch already?" He set aside the mortar full of astringent-smelling heartcure and wiped his long elegant fingers clean on a scrap of old tunic.

"It's late, Papa, didn't you notice?" She set the basket down and kissed his cheek. "Did you make enough medicines to dose the whole town?"

He checked the shadows in the yard, which were already stretched and long. "Two days without emergencies is a gift from the seven hundred gods and goddesses that I couldn't neglect." He stretched his back and teased, "And no one in this house has ever been late, or even forgotten to buy our lunch altogether."

"And someone else in this house will never let me forget it," she said affectionately, "even though I never forget to deliver the medicines." The thick mud walls kept out most of the heat, and Malenie peeled her tunic from her skin, flapping it to funnel some of the cooler air under it. "I know how finicky the—"

"What's this?" He touched her shoulder, his fingers slightly sticky on her skin. Craning her neck, she spotted a short tear in the seam.

"I didn't know it was there. I'll fix it." Escaping the sudden sharpness of his regard, Malenie closed the curtain across the alcove where she slept and changed into her spare tunic. Usually he reserved that look for his patients. When she emerged, Papa took the ripped one from her without a word and mended it with quick, neat stitches. She could have done it, but it made her feel safe, in a way she couldn't explain, to have him do it with the same meticulousness he used to set bones, wrap bandages and tap the healing drum.

Papa said, "Malenie, you have to—"

"—be careful," she finished. "I know." She busied herself washing her hands and then moving his books. Like many of the things in their one-room house, the table had been offered in payment for Papa's services by a grateful merchant. The thought of replacing their rope-strung table with a 'proper' one of solid wood had pleased Papa so much he hadn't been able to refuse, even though it was worth far more than the healing.

As they ate the spicy pies, Papa relaxed enough to ask about her day. She repeated Steph's gossip but not her intention to visit. "Gravin's caravan is arriving soon. I'm going to watch it come in."

Papa finished chewing and frowned at her. "I hope you know enough to stay away from Gravin," he warned. "He's a dangerous man."

"I don't care about him," Malenie said, tossing her hair back. "I want to see his caravan. They're always the biggest."

"There's a reason for that." Papa put down his lunch. Usually he was a little vague, almost always thinking about several things at once. Now all his attention was focused on Malenie again and it made her squirm.

"Papa, everyone knows he's a bandit, as well as a merchant."

"Just because half the men in this town are sometimes bandits doesn't make it right. They kill and rob Gravin's rivals to make him richer. He wants to be an important man, with all of the privileges and none of the duties." The lines around his mouth deepened and he pushed aside the scraps of his pie. "And there are rumors he's involved with the slavers."

"Papa—"

"I won't stop you from watching the caravan come in, but be careful. No, be smart. And keep your sleeves down." Malenie bit her tongue to keep from mouthing the last words along with him. Instead she gave him a peck on the cheek and dashed outside.

Nes, Nes's sibs and their goat were in their yard next door, so Malenie swung on the gate and waved, hoping this time Nes would acknowledge her. Nes had changed when her pa left, gotten surlier and closed off. After her cousins were taken by slavers and her aunt and uncle went looking for them and never came back, she had thrown herself into helping her ma, making soap, taking in the neighbors' wash and caring for her sibs. She stopped talking to Malenie. Malenie had cried her confusion to Papa, who counseled patience, saying everyone dealt with grief in a different way.

Days and moons passed, and Nes stayed away. The bullies had started heckling Malenie, then throwing things and finally closing in for real trouble when Nes didn't come to her defense. They cornered her not too far from home and Malenie was getting ready to give up pride and scream when Nes appeared. She knocked the biggest bully to the ground with one hard blow to his head and the rest scattered. Then, without saying much, she taught Malenie every dirty trick she had learned from her pa, how to hit and how to break holds. Every day they met behind the tannery at the edge of town to practice, their eyes watering and burning from the smells that were too powerful even for the spell stones to sniff up entirely. On the eleventh day Nes didn't show up, or any day after that. Malenie went back for ten more days, hoping, but that was the last time Nes spoke to her.

She knew Nes must be worn-out-exhausted with work and a huge ache inside, much bigger than the emptiness Malenie felt for the mother who'd died when she was born. Emptiness like that could swallow you, and because of it Malenie hadn't stopped trying to be Nes's friend.

Nes's youngest sister waved to Malenie over the goat's back, but the older ones copied Nes and ignored her. Malenie watched them for another moment, pushing down the hurt, before walking away, swinging her arms to show she didn't care.

She beat the caravan to the center of town, but not the rumors that it had been sighted. Standing on the low wall that separated the pools from the dirt of the market square didn't give her the best view, especially as peddlers and shoppers crowded against her, but with the water at her back, no one could sneak up on her. The kids that jumped up next to her ignored her, but out of excitement, not meanness.

"It's here, it's here," one squealed.

"Twenty-five camels," the merchant in front of her counted. Malenie leaned to the side to see around him.

"That's not possible," his companion said. "How'd he manage? The longest train I ever saw was fifteen and I heard they bribed the bandits with half their goods to let them pass without bloodshed."

Camels bawled and the crowd rippled to accommodate the arriving caravan. The two men were jostled away from Malenie's perch, and she caught glimpses of dusty guards, a robed pilgrim, and camels and horses, which were an exciting change from goats, dogs and pigs. She pushed up on her tiptoes and gasped. One of the horses carried a rider with reddish skin, a pointy nose and a turban just like Papa's. Malenie gawked until Steph's husband Jak stepped in front of her and blocked her view. His black fighters' braids had come loose from the nape of his neck and brushed his shoulders. Pale scars marred his leather vest, which had been new when he left.

"Jak, who's that Parthavian?" she demanded. She and Papa were the only Parthavians living in Trader Town, though there were more, in real cities like Pashtin, where the first Family was even Parthavian, or in the far away Outer Cities. "And why aren't you saying hello to Steph first? The line for your wages is over there."

"Eh, now, that's a nice hello," Jak rumbled. He frowned down at her, solid and solemn. He never changed, no matter how far he walked away before walking back. "Since you asked, I came looking for you with a warning. That Parthavian is a mean one, so don't be catching his attention. If he sees you, he'll be noticing you—you're like a wee red chick in a flock of brown ones." He tweaked her nose, just like he'd done since she was little.

Malenie batted his hand away too late and pretended to glare at him. "I'm not so wee any more."

"Promise," he said.

"I do." She sighed and stepped down out of sight. "Will you tell me about your trip later?" she asked instead of the hundreds of questions he'd provoked.

"Of course." The crowd parted around him and then closed back up as he waded away, leaving Malenie with a fine view of a bunch of backs.

"Well, this is useless," Malenie said and slipped behind a few loaded camels as they were led away. Half the town would be betting against the other half on what was in the odd-shaped bundles. She tried to guess the cargo by its shape. It didn't smell of cinnamon or cardamom and it was the wrong shape for bolts of silk, linen or cotton. Once Gravin had brought a whole caravan of spell stones to punish their local shaper for something. The shaper had lived off clandestine charity for two years while Gravin sold spell stones at inflated prices, and everyone bought them, they were that scared of him. But the bundles didn't look right for spell stones, and there was an odd sharp smell she couldn't identify.

Down a side street, Malenie glimpsed the Parthavian man again, head bent as he spoke to the stranger who had exclaimed over the number of camels in the caravan. She scudded past, and they never looked around. At the open ground between Trader Town and Gravin's compound, where she had no way to remain unseen, she gave up and turned for home. The shadows stretched long and the sun was low and red in the sky. In town, poor man's lanterns—tiny flakes of rock like mica that drifted on the wind and were collected by the poor—flickered to life on lintels and along rooflines. The occasional lightcrystal, made by a shaper, shone brightly from a wealthier house. Although Malenie was hot and thirsty, the thought of Steph telling Papa exactly how badly Malenie was taking care of herself slowed her steps.

2

Two broad horses smelling of grass and sweat were hitched to the gate in front of Malenie's house, taking up most of the street. She gawked at the lines of their muscles and fragile-looking legs. Their ears swiveled towards her as she crept forward, wishing they were hers, that she and Papa could ride away. Light from a neighbor's house caught on their dark brown coats, black manes and soft noses that seemed to invite petting, and Malenie didn't even wonder what they were doing there until something crashed loudly inside. She jumped; the horses's ears swiveled the other way. She didn't recognize the voice of the man cursing.

"How dare you. Get out of my house," Papa demanded in a controlled voice. "What are you—get your hands off me!" Pottery shattered as if someone were throwing all of Papa's pots against the floor. Malenie rushed forward in dismay.

"My med—" Papa's shout ended in the smack of flesh against flesh.

As she reached the gate someone pinned her arms to her sides and dragged her away. She kicked back and her heel slammed into the person's shin. Nes swore in her ear, and Malenie's breath rushed out in a gasp of shock and relief and frustration all mixed together.

Malenie sucked it back in. "Let me go." She struggled a little less violently. "I have to get to Papa."

"Shut up." Nes pulled her into the shadows between the neighbor's houses. "There are two more men on the other street."

"I don't care." Malenie broke free, but Nes recaptured her and twisted Malenie's arm behind her back. Nes's hold was firm and her muscles hard from pounding wash.

"Listen to me," Nes said. "That's too many for us to fight."

"Then we have to—"

Papa stumbled into the yard, pushed by a stranger with Papa's precious lightcrystal in his fist. Malenie bit her lip. Papa's turban was loose and some of his hair was showing. She looked away in embarrassment, then forced her gaze back. The stranger grabbed a coil of rope from his horse, looped one end around Papa's hands and tethered the other end to his horse's saddle. A groan escaped Malenie, and Nes clapped her hand over Malenie's mouth. A second man exited the house with a bag over his shoulder. He crossed to the chicken coop and pulled out a laying hen. The bird hung calmly from his hand, stupefied by its upside-down position and the evening hour.

I'm not any better. Malenie shook Nes's hand away. "We have to get help," she whispered urgently. "Get your ma."

"My ma can't do anything against men like that," Nes said but loosened her hold so Malenie could turn to face her.

Malenie dug her fingers into Nes's arm. Up close, Nes looked older, almost like a grown woman. "Then get Jak, he'll help, and I'll follow to see where they go."

"And if they work for Gravin? What is Jak going to do then? Lose his job?" Her bristly shocks of hair bobbed as she shook her head. She looked over Malenie's head. "Ancestors."

Malenie spun around. Both men had mounted their horses and set them walking. The rope jerked tight and Papa staggered behind them. Her hands got cold and only Nes's hold kept her upright. Her lungs stuttered as she dragged in enough air to say, "Death's ashes, Nes, let go."

"Listen to me." Nes's voice was flat and intense. She bent close and her breath puffed across Malenie's face. The scent of the palm oil she used to soothe her skin was weirdly familiar after so long. "They'll be real glad if you jump into their arms." Malenie started to shake. "They'll put a slave collar on you and they'll sell you and you'll have no hope of helping your pa. You got to—" Footsteps scuffed in the gravel behind them. Nes shoved Malenie hard. "Run!"

Malenie staggered. Nes shouted and a man cursed angrily. Malenie righted herself, turning to help Nes, and came face to face with the Parthavian as he stepped around the house. Behind him, Nes fought fiercely with yet another man. The Parthavian smiled. She'd seen men smile like that before they picked a fight they thought they couldn't lose.

She ran, choosing a direction randomly, missing the turn to Steph's house in her panic. The soles of her feet burned in her thin sandals. Breath sobbing in her chest, she passed an alley and glimpsed a group of men drinking and laughing by a brightly lit doorway. The Parthavian was too close to double back. Her scream was so faint she barely heard herself.

At the next street, she turned and turned again. *Those men will help me. They will. If I can get to them.* The words repeated in her head in time to her heartbeat. The street curved the wrong way, leading her further into town. She ran faster, bouncing off walls, and burst into the market. A dog slunk across the square. Where was everyone? It wasn't that late. Still running, Malenie searched for someplace to hide in its empty expanse.

The Parthavian's footsteps slapped against the ground behind her and his hand brushed her arm. Her feet made the decision for her and she darted towards the Wall. His fingers tangled in her hair and her head snapped back painfully. Ridiculously, she thought, *Not again. Stupid hair, stupid religion.* She fell against him, her elbow jab bouncing off his ribs.

Turning, she struck for his throat. He dodged. Malenie grabbed her hair above his fist and jerked against his hold. They both tripped over the low rock wall around the pool and tumbled into the chilly water. Rough sand abraded her elbows as she hit the bottom. She twisted, kicking furiously, and the shock of connection ran up her leg.

He lost his grip and she floundered backwards. The bottom sloped abruptly down beneath her and the pool swallowed her. Water filled her nose and mouth and she flailed, grabbing for anything, even the Parthavian, to save herself from drowning.

Her head broke into the air and her hands met the solid blocks of the Wall. She stilled, blinking water from her eyes, knowing he wouldn't be able to see her anymore. She looked up. Met his eyes.

He saw her, saw the Wall.

No! He can't see me. Gasping in shock, she pulled herself sideways, bruising her cold hands on the rock, and slipped. Water closed over her head. She forced herself deeper, away from him. In the light blurring through the water she saw a thicker darkness, an unexpected absence, near the bottom. An opening.

Strength born in terror propelled her into a narrow black tunnel. It led under the Wall. Her shoulders scraped the sides and she jacked her legs in, dreading the feel of his hands on her ankles. Lungs aching, she fumbled her way through. The darkness thinned. The water seemed to push her up. She found the air and drew in great gasping breaths.

She was on the other side of the Wall.

◊◊◊

The other side of the Wall was dark and smelled of rotting garbage and roasting peppers. Malenie gagged and covered her nose. The water murmured around her in reaction to her movements. As her eyes adjusted, she picked out the shape of a market square and buildings against the starry sky. She was in a town, but its smell stones and lights must have gone missing. Two men shouted somewhere and stopped. Malenie startled and looked over her shoulder. The Parthavian wasn't behind her, not in the pool, not scaling the Wall. He was too big to get through the tunnel, even if he saw things others didn't.

He can't find me. But I have to hide.

Absently, she adjusted her sleeves and scratched one wrist and then the other as she waded out of the pool. She rubbed her chest. The itch flared into hot prickles that spread across her ribs, circled her waist and rushed down her legs. Even her toes itched. It felt like a whole colony of fire ants stinging her. Frantically, she tried to scratch everywhere at once. It didn't help.

And then she began to glow.

A faint blue light filtered through her clothes at wrist and elbow, ankle, knee and hip, around each shoulder and below her collarbones, brighter and brighter. Every place marked by her secret deformity lit up, as if making itself visible for anyone to see, her nightmare made real.

"No. Get it off!" She whimpered, scratching furiously, desperate to escape herself, and willing to peel her skin right off to do it. The light intensified. She was a human lightcrystal, lighting up the night around her.

"Don't be afraid, lads," a man ordered.

Malenie swung around. Men with flickering hand lamps and cudgels surrounded her. The light was too confusing for her to make out individual faces, but their attention and animosity made her neck tighten. It was too much. Panicked, she ran, staggering, straight into one of them and bounced off. He looked huge from the ground, his face warped by the same fear gripping her.

His fist filled her vision. Her head rocked back in pain and all the lights went out.

3

Seven hundred gods and goddesses, where am I? Malenie's head ached, front, back and everywhere in between. A gag cut into the corners of her mouth and her tongue felt swollen and dry. She wiggled in alarm, knocking herself in the chin as she felt at her neck for a slave collar. Her neck was bare, but her hands were tied together. Her head thumped onto the tile floor in relief and pain blazed sharply again.

She blinked up at the ceiling until the pain lay back down. Bunches of dried herbs and flowers hung from its dark wooden beams, the numb-root tauntingly out of reach. Sunlight slanted through the open pattern of bricks of the ventilation lattice high on the white plaster wall. It was day; her clothes and hair were dry, but the desert air drank moisture like a thirsty man sucks down water when he finds an oasis, so that didn't tell her much about whether it was morning or evening.

Thinking about her clothes reminded her, and she inspected her arms with the same suspicion she shook out her bedclothes at night to dislodge scorpions. Not a hint of blue light or the secret under her clothes. Her body looked normal, the same one she had woken up with…yesterday?

Voices murmured beyond the door. Alarm surging through her, Malenie bent her knees and wrenched at the knot around her ankles. Her fingernails were too short. She scanned the pantry for a knife, too late. A key scratched in the lock and the door swung wide. In the opening a very young man hesitated. He looked like anyone she might see in Trader Town, his skin as brown as hers without the red. Geometric patterns were shaved into his hair like the ones that had been popular in Trader Town a few years ago. Only the crisp orange ribbon tied around his left arm was odd.

They stared at each other, and he swallowed hard before stepping slowly towards her as if approaching an animal he didn't know the temper of, as if she weren't the one tied up. Indignation rose up for a moment and then she remembered the blue glow under her clothes. Fear soured her stomach in its place. His hands were clammy as he fumbled the rope off her ankles and pulled her to her feet.

"Move," he said. Even though he spoke the Trade tongue, she felt as far from home as a person could get and still be alive. He pushed her past gleaming copper pots in an empty kitchen into the next room. Between a row of low tables, two men waited, both with orange ribbons on their arms. The first was old, at least Papa's age, with different patterns in his dark hair. His grip was firm as he took hold of her.

"Wait outside," the second said to the young man who'd untied her. This one was older still, with gray hair twisted up and wrapped in wire. No one wore their hair like that in Trader Town. His expression didn't change as he examined her. Malenie looked away, but the rich blues and browns of murals depicting robed pilgrims and crowded streets dizzied her.

"Well?" asked the older man.

"She's marked, Patriarch. She was screaming when they found her, glowing and trying to scratch her own skin off. Alone. She's probably not sane. She's definitely not safe."

"I am sane," Malenie tried to protest, but the gag muffled it and the men ignored her.

The dark-haired man continued, "None of the other Families have reported missing any children."

"Which marks?" the Patriarch asked. The one holding her slid his hand up her arm, pulling her sleeve with it.

"No." Malenie wrenched free and stumbled away. They caught her easily and shoved up both her sleeves, exposing the secret she and Papa had hidden all her life.

Bitterly, she stared at the tattoo-like lapis-colored diamonds, points touching, like manacles around each wrist and elbow, the size of her smallest knuckle of her smallest finger. She'd been born with them; they were under the skin; she had tried and tried to scrub them off when she was younger and had only rubbed her skin raw.

"She has thirteen sets of marks, Patriarch, at each major joint. Only the joints on her hands and feet are unmarked." Malenie flushed hot and trembled as she understood they had looked at her while she was unconscious, pushing aside her clothes. They had no right. She struggled against the casual strength of their hands.

"So many?" The Patriarch let go and began to pace. "I've never seen so many."

What? Malenie stilled. *He's seen these marks before? I'm not the only one?* She didn't have time to think what that meant; he was still talking.

"And no one's come forward to claim her?" He didn't wait for an answer. "This will mean delay, messages to all the Families, while the town panics. There's not an arm without a ribbon on the streets of Raleton already. It's a pity so many saw her, or we could have—" he cut himself short and stared at her, but his eyes looked through her to the problem she represented. The dark-haired man's grip pinched tighter and tighter, but Malenie didn't dare move. "I would rather not delay so long. But I don't see any other option. We can't deal with this on our own."

"But there'll be riots! No on has forgotten what happened in Suntin."

The Patriarch shook his head. "I know," he said. "But there's nothing—"

"I wish they had never caught her!"

The Patriarch's head jerked back. "What have you—" Malenie followed his gaze. Her breath caught, and time stretched.

Light sparked at the center of each diamond, spilling to their edges as a thin film of water spreads in a shallow pan. Malenie blinked rapidly as more light shivered through her clothes, the color of the sky in the morning before the harsh sun paled it. *What's happening?* The light burned, and she shook with the pain. Her ears roared, the sound of her blood pulsing through her veins magnified a hundred times.

She looked back up and saw her captors' faces, their horrified and awe-stricken expressions, go dim and gray. Blackness closed her vision in.

"—done?" the Patriarch finished.

Time snapped into motion and the world rushed back. Her head thunked against dirt.

Sunlight dazzled her, and shadows. Noise deafened her. Her stomach roiled with vertigo and the onslaught of new smells. The room, the two men, the light, the pain were gone, and her body ached with weakness and hunger as if she had run from one end of Trader Town to the other without stopping. Five times.

The gag was gone, and when she raised her hands to press her palms against her eyes, she realized the ropes were gone, too. She blinked, and the dark blurs became barrels stacked around her that—by the slightly putrid sweet smell—held barley liquor. The noise rolling over her separated into the sounds of a market in full spate.

The frantic clucking of chickens bound for the pot evoked a sudden fellow feeling, and she hastily levered herself up to peer over the nearest barrel. Brilliantly dyed clothes bewildered her eyes, some indigo like her own, but more saffron or cream, and orange, like the ribbon on the old auntie peering at her now. No, the woman's filmy eyes were blind and her head was cocked to listen.

"Who's there?" the old woman asked. "What was that noise?"

"I, I fell, auntie," Malenie stuttered. She didn't understand what had happened, not anything since she'd seen Papa tied up yesterday, but she would not be captured and tied up again. Everything else had to take second place. She pushed away the thought of the blue light, the memory of pain, the mystery of her arrival here and focused on one thing: escape. The question of where she would escape to could wait.

Right now, right here, she needed to fit in and for that she needed…. She looked around quickly. It was true, everyone wore a ribbon. "The boys chased me and took my ribbon." Her voice quavered and she let it go high like a child's, letting all the anguish of the last day help her story.

"Come here, let me touch you." The ancient woman gestured and Malenie put her hand out timidly. But nothing strange happened when the woman groped Malenie's arm, measuring the width of it. "We can't have that, and I thought you might be small enough to share mine. My great-great-grandson is generous—and scared, for the last glowerer destroyed half my grandson's cattle with half of Suntin before they could stop her." As she spoke she slipped the knot from her ribbon and, with the scissors tethered to her belt, cut off a length, which she tied around Malenie's arm with an elaborate knot. She handed Malenie the larger piece. "Careful of the knot, it's important to get it right." Malenie concentrated on tying it exactly as the woman had.

"That's it," Malenie said when she finished. She held her breath while the woman tested it with calloused fingertips.

"You're a good girl." She patted Malenie's hand. "Stay away from those boys."

"Thank you, auntie. I will." Prompted by guilt, she added, "Blessings on your family," before she walked away.

Luckily, it seemed no one else had noticed her sudden arrival, half hidden as it had been behind a stack of barrels. Malenie pulled at her sleeves with more deliberation than usual, and touched the bag at her throat. The necklace was a comforting weight but otherwise the bag was empty. She'd given the extra coins to Papa. No money for food. She had to think what to do next.

Those men, the Patriarch and the other one, seemed to know more about her than she did. They thought she was a danger and they wouldn't give up searching for her. The market was bigger than the one in Trader Town and it would be easy to disappear in the confusing maze of wooden stalls, beige awnings and crowds. Especially as there were plenty of Parthavians mixed in with the Thessem—like Jak, Steph and most of the people in Trader Town—and a few lighter skinned Hennites. Malenie stepped into the flow, but couldn't help gaping at the women with long straight hair and the men in turbans.

A woman balancing packages cursed as she pushed past and an elbow poked the soft spot above Malenie's hip. She shifted away and suddenly felt light hands at her neck pulling on her coin bag. Her head pounded with anger, all the stronger for her earlier fear. *This is too much.* She grabbed a hand and hauled on it until a face popped out of the crowd. Surprise loosened her grip. The boy could be mistaken for her younger brother. A dirty rag wrapped his head in place of a turban and his too-large tunic hung off one bony shoulder. Their eyes met, and his widened. He jerked his hand out of hers. With the same motion he sliced the thong of her bag with a razor hidden between two fingers. He threw himself backward, bag in hand, and ran.

Mama's necklace. Malenie felt like he had slashed his razor across her heart. Shoving and pushing, she chased after him, forgetting she wanted to go unnoticed. The boy slipped through the crowd, barely disturbing the flow of traffic, like a scorpion burrowing in the sand, displacing only a few grains behind it. But Malenie's legs were longer. He was almost in reach when he dodged sharply to the left and wormed through a gap between two stalls. She squeezed in after him, stretching, and grasped his sleeve. He wrenched free and burst out the other side. By the time she clambered through he was gone. Malenie turned frantically in a circle, searching for him.

Behind her, a date seller started screaming abuse. "Sun-rotted thief! Get out of there. I'll have the guard on you!" His stall shook, shedding dates, and the boy slipped out the other side. Malenie sprinted after him. Dates squished and slid under her feet as she ducked the merchant's grab. Saliva flooded her mouth at their sweet smell.

The thief ran between two tall, dark buildings with white triangles painted along the roofline and white arches above the windows and doors, very unlike the one-storey sand-colored houses of home. Malenie's legs dragged. She was slowing down, too tired and too hungry. He disappeared around a corner. She called up a desperate burst of speed and reached the next street in time to see him fling open the woven brush door of a small house. Irregular sections of plaster were missing on these smaller houses, giving them an abandoned look. No chickens scratched in the dirt. No wash hung on the crooked fence. It must be his hideout.

Malenie rushed inside, shouting, "Give it back!" and came face to face with four angry boys and girls about her own age. "Ashes." She dove for the door. A fifth girl, another Parthavian and the biggest of them all, planted her feet in front of it and folded her arms across her chest. The brass knuckles on her right hand looked heavy enough to break bones. Her stare dared Malenie to try to get by.

"Right, I'll just stay awhile, then," Malenie muttered.

"You're useless! You let her follow you," a boy shouted behind her. Malenie turned. The oldest boy threw Malenie's bag at the thief and smacked him viciously. The thief staggered back. Blood welled in a slice across his cheekbone. The leader smirked and showed his palm and the heavy ring there, turned inward and wet with blood.

The thief flipped up the back of his hand and the leader's smirk disappeared.

Veins stood out on the older boy's forehead. He shouted, "If you want to trade with us—"

"Maybe I don't want to," the thief snarled back.

Everyone was focused on the argument and not looking at Malenie. Slowly she sidled backwards at an angle to the door. *Maybe I can get behind the Parthavian girl. Even if it means leaving Mama's necklace*, she thought, anguished. *For now.* Plans to recover it rushed through her head: she could wait outside, follow either the leader or the thief and fight them one on one.

"You came crawling to me."

"I never! It was a fair trade—"

The Parthavian girl uncrossed her arms, head tilted as she listened. Malenie was almost even with her.

"—think you're so high and mighty—"

"That's not what you said before," the thief flung back, chin high and nostrils flaring. He was brave, if not very smart. Malenie felt a pang of empathy. She'd been in his place often enough.

It doesn't matter, Malenie reminded herself. *It's all his fault anyway. It's time to go.* She lunged for the door. A shove to her back sent her spinning to the floor in the center of the room. She rolled as Nes had taught her and, on her feet again, slammed the heel of her palm into the big girl's chin—not the vulnerable nose. Malenie didn't want to kill anyone. It hurt, but the girl crumpled, and Malenie whirled to find who had shoved her.

The biggest boy of the bunch stepped out of the corner where he had been lurking. He swung wide, strong but slow, and she ducked under his arm, trying for the door again, even though she knew her chances were better if she knocked him out in a way that kept him out. He hooked his fingers in her tunic and pulled her straight down. Her head smacked into the dirt floor. "Ow, ow, ow," Malenie gasped and went limp.

The big kid rolled her over like she was a baby, twisted her arm behind her back and ground his knee into her spine. Malenie sucked in dust as she struggled to breathe. Two sets of hands patted her down, efficiently searching for more loot, and stripped off her ribbon. She'd had it for such a short amount of time.

"Nothing," announced a voice above her head.

Are they more or less likely to let me go now?

"I told you she wasn't worth trading with, Deek," the Parthavian girl said. She sounded muffled, as if it hurt too much to open her jaw properly. Good.

"Shut up," said the thief. "I am too worth trading with."

She's a girl? In a turban? Malenie twitched in surprise and the bullyboy pressed harder on her arm. She froze.

"You shut up." The leader turned away dismissively. "Who is she?" Malenie grunted in pain as the bullyboy yanked her head up by the hair. The leader and the Parthavian girl stared at her. The others hovered behind, nervously looking from Malenie to the leader and back again. Except the thief. Her lips shaped a silent 'oh' and the clotting blood on her cheek cracked. Malenie glared back defiantly through the tears leaking from her eyes.

"Dunno."

"Never seen her."

"I don't recognize her," the Parthavian girl said. Malenie swallowed hard. *What now?*

"Look at her arm."

They all looked down. The blue diamonds around her wrist were fully exposed. Malenie jerked her arm to her chest.

Slowly, the leader said, "She's got to be the glowerer everyone's been talking about. Do you know what this means?"

The Parthavian girl backed away, pulling a smaller boy with her. "Deek, you better turn her loose. If they find her with us…I don't like to think what they'd do." Malenie looked at the thief, who shook her head frantically, attempting to communicate something.

"Don't be such a cowardly rotter. Don't you see? We found her. That makes her ours." Deek darted forward and jabbed his fingers cruelly into her shoulder. The bullyboy twisted her other arm, holding her in place. "Give Paza blisters on her tongue!" A hysterical laugh hiccuped in Malenie's throat. It died as they stared expectantly at the thief.

Nothing happened. The thief scowled at the leader and said, "Deek!"

"I wish Paza had blisters on her tongue!" Deek yelled.

Malenie yipped in pain. It felt like needles were poking her all over. The thief yowled. She stuck out her tongue and crossed her eyes trying to see it.

No. Malenie closed her eyes in denial. Willing them to see clearly, she opened them. The thief's tongue was covered with huge distended blisters. One burst, spilling yellow liquid. She whimpered and clawed at her head.

"Gross," one of the other girls whispered.

No, oh, no. Malenie thrashed wildly. "Shut up, shut up. Stop it!" she screamed.

"I wish I had a sword," he said, ignoring her.

They all looked around, even up at the ceiling, and Malenie quieted as nothing happened. *It's a hallucination, from hunger or from getting knocked out. It is.* She kept her eyes away from the whimpering thief.

"What is this rot, you sun-rotted glowerer? What are you doing?" Deek demanded.

"Everyone knows it don't work that way." The Parthavian girl seized Malenie's other arm, almost wrenching it from the bullyboy.

Malenie bit her lip, refusing to whimper. She felt like the favorite toy of rough two-year olds.

"It's gotta be something live. I wish..." The girl stuttered to a stop, apparently overwhelmed by the options or stumped by the limits.

Malenie didn't care. She whispered, barely moving her lips, "I wish I was home safe and everything was back to normal." She held her breath and closed her eyes. Opened them again to the dirt floor. "Then I wish I was back in Trader Town… I wish I was back in this town's market."

Deek pushed the Parthavian girl. "You going to do something or just stand there in the way?"

"I'm thinking." She shoved him back.

"Think faster." They started shouting insults in each other's faces. The bullyboy's grip on Malenie's hair eased and she pressed her forehead into the floor. A sob shook her. *Rotting useless…. And crying is useless, too.* One more sob scraped its way out of her throat. She gulped down the rest and tried to think.

Footsteps whispered behind Malenie, light familiar hands touched her neck, and the thief murmured above her head. Magic pulsed through Malenie and the bullyboy released her arm and removed his knee from her back. Malenie sat up. Her hands were shaking. Her everything was shaking.

Finger to her lips, the thief crouched in front of Malenie. The bullyboy was sitting next to her, rubbing his head and looking around dazedly. The thief tucked herself under Malenie's armpit and levered them both up. The rest of the gang was too intent on the fight to notice them creep to the door and nudge it open. They slipped out.

The thief paused to tie the door to the frame with a bit of hanging rope before pushing Malenie down the alley. Malenie hobbled as fast as she could. Her vision blurred and her stomach turned over sluggishly like she might puke.

They were passing the last crumbly house when Deek howled, "You stupid rotters. Find them." His gang yelled angrily and the door splintered apart with a loud crack.

"Uhnnkey balls," the thief cursed, and lisped something Malenie didn't understand.

Malenie's bones ached and the air turned blue. Pain licked at her skin. Black dots burst in front of her eyes. They fell, missed the street, and slammed into a roof.

4

Malenie stared at the pale sky, stunned by more than just the fall. Magic. In a person. Not in a spell stone, a slave collar or a blanket made by a shaper. *In me.* She tried the thought out: T*he diamonds are magic. I'm magic? Impossible. Except…*

The thief bent over Malenie and pointed to her tongue. Malenie scrabbled away. When the thief didn't follow, Malenie sat up and looked around. They were on a flat adobe roof. In front of her, two narrow windtowers, which funneled cooler air to the rooms below, stretched higher than Malenie's head. Behind her, the lip of the roof cast a thin slice of protective shade where nutmeg, mint, fenugreek and purgewort struggled to grow. And past the neglected herbs, adobe rooftops with narrow windtowers stretched out in every direction, finally giving Malenie an idea of how big this town was. Big. Way bigger than Trader Town.

The thief gestured urgently. "Lemme tuss you."

"Death's ashes, no." Malenie shook her head vigorously. A headache clamped down, and she stilled. "I don't want anyone coming near me ever again. You could do anything."

"Ick hurcks."

Malenie wrapped her arms around her knees. The blisters looked painful and foul, especially with her tongue hanging out like that. *Nothing in this garden will heal those.* The habit of helping Papa help others was strong. *I should say yes. She could help me, too.* But this was more serious than tending a patient. Malenie was vulnerable. She didn't want to be used by anyone else.

The thief growled in her throat and the crease between her eyebrows got deeper. Malenie uncoiled, readying for an attack. They stared at each other. Finally the thief fumbled with a purse under her tunic and drew out the stolen necklace. "Peaf?" It glinted gold in the sunlight. Malenie felt like someone had put a finger on her heart. Involuntarily, she rocked up on her knees. The thief placed it on the roof between them and nudged it towards Malenie.

"Oh," Malenie said in a soft voice and picked up the peace offering. Her bag was gone, so she fastened it around her neck and fingered its flat links. "Please don't wish for anything else," Malenie said and tensed, waiting for it to hurt.

The girl nodded and shuffled forward. She touched Malenie with the tips of her fingers, whispering, her face screwed up in pain. Gentle warmth flickered softly, almost soothingly, through Malenie, and the other girl slumped in relief.

"Let me see," Malenie demanded and the girl stuck out her healthy, pink tongue. It was unremarkable once more. Malenie scooted backwards. "I don't understand. Why does it only work sometimes?" she asked herself out loud.

The girl sat up straighter and surprised Malenie by answering. "Don't you know nothing?" She wrinkled her nose scornfully at Malenie. "It only works on things that are alive, you can't use it yourself, only someone touching you can, and they have to say it the same way every time."

"Then it's rotting useless." The bubble of hope that had been growing in her chest shattered into jagged pieces, erasing Malenie's image of marching into Trader Town and rescuing Papa by pointing her fingers and making wishes. She rubbed her hands over her face and tried to pay attention.

"And if it hurts someone else, you'll feel the pain, too. And if the magic is too big that'll hurt." A little kid screamed shrilly in the street and both girls flinched.

Paza—that was her name, wasn't it?—peered over the edge of the roof, keeping her head down so no one below would notice her. "Just some kids playing." When she turned back the expression on her face was a mix of longing and distaste, quickly smoothed away.

"What else do you know about it? And how do you know so much?" Malenie asked, leaning forward.

Paza backed away and shrugged. "I only know what everyone knows about glowerers. Everyone knows. You got to. There ain't—isn't much else to say. If you have the marks, you have the magic. If the wish is too big or you do too many, you can get hurt, or dead." She paused and added, "It runs in Families."

"Families?" Malenie bit her lip. *Papa would have told me. He would have. And I know he doesn't have them.*

"Where did you come from?" Paza asked. "Everyone's saying you were trying to poison the market pool. You know they hang people for that."

"I was not," Malenie said. "I'm not a, a bandit."

"What were you doing then?"

"I was lost."

"You're a terrible liar," Paza accused her. "You weren't poisoning it, but you're not from here and none of the Families are visiting Raleton. You ran away," she tested, watching Malenie's face. "No. You were kidnapped." A longer pause. "No. Your Family sent you here, you flew, you fell out of the sky, you came from the other side of the Wall—holy gods and goddesses," she breathed.

"What? No—how do you….How could you guess that?" Malenie scrambled up and then thought better of getting any closer to Paza. She settled for planting her fists on her hips and trying to loom.

Paza raised her eyebrows scornfully. "Everyone knows there are Gates where the Families go through the Wall."

"I didn't know that."

"But you don't even know about the Families, do you?"

"Nooo."

"You don't know anything, really."

Malenie sat with a thump and pressed her hands to her head, trying to squeeze her headache away. "I guess I don't."

"You look worse than camel spit. What's the matter with you?"

"You mean besides being chased, tied up, beaten up and sat on by a whole gang that wanted to use me as their own personal wishing pool?" Paza snorted a laugh through her nose. "I'm hungry," Malenie admitted, though her hunger pangs had long since turned into nausea and exhaustion. "I haven't eaten since yesterday. I think."

"Me, too." Paza eyed her. "Will you let me use your magic to get us food?" she asked in a rush. "That's what I was going to trade your necklace for, but using your magic will be even better. We could have a real feast," she added wistfully.

Malenie eyed Paza's skinny arms and the sharpness of her bones under the skin. Her own lightly muscled arms looked plump in comparison. "What would you do?"

Paza stripped a handful of leaves from the nutmeg plant. "Use the magic to make these look like coins."

"But that's stealing." Malenie snapped her mouth shut too late to stop the words, but Paza just narrowed her eyes. *It's wrong, and it's stupid to trust her.* Her stomach gurgled around its emptiness. *And I'm going to do it anyway. It's life and death, right? For Papa. For me.* She nodded abruptly.

Paza barely touched her. The faded leaves flushed bright green, then gold crept in from the edges of one and silver and bronze for the others. They shimmered, the ridged ovals contracting into circles and half circles, and Paza cupped a handful of coins.

"Wow." Malenie poked them. They rattled like coins and felt hard and slick like coins. Paza pulled away and dumped them into her purse. "Hey, how do I know you're coming back?"

"If you keep insulting me I won't. But I said I would, so I will."

Malenie rolled onto her back and tried to think what she would do if Paza didn't return and how to rescue Papa and what everything meant, but it was warm and she was lightheaded and tired. She drifted off to sleep. She woke to the smell of chicken roasted with lemon and mint and Paza plunking down sturdy clay bowls of plump dates, creamy thick yoghurt, shiny red pomegranate preserves and steaming dark tea that smelled of citrus and smoke.

Malenie's stomach clenched painfully as she tore off a chicken leg. The skin crunched under her teeth and the rich taste of the meat on her tongue woke up her hunger. "Mmm." She couldn't eat fast enough, and neither could Paza.

By the time Malenie's stomach ached from being overfull instead of empty, Paza was running her finger along the bottom of her bowl and licking up the yogurt dregs. "What?" She glared at Malenie. "This is the best yogurt I've ever tasted." She popped her finger in her mouth and sucked on it.

"This is the best everything I've ever tasted." Malenie tried not to let the pity show on her face. The food was good, but hunger made it taste better. She nibbled the last of the flesh from a date pit and assessed her companion, who was now licking up the last of the pomegranate preserves. "Why are you wearing a turban?" she asked.

Paza rubbed the back of her hand over her mouth. "My hair is gone. I—he sold it, and now it won't grow back. It's been years."

Malenie ducked her chin to hide her shock. Parthavians were not allowed to cut their hair, girls or boys or adults. It was one of the rules all seven hundred gods and goddesses agreed on and they didn't agree on much. The body was sacred, all of it. "What did they want your hair for?"

Paza's eyes were enormous in her thin face. "I don't know. I don't— Why are you so rude?

"I'm not usually rude. But my papa…" She wrapped her arms around her knees.

"Did something happen to him?"

Paza had shared something personal. Malenie could reciprocate; it was too much to keep inside anyway. "Yeah. Some men took him away tied up like he was robbing caravans in the desert." She shrugged. Her eyes burned, but she refused to cry. "Before I could get help another man chased me and I wound up here and I haven't stopped running since. For a little bit I thought I could, you know, use the, um, thingy," she was not quite willing to say 'magic' out loud, "to rescue him, but you said I can't do it, by myself anyway. So it's useless and I still can't help Papa." *Magic should be good for something. For me, not just everyone else.*

"Maybe we can help each other," Paza said, holding very still. Her voice was intent, and excitement and anger mixed on her face, making her look a little crazed and feral. Malenie got her feet under her, ready to jump away if Paza decided she wanted to use the magic without asking. "I'll help you make the magic work so you can find your papa, but first you have to do something for me."

"What?" Malenie asked. *It's going to be bad. I can just tell.*

"We have to kill a man," Paza said flatly.

"No!" Malenie jumped up and backed towards the edge of the roof. "Stay away. You are crazy! You said I would feel any pain wished on someone else. Your blisters hurt me and that's tiny compared to that." She shuddered. "And wrong!"

"I didn't mean with magic. And it wouldn't be wrong. You don't know—but I can't help you unless we stop him."

"Stop who from what?"

All the expression disappeared from Paza's face. "I can't leave," Paza said. "If I leave, he'll know and he'll hurt my family. What's left of them." Malenie sat down, her knees weak. "I know he'll do it," Paza said. "He killed my sister. He'll kill the rest of them, or worse."

Each time Paza said "kill" Malenie flinched. "Who?" she whispered.

Paza fidgeted with her turban. "This man, he snatched me from my family. He has a, a crew of kids, all of them taken from their families. That's why I could stand up to Deek, they all know I'm a part of his group, and they're afraid of him. I have to do something about him so I can help you. If I'm gone…" Now she was all pleading sincerity.

"How can I trust you?" Malenie asked, unwilling to feel like nothing more than a tool in another's hand. And in truth, more than a little afraid of what kind of tool this reckless brave girl would make her. *But who else is there?*

"I don't know. I don't know if I'd trust me either. But I stopped Deek—he would have hurt you, hurt a lot of people if he kept you. And I gave you back the necklace." That had felt like a promise. "How about this: my first wish will be that only the wishes you agree with will work."

"That's smart," Malenie said.

Paza leaned in like someone might overhear. "They hunt for kids like you. Like the Suntin girl. You need protecting and help."

"The Suntin girl?" The Patriarch had said that name. The old woman in the market had said it too, with fear.

"She was like you. She got snatched—like me—and used for her magic. She destroyed half of Suntin before…"

Malenie listened to the noise of the city around her. Its dangers seemed far away, but even so she didn't feel safe on the roof. She carried danger with her, everywhere she went. It might be a trick. She might be lying. She considered Paza, who was picking at the blood on her cheek. She did seem to know a lot about what was happening. Things Malenie needed to know. *Everything she's said so far made sense. Partial control is better than no control. Better than just anyone being able to use me and the magic.* That reminded her. "Why is everyone wearing orange ribbons? Is it because—because of me?" Paza's sleeve was tattered and patched, but she wasn't wearing one. None of the gang had.

"Yeah, but it's just a superstition. Nothing will protect against the harm someone like you can cause," she said bitterly. It didn't sound like something she'd say to get Malenie to help her. That decided her.

"Do you swear that'll be your first wish?" Malenie asked.

Paza nodded and touched her fingers to her lips, the same oath they made at home. "On my dead sister," she swore.

"Do it." Malenie crouched near her and held out her arm, ready to leap away.

Paza stayed seated, touched her fingers lightly to Malenie's skin and said, "I wish that—what's your name? I wish Malenie has to agree for the magic to work." Blue light lit up the bones in Paza's hand through the skin. Swallowing hard, Malenie rubbed her arms as the tingling faded. It was still so unreal. Paza asked, "Can I wish that he can't hurt my family?" Malenie nodded. "I wish that man can't hurt my family." Nothing happened. Paza jerked back like she had been slapped, but her hand clamped hard on Malenie's arm. "Why didn't you agree?" she shouted, her face almost purple with rage.

"I did!" Malenie shouted back. She frowned, thinking about the times the magic had worked. "Maybe it was too vague?" she guessed more calmly. "All the other wishes were very specific."

"Sorry," Paza said roughly and dropped her hand. The angry color faded from her cheeks. "I don't know his name. We just always called him the man in the blue robe. I can't be more specific. I was picturing him in my head, but I guess that's not good enough."

Malenie chewed her lip while Paza stared at her feet, shoulders hunched. "What if we were looking at him?" Malenie suggested.

Paza raised her head. "It'd be awfully dangerous."

"Freeing Papa might be, too. I don't even know who has him. I'll need your help."

"You'd really do that?" Paza asked. Her shoulders relaxed a little.

"Yes," Malenie said decisively.

"All right!" Paza spit in her hand and held it out to Malenie. "Deal?"

Malenie copied her and they shook on it. "Deal."

5

Malenie and Paza crouched next to a warehouse. In other parts of
Raleton, lamplight spilled from doorways and ventilation lattices, and
people carried hand lanterns that smelled foully of old, burning animal fat. But these buildings had few windows, and the stout wooden
doors were locked up tight. The city made Malenie's hometown seem
like a temporary desert camp. They had walked through four markets
surrounded by houses of all different sizes, past a merchant's quarter
where the buildings were hidden behind high walls, and down streets
lined with warehouses for longer than it took to cross Trader Town
from one end to the other.

No one had paid much attention to them through the city, but in this
isolated area they were as noticeable as spots on a camel, so they were
waiting four buildings away from the one Paza said belonged to the
man in the blue robe. Malenie's imagination failed as she tried to picture the man Paza hated enough to want to kill. He must be a monster.

"There," Paza said in a strangled whisper. Malenie followed her
pointing finger to a man rounding the corner. She couldn't see much,
just the glow from his lantern across fine indigo robes and the lower
half of his face. He didn't look evil. He looked like a merchant, and not
even a smug self-satisfied merchant. He looked like someone's uncle.
Raising the lantern, he illuminated the door in front of him and all of
his face.

Malenie bit back a gasp; he could be her uncle or Paza's. She hadn't
said he was Parthavian or that his long black hair fell down his back
without a ripple or a kink. Malenie turned her eyes away, hotly em-

barrassed. She had never seen a Parthavian man without a turban. It was as if he were walking down the street naked; as if he had invited strangers in to pray at his family altar. Papa's hair was never loose; maybe a few strands escaped after an exhausting stint at a sickbed, or his turban tilted askew, but never like this.

Paza's cold hand clenched tight on Malenie's shoulder. Malenie waited for her to do something. The man took out his key and turned it in the lock. They had to act now. Malenie poked Paza hard. "The wish," she hissed.

"I know," croaked Paza. Malenie pressed both palms to the ground for luck. "I wish this man can't hurt my family," Paza choked out and the blue light flared like a torch. He startled and looked right at them, meeting Malenie's eyes. And he still didn't look evil.

Pain stabbed through Malenie's skin to her bones "Paza," she managed to whisper before the scream came. Paza's face was terrified and her mouth moved but Malenie couldn't hear over the roaring in her ears. Then something was in her mouth, blocking the scream, and she clenched her teeth against the taste of blood. The pain grew splinters to jab her eyes. She couldn't see. Her silent screams echoed in her head.

◊◊◊

"Ugh." Malenie spat blood. She probed her face and scalp for its source, but she seemed to be in one piece, though her eyes weren't focusing properly. As they cleared, she realized they weren't by the warehouses anymore. They were in a market, the one by the Wall, the pale awnings flapping in the night breeze. Sitting up, she called softly, "Paza?"

"Here."

Malenie's neck creaked as if she were a thousand years old. Paza was hunched forward, cradling her hand, her face twisted in pain.

"What happened?" Malenie scooted closer. "What's wrong?"

"You were going to scream." Paza stopped speaking and rocked a little.

"I remember that. You gagged me," Malenie prompted. "What... with your hand? Seven hundred gods and goddesses, Paza, let me see." Paza shook her head, but Malenie gently pulled at her arm. The hand was limp like a damaged bird, and the deep impressions of Malenie's teeth seeped blood. "It's broken. We have to get you to a healer!"

"No!" Even whispering, Paza was fierce. "You do it. Hurry."

"Me?" But she knew what Paza meant. *I healed her blisters. I could do almost anything.* The thought scared her. The pain and responsibility scared her. *I don't want to. I just want to go home.* Immediately, she felt guilty. *And leave Paza like this when I could help? It can't be worse than what I just did.*

She reached for Paza. Her stomach turned over and she swallowed thickly, averting her eyes. "I don't…Paza, I want to, but something is wrong. I feel ill."

"You have to eat," Paza managed to say. "It's like running a race, magic…" She reached for her purse and hissed with pain, curling over her hand again.

"Don't move." Malenie unwrapped the oiled cloth from the last of the chicken and dates and forced herself to eat. An aching hunger grew in her middle the more she ate, until she was shoving the food in her mouth and barely chewing. Then she wiped her hands and grasped Paza's ankle. "I'm ready."

Paza mewed and bent further over her hand. Malenie shook her lightly. "Come on, Paza, make the wish. You have to do it. I can't." The other girl ignored her. Malenie set her teeth and dug her nails into Paza's skin. "Paza!"

"Let go of me," Paza snarled like a cornered dog.

Malenie tightened her grip. "Make. The. Wish."

"Ow. Ow, gods…wish…my hand, heal." That stuttered wish seemed to be enough. Malenie felt an answering twinge of pain and watched, fascinated and repelled, as the little puckered mouths of the wounds closed up and disappeared as if they had never been. Paza moaned once, and then all that was left was a smear of blood across her hand and the creases pain had engraved on her face. The cut on her cheek had not healed.

"Eat this." Malenie handed her the dates and a piece of chicken she had saved for Paza, who took it with a revolted expression but, surprisingly obedient, ate. Her face had eased and her hands shook less by the time she finished. "Better?" Malenie asked. "Now tell me what happened. I remember the, *him*, but not after that. That wish felt huge.

He must have had a world of hurt in him for—for your family." She fumbled to a stop. Paza screwed her face up, and Malenie thought, *What a stupid, hurtful thing to say.* She was so tired—and starting to admire Paza's determination. She didn't want to cause more pain.

"I'm sorry, Malenie. I had to make another wish to get us here. He knew. He saw us."

"You're sorry?" Malenie asked incredulously. That's what that face meant? "After what you told me about him? After what I just said about him? You had to get us away. And you put your own hand in my mouth so that all of Raleton—the Patriarch, Deek and, and the man in the robe—didn't know exactly where we were by the scream I was going to scream. That was so brave. Risky, but brave. You probably saved us."

"But that second wish hurt you." For the first time she seemed young and unsure.

"I must have agreed, or it wouldn't have worked."

That made Paza stop arguing. "I think we better get away. He'll be coming after us."

"We've been sitting here for a while," Malenie said uneasily. "You're sure though, about coming with me to get Papa?"

"I said I would! Besides," she said in a quieter voice, "I don't think the man in the robe can follow us there."

They turned to the Wall. Paza's gaze slid away so she stared at the water even when they stood right in front of it. "You can't really see it, can you?" Paza's chin jutted out and Malenie hurried to say, "I mean, can you touch it? Will it let you?"

Paza reached out. Her hand veered left. She pressed her lips together and tried again. Her hand veered right. She made fists, violently drove herself forward, tripped and fell face forward into the water. When she came up, spitting water and curses, she was facing Malenie.

"Fine," Paza bit out, wrapping her arms around herself. "You lead me."

Malenie had never seen anyone look less like they wanted to be touched. "Don't you think…maybe that won't be enough and you'd better…"

"Use your magic? Alright, yeah."

Malenie thought it was the prospect of having control, not of using the magic, that made Paza relax a little, and that made it easier for Malenie to offer her hand.

They struggled through the narrow tunnel and surfaced, gasping, in Trader Town. The night was brighter, the darkness tamed by the soft glow of poor man's lanterns and the sharp light of crystals. The air smelled fresh. "It worked," Paza said, staring at the Wall. "Donkey balls and maggots, we're really here." She laid her palm flat against its rough stones, testing its reality and then swiveled to absorb the sight of Trader Town.

"Yes." Malenie pushed wet hair from her face and pulled it free of her armpits as she clambered out of the pool. She spared a thought for the people and beasts that would be drinking the water tomorrow and hoped they hadn't fouled it. "And now we can find Papa." As she wrung her hair out she was already thinking ahead. *We'll have to leave tonight. Papa will know where to go.* A healer could find work anywhere and Papa would take Paza in, like another daughter. They would all be safe.

"What now?" Paza asked.

"Wish for us to find him," Malenie said impatiently and waited for something to happen after Paza spoke. When nothing did, she prompted, "Say, 'I wish to know where Serliac, Malenie's papa, can be found.'" More nothing.

"Do you feel all used up?" Paza asked uncertainly, straightening her turban.

"Not like before. I feel fine. Try something else."

"I wish for my hair to grow back." Paza stuck her fingers under her turban and made a face. "I wish the cut on my cheek would heal, I wish we could know where Malenie's papa is, I wish these leaves would look like coins," Paza said all in a rush. No tingle, no glow, no results. Malenie cursed and kicked at the stones bordering the pool. Neither dispelled the numbness spreading through her chest. It should work.

"What are we going to do?" Paza asked in a small voice. She sounded afraid Malenie would crumble at this new obstacle, leaving her alone in an unfamiliar place. *Well, I won't.* Responsibility pulled Malenie back from immobility and despair. *I have to take care of her. Even if I don't know how.*

"We'll decide in the morning," Malenie said, trying to inject decisiveness into her voice. For lack of a better place, and out of habit,

Malenie led Paza home. The house was empty of Papa and squatters but stripped of everything that had made up Malenie's life. They huddled together in the alcove where Malenie's bed had stood and waited for morning.

6

Malenie sat crosslegged in her empty house and watched the shadows in the yard shorten. They drew away from Papa's herbs, heartcure and bloodstrong, numb-root and purgewort, which drooped under a layer of dust, missing their morning water. That had been Malenie's job. The light crept inexorably forward and gleamed on the shiny black and red fragments of the shattered water pitcher. A traveling shaper had given it to Papa. Its magic had kept water as fresh and cool as the moment it was drawn from the spring. Now it was broken and useless, as useless as Malenie because she didn't know what to say to Paza when she woke up and asked the question Malenie was asking herself: Now what?

Paza groaned and sat up all at once. Pity jolted through Malenie at Paza's automatic and suspicious scan of her surroundings before she rubbed the sleep from her eyes. *I can't say 'I don't know' to her.*

"What are you doing?" Paza asked.

Malenie stared past her. The shadow of the house bowed out on one side now, as if someone were below the ventilation lattice. Malenie's palms began to sweat. *Why did I think it was a good idea to come home?*

Paza shifted uneasily and squinted out the door. "What's—"

Malenie shook her head and put her finger to her lips.

"—for breakfast?" Paza finished with only a slight hesitation.

Malenie pointed to herself, to Paza, held up three fingers, and pointed outside. Paza nodded.

"I saved some food last night," Malenie said, gathering her feet under her and trying to sound normal. Paza sidled closer to the door and on Malenie's gesture rushed out to the left. Malenie dashed right. A dark silhouette, too short for a grown man, detached from the wall.

Malenie threw herself forward and tackled the eavesdropper. "Got you!" They slammed into the ground and skidded through the dirt. The eavesdropper twisted under her and Malenie's grip loosened with surprise. "Nes?"

Nes bucked her off and rolled free. Paza flung herself atop Nes and pressed a sliver of sharpened metal to the hollow under Nes's ear. Nes froze.

"By my ancestors' bones, tell your friend to get off me before I hurt her," Nes said, through her clenched teeth.

"Don't—"

"She was spying!"

Blood beaded under the point of the shiv, and Nes's lips pressed together in a thin line.

"Let her go now," Malenie said, her voice tight with anxiety. "She's a friend." Paza lifted the shiv a hair and Nes knocked her arm away.

"Don't do that again," she growled and sat up.

The two girls glared at each other, as spitting-wary as two cats contesting territory.

"What are you doing here?" Malenie asked. "What happened to you and have you seen Papa?"

Nes looked around. The street was empty and the houses turned blank faces to them. "We better get out of sight." Inside, they sat on the packed dirt floor in an uneven triangle, her two—friends?—the wide base with plenty of unfriendly room between them. Malenie wrapped her arms around her knees, chilled by the emptiness of the house. It didn't feel like home anymore.

"When you didn't show up anywheres I was afraid they'd caught you." Nes scratched her neck and winced as she re-discovered the cut. "But they were back yesterday, searching for you, so I knew they didn't. You shouldn't be here. If I can find you here, so can they. Where have you been? And where did you find her?" She jerked her thumb at Paza, who scowled at this rudeness but held her tongue.

"It's a long story," Malenie hedged.

"Fine. Trader Town is full of rumors. The strangers are saying your pa made that Parthavian's wife get sick."

"He'd never!"

Nes talked over her. "But most people got more sense than to believe it. Not of your pa."

When she didn't say any more, Malenie asked, "Do you know where Papa is?"

"Yeah," Nes said and clamped her mouth shut.

"Yeah…?"

"It's going to cost you."

"Hey," burst out Paza. "What kind of friend is that?"

"What do you mean 'cost me'? Just tell me!"

"I'm not giving it away for free."

"I haven't got anything." Malenie gestured around the bare house. Even the hearthstone was cracked.

"I want your hair."

"Wh-what? That's…" Blasphemous. Involuntarily her gaze went to Paza's raggedy turban.

Paza jumped between them. "No, Malenie, you can't!" Her voice shook and she turned on Nes. "How can you even ask? You aren't a real friend."

"It's none of your business anyways, is it?" Nes said calmly, but her knuckles were shiny yellow on her clenched fists. "Whoever you are."

"A better friend than you."

"Just, wait," Malenie said. "Why? Why my hair, why are you doing this?"

"We're not friends anymore," Nes said. "I just helped you before because of your pa."

Malenie stared hard at her. She didn't believe her. Their friendship might not be of the usual type lately, but when Malenie needed her, Nes had been there. She'd been her friend and her protector for as long as Malenie could remember. Together they had laughed and complained about their parents and made themselves sick on too many honey and milk pastries far longer than this strained silence had lasted. Maybe Nes said she didn't want her friendship, but she still had it, all the same. That's what friends did.

"Just give it to me," Nes repeated, and Malenie touched her hair, the hair she hated because it made her different, that she had repeatedly wished was like Nes's. She'd cut it all off to find Papa if she had to.

"You know where Papa is? And you'll help us get him?" Nes nodded. Paza shot her a disgusted look, brushed past her and leaned on the doorframe, facing the street. "I can't give you all of it. You know my religion forbids it," Malenie said slowly, "but I can give you the ones that pull out naturally, the ones I'd usually burn. Will that do?"

"Yeah." Nes produced the wide-toothed pick she used on her sister's puffy hair. Malenie took it doubtfully, but she didn't have anything else and her hair was in an awful snarl. It might even do better than her fine-toothed one made of camel bone with dark wood insets. Malenie yanked too hard and stopped thinking about what was gone. By the time she could comb through from the roots to the tips she had a tangled ball big enough to cover her palm.

Nes twisted it tightly and tied it with a piece of string she pulled from her own hair. It and the comb disappeared into her waist pouch. Malenie had the feeling that little twist of hair had been all that Nes had been expecting to get. "You're really not going to tell me what you're going to do with it?"

"They took your pa to Gravin and locked him up in his house."

Malenie groaned. She was going numb, crashing from hope to despair and back again.

"Who's Gravin?" Paza asked over her shoulder.

"Only the richest, meanest bandit this side of Pashtin," Malenie said. "There's no way..."

Nes interrupted. "The washerwoman there, Salla, is a friend of my ma's. And she didn't take to the strangers or what they were saying about your pa. He fixed her daughter when she broke her leg bad, for nothing. He said no one deserved to limp 'cause they couldn't afford a healer."

"I remember," Malenie said. "She's Steph's cousin."

"Salla is a special friend with one of the guards. I'm betting he'd let you in to see your pa."

"All this for my hair?" The question burst out of her, even though it might make Nes take back her help.

For the first time the other girl looked away. "Men came and put the collar on my sibs," she said stiffly, sharing with Malenie now the story she'd refused to tell when it happened. "Aunt Stel took our clothes to wash in one of the pools north of town and brought the kids. It was a treat for them." Among the Thessem, cousins related through the mother were counted as brothers and sisters. "She said they were splashing and paddling in the water more'n helping, but she didn't mind to see them happy. It was just her. She never expected—the slavers never took kids from parents before. Just orphans that no one wanted or claimed.

"When she came back, alone, her head and arms were all cut from fighting the slavers. They took my sibs. There wasn't anyone around to help. Uncle Den and Aunt Stel went off following them and never came back. One day I had nine sibs, and the next I had three."

Nes looked up, her face creased with anger and pain. "Ma begged Gravin for help, and he told her it wasn't none of his business. After all the years Pa worked for him! There wasn't anyone else to go after them. That shouldn't happen to nobody. Not you, not your pa, even if locking him up is a different kind of collar, one you can't see."

Her story shamed Malenie. She had never thought about slavery until Nes's sibs disappeared, childishly believing it was something far away from her life. There weren't too many slaves in Trader Town, and the ones that passed through with caravans had just seemed a fact of life, like the sun or the sand. Nothing in her life had ever made her ask whether it was right or wrong, until it was her own neck threatened. Nes had though, had thought about it and was living with it.

"This is what you're going to do," Nes said, her passion once more closed off from view. "I run errands for Ma and Salla, and I have one today. Gravin's got a new fancy lady and Salla needs expensive soap to clean her clothes and fripperies. I'll bring her the soap and tell her you're coming. Then you'll pretend to have messages to deliver and you won't leave. When it gets dark you can talk to your pa."

"They'll know Paza's not from here, but they'll know me."

"Say you're caravan brats. Another one came in with a bunch of Parthavians. And pretend to be boys. A turban makes a good disguise." Nes cut her eyes towards Paza's back.

Malenie ignored it. "Do you think Salla and her guard will help me get Papa out?"

"We can't know until you're inside."

"That's not much of a plan," Paza said.

Nes didn't look at Paza. "It's the only one you got, I guess." Behind her, Paza shrugged.

Clearly, it was up to Malenie. She picked at the dirt ingrained in the knees of her trousers. *I don't have another one.* "Yes, we'll do it," Malenie said, hoping she sounded more confident than she felt.

◇◇◇

Malenie panted up to the gate, hair tucked into a makeshift turban, Paza a few steps ahead. Her knees wanted to fold from the sprint across the hot sands, the guards' heavy stares and spiraling nervousness, but she locked them straight. Paza didn't even try; she supported herself with her hands on her knees to catch her breath and squinted up.

When she could breathe easier Paza called to the guards eyeing them, "This Gravin's place?"

"You seen anyplace else it could be?" the guard on the left shouted back. Luck was with them; Malenie knew them by sight only. Neither had ever been a patient of Papa's.

"How the rotting donkey balls should I know?" Paza hollered back. "You seen one no-horse town, you seen 'em all."

"Merchant brats," the other guard said and lifted his leather helm to wipe sweat from his hairline, revealing his short hair. "You seen one you seen 'em all."

"So what do you want, brats?" The first man ignored the second with familiar contempt.

"Message for the boss."

Malenie bit her lip. This was it—they didn't have a name, just the assumption that Gravin had to be in contact with someone that had arrived with his caravan. Merchant, trader, slaver or the men who had taken Papa, it didn't matter, as long they were used to message runners coming and going.

"Who from?"

"Who do you think?" Paza sassed him.

"Garth, just let them in. These brats have been running back and forth all day, and I'm tired of you grilling all of them."

"Awright," Garth said and disappeared from sight. A moment later, the gate swung open on well-oiled hinges and he waved them through. "Straight up to the house, mind."

Paza swaggered along the path, nose in the air, without a glance at Gravin's porticoed house with its glass-encased lightcrystals and the lady's sedan chair in front in pride of place. Malenie gawked at the fine shiny wood left out in the sun. It was a distraction from the tension that made her feel like she was going to pass out.

Paza halted and fished an imaginary pebble from her sandal, stalling, stalling… Another of Gravin's men jogged from behind the sedan chair and intercepted them. "You looking for Salla?" he asked under his breath. Malenie almost swallowed her tongue. He was young, a handful of years older than Malenie, and Salla old enough to be her mama—or his. Paza jerked her head once in a sharp nod. "The chief is this way," he said in a carrying voice and led them around the house to the back of the compound where the smell of manure was strong and a woven brush fence enclosed a herd of camels. Past the pen there was a cluster of outbuildings and then the wash yard, which had its own chest-high walls spread with Gravin's linens. Their guide glanced furtively around the yard—empty, except for Salla's tall figure—and led them at a trot.

"These are them," he said to Salla. She shooed the girls into hiding among the huge tin washtubs, some filled with steaming water, others empty.

"Thank you, Char," Salla said. Malenie, looking over her shoulder as she slid into place, saw her grin. The guard's eyes lit up and he stole a kiss before hightailing it away.

"He really likes her—and I think she does too," Malenie whispered to Paza.

"Huh," Paza sniffed, and banged her elbow as she folded her legs to fit into the cramped space. Malenie squirmed until her back was braced against the wall and her feet were tucked up against a tub. An awning kept the sun off the enclosure, but trapped the humid heat so it wasn't noticeably cooler than in the sun.

Salla took up her paddle at a tub one over and stirred, the rhythmic thwack punctuating her words. "Malenie, girl, are you in one piece? Steph's oldest son's friend's grandda said he saw you being chased by a stranger. He and some other men found him wading like a sun-addled fool in the market pools and gave him what-for," the paddle banged angrily, thump, thump, "but you were nowhere in sight."

"Yes'm. He didn't get a finger on me."

"So he was chasing you! Nes did say so. You should have come to us—although seeing where we're standing with your pa locked up here, I can see why you didn't."

Malenie didn't know what to say. Most of Trader Town was dependent on Gravin one way or another, and if they weren't, their sister or their uncle or their cousin was. She scratched under the turban, thinking maybe Parthavian men didn't have it any easier with their hair than women; her hair pulled where the turban was twisted too tightly and her scalp itched with sweat and the unaccustomed confinement. At her side, Paza was as still as a stone.

Salla put the paddle aside and plunged her hands into the steaming water. She pulled out a length of cloth and twisted, her muscles bulging as she squeezed out the water. "Getting you girls in here was maybe easy," she said. "But we've got a way to get you out again. Don't worry, you'll know it when you see it. She's got it coming to her." She grinned in pleased anticipation and throttled the cloth with extra vigor. "You stay low now and quiet. I'll be back and forth all day." The wet laundry was spread to dry on a bare patch of wall, and she bundled up her earlier efforts and carried them to the house.

It was a long, cramped day. Each position Malenie squirmed into was as uncomfortable as the last and there was nothing to do except listen to Salla hum or sing off key and nothing to see except each other and the curving sides of the tubs in front of them. During Salla's frequent trips to the house, Paza and Malenie tested the magic in whispers, without much hope of success, until they were hoarse.

Finally Malenie had to admit the obvious: this magic only worked over there. Otherwise the magic coming on just as she found her way under the Wall was too much of a coincidence. And that raised even more questions like, *How did I get it if it belongs on the other side?* and *What does Papa know that he's not telling me?* She felt helpless without her new-found magic. *Funny how quick I got used to it, even with all the pain and terror.* Rescuing captive fathers seemed to require more than a few guards willing to look the other way; it seemed to require magic like out of a storyteller's tale. Sick fear made a home in her stomach, adding to the anxious boredom of the day.

As the sun set, Salla dropped packages of greasy mutton and another waterskin into their laps. The chili made Malenie's eyes tear, but she didn't take more than a few sips of water. The pressure on her bladder was already uncomfortable, and no chance of relief in sight.

Finally the reds and golds in the sky faded to gray and deep blue and it got dark. Nes slipped up beside them, smelling incongruously of heavy perfume. Paza sniffed loudly and Nes muttered, "The fancy lady's soap."

"Help us up," Malenie said, and Nes levered her out of the corner. The sensation that had vanished from her legs during the afternoon came rushing back as pins and needles. Nes supported Malenie while she groaned and pounded on her legs to get them working again.

Disdaining help, Paza unfolded herself and crabbed slowly to the edge of the wash yard where she massaged her legs in aloof silence. When Malenie could stand on her own, they joined Paza among the empty tubs standing like stubby guards.

"You tell your pa we're getting him out, and Char will open the door. We just got to wait for the guard to change again," Nes said and tilted her head towards the dark huddle of outbuildings. In front of the last one on the left, a guard spat a wad of bloodstrong into the scrubby plants.

They were so close she could smell the musty herb. Papa was probably lecturing the guard's ear off about the dangers of its non-medicinal use.

A man sauntered across the yard. Malenie couldn't tell if it was Salla's friend, but Nes breathed, "This is it." Malenie's heart seemed to beat hurry, hurry, hurry and she clenched her fists. She twitched, ready to move, and Nes held her in place with sweaty hands. "Not yet." Nes's breath tickled her ear, and Malenie fought a sneeze.

"Hey," the new guard greeted the old.

"Hey, Char, can you move any slower?" he crammed another wad of bloodstrong into his cheek. "I want my dinner."

"Go on, then."

The old guard stomped away. Nes watched him out of sight, while Malenie's gaze stayed pinned on Char, who rounded the corner of Papa's prison. Malenie held her breath until he reappeared, paused and waved, hand tight to his body and the gesture small. Her friends recognized the come ahead before she did and hustled her across the yard.

7

Nes pushed Malenie between the hut and the compound's walls, and Paza squeezed in last. They crouched next to a low ventilation lattice. Even proud Gravin built with mud bricks, Malenie noted, although this outbuilding was as big as Malenie's house. Her mind raced with nonsense, and she bit her lip to steady herself. "Papa?" Her voice was a bare thread of sound, but a cough and the rustle of clothing answered.

"Mellie? Is that you?"

She pressed herself to the wall as if she could touch Papa through it. "Yes, Papa," she said on a half sob. His long fingers poked through the opening between the bricks and she clutched them. They were cool against her palm. "We came to get you out."

"Mellie, you have to get away. They're looking for you." His voice was hoarse, but as calm as ever. A thousand times she had listened to him soothe sick or injured patients, whether he knelt at their bedside or in the chaos of a market accident, and now he soothed her.

"The guard is going to open the door and we'll walk right out of here," Malenie said.

"I can't walk—they have my feet chained together." Beside her Nes cursed Gravin's ancestors and cat-footed around the building to notify Char. *Maybe he has the key.* Paza shifted restlessly, restraining who-knew-what impulse, and took up the lookout position at the corner.

"We're going to get you out," Malenie said with more certainty than she felt.

"Listen. I believe Gravin is holding me prisoner for someone else, someone he's working with, or someone he double-crossed. A man named Harashan—maybe. A Parthavian, definitely. They're looking for you in particular, and they're not just slavers." The tumble of words slowed, and Papa spoke hesitantly. "Mellie, I never told you this and there's no time to explain, but you should be able to cross the Wall. Maybe the pools—"

"You know? How did you know? Why you didn't tell me?" She clutched his hand tighter, feeling disoriented.

"Listen to me, you have to get under the Wall and—"

"I can't, Papa," she broke in. "They're looking for me there, too. It's a long story, but I did, I went under the Wall." For the first time the wonder of the experience reached her. "It's just like here, but different. And I—"

"Are you certain you can't hide there?" He sounded sterner and sharper than she had ever heard him.

"I can't," she answered quietly, the reminder of danger chasing away the awe. She thought he cursed, but Papa never cursed.

Nes gripped Malenie's shoulder, a warning she didn't bring good news. "He doesn't have the keys. Gravin's keeping them and Char said he can't get them."

"No." The word seemed to tear her throat.

"Mellie, you have to go," Papa demanded. "Go to Pashtin." Paza looked over her shoulder at Malenie's gasp. "And find my sister, Emelenie, there."

Nes's fingers gripped harder as Malenie sputtered, "What? You don't have a sister. You have a sister?"

It was Papa's voice, his fingers, elegant even with grime caking his knuckles and ragged fingernails, but Papa didn't have family, didn't keep secrets. "You never told me." It wasn't right to be angry at him, he was locked up, they were in danger, but his words made the familiar things of her life as strange as the town across the Wall. Made Papa a stranger to her.

His fingers tightened on hers. "Follow the road north to Pashtin and find my sister. She's a Pashtin—she can help both of us. Everything will count on you finding her, do you understand?"

"North, to Emelenie Pashtin," Malenie repeated, thoughts whirling.

Papa said, "Ask—"

Char's harsh whisper cut him off, and Malenie startled, almost falling over as he loomed over them. "Now! You have to leave now."

Papa released her hand. He said something more, but Char hooked his arm through hers and urged her to move. "No, wait," she said as loudly as she dared, straining back towards Papa. "I have to—" Char hustled her away. *I have to find out what he said. I have to find out everything about me.* Nothing was the way she thought it was.

Next to her, Char made a strange sound. Malenie looked around wildly, thinking they had been spotted. The yard was full of activity, but everyone was running towards the house and the flames devouring the fancy lady's brand new sedan chair.

"Never thought that heavy thing would make such a great show," Char hooted quietly, and a hot flash of indignation rushed through her. He was laughing while her world fell apart. It died again when none of the guards at the open gate noticed them sneaking by. They were too busy choking on their own howls of laughter.

◇◇◇

Nes wouldn't come with them any further than the edge of town.

"Can't," she said when Malenie asked her to. "Have to help my ma with my sibs." But she gave them a packet of food, full waterskins and bags to carry it all. "Give me your hand." She dumped a few coins on Malenie's palm. "Only fair, they came from your house," she said. Pretending to be mad made it a little easier for Malenie to part with her.

◇◇◇

Malenie and Paza followed the Wall north by starlight. In a few places water gleamed and dripped from its stones before disappearing into the sand or collecting in pools. Some were improved by low walls and troughs so beasts of burden could drink separate from their owners, and others were in their natural state, tiny gems draped with lush—for the desert—grasses and the leaves of trees, all gray in the night. To the west, the desert rolled away in gentle up and down hills, some topped with squat trees, everywhere thick with low-growing bushes, and all of it ready to prick, trip or stab an unwary traveler if the shale and loose gravel didn't.

The north-south road along the Wall ran far beyond Malenie's knowledge, linking cities like an artery, caravans and their goods the blood pumped along its length. Pashtin was a seven-day journey north, for travelers on horse- or camelback. For the two of them, it would take much longer.

"Our food won't last. We might buy or beg some from other travelers," Malenie said.

"And how do we know we won't walk right up to the people hunting for you?" Paza answered. "Or someone willing to sell you to them? Or slavers who don't care who we are?"

For now the road was empty. It was late and most travelers had ended their day's journey long before they had started theirs. They trudged along, Malenie wrapped in bewilderment and apprehension. It was one thing to imagine leaving her home with Papa at her side; it was another to leave him behind and search for a family she had never heard of.

"What is that?" Paza asked, voice high in delight. She pointed with her chin. Small rocks glittered and twinkled like a constellation fallen from the sky across the road and trailed into the desert.

She walked differently here than on the streets of Raleton, lighter and more upright, not so hunched. As if remembering life before a terrible time. And no wonder, with the Wall and magic between her and the man in the blue robe. Impulsively Malenie threw her arm around Paza's shoulders. Their thinness surprised her again. Paza shifted slightly to avoid an uneven patch and Malenie's arm slipped away.

"I'm glad you're with me. Those are poor man's lanterns. People collect them and use them as lamps."

Paza stalled. "They're beautiful."

"We should go," Malenie said. Paza didn't complain, although she walked with her head craned over her shoulder until the glittering motes were out of sight. She said little, but just her presence at Malenie's side eased the night fears that crowded Malenie's thoughts. *I wouldn't lay a bet in our favor, but I can't fail Papa. He's depending on me now, instead of the reverse.* Malenie threw her shoulders back under the new burden. *We have to make it.*

Late in the night they stopped, stumbling on heavy feet, when they spied a caravan, a great hump of humanity, beasts and cargo, camped close to the road. They backtracked quietly and then struck out into the desert to make their beds in cold hollows in the sand.

◊◊◊

A shadow moving over her face woke Malenie. The sun was already fierce and the gray brittle bushes hugged the ground; there shouldn't have been a shadow. She opened her eyes. A thin youth sat on his haunches out of arm's reach, blocking the sun. Malenie blinked and sat up, nudging Paza, and rubbed sand from her face with the back of her arm. He was skinny, a little grubby and wore the twist of cloth desert travelers used for protection from the sun pulled over his close-cropped hair. By the hair and the thin metal collar around his neck, he was a slave.

"What are you doing here all by yourselves?" His accent, like his light-toned skin, was Hennite; he was far from home.

"What are you doing here all by yourself?" Paza echoed back, jerking her chin up.

"Shall I tell you instead? You are running away; you are not slaves, so you are running from slavers or a family that makes life intolerable or some other trouble, although I think that this trouble may be different for each of you."

Malenie and Paza both crossed their arms across their chests and glared at him. "I don't know what you're talking about," Malenie said. "We're meeting Papa and his friends here."

"Hmm." He did not look like he believed them. "Shall I tell you a thing? The first, I am named Shay Genalen Toph."

"Your mama didn't say all that every time she called you," Malenie said.

He grinned, displaying a gap between his front teeth. He was under-fed, not young. Old enough to be sent west. "No, she called me Shay or Shay-Jah. You can call me that." His smile dimmed. "The second, I saw your tracks when I stepped off the road to piss. You must hide better."

"Why do you care?" Malenie challenged him.

He ran his finger under the slender collar and lifted it. His neck and the tops of his collarbones were cut by heavy raised scars. Malenie looked away. But she forced her eyes back. His voice was quiet, not bitter, just old, too old for his body, older even than his smile. "This master is not too bad. He does not beat or whip me. But he will never let me free either, like some do. No one should have to wear this." He slid his fingers out from under the collar and it slipped down to rest in the furrow it had dug in his skin. The scars weren't hidden, once you knew to look for them.

No one spoke for a long time. He watched them while Malenie imagined what his life must be like. Finally, she offered him their waterskin. "Water?" Paza didn't protest. He accepted, sipped a mouthful and returned it. The hot water tasted of leather when Malenie took her turn.

"You cannot travel on the road," Shay said, his posture open and relaxed. "It is too dangerous—they are always looking, the slavers, even if you had nothing to escape."

"It's the only source of water," Malenie said. "And we'll need food soon."

"I know this desert. I have crossed it many times. I will show you which plants hide water. If you walk the road, you will be taken and sold. Therefore you must not walk the road." He raised his hands, palms up in offering. "If you travel parallel to it, I will bring you water, and food."

"You can't," Paza said. "If they found out…" Her voice wavered. Sweat tickled Malenie's ribs. She was used to buildings that shaded alleys and marketplace pools that never ran dry even in the years no rain came. The wide emptiness of the desert made her shiver, and she knew they weren't prepared for it.

"They know I cannot run away," Shay said. Metal shapers made the collars, as stone shapers made spell stones, and only their hands could seal or unseal them. Anyone who escaped still wearing a collar was known as a slave, captured, and returned. "I hunt the hounds, and bring game to the caravan, sometimes staying away all day. As long as I return at night, they will not remark on it."

"But why would you?" Paza asked.

"No one should wear the collar," he repeated fervently.

Malenie and Paza shared a glance. Paza shrugged, not any more distrustful than usual. "Shay," Malenie said, trying out his name. "We can't let you." *Even if he's our only chance?* But it was his life he risked. "If you were caught, they'd think you were stealing even if you weren't."

"You do not let me do this. I will do it," he said, and Malenie heard the same awareness in his voice that she felt: they couldn't deny him, couldn't deny they needed him. Without help they wouldn't survive.

8

Shay kept his promise. He brought them stringy hares, desert fowl and ground squirrels. He brought them water, ointment for their skin and dung for their fires and lent them his flint. Even so, their faces and hands burned redder, peeled and burned again. Their feet bled. Malenie's legs never stopped aching, and Paza's cheeks were so hollow it seemed the bones would poke through her skin.

On the eighth night, Malenie sucked on her lip and grimaced at the taste of blood and grit. "Paza. Are you thinking what I'm thinking?"

"The desert is killing us," Paza mumbled, bending her head so all Malenie could see was her dirty head covering. "You think we should cross the Wall and use your magic."

No, I don't, Malenie wanted to say, although she had made the other girl say it first. Thinking about using the magic to move them again made her feel sick. The agony of the last time lingered in her bones. But she had also thought about how easy it would be to just make a wish. "And Shay is taking too many risks for us. We're risking his life, too," Malenie said.

"What about *him*?" Paza asked, hugging a waterskin to her chest.

"What do you think?"

"Maybe death here versus maybe being captured by *him*." Paza's voice made it clear which she thought was worse.

Malenie thought Paza had finished speaking. She uncrossed her aching legs, trying to find a more comfortable position. The desert then. But Paza surprised her.

"If it weren't for Shay," Paza ventured, "I wouldn't… but…should…

should we try to, um, go to the Wall tomorrow?"

"After we talk to Shay," Malenie confirmed glumly, not as excited as she should be to avoid certain death.

◇◇◇

Something cool and wet poking in her ear woke Malenie before dawn. She bolted upright and whacked her head on the bony skull of the hound standing over her. "Ow. What?" One hand to her head, she squinted in the uncertain light, heart pounding, and spotted Shay squatting an arm's length away, bracketed by two more hounds. They were tall, rangy and gray-brown, darker than the yellow-brown of the sand.

Without a hound's nose in her ear, Paza awoke more slowly. She pushed up on one elbow.

"I thought you were coming—don't do that!" Malenie said, pushing the hound and its tongue away from her ear, a little surprised it—she—didn't snap or growl. "What are you doing here, Shay?" The hound sat heavily on Malenie's feet.

"I was worrying. You do not look well. I brought you some things." In a folded cloth he showed them fresh bread. "The fabric can make better head wraps. And camel milk." He gestured to a skin that usually held water.

"It's too much!" Malenie protested, appalled at the risks he was taking for them.

At the same time, Paza said, "Shay, no."

The hound shifted and swung her head around to stare at Malenie with yellow eyes. No teeth showed, her hackles were smooth and her ears pricked forward, but she was big, and close. "Um."

"You do not look well," he repeated stubbornly. "These hands can help you," he said, spreading them wide. Crimson and gold streamers lightened the horizon, making it easier to see, but Shay wouldn't meet their eyes. The expression he had been suppressing the past few days was now a full-fledged frown.

"It doesn't matter, anyway," Malenie said, and that brought his head around, offense and concern clear on his face.

"We decided last night to return to the road—"

"No! Please think," he said. "It is not safe. I do not take as many risks as you think. I know what I do. But you…there are many travelers on this road. You will be seen." His hand touched the collar at his throat. "They will want you and they will catch you. You are young, sturdy… different." He forced his hand down stiffly.

"Like you," Malenie said, momentarily sidetracked.

"Like me." He sighed and pushed back the cloth covering his head, sending a sprinkle of sand pattering across his shoulders. Malenie looked at the collar again. If you didn't know, it might look like a piece of jewelry. It wasn't though, and they had no way to help him…here.

"Wait," she said loudly and pulled Paza near. "We can take him with us," Malenie whispered. "And there…" she squeezed Paza's arm, not wanting to say "use the magic."

"Yes!" Paza said.

"Shay, Shay-Jah." Malenie beckoned him closer and grabbed one of his callused hands in hers. The first finger was bent, as if it had been broken and set badly. Paza shifted out of the way. "We're not just going to the road, but to the Wall, and beyond it. And we want you to come with us." His entire body stiffened. "And this," she kept hold of his hand with one of hers and touched the collar with the other. It was warm under her fingers. "We can take it off, there."

He folded his thumb over the fingers of his other hand, until only the pinkie stood up straight, and kissed it softly. Malenie had never seen the gesture before. "The Wall. You go beyond the Wall?" His hand tightened on hers.

"You know about it?"

"I know a little." The colors in the sky had faded to steel blue. Shay's eyes were intent. "We are taught—my mother taught me the Wall was a working of great desperation to save the world from fragmenting. Instead it broke the world in two, here and there." He pointed to the ground and then to the east. "That is all I know." Malenie's fingers were growing numb in his tight grasp, but she felt Shay needed that contact more than she needed working fingers, and didn't withdraw from his grip. Actually, under the hound, her feet were going numb, too.

"A breaking," Paza repeated. "That's why the people and places on both sides are so alike, and so different."

"You've seen it?" The words were barely audible.

"Oh, yeah, I've seen it." Paza snorted a laugh. The hound's ears twitched, but she was watching Shay.

"And you can take this off?" His hand hovered over the collar, his eyes wide with hope and fear. The hound whined and deserted Malenie in a scrabble of claws and scattered sand. Her tail waved anxiously.

"Yes." Blood tingled as it rushed back into her feet.

"I will come." His voice cracked, and the hound licked his cheek, hiding Shay's face from view.

◊◊◊

They pushed their way through prickly bushes that were startlingly green and tender looking against the browns and grays of the desert. The untender thorns, gray and as long as Malenie's thumb, tore a jagged scratch in Paza's arm. "I hate the desert," Paza fumed, blotting the blood on her tunic, and stopped so abruptly Malenie walked into her.

"What?" Malenie asked and then saw the Wall, like an old friend, and the spring at Paza's feet. It was small but deep, with a pretty border of alternating white and matte black rocks. Saliva filled her mouth, and she dropped to her knees and plunged her head into the pool. The cold water swirled against her hot scalp and filled her mouth and glided down her throat until her stomach felt like a waterskin about to burst and she had to come up for air. She rolled onto her back. The smell of water and growing things was almost as good as food, and for a moment she didn't care about the gravel digging into her spine or the man in the blue robe or the pain she would feel when she used magic to move three people.

Shay was frowning with the effort of focusing on the Wall. His eyes slid away to the hounds and he forced them back. They slid to the spring and he forced them back.

At the sight Malenie's stomach squirmed like a tail that had lost its lizard. "What do you see?" she asked.

Paza dunked her head in the pool again. After a long moment she came up for air and gasped, "The water feels so good." She wiped her face. "But I couldn't really tell if there is a tunnel." She beat sand from her clothes, swung her legs over the lip and into the pool, grimacing at the cloud of dirt that spread out around her, and slipped in. She seemed to hang, motionless, just under the surface. Bubbles ornamented her hair.

Shay finally answered. "I see a Wall, but I cannot tell you how tall it is, or if it is made with small blocks or large, if it is weathered or raw. It makes me unsteady, as if I had not eaten in many days. What do you see?"

"There's a tunnel!" Paza shouted, surfacing in a wave that splashed the nearest hound, who sneezed and danced away. "I stuck my head in."

"What is wrong?" Shay asked Malenie. "Something is worrying you." She tried to make her face a mask. "And—I should have asked this at once—why is this way not your first choice?"

"Well, it could be dangerous. It will be." Paza did not look like she was about to explain, and Malenie didn't know how to in front of her. *The man in the blue robe probably doesn't know where we are. I can tell him later, when I'm not so worried about the magic.* "Do you mean to bring the hounds?" she asked.

"Mora, yes, if you agree. The others I will send back."

"Let's try it with just you at first," Malenie said nervously. "I don't know how hard it will be..." Her eyes flew to his. "I shouldn't have promised you, when I don't know if we can even get you to the other side."

"Peace," he said quietly, like he meant it. "The Wall is obviously a great, complex magic. I know this might not prove possible. I cannot say the outcome does not matter." He huffed a breath of laughter. "It matters very much. But so too does your offer and your intent."

"It will work," Malenie vowed.

"So are we going?" Paza asked, her voice wobbling.

"Are you sure?" Behind Malenie, Shay commanded the hounds to stay, and they sat, their feathery tails wrapped over their front paws.

"I think I should go first," Paza said. "Shay, grab my foot. Malenie, you push him."

Paza dove and Shay and Malenie followed. Under the water, Shay seemed muddled, but went where she pushed him. Once in the tunnel he moved faster. She barely had time to think, *What if it doesn't go through?* and she was blinking against the light and sucking in air.

"We did it," Malenie crowed, shaking water out of her eyes. Shay would be safe.

Brittle grass crunched nearby, smelling sweet, and Malenie looked up, her heart constricting in her chest. The man in the blue robe surveyed them benevolently from the height of a camel. He was alone.

"How did you find us?" Malenie blurted out.

"Paza told me, of course."

Shay's hand encircled Malenie's arm as she bumped into Paza's rigid body. Doubt flared in Malenie's mind. Paza made a small sound, as if she had been kicked in the stomach, and stared up at him, her eyes dark with terror.

"She's been with me the whole time," Malenie said. *It was Paza who suggested we cross the Wall—after I brought it up.*

"I didn't," Paza said, her voice a thin thread of sound. "He's lying."

"Do you still believe only in what you can see? I should have thought you were learning better." He swung his leg over the camel's neck and dismounted lithely, knees flexing as he landed. "What a charming spot." He strolled closer, propped one foot on the low edge of the pool and smiled at them. Behind him, the camel ripped at the grass noisily.

"Who is this man?" Shay asked. Malenie made a helpless gesture with her hand. Paza didn't respond at all.

"My dear, I'm so glad to see you've returned to me," he continued, as intent on Paza as the camel on its meal. "You have been a naughty girl—and you've forgotten about the danger to your family," he chided gently. "Luckily for you, I was a naughty child myself. You seem to be following in my footsteps in other ways." He turned his smile on Malenie. One of his bottom teeth overlapped another, and he had a faint scar through his right eyebrow. It didn't make him less beautiful.

As she met his eyes, Malenie flushed hot in shame for his exposed hair. It was too weirdly intimate and, and, and perverse.

"You must be the girl who upset Raleton and its Family so badly," he continued. "And me. I'm looking forward to knowing you better." The words must've held a threat, but his tone was so nonchalant, so opposite everything Malenie would have expected, that she couldn't think, couldn't move.

"What is your name, my dear?" She glared at him and he turned back to Paza, as if it didn't matter, but his shoulders were stiffer than they had been. "Come, Paza, let me help you out, and you can tell me what you've been doing while you were away." He extended a hand, almost, but not quite, close enough to touch her. When she didn't move, he said in the same caressing voice, "You remember your sister, my dear. She screamed quite loudly as she died. It was an agonizing death. Surely you haven't forgotten?"

Bile burnt the back of Malenie's throat. Under the water, she interlaced her fingers with Paza's and squeezed.

"Stop," commanded Shay, striking the water with his fist. "Do not say such things to her."

"Boy. Slave." He raked him with a contemptuous glance. "She belongs to me as entirely as you belong to someone. She is mine."

"I belong only to myself," Shay said with dignity. "She belongs only to herself." Shay stepped forward and everything seemed to happen at once.

Malenie raised an arm to block him.

He reached for Paza's arm.

Paza screamed "No!" and threw herself backwards into Malenie and Shay. She fumbled for a hold on Shay and clutched his collar. The man's smile slipped. Paza ground the bones in Malenie's hand together and shouted, "IwishtobebackontheothersideoftheWallwithShay-Jah-andMalenie!"

Death's ashes, no, Malenie thought as the fire and the pain took her and everything went gray and indistinct and disorienting. Water burned her lungs and the back of her throat and there was no air. The darkness was swallowing her. Her flailing arms scraped rock and her feet smacked against skin. *We're in the tunnel, under the Wall.*

Even if she had known which way was out, her arms were too heavy to lift now and she was too weak to go there. She kicked and kicked her heavy legs, and hands tangled in her hair and closed around her arms, dragging her up, and the world had direction again. Her head broke the surface and air rushed into her, fighting with the water. She choked and struck out at the hands holding her.

"You are safe," Shay said.

The fight went out of her, and she let him pull her all the way out of the pool. She collapsed in almost the same place as before. The leaves of the prickly bushes were still painfully green against the white-blue sky. But everything had changed.

Shay half sprawled beside her, his chest heaving as he caught his breath. The gravel darkened with the water dripping off him. His expression was shuttered. There had been no irony in that simple statement, but of course they were not safe, merely safer. Malenie's heart went out to him; to be so close and have salvation snatched away…

Malenie bolted upright. "Where's Paza?" Her voice climbed high in fright. Shay pointed with his chin at the three hounds lolling in the shade. Paza's shorn head was just visible between the furry bodies curled over and around her, and they shook as sobs tore through her.

Sympathy tears clogged Malenie's throat, and her voice was hoarse when she asked, "Did you—what are they doing?"

"They are kinder to pain than many people, and maybe they are more welcome right now." He frowned absently at the hounds. "That man, he did not seem so evil in most of what he said, just concerned for a wayward girl. Until the end."

"Yes," Malenie said. And then, "It's not my story to tell." *If I even knew all of it.* "Can you help me up?" Her knees were trembling so with shock, fear, anger and the aftermath of magic she wasn't sure she could stand, much less walk. Shay half carried her to Paza's side.

The hound Mora lifted her head, looked at Malenie and returned to exactly the same position as before: muzzle resting on her outstretched legs, her nose touching Paza's neck. The dog over Paza's hips wagged his tail, raising a miniature dust devil.

"Paza," Malenie said tentatively, and the girl exploded up. The two males fled, tails between their legs, but Mora stepped disdainfully out of the way. Paza's shiv glinted in her hand, and her face was distorted with hatred and the sobs that tore her chest.

"I'm going to kill him this time!"

"Wait—"

"Don't you try to stop me." She flashed the shiv and Malenie stepped back. Mora growled. The rumbling menace of it died at Shay's low command. "You keep stopping me. I should never have listened to you." She stomped forward.

Malenie retreated, fear lending her new strength. "No. You can't blame me for this. You knew attacking him wasn't possible. You made the wish to get us away. You. You chose safety over a suicidal attack." She trembled almost as strongly as her friend, afraid for her, afraid for herself. Terror and rage seemed to hang around Paza in the air.

"You do not want to do this," Shay said.

"Shut up!" Paza's lips pulled back in a feral smile and she raised the shiv.

"Mora, guard. Het, Shet, guard." The hounds flowed in front of Shay, their low growls vibrating in Malenie's chest. Their hackles bristled, their ears flattened to their skulls and their lips peeled away from their teeth in a grin very like Paza's.

"I'm not afraid of you!" she shrieked hysterically. She swiped at the nearest hound, who leaped away, then returned to position.

Hesitantly Malenie stepped forward. *How can I protect everyone?* "Shay, no."

"Het, guard," Shay reinforced his command.

"We got away, Paza," Malenie said in as steady a voice as she could manage. "He can't hurt us here. You're safe."

"I'm not listening to you!" Paza darted forward and Het blocked her. She swung wildly and scored his shoulder with her shiv. He yelped and jumped away. Blood stained her hand. She froze, and it was terrible to see the guilt and anger warring on her face.

Guilt won. She wailed, "No!" and fell to her knees, throwing the shiv away. She reached one hand towards Het. As he shied out of reach, her face crumpled, the rage draining out of her. "Sorry," she whispered. "I'm so sorry." She plunged her hand into the sand and scoured it, until the skin was red with irritation, not blood.

"Go," Shay told the hounds, his voice troubled.

Paza stared after them. Her turban was gone and she rubbed her hands over her hair, until it stood up in pitiful spikes. Her shorn head was almost as disturbing to Malenie as *his* exposed hair. It went against everything she had been taught was right.

When Paza turned back, her face was controlled. Too controlled. "I don't know what happened."

I think I do. Malenie knew a little about the effort to not feel her own emotions, the pressure that built up and what it felt like to release that control. The first time she used what Nes had taught her to protect herself from the bullies' escalating harassment, the rage had taken over her body and defense turned to attack. It was as if she watched from someplace in her head while her body hurt them worse than they had ever hurt her. But that was nothing compared to what she had seen in Paza. Malenie began to suspect that what *he* had done directly to Paza was very bad. Bad on top of killing her sister and threatening her family. The pressure of everything Paza was hiding must be enormous.

"It won't happen again."

"All right," Malenie said, trying to keep the doubt out of her voice.

Paza pushed herself up and stood, swaying. "We gotta go, right?"

"Yes, it is now getting late," Shay agreed anxiously.

They scattered to recover their discarded bags, saying little. Before they left Malenie circled the spring once more. The bloody shiv no longer rested in the hollow where it had fallen.

9

Fifteen days later, Shay pointed to a smudge on the horizon and told them they were two days outside of Pashtin. "I cannot be absent from the caravan again. You should be safe—safer," he corrected himself, "in the city."

"Shay," Malenie started, but didn't know how to end. "I wish…" Malenie tried again. But those words held a different meaning than they had in the past, and besides, there were so many things to wish for once she started.

He surprised her by taking her hands, and she looked up from studying her dirty feet. "I wish many things. But you did not take anything away from me," he said, and she remembered how strange his accent had sounded when they first met. It didn't sound strange now. "I asked for your trust without fully giving you mine. I give it to you now. I helped you in the desert because it is what I do. I help those who do not yet wear the collar, but might or will. I steal for them, and when it is possible, I steal the would-be slaves."

Malenie gaped at him. "Shay…I didn't know anyone tried to stop slavery beyond protecting their own kin."

"My birth kin are dead. There is no one to protect me. Many children have no one to protect them. I am not free, but I will keep others free. Maybe you will too.

"Let us meet again."

He's even thinner than when we met, Malenie thought, hugging him tightly. *We did take from him. His food, his help. We'll come back and find you,* she promised silently because it was a promise she might not be able to keep. Hesitantly she patted Mora. The hound accepted her caress and even Paza's fervent hug, her attack forgiven or forgotten. *We're all too thin. But we're not dead.* In the sky-high quiet of the desert they turned their faces to Pashtin, and they did not look back.

◊◊◊

At the first fountain on the outskirts of the city, they gulped sweet cold water until their stomachs sloshed full. Malenie laughed at Paza's face, dark from the nose up with sweat and grime, light around her mouth where it was clean. Paza smiled and splashed Malenie. Together they tumbled into the trough for watering beasts, splashing and scrubbing at skin and clothes. Malenie imagined she felt her skin lose its tightness and plump up with water. An older matron, water jug balanced atop her head, sniffed and turned away, but a young mother with beads in her tight braids and children clinging to her winked and smiled at them. They smoothed each other's clothes as best they could.

"How are we going to find any one person in all of that?" Malenie asked. Even this marginal neighborhood, with the desert air tapping at its doors and desert sand as its streets, was crowded and loud. Houses seemed to loom over them and close them in after the wide-open desert. But the shade was very welcome. Pashtin was bigger even than Raleton, and there Paza had been her guide.

Paza led them further into the city, whispering, "This neighborhood is too poor." To Malenie's eyes it looked a lot like Trader Town, clean and tidy, with gardens around the small houses. Remembering the grand multistorey buildings of Raleton, she kept her thoughts to herself and her eyes open.

In the neighborhood Paza picked, the houses were bigger and plastered and the fountain had an engraved metal spout that splashed water into the air. Its market was crowded, and according to Paza, the shoppers were neither wealthy nor poor. The dye vendor she singled out had a kind face and spoke easily with all her customers, greeting them by name. Malenie hung back, painfully aware of every sun-bleached patch and dark seam on her clothing.

"Missus," Paza said, "I'm new to town with my father, a merchant. He sent me with a message, but now I'm lost and I don't know how to find where to deliver it."

"Well now," the woman said, fanning herself with one hand and holding down her samples of dyed wool, linen and leather with the other, "had yourself a bit of a scramble 'bout the city did you?" Paza ducked her head and grinned shyly. "Who's the message for, dear?"

"Emelenie Pashtin."

"Madam Emelenie? You are far and gone from where you should be, but it'll be the easiest thing in the world to find her," and she gave Paza directions, making her repeat them back until she was satisfied Paza had learned them.

The directions took them through more and more imposing neighborhoods. Plastered houses with ornately carved wooden balconies gave way to large stone houses with shallow steps leading up from the street and metal-banded doors of wood.

"We're close now," Paza said as they turned onto a wide street lined with walls that hid all but the red-tiled roofs. Halfway along, Paza halted across from iron gates worked with repeated motifs of flax and sheep.

"This is it," she said with satisfaction.

"This can't be it," Malenie said in a voice barely audible to her own ears. Thessem guards flanked the gate, inside and out, and a crushed gravel lane—wider than the alley Malenie lived on—stretched from their feet to the raised verandah of a huge stone house. The light smell of flowers escaped its gardens.

"It has to be," Paza said and stepped forward.

The guard on the left blocked their approach. "Run along. There's no bread handed out today." His voice was kind enough, but he was armed and armored, and somehow reminded Malenie of the strangers who had taken Papa away. Papa hadn't known for sure who was behind it, and neither was she. *What if…?*

Malenie tried to back up, but Paza tugged on her arm. "Whatever you're thinking, stop," and whispered. "We came all this way. We almost died. Do not chicken out now."

"You're right, you're right," Malenie muttered back. She straightened her shoulders, lifted her chin and flipped her hair back. Looking squarely at the guard, she announced, "I'm Malenie, daughter of Serliac, brother to Emelenie. I need to speak to her. Urgently."

The guard's expression didn't change, but Malenie knew he didn't believe her before he spoke. "Madam Emelenie does not have a brother named Serliac. Clear off and don't come back."

Malenie glared at him, refusing to feel small. "You're making a mistake." Past him, she caught a glimpse of movement in the garden. She dodged past him and wedged her head and arms through the bars. The woman in the garden turned and Malenie shouted, "Emelenie Pashtin, your brother Serliac is in danger!"

"Stop that, you cheeky urchin." The guard's hands clamped around her waist. "I'll send you to the Council myself."

"You have to help him!"

"Let go of her," Paza shouted.

The woman reached the gate. Shock and some other emotion Malenie couldn't guess at passed over her face, a younger, female version of Papa's. Malenie's hands slipped. The guard plucked Malenie out of the gate, and she thought Papa's sister was going to just let him. She couldn't say anything around the lump in her throat. She couldn't even kick the stupid guard while she dangled there.

"Stop," Papa's sister said. Her voice was husky as if she spoke around a lump in her own throat, and her hands trembled as she touched Malenie's arm through the gate. "Put her down. I do have a brother named Serliac."

The guard dropped Malenie and then steadied her, blurting out a garbled apology. Paza scowled at him and pulled Malenie out of his reach.

As the gate clanged shut behind them, the woman shocked Malenie again. "I'm not Emelenie Pashtin. I'm Yasmin Pashtin."

Papa has more than one sister?

Yasmin examined Malenie. "So you're Serliac's daughter."

Malenie nodded numbly and looked her over, too. Yasmin's dark hair was twisted in one long braid twined with green ribbons, just as Malenie wished she could wear her own. Her green tunic was perfect, like new. Malenie kept her hands from tugging at her own worn one.

"What's happened?" Yasmin asked. "No, come with me and tell us all at once. My sister and the others are inside."

The others?

Yasmin nudged Malenie's shoulder and gestured for Paza to follow.

Malenie stumbled through the verdant garden, up three blindingly white stone steps, across the shadowed verandah and down the gullet behind the broad double doors. The warmth of Paza's arm brushing against hers was reassuring in the cool house. Yasmin glanced over her shoulder several times, mouth open to speak, but each time she faced ahead without voicing her thoughts. The guard tramped noisily behind them all.

Finally Yasmin paused at a curtain in shades of cream and ivory. "This is Emelenie's parlor." Stepping into the room, Malenie's eyes went first to the woman seated in the middle, the one who must be Emelenie. Her face was stern but not mean. Gray streaked her dark hair and her ankle-length tunic was split high to the hip, revealing loose trousers beneath it. A heavy gold chain encircled her neck. On one side was a woman who didn't look at all like Papa and on the other a man who looked disturbingly like an older version of him. A turban covered his hair properly, Malenie was relieved to see. Behind them, wood screens, carved in the shape of trees and flowers, filtered light from the windows.

"This is Malenie, Serliac's daughter," Yasmin said, each word precise. The man's wooden chair screeched across the tiles as he jumped to his feet. Yasmin's next words stopped him cold. "She says he's in danger." The other woman's hands flew to her mouth; only Emelenie held still, just her brows crinkling in the middle.

"Malenie," she said, as if testing the name. "And who is this?"

Paza supplied her name without the least sign of intimidation. Malenie huffed in annoyance at her own nerves.

"This is your Uncle Liac and Aunt Salenie. Liac, please."

The blood rushed from Malenie's head, and she half fell into the chair Liac drew up. Deep down, she hadn't really believed in the existence of Papa's family. "There are so many of you." The words fell out of her mouth before she could stop them. She felt stupid under Emelenie's measuring gaze.

"Please, let me take your headwraps. They're so…in need of washing." Salenie fluttered over her, almost but not quite patting Malenie's shoulders and arms. Automatically, Malenie began to tug at hers and then stopped, arrested by the thought of the humiliation Paza would have to face. They might even kick her out if they were very religious.

Inwardly, she sighed. *This is not a good start.* "You're right, they are dirty. This is probably not the best place to take them off."

"Oh, no—" Salenie protested.

Emelenie overrode her. "You will obey your aunt's request."

"But—"

"Malenie."

"No." Malenie gripped her knees to still their trembling. She tried to look resolute and not insolently disobedient. From the way Emelenie was glaring, it wasn't working.

Emelenie tilted her chin. Before Malenie could turn around, Liac unwrapped her headscarf and her hair fell heavily down her back. "Hey!" Malenie protested.

Paza screeched and kicked her chair over as the guard seized her shoulders. "Let go of me!" She twisted and kicked, and everyone started shouting.

Malenie thought she glimpsed a flash of metal in her hand. "Don't hurt him, Paza," she pleaded.

Startled, Paza met her eyes, her own wide and dark with fear. The guard took advantage of her distraction to pull her headwrap off. Everyone stopped and, except for Malenie, stared at the bristly spikes of her hair. Paza's breathing was loud in their silence.

"Seven hundred gods and goddesses," Yasmin finally whispered. "Who did that to you?"

Paza's chin went up like she'd been hit in the face. "Nobody."

Salenie pressed her hands to her mouth. "Are you saying you did it to yourself?"

"No." Paza scowled, but she was shaking so hard the guard was holding her up.

"Pull up her sleeves," Emelenie commanded, and the guard obeyed, exposing Paza's red-brown skin and a faint tracery of old scars on her forearms. Even though Malenie was sure Paza's shiv was in her hand, she stood there like a stick and did not look in Malenie's direction.

It didn't matter. Liac thrust Malenie's sleeves up. She flinched, but managed not to kick him for Papa's sake. The blue diamonds seemed like the brightest things in the room, and everyone stared. She straightened her shoulders under the weight of their regard. It felt like every bad dream she'd ever had. But at least they weren't staring at Paza any more.

"Very well," Emelenie said, after what seemed like an eternity. Liac let go, and Malenie deliberately pulled her sleeves down to her wrists. "Let the other girl have her headscarf. We're wasting time while my brother needs help."

Yasmin retrieved the headscarf, the guard righted the chair, and Paza sat stiffly with the scarf in her lap and her arms crossed over her chest. Malenie sat on the edge of hers, wondering what would happen next.

"Surely we should feed them, the children are quite gaunt and famished looking."

"That will have to wait, Salenie," Emelenie said, "but ring for water and tea. Now, Malenie, stop scowling at me like that. I am your aunt. I helped my brother care for his young daughter for a time. I know what you are."

What am I then? Malenie wanted to say, but couldn't, any more than she'd been able to ask Papa for help with the bullies. Even when everyone knew more about her than she did, she could not break the deep-seated habit of silence. She squeezed her hands between her knees to stop herself from checking her sleeves again.

"Tell me about my brother and how you came here."

Papa sent me here. He must have known this would happen. She couldn't force herself to talk about the marks on her skin, but she told them about the man that had chased her in Trader Town and Papa's guess that it was Harashan, the same man that had put him in Gravin's outbuilding. She said Paza was an orphan and emphasized that she had helped Malenie avoid the men chasing her, although she was vague about how exactly. She left out everything about the other side of the Wall, Paza's story and the man in the blue robe, but by the time she finished, her voice was hoarse in spite of repeated sips of honeyed water that had done nothing to calm her sour stomach.

Emelenie spoke in a low voice to Liac and he left. The silence was broken by the tap-tap-tap of Emelenie's fingers on the arms of her chair and growls from Malenie's stomach. Liac returned with a Thessem man with graying hair.

"Captain," Emelenie said. "Take thirty guards to Trader Town. The one that bandit Gravin has laid claim to. He's holding my brother, Serliac. Get him back any way you can. I don't care if you have to raze the place to the ground to get him."

"But we have friends there!" Malenie cried. "You can't do that."

Emelenie gave her a cold look, but added, "They could be useful. A washerwoman named Salla, a guard she has…a friendship with and an errand girl."

"That's not what she meant," Paza muttered under her breath.

Emelenie took no notice of her. "Liac," she told the captain, "will go with you."

"And us," Malenie and Paza said as one.

"No," Yasmin said.

"No," Emelenie said. "I suspect Serliac was right, and you are the target, Malenie. I will not let them have you."

"But you need us," Malenie said. "We know who can give you information, who you can bribe, who hates Gravin and will help you. We've even been inside his compound and can show you where Papa is being held!"

The guard captain looked like he might agree. "Madam—"

"No."

"It would improve our chances of success," he bulled on calmly. Malenie swallowed against hope. "We could keep them safe. Leave them with guards outside of town during the action."

"Thank you for your input." She folded her hands in her lap and straightened even more in her chair. "Understand that I don't know what you are facing. It may be a small band of men organized under this petty tyrant. Or it may be a much larger force answering to this Harashan, who may have decided to use my brother and my niece in some sort of power grab. I cannot risk her safety, and I will not permit you to divide your force."

He nodded, and hope leaked out of Malenie like water from a cracked pitcher. "Yes, Madam. If you are concerned about a power grab—or possibly a feud?—do I have your permission to hire temporary guards? Thirty fighters will leave you depleted."

"Mercenaries." She flicked her fingers in disdain. "I trust your Family to guard us, Captain, no other." A faint smile pulled at the corners of his lips.

What can we do? Malenie asked herself. *We'll follow—*

As if she had heard Malenie's thoughts, Emelenie said, "And Captain, please tell my niece and her friend that if she follows you, you will send her back to me, even though it will reduce the number of your force and your chances of success."

Malenie glowered at Emelenie, who returned her gaze evenly.

"It will be as she commands." The captain bowed and Liac kissed his sister's cheek with a murmur too low for others to hear.

"Wait," Malenie said to Liac. "Someone helped us even though it put him in danger…his name is Shay and he's a slave and Hennite and…" What if Emelenie kept slaves?

"Are you asking us to free him?" Liac asked.

"Yes." Malenie straightened her shoulders and looked him in the eye. "We wouldn't have made it here except for him. Isn't that worth it?"

"I'll look for him," Liac held her gaze even when Emelenie said his name. "She asked me, Emelenie. You'll have to live with that." He asked Malenie for details about Shay, nodded to her and left with the Captain.

"Baths and food for you," Yasmin said, ushering Malenie and Paza out of the parlor. "And then I'll show you where to sleep."

Malenie let Yasmin lead her, feeling disillusioned that Papa's family hadn't lived up to her high expectations and tired and lost now that she had finally done as he had asked.

10

Yasmin guided them through the house. The mosaicked floors seemed too beautiful to walk on and the wall hangings too plush to touch. Everywhere Malenie looked there was more evidence of wealth: light-crystals in bronze settings, a gilded niche holding red candles and a white ivory cup, a tiny dancing figure carved out of lapis lazuli. At the end of a hallway, stone steps with worn hollows in their centers cupped her feet and led down to a cavern with six pools. It was more water than Malenie had ever seen in one place. Steam rose lazily from some and a cool draft flowed from others, churning the steam where they met. Embers glowed red in the belly of a small brazier, which released the clean, sweet smell of burning herbs.

Yasmin showed them thick nubby robes just for wrapping up in and thicker towels, wooden combs, and glass bottles of ready-made skin creams that Malenie would not have to mash and boil and render herself. "I'll come back in a while," she said and left them alone.

Paza stripped off her clothes without embarrassment, but Malenie, not used to being naked in front of anyone, prowled the room first, testing the temperature in the pools. She found the spell stones that heated three of them, carved in the shape of flames, and puzzled over the ones that kept three others cold: they were carved in uneven circles of speckled stone that glittered and reflected light.

"Six spell stones just in here," Malenie observed, "and all those light-crystals. The Pashtins must be hugely rich."

"What's a spell stone?" Paza asked, just her head above water, her hair plastered closely to her scalp.

"It's how magic works here," Malenie said. "The magic is in things, rocks mostly, but sometimes metal or cloth." She paused, thinking about the slave collars. "Rocks are carved into the shape of the spell, like the flames there for heat. Smell stones are carved like noses and they sniff up smells in places that would smell bad otherwise. Only special craftspeople, called stone shapers or metal shapers or weave shapers, can make them."

When Paza looked away, Malenie quickly shucked her clothes, feeling awkward and exposed. The warm water dragged a sigh out of her, and her body at least, started to relax.

"Do you think we're in trouble here?" Paza whispered, and Malenie opened her eyes. A thick dark scar ran across Paza's shoulder and down her arm, crossing older, fainter ones.

Malenie looked away hastily, feeling rude, and nodded. "They just told us we couldn't leave, didn't they?" Her stomach ached with indignation and worry, and she kicked her legs, roiling the water into white froth. "The captain would have let us go with him except for her." She kicked harder. The bathing pool looked how her stomach felt now. "I can't help thinking there was a reason Papa kept away from his family."

"That Emelenie was looking at you the way you looked at that roast chicken after we first met. There's no doubting they're your family though. There's your names: Serliac and Liac, Emelenie, Salenie and Malenie. The old lady kind of looks like you, too, you know."

Malenie hadn't seen anything familiar in that woman and she didn't want to. Yasmin seemed kind and beautiful, exactly how an aunt should be. She had always wanted at least one aunt. *I don't know if I want any now.* She stopped kicking.

Paza frowned down at the ripples. "Did you notice how few Parthavians there are in this city? We're too obvious. And there are probably still men looking for you. They all think so: Nes, your father, your aunts." She slapped the water, sending waves sloshing over the edges of the pool. "At least they said they'll feed us." Underneath the forced optimism Malenie heard the same worry that was worming its way through her own stomach.

◊◊◊

They were wrapped in the luxurious robes and Paza was combing Malenie's hair when Yasmin returned to collect them. Paza had offered once she hid her cropped hair under a clean scarf. Malenie had held very still, thinking, *That's the first time she has ever touched me outside of wishes or danger.* It seemed to cheer Paza up. Maybe she had combed her sister's hair in happier times.

At the sound of footsteps, Malenie had thrown the loose hair from the comb on the brazier and muttered, "Please take this offering and excuse the lack of proper prayer." Her voice wavered as she wondered if the god Papa had taught her to worship was his family's god. Or would it be Mama's? *I really don't know anything.* She didn't like the feeling. She clutched the robe closed at her neck to hide the diamonds below her collarbones, glad it was long enough to hide the ones on her ankles.

Yasmin ignored the stink of burning hair. "Leave your clothes. A servant will clean them, and we have other things you can wear meantime." At the top of the stairs she turned in a different direction, past more beautiful furnishings. Malenie had to admit, even just to herself, that the cool tiles felt marvelous under her bare feet. It made her feel guilty to compare them to the dirt floor of the little house she had shared with Papa. *We were happy there*, she thought. *Weren't we?* It was strange to think that what made her happy might not make Papa happy. Maybe he missed this house and his family. It was a lot to give up, servants and luxury and a family name everyone knew. The Pashtins seemed more famous than Gravin even. The world she thought she knew kept changing, until she didn't know herself anymore.

Yasmin opened a half door into one of the rooms; the top half already stood open for ventilation. "We thought you'd like to share." The sound of falling water drifted through the screened windows. There was a raised bed almost as wide as Malenie's house, and more swirly blue and green tiles framed the curved windows.

"It's very nice," Malenie said politely and picked up a tunic from the pile on the bed and shook it out. The cloth was fine and the dye even, but cutouts at the neck, elbows and wrists were meant to expose skin, and it was split at the hips, too. "No!" she shouted, flinging the tunic at Yasmin, her voice echoing off the tile. "It's not enough that you want to know everything. Now you want to see it too?" She was so furious she was shaking and, under that, scared. "I've done everything you've wanted, for Papa. I am not wearing that."

Paza jumped away from the window, ready to attack, then hurriedly sorted through the clothes. Everything big enough for Malenie to wear was the same, even the trousers, which were discreetly cut at the hips, knees and ankles.

Every single mark on my body would show if I wore that. Malenie wrapped her arms around herself.

"No," Yasmin said, hurrying over to the wardrobe and riffling through more clothes than Malenie had ever seen before. "This was a mistake, I assure you." Not finding what she wanted, she pulled a braided rope in the corner. They stared at each other in silence until the patter of feet sounded in the hall. A maid came in. "Dessie," Yasmin said, "take all these clothes out and find suitable replacements."

"But Madam said—"

"I don't care what you heard. These clothes are not appropriate for our guests." Dessie gulped, gathered up the clothes and hurried out. A few garments slipped free and floated to the floor. Yasmin ignored Paza kicking them into a twisted pile. "Food is coming, too," Yasmin said. Her face softened, and she looked less like her sister Emelenie and more like the pleasant woman who enjoyed walking in the garden. "We want you to be happy here, as happy as is possible, under the circumstances. We have waited a long time to meet you again, Malenie." She seemed about to touch Malenie's shoulder.

Malenie stiffened, thinking, *Don't touch me. I don't know you and I don't trust you.* Yasmin must have seen the thought on her face, and she turned to go instead. "Wait," Malenie said, not quite daring to grab her sleeve, but her aunt paused. "If there's any news of Papa, you'll tell me, won't you?"

"Of course. But it will be at least fifteen days before we can expect any," she said gently.

◊◊◊

"What does it mean that they had those clothes?" Malenie asked around a bite of the last fig stuffed with goat's cheese. The feast Dessie had brought was mostly crumbs, and Malenie's stomach made a satisfying bump under her new—normal—tunic.

"I've seen them before," Paza admitted reluctantly, putting down her spoon. "The Families wear those clothes sometimes, the ones that have the glowerer magic, anyway."

"What? I thought—I thought it was unusual, to have, to have—the way everyone reacted, the orange ribbons, and the Patriarch in Raleton…"

"Unusual, yeah, for someone not part of a Family, unprotected. A Family has magic or it doesn't, and usually it stays that way."

"But the way everyone reacted. They called me a danger and questioned my sanity." Paza hunched her shoulders, and Malenie recognized that look, the reluctance to expose old hurts, but she had to understand. "Please, Paza, I wouldn't ask if it weren't important." In the desert they had concentrated on survival, but now survival might depend on how much she knew.

"I know," Paza said, fidgeting with her cloth napkin. "It's what the people outside the Families think because they're ignorant. Mostly the Families like it that way. I guess it used to be different. But they didn't want people doing what he's done." Her voice got even quieter. "Stealing kids from all over, Suntin, Sarnath, I think, and even further east, and used them and their magic up like rags. Until he went too far, and the Suntin girl went mad and destroyed herself and lots else besides."

"You saw that," Malenie whispered. Paza picked at a fingernail and didn't answer. "But Paza, how do you know so much?"

Paza lifted her head, her eyes wide and her face gray and pinched. "I saw it," she said, "and the Suntin girl told me before…

"The man in the blue robe had me and her both. He ran a lot of kids, for different stuff, stealing, running messages, but always he looks for the magic ones. The things he used her for… He made her hurt people…. It was too much. She went insane, and when that happens glowerers can control their own magic. But, you know, the kind of control someone has when their mind is broken." Her voice cracked. "I don't know why it works like that."

Malenie wanted to tell her to stop, but she couldn't. She had to know.

"The Suntin girl was ripping the world apart…with fire and making the ground break…" Paza's words came slower and slower. "We were right in the middle of it. He had a boy, I don't know from where. The boy didn't have as many marks, just the ones on his arms and ankles, so he wasn't as strong. He—the man in the blue robe—made the boy use magic so the fire couldn't burn them—us. It really hurt, because it kind of did burn, but then he kept healing us….So I was saved, too, but the boy died after because of using too much magic."

She pinched her lips shut and methodically started separating her food on her plate. Pork and onions on one side, raisins and almonds on the other. She shredded her soggy bread and piled it in the middle, dabbled her fingers in the sauce, and frowned at the mess. "I have to tell you something. That I didn't tell you when we met. The Suntin girl had the same protection on her that I did for you, that only the wishes you agree with will work, but he broke it and made her do what he wanted. It hurt her when he did it. I thought if I told you, you wouldn't help me, but it does protect you from most everyone else."

"Donkey balls." Malenie turned the information over in her mind and shivered. "I kind of wish I still didn't know that." Paza jerked and almost dumped her plate in her lap. "I see why you didn't tell me. It's alright. I hope I would still have helped you. I probably would have." *Because I had no idea how scary he was until I saw him, and by then it would have been too late anyway.*

Paza resumed eating with a set face.

She's probably eaten worse. Or nothing at all. The half-eaten fig weighed heavily in Malenie's hand. She copied Paza's pragmatism, though all the flavor had gone out if it. Maybe to the same place as Paza's innocence. *Papa needed her strong. So did Paza.* When the silence got too long she asked, "So do you think the Pashtins are a Family like across the Wall?"

Paza nodded her head and swallowed. "That would explain you having the marks and the clothes, but why would they be here and not on the other side? There's no magic in people here, you said. And they weren't wearing the clothes."

"I don't know," Malenie said, feeling as if there was very little she did know. *And right now, the more I learn, the less I want to know.*

11

"Why do you suppose there's no one our age?" Paza asked yet another question Malenie couldn't answer. They had tried to nap, but even in the huge bed, Paza had managed to kick Malenie several times, and too many thoughts were tangled in Malenie's head to allow her to sleep, so she suggested they explore. Not just the house, but how close the Pashtins held them. Of course Paza had agreed.

No one had stopped them as they explored the house and grounds from end to end. Not any of the guards and servants and the kitchen staff who greeted them in the big house; not the women and men in the outbuildings working at looms and spinning wheels, chatter and dust swirling around them in diffuse sunbeams from the tall windows, although their rhythm and conversation faltered at the intrusion. And the horses, camels, goats and chickens in their pens didn't care once they'd proven not to have food.

"I suppose the rest of the adults are off working," Malenie guessed based on Papa's routine, which started early, ended late and was often interrupted by middle of the night disturbances. Babies, injuries and illness always seemed to wait for night. "But the kids my age and younger can't be all 'prenticed off. Some at least must be too young, and I didn't think rich people sent their kids for 'prentices anyway."

"Me neither. Let's ask," Paza said, sliding out of the tree she had climbed and showering Malenie with its tiny flowers. "You're all yellow." She giggled, brushing the pollen and petals away. Malenie laughed with her, even though her heart seemed to pinch to hear a real laugh from Paza.

Outside the barracks, they found a guard oiling a piece of leather and whistling between his teeth. "Hey now, misses. What can I do for you?"

Paza ducked behind Malenie, suddenly wary again, so Malenie asked their question. "We were wondering where all the people our age and younger are. There must be some."

"Why sure, and more'n some. A whole passel of 'em. But they're out at the farms today. Soon enough they'll be back and then this place won't feel like a ghost town after the water's all dried up."

"Thank you," Malenie said, wondering about the farms.

"What're you doing?" Paza asked from behind Malenie's shoulder.

The guard shook his work out so they could see it was a jerkin with neat stitches down one side and a lighter patch of newer leather sewn in on the other. "A mate's leather armor. I gave him mine when they went off to see to your pa, since his needed fixed." He laughed at the surprise on their faces. "Not too many secrets here, misses."

Emelenie really did send them, Malenie thought, not realizing how much she had doubted. A tightness in her chest loosened, and she allowed herself to think the captain would succeed. *Thirty fighters is a lot.*

"Don't you worry," he added. "Pashtin-Hafz Family guards are the best there is, and we don't let anyone get away with messing with one of ours. We'll find him and get him out safe." It felt strange to be claimed that way. She and Papa had been on their own for so long, when everyone around them had family to protect them and look after them and ease their way. She thought she liked it, but family was also more complicated than she had imagined back when the bullies were calling her "orphan" every day.

He bent back to his task, and they wandered, purposefully casual, to the gate without having to discuss it. The guards had changed, and the iron gates were closed. And locked, as Malenie found when she put out a hand to shove them open.

"Good afternoon," said the man on the left, gruffly but not unkindly. He looked in towards the house while his companion faced out, and a woman stood on a wooden platform to look out over the wall. She glanced down quickly and then resumed her vigilance.

They seem much better at guarding than Gravin's men, Malenie thought, both concerned and reassured. Her heart pounding, she said,

"We would like to go out."

"You'll have to speak with Madam Emelenie," the guard said.

Until the guard said she couldn't, Malenie hadn't really wanted to leave, she just wanted to know it was possible. Now she really wanted to walk out through those gates. She had been taking care of herself for a long time and wasn't used to being told what she could and couldn't do. She didn't like it. For Paza it must be even more constricting. Impatiently, she tucked her hair behind her ears. "But we're family, not prisoners," she said more belligerently than she had meant to.

"Of course you're not prisoners!" he said, shocked enough that Malenie knew he at least believed it. She wasn't so sure. Emelenie seemed to have very set ideas about who was allowed to do what. The other guard glanced back with one of those looks adults must practice, that said clear as anything, 'What will these youngsters think of next?'

"Madam's orders, for your own protection," the first guard continued, unaware he was confirming suspicions Malenie was ashamed of having about her papa's own sister. *But still… here we are, unable to leave.* "None of that," the guard said to Paza, who seemed to be judging whether she might slip through the bars.

Paza would fit, too, but I won't. Malenie hugged her arms to herself to keep from clutching Paza and begging her not to leave. She did not want to be alone again.

In her best haughty accent, Paza said, "We wouldn't dream of it." Malenie grinned at her in relief.

The guard winked at Malenie behind Paza's back. "Sounds just like Madam Emelenie, when she talks like that."

"We'll find another way," Malenie reassured Paza once they were out of earshot. "There has to be one." Though she was thinking, *Maybe we're safe here. Maybe we shouldn't try to get out.*

Avoiding the barracks, they circled the grounds again. "There's only one gate," Paza said.

"But that tree might hold us," Malenie pointed out. "And look there." The corner of the wall furthest from the house looked promising—the rough mortar had crumbled and fallen, leaving plenty of finger- and toeholds. "But if we left that way we wouldn't be able to get back."

"It's not so bad," Paza said. "They are feeding us." Malenie felt another rush of relief that Paza wasn't ready to leave her just yet. She wanted to hug her. Instead, when Paza asked, "Are you going to talk to Emelenie?" Malenie accepted the dare.

◇◇◇

Paza hung back as they entered the parlor where Emelenie was enthroned, a walking stick propped against her chair. She finished speaking with a messenger before turning her unreadable dark eyes on Malenie. *She really doesn't look much like Papa*, Malenie thought. She had dithered in her head about what to call this woman, whether aunt or madam, but Emelenie didn't feel like family and suddenly Malenie didn't feel polite. "Emelenie," she said straight out, "the guards stopped us at the gate, at your orders, they said."

"Yes."

Emelenie was so calm, her expression so smooth, it made Malenie want to provoke a reaction. She wanted Emelenie to see her, not whatever Emelenie thought Malenie was. "But we want to go into the city."

"You may not."

"We got here alone, through the desert—you can't keep us in!" Malenie stood as straight as she could. This woman was not her mother.

"If you would allow me to finish, I was about to say it is for your own safety. Regardless of how you were forced," just the slightest stress on the word to show her disapproval, "to come here, I could never look Serliac in the face again if something were to happen to you while you were under my care."

Just like that she silenced Malenie and made it impossible to challenge her, as she had certainly meant to. Paza poked Malenie on her hip, trying to communicate gods and goddesses knew what.

"When your father has been retrieved and this situation has been resolved—"

A tumbling, rowdy crowd of young people burst into the parlor. "Auntie, you'll never guess—" the speaker, a youth about Malenie's age, stopped abruptly at the sight of two unknown girls being dressed down by his aunt. Malenie lifted her chin proudly and Paza scowled.

The others, all Parthavian, jostled for a better look. Malenie had never seen so many Parthavians her own age before. And there were so many. Malenie swallowed, unsure, and stared back. These were the cousins. They were sleek, well fed and well dressed even in work clothes. The girls' hair was tidy and the boys' turbans were neat. Even in her equally fine borrowed clothes Malenie felt out of place.

"I guess it wasn't a whopper," someone said into the silence. Malenie blushed. There were a few titters but no one else spoke. Emelenie looked a tiny bit less awful as she surveyed her nieces and nephews— *Her real ones*, Malenie thought bitterly, surprising herself—although they didn't seem intimidated.

"Indeed," Emelenie said. "If what you were told was that my brother's daughter and her friend are here. You may get acquainted," her voice rose over the swell of sound, "elsewhere."

The cousins surrounded Malenie and Paza and swept them down the previously hushed corridors to the children's hall, bombarding them with questions. After a brief squabble, they went to the girl cousins' rooms first, a suite of four rooms around a common area cluttered with brushes and shoes and pens and more clothes.

The girls tore off their clothes, which were muddied at the hem and stained in spots, and replaced them with clean ones. The boys' rooms were identical to the girls, except for a shelf of rocks and the discarded turbans. The boys stripped as unselfconsciously as the girls. Malenie turned away and caught Paza slipping a gold bracelet into her sleeve. Malenie shook her head and Paza shrugged. By watching out of the corners of her eyes—flustered and embarrassed—Malenie was able to see that boys' bodies were interesting when their owners were not trying to beat her up and that not one of the cousins had mysterious marks on their skin, just the odd bruise or scrape. They were not glowerers. Malenie wasn't really surprised, but she had wanted the simplest explanation to be true.

She began to sort out the individuals by the questions they asked. Leocarl, the boy who had spoken to Emelenie, asked, "Where have you been all your life?" That was easy enough to answer in spite of the intimidating experience of having so many strangers staring at her. There were only fifteen of them really, not the twenty she had first thought, from about age thirteen to six.

"Where do you live?" asked one of the girl cousins, the one with dark freckles on her cheeks. "What does your family do? Hey, my name is Marlassa."

"Papa is a healer."

"Lots of our older cousins are healers," said one of the youngest boys, unimpressed. "What about the rest of your family?"

"It's just the two of us," Malenie said, keeping her voice even. Even though she expected their reaction, their silence and shocked faces seemed to accuse her of being no better than an orphan.

"Really?" the young cousin asked, his dark eyebrows arched in surprise. "How do you make alliances? How do you trade? Who guards your home?"

"Leave her alone," Paza said, stepping in front of Malenie, her hands raised and balled in fists. "Lots of people don't have no one."

"Yeah, shut up," whispered Marlassa, pinching her cousin's arm. "Is Trader Town really full of bandits?" she asked loudly. "Why don't the caravans get together to get rid of them?"

A deep-voiced bell rang, saving Malenie from trying to explain Gravin and Trader Town politics. "That's the signal for our dinner," another girl cousin, one with a sharp nose and a stubborn chin, told her. "I'm Jalene. Come on."

Malenie nudged Paza, who unclenched her fists. She seemed willing to follow the swarm of cousins if it meant food. In the dining hall, three low round tables were already set with plates and mugs and serving platters full of food. Paza folded her legs under the low table without difficulty. Malenie settled more awkwardly on the pillow between Paza and Leocarl and finally got in a question of her own. "What does your family do?"

"Shapers," he said around a mouthful of lamb. "Weave shapers mostly, though I'm a stone shaper. We grow the flax and raise sheep on the farms. That's where we were today."

A whole family of shapers? And farms? That explains the wealth.

"The dyeing, spinning and weaving happen here, and then we trade it. And Aunt Emelenie is on the Council, the head really, and makes a lot of decisions about the town. And we guard the Suntin Gate of course."

"Guard the Suntin Gate?"

There was a sudden silence at their table, although the younger kids continued chattering behind them.

"Leee-o," Jalene said.

"What? She's a cousin." He shifted uncomfortably and swallowed his food. "You know there's a Gate, right?" Malenie nodded, remembering what Paza had said when they'd first met. That there were Gates in the Wall and the Families used them. "Well, there's always a guard to keep people away—if they can even see it—and a courier for when there are messages or a visitor."

"What do you mean, see it?" Malenie asked, not sure if this meant the cousins did or did not see the Wall clearly. She desperately wanted to ask him about the messages and visitors but suspected he'd stop talking if she did.

He shifted again, and this time Malenie saw Jalene elbow him in the ribs. Leocarl shot her a look and edged a little further away, but he kept on doggedly. "Have you ever noticed that your eyes slide away from the Wall and that you can never really remember what it looks like, to describe it?"

"Ummm…" *They don't see it.* What else could she ask that he would answer? "Isn't that a problem for the guard?" *What are they guarding against?*

He glanced nervously away and back. "Uh, they… I don't know." Or didn't want to say. Jalene was focused on shoveling food into her mouth as if she had been eating gamey hare and stringy birds in the desert with them. *They know, but they're not supposed to tell.*

Malenie relaxed her fingers on her fork. *I'm not going to find out this way.* To fill the awkward silence she asked, "Where do all the adults eat?"

He rushed to answer, relieved. "They eat in the formal dining hall. There are usually important guests, so us kids eat in here. Probably this year me, Jalene and Marlassa will have to eat there every few days."

They made faces, except for Marlassa, and Jalene said, "It's boring." Marlassa stared dreamily into the air. "All she can think about are the boys that will be there," Jalene said. "But she never thinks all our parents will be there, too." She seemed to remember her manners and turned to Paza, who had barely said two words together. "Excuse us, we didn't mean to be rude. We thought we knew everyone we're related to. What's your family name? Have we met before? You seem familiar."

Paza looked up and knocked her mug over, spilling mint tea in a slash across the yellow and turquoise tiled table. Seven sets of hands quickly mopped it up, and a servant appeared to carry off the stained cloths, responding to a signal Malenie missed.

Malenie asked, a little desperately, "Are you all my cousins?" The question about Paza was forgotten as they tried to straighten her out, and Malenie got a chance to eat instead of talk. And she was hungry again. The lamb was really good. Not stringy, not cooked dry and not over-salted. Actually, it was perfect, far better than anything she ate regularly with Papa, Malenie admitted reluctantly to herself.

"Almost all of us here are first cousins," said Jalene, "except for those two and those two." She pointed to the youngest kids at the other tables, two girls with chubby, happy faces, a boy with a thin serious face and the boy who'd asked all the questions about Malenie's family. "They're Emelenie's and Liac's children's children."

Malenie missed what Jalene said next at the thought of what life in Trader Town would have been like as part of this family: she and Leocarl, Jalene and Marlassa facing down the bullies that had tormented her, and an unlikely image of Emelenie presiding over a scrap of fabric at the market, dickering over the price of camel hide. But she would have been here, wouldn't she have? Eating like this every day and taking family and servants and guards for granted. She had always thought it was bad luck it was just her and Papa, but he had chosen to leave his family, to make life harder for them, hadn't he? Why? Malenie didn't know whether the ache in her chest was a laugh or a sob.

12

Two nights later, Malenie lay in the huge bed and stared at the play of light across the ceiling. Beyond their room, the fountain gurgled, footsteps tapped in the hallway and the murmur of voices drifted from another room. In a moment of paranoia, Malenie had drawn the light sheet up to their chins to hide that they were fully clothed, and now she stroked her hand back and forth over it for the pleasure of its softness against her skin. At her side Paza was a warm, comforting presence in what felt like the vast emptiness of the house, even though she knew it was full of people. Papa's family. Her relatives.

"You barely talked these last two days," Malenie said. "What's wrong?"

"Most of the time we were sleeping. I thought we were going to sleep forever. Besides, they were talking to you," Paza said. "I don't like not being able to leave. I don't belong here."

"You belong anywhere I do," Malenie whispered fiercely, rolling to face Paza and daring to squeeze her hand. In a lower voice she admitted, "I don't know if I belong here either. But I know about you and me." She let go before Paza could and kicked off the sheet and slipped out of bed.

"Is it late enough?" Paza asked, and Malenie felt hurt Paza didn't even acknowledge what she had said, either the doubts or reassurance. *She hasn't had a normal life,* Malenie reminded herself as she pressed her ear to the chink between the top and bottom halves of the door. *She's been in the hands of a monster.* Paza untangled their sandals, handed Malenie a pair and bent to put hers on. *Anyway, it's what she does that important.*

The fountain was louder than anything in the corridor, so Malenie cracked open the door and peered out, head cocked to listen. The hallway was empty. She beckoned to Paza and they ghosted through dimly lit corridors to a side door near the kitchens. Outside, the back of the house was dark, but light glowed from the front. Moving slowly, clinging to the shadow of the house, they walked towards the light. The verandah, the steps and the area around the gate and its guards were brightly lit.

"Rot it," Malenie said, not quite as softly as she should have. "We still can't get back if we leave." She wanted Paza to stay, and if that meant having a way in and out of the compound, she was determined to find one. "It's ridiculous that we can't see Pashtin. I've never been to a city."

"I know but—"

A boy's voice intruded, scolding, "Shh! Do you want them to see you?" Malenie jumped, whipping around. Paza slipped around the corner, out of view of the guards, and Malenie hurried to follow. It was Leocarl, hands on hips. "What are you doing?" he said, sounding aggrieved. Malenie glared back, annoyed and ready to take her frustration out on him. "You're going to get us caught. I said I'd meet you."

Malenie drew in a sharp breath and switched her glare to Paza. "What did you do?"

"He has a way back in that we didn't find."

"How do you know and why didn't you tell me?"

"Shhh," Leocarl said. "Are you coming or not?" He wheeled around and headed for the corner they had noticed the other day.

Malenie blocked Paza from following. "What's going on?"

"I saw him sneaking out last night. What? I couldn't sleep."

"So…"

"So I told him I'd tell unless he took us with him."

"Paza!"

"He expected me to blackmail him! He would have done the same. You just don't know because you don't have any brothers or sisters."

Malenie fell back a step, feeling like Paza had stabbed her.

"No—I didn't mean it like that." Paza reached out for Malenie's hands, but didn't quite touch them. "I'm sorry. I just meant, death's ashes, I don't know." She paused. "That's what it was like with my sister, before…"

"I guess I know what you mean." She'd had Nes, and Nes had lots of siblings and they had acted like that. "It's alright."

"Besides," Paza wheedled, "I didn't have to threaten him that much. I think he likes you." Malenie gaped at her and Paza laughed and loped off.

"But…" Malenie didn't know what she wanted to say. She closed her mouth and trailed after them.

"You scraped the mortar out," Malenie said, just realizing. Leocarl grinned. They climbed easily to the top and hunkered flat to avoid being seen. Leocarl fumbled with a rope and dropped one end into the alley. "Where did you get that?"

"Wait and see," he said. He made quick work of climbing down.

When it was her turn, the rope scratched Malenie's palms, and the smooth soles of her sandals slid across the equally smooth surface of the wall's outward face. A deep breath as her feet met the dirt yielded no difference in the air, but a hard knot dissolved in her stomach.

They were out.

Paza barely waited for Malenie to release the rope before she shimmied down. Lightcrystals in metal settings at the end of the alley lit Leocarl's frown as he wiggled the rope from side to side. With two sharp jerks the end came unanchored and tumbled to their feet. A soft sound of dismay escaped Malenie's lips.

"Don't worry," Leocarl said with another grin, coiling the rope. "It won't do that while we're climbing it."

"But how will we get back?" Malenie asked.

"Look." A flat piece of rock was enmeshed in one end of the rope. "It's half a spell stone. One half on the wall, one half in the rope, and they attract each other. Once they touch, they won't come apart unless I make them. I shaped it myself. I figured if metal shapers can do it with slave collars and stuff, I should be able to do the same thing with rock." He puffed his chest out proudly and then quickly bent to store the rope at the base of the wall as if he had embarrassed himself.

Malenie had half a dozen questions, but chose the most important first. "You're not just leaving it there for anyone to use?" she asked incredulously.

"It's in a shaped metal chest, and only I've got a key. It's safe."

Malenie and Paza exchanged looks, and Malenie suddenly felt much older than him, as she thought of all the ways it was not safe. But… he'd obviously been doing this for some time and nothing had happened. Yet.

"We can meet here before dawn if we get split up or if you want to go off on your own. But," he hesitated, and continued almost shyly, "I'm going to the night market. I thought you might like to see it."

"Night market?" Malenie and Paza asked at the same time.

"It's a hundred times better than the regular day markets," he said.

◊◊◊

"That's beautiful," Malenie said, entranced by the complex patterns made by the flaming torches the jugglers hurled at each other. The audience pressed close together, the drumbeat incited the jugglers to go faster and faster, and hushed voices murmured on all sides. The breeze turned, and Malenie's eyes and throat stung with the harsh smell of burning pitch. The drum sped up even more. With a flourish the men flung the torches higher than Malenie thought possible, snatched them out of the air as they dropped and posed with three in each hand above their heads. The audience roared its approval, clapping, whistling and stomping.

The drummer flipped his instrument over and shouted, "The amazing Tan Brothers! They have performed all over the known world! Show your appreciation!" As he walked the edge of the crowd, the spectators threw silver and copper coins in his drum. Malenie drew back, avoiding his eyes so he wouldn't realize she had nothing to give, but Leocarl threw in enough coppers and silver half coins that the boy grinned and thanked 'the gen'lmon.'

The jugglers announced a break and the crowd milled in all directions, breaking off into smaller groups of laughing, chattering, arguing people. Mostly the crowd was Thessem, but Malenie saw Hennites, Samthanians and a few Parthavians. A woman dressed as finely as Emelenie in long tunic and trousers jogged her elbow on one side and a woman with the braids, leather jerkin and long knife of a professional hire-guard strode by on the other. Malenie even spied a pickpocket, who ducked his head and disappeared in the press of people when he caught her looking. Leocarl led them on a wandering route through more performers and past an energetic band playing for dancers.

"Look, seers." Paza stopped abruptly in front of a gold and scarlet striped tent, and Malenie tripped on her feet to avoid crashing into her.

"Come on, I want you to meet someone," Leocarl said and tried to hustle them onward. Paza ducked his hand and held her place.

"How much do you think they charge?"

Leocarl circled around. "Who cares? They're just charlatans."

"What?" Paza asked, shocked.

"That's what Aunt E says: 'fakes that cozen the witless.'"

Malenie laughed. His imitation was perfect.

"No…Really?" Paza asked Malenie.

"I don't know. But Papa would get mad when seers would tell someone who was sick that they would get better, because then they wouldn't go see a real healer."

"Come on," Leocarl said, and Paza shrugged his hand off but followed, craning over her shoulder to keep the seers' tent in sight until she collided with a well-dressed young man. She jumped back with a cut-off shriek and the man dropped all his packages.

They hurried away and entered a quieter section of the market that smelled of cinnamon and fresh baked bread. Malenie caught glimpses of luxury wares: the glint of gold jewelry and the graceful curve of fine pottery. A perfume stall with curious little bottles made her sneeze. Finally they stopped in front of a fruit seller's cart. Malenie had never seen such fruit: a misshapen green ball with scales, cut to display a creamy white interior and glossy brown seeds as big as Malenie's thumb, a brown fuzzy ovoid with flesh of palest yellow, and a green melon cut into the perfect crescent of a dark red moon.

"This is Harris," Leocarl said and Malenie looked at the proprietor for the first time.

He was Hennite, rakish with a missing earlobe, but he grinned at Leocarl as he said, "What are you doing out past bedtime, you scalawag?"

"Learning things I can't in the classroom," Leocarl answered impudently. "This is Malenie, my cousin, and Paza, her friend, from Trader Town." He turned to Malenie to say, "His son is the best spell stone shaper in Pashtin and my teacher," and missed the frown that briefly transformed Harris into the kind of person that had earned a missing earlobe and doled out worse to the one responsible. It was gone again by the time Leocarl turned around, but Malenie and Paza edged closer together.

"I wouldn't be saying those names out loud in this market, young sir," Harris said.

"Why? What have you heard?" Malenie demanded, jostling the fruit as she stepped up to the cart.

"Those names, and a hint that the man or woman who can catch the ones bearing them stands to gain a great deal." Leocarl stared at them, mouth open, while the knot tied up Malenie's stomach again.

"Anything else?" Malenie asked through her constricted throat. "Just our names?"

"Those two names." He hesitated and added, "In the mouths of those that sell drugs and slaves and poison. Were you looking for another name?"

"We have to get back," Malenie said. Walls kept things out, as well as in, and Emelenie's restrictions suddenly seemed a reasonable price to pay for safety and freedom.

"Hold on now, young misses. I'll send my man back with you, but first I have somewhat to give you." He bent down and rummaged beneath the cart and came up with a battered leather satchel. "It seems to me you might be leaving Pashtin suddenly. I'm thinking as how some supplies might come in handy." His eyes were serious and intent, with none of the hardness they had shown before.

"Ah," Malenie said, wondering if they should take it.

"The world is full of mean people aiming to do evil things. The rest of us have to work to make it the kind of place we want to live in."

"You should take it," Leocarl said.

"Thank you," Malenie said, feeling it would be unforgivably rude to refuse.

"Kal," Harris beckoned to a big man who had stood just out of hearing the whole time, "will take you home. But first let me give you a gift just for the pleasure of it." With the knife from his belt he sliced slivers off the dark red melon and handed them out, juice running down his wrist. The taste tingled across Malenie's tongue, and she closed her eyes in delight. It was like paradise, like the smell of the night blossoming flower that died at dawn.

◊◊◊

They didn't have time to open the bag until the next afternoon. Kal had escorted them back to the Pashtin house and confiscated the rope with a gruff, "Harris's orders," over Leocarl's protest. Then, way too soon after they crawled into bed, they had breakfast with the entire Pashtin family, which only seemed larger than the entire number of people living in Trader Town, more clan than family, all the relations introducing themselves, sometimes hugging Malenie and even Paza in their enthusiasm, except for the youngest, who squealed or cried or threw food. Even the haughty Emelenie—who, Paza pointed out, was the matriarch of this Family, and therefore the most important personage in the city—didn't escape the hurled food. Dishes were moved out of the babies' reach with barely a scold and everyone continued on in a cheerful chaos that bewildered Malenie, used to solitary meals with Papa. Paza took it well, dodging the grubby fists of toddlers nonchalantly. Then Emelenie had swept them off to the parlor (picking raisins from her hair) and tested Malenie for the shaper's magic. The rocks felt like rocks to her, the bits of metal like metal, and the textiles like bits of woven wool and linen, however beautiful they were.

"Hold still," Emelenie murmured, pressing a small metal disk to Malenie's hand. Her eyes refocused and she said, "You don't have it; I might just be feeling the other gift. For now you'll join the others in their classes. And no, I haven't heard anything about Serliac."

"Are you going to test Paza?"

"She is not a Pashtin."

"Neither am I," Malenie muttered to Paza in the doorway, maybe loud enough for Emelenie to hear.

A woman was cleaning their room so they grabbed Harris's satchel and ran to the garden. Leocarl, looking as droopy as Malenie felt, found them just as Malenie pulled out a sewing kit, a bunch of leather thongs and a piece of oil paper that had a list of places and the travel times between them. Paza already cupped a piece of clay studded with poor man's lanterns, attempting to see their glow.

"Hey, those are slingshots," Leocarl said, reaching for the leather thongs.

Paza snatched them from under his hand and clutched them to her chest. "Those are ours!" She bared her teeth like she might bite him and Leocarl startled back.

"Paza!" Malenie said. "He wasn't going to take them."

Leocarl dropped to a seat beside Malenie. "Yeah, I just wanted to see them. Harris taught me. Herders use them to keep wild dogs from their sheep. I brought mine to the farm the other day, but we didn't see any, wild dogs I mean, not sheep. We saw lots of those."

Paza's hands had loosened as he chattered, but her shoulders were hunched in embarrassment.

"Do you know how?" Leocarl asked. "Because I can show you if you don't."

"Here." Paza shoved the slings at him. "But you have to give them back."

"I will, I promise." Untangled, there were three. "Perfect! For practicing, I mean. This is the hold cord." He pointed to the cord with a loop on the end and a slipknot. "It goes over your finger or your wrist, whichever you want. The other is the release cord." It ended in a simple knot. "And it's the one you release to throw your rock." He plucked an ornamental rock the size of his fist from the ones lining the path. "Look for ones like this."

Malenie shoved everything else back into the bag, which was big enough to hold a few more rocks, but nothing like the numbers Leocarl was plundering from the garden. Lifting her tunic to make a sling of it like Leocarl and Paza were doing would expose the diamonds on her waist and above her hips. Only a few more rocks fit in the cradle of her arm.

"I have rocks for you," Paza said, popping up behind Malenie. Her tunic strained at the weight. "I mean, I'll share. With you."

"Oh, good. Let's try them." Malenie bounced on her toes, happy the marks weren't going to interfere again with being part of the group.

Leocarl was already hanging dark fabric scraps from hooks set into the wall of the compound. "For some foreign trees the gardener planted," he explained. "They died."

Paza went first and whooped in delight when she hit the target. The rock left a little puff of white dust to mark the spot.

"Nice!" Leocarl said.

Malenie grunted in pain as the rock-laden slingshot smacked her temple on her first try. Rubbing her head, she asked, "What was that fruit last night?"

"Gaisha melon. Only Harris ever has it and he isn't telling where it's from. That little bit he gave us was probably equal to the cost of a young she-goat." He didn't seem to notice the dismay his words caused her.

If I had known… Malenie thought, but it was too late now to refuse the gift, and there was no way to give it back. She practiced without a rock, trying not to care that Paza and Leocarl were much better than her. Her slingshot writhed in all directions but the one she aimed for, even when the others helped. She kept on stubbornly; if they had had slings during the trek to Pashtin, they might not have arrived so hungry, and Shay wouldn't have had to risk so much.

"Here now, miss," an unexpected voice said behind her, and Malenie turned to see the guard who had answered their questions about the cousins. "You're all turned around, on account a being a lefty like me. You've got the right foot forward, but you have to turn sideways a bit more. That's right. Now it's all in your wrist." Malenie twirled the sling, hopping forward and releasing the cord as it swung forward. It made a tremendous snapping sound, like the crack of a whip.

"I did it!" she crowed.

The guard grinned back at her. "And right fine it was."

"Nice shot, Malenie," Yasmin said behind them, and they all spun around in surprise, even the guard. "I came to invite you to tea." Malenie straightened her shoulders in unconscious imitation of Yasmin's confidence and brushed at the dust on her tunic.

"Super!" Leocarl wrapped his slingshot into a neat coil and, with a look at Paza for permission, tucked it into the satchel.

"What do you say, Malenie?" Yasmin asked.

"There'll be sweets," Leocarl added.

"I would like that," Malenie said a little awkwardly and then looked anxiously at Paza, who shrugged.

"Super!" Yasmin said, and Malenie giggled because she sounded so like Leocarl. Struck by a sudden thought, she examined cousin and aunt closely.

"Are you—is she…?"

"My mother? Naw. Salenie is."

"I've only contributed two children to this clan that thinks it's a family," Yasmin confided, leading them into the house. "And they're in the nursery still."

To Malenie's relief they passed Emelenie's parlor and continued to a room further down the hall. Yasmin gestured for them to sit at the low table and tugged on the bell cord near a desk covered in papers. Malenie lingered at the desk to look at the meticulously drawn patterns, like the ones on the blankets and the wall hangings that seemed to hang in every room.

Her aunt caught her looking and lifted a large thin sheet of paper, spreading it out for Malenie to view. "I don't have the Pashtin gift, but I'm very good at designing patterns that work for those that do." A striking design of stylized flames was inked in black and red.

"Is that unusual?"

"Didn't Emelenie explain when she tested you? At most only a quarter of us have the gift." Yasmin drew Malenie, and Paza, who hovered at Malenie's shoulder, to the table.

"Not really," Malenie said, folding her legs under it with a little more grace than the first time.

Leocarl muttered something that sounded like 'typical' as Dessie came through the doorway with a large tray. They helped her unload cups, plates of cheese, olives, bread and pastries. "Thank you. I'll take care of the tea," Yasmin said. She spooned loose tea into the pot, filled it with hot water and set it aside to steep. "The rest of us tend the farms north of the city or sell some of the linen and wool we produce directly or keep the books or all the other things that need to be done. But the best materials come here, and family members with the gift shape the yarn and fabric, adding extra warmth, protection against fire and the like. Some can even shape fabric that speeds healing, but that's rare."

"Wait, you mean all those people weaving and spinning are related to you—to us?" Malenie asked.

While Yasmin poured tea and more hot water into brass cups, Leocarl answered: "All of them. Fifth cousins four times removed to first cousins not removed and their husbands, wives and children." Yasmin passed a cup by the rim and Malenie almost burnt her fingers as she tried to take it all in. It seemed incredible Papa had managed to hide such a large family. *I still don't know why. And what did he think of just the two of us?*

Malenie took a pastry sticky with honey and covered in nuts. She passed the plate to Paza and poured her tea between cup and the deep saucer to cool it. "Do they all live here?" she asked hesitantly.

Leocarl snorted tea out his nose he laughed so hard. While he patted the damp spot on his tunic, Yasmin wiped the table and said, "Your face, Malenie! No, they wouldn't fit. There's about seventy of us here at the house and more live in the city and on the farm. Do you come from a large family, Paza?"

Paza didn't have anything in her hands to spill or knock over this time. If she'd had hair to hide behind she would have; instead she looked down at her plate and traced the graven rim. "Ah, no, not so large," she mumbled.

Malenie rushed belatedly to her rescue. She had wanted to hear the answer, too, and felt guilty for it. "Do you care that you don't have it, Yasmin—the gift?" she asked randomly. Leocarl paused in chewing his third pastry and looked at her. Nervously Malenie untangled her hair from her necklace and smoothed it. "That was rude. I'm sorry." But Paza at least had relaxed enough to pick up her untouched tea and blow on it.

"Don't worry," Yasmin said. Her cup clicked against her saucer as she put it down. "Are you wearing your mama's wedding necklace?"

"Wedding necklace?"

"Look." Yasmin fished a chain from the collar of her tunic. It was very similar in color, a warm yellow gold, and style, flat, with three heavier links etched with words Malenie couldn't make out. Mama's said 'joy, partnership, fruitfulness.' "May I see it?" Yasmin asked.

Malenie fumbled with the clasp until Paza pushed her hands away and helped. Yasmin handled it carefully, Malenie was relieved to see, but it gave her a funny feeling in the pit of her stomach to watch someone else touch it.

"It is! Look, these are hinges." Yasmin pointed to tiny moldings Malenie had thought were decorative when she had held the chain in her hands, imagining her mama. "Inside should be a strand of your papa's hair. I won't open it. That's too intimate." The knot in Malenie's stomach unclenched when she had the necklace back in her hands, but not enough to eat. She refastened it around her neck.

"It's not quite… proper for you to wear it," Yasmin said.

"I didn't know what it was."

"Didn't know!" Leocarl subsided at the look Yasmin sent him and busied himself refreshing their tea. That worked a lot better than Jalene's elbow, Malenie thought.

"Did you know?" Yasmin asked Paza, who shrugged, but even Malenie wasn't sure if that was an answer or not. "Married men wear a ring, or a brooch, with a strand of their wife's hair inside, although they're generally not as constant in their use as women," Yasmin said. "Did Serliac wear…? I think it was a brooch."

Malenie shook her head. "We were the only Parthavians, and he didn't talk about Mama much."

"They lived here for a short time. She was a lovely person."

Yasmin knew her mama.

Yasmin could tell her about Mama, more than a bare, 'You look like her.' Malenie had been waiting all her life to learn what Mama looked like when she smiled, if she was a healer, too, what advice she would have given about the bullies in Trader Town. A memory of the grief in Papa's eyes formed in her mind. Their meals together might seem lonely to the Pashtins, but they had been companionable, Papa talking about patients and healing, Malenie talking about neighbors and the market gossip. She had always thought he would eventually tell her about Mama, and that maybe a little of his sorrow might lift as he did. And she felt, maybe foolishly, that if Yasmin told her… it might jinx Papa's safe return. But the need to know beat in her chest in time with her heart. She wouldn't say 'No, stop,' if Yasmin started talking about her.

"She was here such a short time," Yasmin said, "none of us got to know her very well."

Her words were like a blow. The confused anticipation drained out of Malenie, leaving an emptiness behind.

Yasmin looked away. "Leocarl!" He dropped the last pastry on the serving dish and folded his hands in his lap. Yasmin bit her lip, then said tentatively, "They seemed happy together, and she was very excited to have you."

Malenie hugged herself as if she could catch the words and lock them in her heart.

13

Now that Malenie was recovered from the desert, Emelenie insisted she join the cousins' lessons on accounts keeping, writing and weaving, which Paza avoided like a dog dead ten days in the sun, and teatime with family members, who were about as determined to avoid conversations about Papa, Mama, the Wall and the Gate or anything else Malenie wanted to know. During the day, she started lurking in corners, next to windows and by the gate, hoping to learn something, anything, and at night, unable to sleep, she paced the hallways. Watching the sharpness leave Paza's face was the only thing that kept the wildness growing inside her checked.

One night Paza was trailing sleepily behind Malenie, who was thinking, *I should go back to bed, she won't sleep until I do*, when a commotion in Emelenie's parlor caught her attention. They crept up to the doorway to listen.

"…got our message." That was Yasmin. Her voice rose loudly and then dropped softly, as if she were pacing past the door. "… a coincidence… Suntin."

The word sent a frisson of anxiety through Malenie. Paza whispered frantically, "Here? There's a town with the same name?"

Malenie shook her head. "No, there's no place named Suntin on this side of the Wall. Shh." She strained to hear, leaning as close to the doorframe as she dared, but Yasmin had stopped on the other side of the room, her voice calmer and the words inaudible.

"Salenie, ring for a maid," Emelenie said. "I want wine, and Yasmin can at least wipe her hands and face."

Rot it. Malenie started to sidle away, but Yasmin's next words rooted her feet in place. "…Paza, as you thought…send her… They're waiting now." The words seemed to strike like arrows into her heart. Not Yasmin! Betrayal and panic squeezed her chest. *I liked her, thought she liked us. It can't be how it sounds.*

Stricken, Paza clutched at Malenie and mouthed, "We have to go." The maid's footsteps clattered in the hall, approaching the turn. They darted into a nearby room and let the curtain swing closed. Voices murmured indistinctly. They waited, every rustle of clothing and breath echoing off the tiled walls. *They're going to find us.* Time stretched out. Finally, the maid's footsteps retreated.

"We have to think what to do," Malenie whispered.

"We have to go! They're going to get rid of me. I won't go back to Suntin. I can't." Paza's voice was as ragged as her breathing. Sweat from her hands dampened Malenie's sleeve as she dragged her to the door.

"Wait, there's got to be another explanation." *Papa's family wouldn't betray me. But this is about Paza. Would they see it as betraying me?*

"Not here." Paza let go of Malenie only long enough to twitch the curtain aside and then grabbed her again.

Malenie hissed in annoyance at being tugged along as if she were unwilling. She yanked her arm away and tiptoed behind Paza, thinking furiously. Past the first turning, Paza began to run, bare feet squeaking on the tiles, and Malenie raced to keep up. *Who is waiting?* Her feeling of constrained safety crumbled into suspicion. *Have they been lying to us while they arranged to get rid of Paza? If they lied about her, what else have they lied about?*

Back in their room, Malenie shut the door quietly and leaned against it. Paza slid out from under the bed with their satchels. "Do you know what that was about?" Malenie asked, hoping against hope that Paza had an explanation that did not involve Malenie's family conspiring with Paza's kidnapper.

The nuts and dried fruit Paza had been hoarding tumbled from her hands and skittered across the floor. She stood there staring at the mess. "I can't go back," she whispered. "I can't stay here. He's coming for me." She touched the cloth covering her hair and then snatched her hands away.

All Malenie's confusion, fear and feelings of betrayal coalesced into a hard knot in her stomach. Nuts crunched under her feet as she crossed the tiles. "Paza." Malenie gripped her shoulders and, when she continued to stare at nothing Malenie could see, gently shook her. Paza blinked and looked up. "I'll keep you safe," Malenie soothed. "I won't let them… send you anywhere."

"You promise?" She clutched Malenie's wrists, as if she were dying of thirst and Malenie had offered her water.

"I promise to keep you safe." The tautness of Paza's shoulders relaxed a little, but she still thrummed with tension. "But I don't think they would… they're my family, they wouldn't just, just turn you over to someone like him."

"You saw him. He looks normal. How would they know what he is?" She pressed her lips together. "They're your family, not mine. They look at me and see a godless monster. What they wouldn't do to you, they might to me."

"I guess…" *I just can't believe it of Yasmin.* That the Pashtins could know him, but not what he was or what he had done, that seemed much more likely. *Either way, I can't take that risk for Paza.* No matter how dangerous it might be out there.

"We have to hurry. Please," Paza said.

"Right." Hurry, hurry—the word beat in Malenie's ears as she stripped out of borrowed clothes, folded them and put them on the bed. It was the only note she was going to leave, and she hoped they read her intention. *I don't steal. We left on our own.* She changed into her own threadbare tunic and trousers and gathered together her meager belongings. Harris's bag with the slings, a few rocks that fit perfectly, waterskins and the bag Nes had given her. With an unexpected sense of loss, she glanced at the bed with its fat mattress, the blue and green mosaics on the walls, and the carved screens. Impatiently Paza tugged at her hand and cracked the door open to peer down the hallway. As they passed Marlassa and Jalene's rooms, the cousins laughed and dice chattered on the tiles. *I'm not sure I want to go.* Paza dragged her on.

Outside, as they climbed the wall, Malenie wished the Pashtins a silent farewell. No matter how frustrating they'd been, she'd wanted to be a part of their family. Even now, with the sharp rock digging into her palms as she hung suspended on the street side, she wanted to believe it was a mistake. *I should have talked to them.*

Her feet slid over the smooth plaster and she dropped, bent knees absorbing the shock as she hit the ground. Paza landed beside her, jostling the satchel on Malenie's shoulder, and they both overbalanced and landed on their butts. The lightcrystals' sharp glow revealed the straight line of Paza's lips and the shadows pooled under her eyes. She looked hunted, wound tight with tension. Malenie's stomach did somersaults, half fear, half excitement at escaping the confines of the Pashtin family. The cold night air bit at her lungs and seemed to clear her mind, enough for her to think about what was ahead of them and where they would run to.

"Paza," she said slowly, "Emelenie will find us in Pashtin, and the desert… There won't be any Shay this time." She heaved a deep breath, mentally reviewing the last six days. "Maybe they lied to us about everything. Maybe they never sent any guards for Papa." She choked on the thought. Emelenie, she could believe anything of, but Yasmin… "I don't know what to think, but I have to know. Liac and the guards must be about to arrive in Trader Town if they were sent at all. If we got there first, we could wait for them, watch what they do. Help, if they…" She couldn't voice her hopes; she had been close enough to touch Papa's hand before and still hadn't been able to do anything except run away.

"There's only one choice, isn't there?" Paza said. Her hands jerked as she brushed dirt from her trousers, and Malenie could almost see her struggling to think in spite of her panic.

"Is there?" Malenie licked her lips nervously. Like an untamed horse Paza's fear could run away with her at any moment. *I have to ask anyway. It's too important.* Remembering Paza's rage in the desert, she watched closely as she asked, "He's using to magic to find you, isn't he? Why does he want you so bad?" *Why didn't I ask before this, before we were crouching in the dirt and the dark again?*

Because she hadn't wanted to see fear behind Paza's eyes. Because she was afraid of the rage Paza kept pent inside and that asking questions would set it free. Because she had chosen to trust her on that rooftop the day Paza rescued her.

"I messed up that time, but I won't this time. I should have wished us somewhere, anywhere else than on this side of the Wall. And I should have put a protection on both of us, so he couldn't use magic to find us. If he's there…" her voice wavered, gained force. "If he's there, we'll be ready. I'll be ready. I'll wish for protection and I'll wish us to back to Raleton." Conviction rang in her voice, but she hadn't answered the question and she wasn't looking at Malenie. Instead she stared at the stars and blinked rapidly.

Malenie touched the back of her hand with her fingertips, hoping she would face her. "Paza."

"I don't know, honest." Lips trembling, she said, "Do you think I haven't thought about it and thought about it? If I only knew…." Her voice cracked.

Malenie had to look away from the fear on Paza's face. It didn't make her own fear any easier to deal with. *We're begging him to find us if we do this. All I have to do is go up to the gate and demand to be allowed back in.*

Two things stopped her. She had given Paza her trust, and she had promised to protect her. Sure, she could change her decision to trust. But Paza had rescued her, trusted her, helped her, suffered with her in the desert, needed her. She had no one else, and so Malenie really couldn't and really wouldn't take back her trust. And she had just promised to protect her, and this place was no longer safe for her.

Just as she came to that conclusion, Paza added: "I need you, Mellie. We need each other."

Malenie flushed warm at the affection in Paza's voice and the trust implied by her exposure of vulnerability. It was enough to push away the fear for a little bit, enough to make something hard in her chest crack, enough to make her believe they could face him and survive.

◊◊◊

Finding the Wall was easy. Leocarl had pointed the way the other night. The Pashtins' house was close to the temples, which smelled of flowers and wood smoke and lined the north-south road in the center of the city, and the temples were close to the parade ground, which smelled of dust and animal dung, and extended from the temples to the Wall. The light of the waxing moon reflected off its pale stones, except where it was absorbed by a darkness that was not stone, but wood.

"The Gate," Malenie said softly.

"Don't stop," Paza pleaded. "We can't go that way, anyway."

Try as she might, Malenie could only make out one figure, standing at attention. The courier was either hidden in the shadows or away on an errand. Was she on her way to the Pashtin house or on the far side of the Wall with a message about Paza? It was too far to see much else, except that the Gate loomed higher than the stone enfolding it on all sides. *Rot it*, Malenie thought. *This is something I need to know about and instead we're hurrying by like thieves.*

The parade ground was otherwise deserted at this late hour. They skirted its edge, Malenie's back tense with the thought of the guard's watching eyes, and her ears strained for the sound of an alarm. Her feet wanted to hurry, but she knew they mustn't. *We're just two girls going home*, she thought and tried to project normal, not fear and definitely not daring escape into the unknown. As they got closer to the Wall, the shadows ahead resolved into trees exhaling cool moist air. The croaking, chittering chorus of frogs and crickets reached out and surrounded them, blocking out all other noise, and then cut off. Malenie stumbled in surprise.

"Come on." Paza pulled her into the tangle, ducked under a trailing vine and slithered past a spiky plant like an open fan that caught at Malenie's clothes and hair. Every step was a battle.

By the time they found the first pool, even Paza's feet were dragging. The unsuccessful, chilly dive sapped their strength. After the second pool, they gave into exhaustion and slept.

14

Malenie rested her head on her arms, closed her aching eyes and waited for Paza to emerge from the pool. This was the third one they had
checked since Paza had nudged Malenie out of a dreamless sleep at
first light, and Malenie's late night belief in their invincibility had faded. It was no longer dawn, Malenie's clothes stuck to her with sweat
and Paza was taking a long time. Malenie rolled her head on her arms
and frowned at the limpid water. *She's found something.* The thought only
intensified Malenie's worry. A welt on her cheek throbbed, the gift of
a whippy branch. Waving away the tiny insects attracted by the blood,
she bent to peer into the pool. Her blurred reflection rose to meet her.
Tendrils of her hair dropped into the water and fanned open, hiding
everything beneath the surface.

Paza erupted into the air, snorting water from her nose, and Malenie
reared back. "It's deep, but it's there," Paza gasped, grabbing a rock at
the edge as an anchor.

"Oh, good." Malenie sat on her heels and wiped moisture from her
face. The humid, green heat under the trees no longer seemed so op-
pressive, now that she knew they'd be leaving. The lack of sky above
her had been wearing at her nerves. It was almost enough to make her
glad they had found a way under the Wall. Almost. "Are you sure about
doing this?" Malenie asked, although she didn't know if she wanted
her to say yes or no. It gave her the creeps, and worse, to imagine him
as they'd seen him last, lounging, waiting, expecting them.

The flicker of matching fear on Paza's face was impossible to miss,
but she answered "yes" as stoutly as she had every other time they had

discussed it. This time she added: "I'm not going to let him, let my fear of him decide what I'm going to do. I might as well be—it'd be like I was still—that he was still telling me what to do." Her voice trembled, then steadied. "This is what we have to do. So we should just go, before I forget I'm being brave," Paza joked, but it wasn't a joke really.

"Right. You'll go first," Malenie said. "I'll keep a hold of your ankle."

"You remember what I showed you about swimming?" Paza asked, referring to her brief lesson that morning. That Paza knew how to swim was just one of the many mysteries about her. "Just keep kicking." She waited for Malenie to nod. "And at the first sight of anything I'll use the magic to get us away, quick as a striking snake."

Malenie dangled her legs in the water. It felt good, although earlier she had thought her feet were going to fall off from the cold. "Ugh, I wish you hadn't said that." *I'm not sure we're the snake in this scenario. I feel more like the mouse.* But she wouldn't let Paza see her doubt. She slipped into the pool and sucked in her stomach at its chill. "It's not much of a plan," she said, thinking of Nes and the stratagem that got them into and out of Gravin's compound. That had been a real plan, no matter what Paza had said at the time. What was Nes doing right now? Laundry, probably.

Paza tried to grin, but it wobbled. "How is this for a plan? Take a deep breath. You're going to need it." She flipped over and pushed off the rocks with her feet, propelling herself downwards. Malenie took several quick deep breaths and one longer one and let the water swallow her. Everything was dim shades of green and blue. Her ears popped with the pressure as she thrashed in an attempt to imitate Paza's more graceful dive. Her fingers raked the sandy bottom as Paza kicked into the rounded mouth of the tunnel. Malenie caught her heel and used her free hand and feet to scrabble and kick forward into the darkness.

Malenie's shoulder scraped the side of the tunnel. Paza's foot jerked almost out of her grasp and her lungs ached for air. A tiny bubble of fear grew in her stomach. The tunnel seemed to be closing in on them, tighter and tighter. *I need to breathe.* Suddenly Paza's foot swung wide and Malenie's fingers clawed water, not stone. It was still so dark that it made no difference whether her eyes were open or closed, but the feeling of being closed in lessened. Paza swam faster. *I hope that's up.*

Malenie kicked strongly and fought to hold on to her. *I can make it*, she thought as the pressure on her chest clamped down.

She broke into the air. Their shoulders bumped. She panted, opening her eyes wide to see something, anything besides darkness. Water slapped her in the face and she kicked harder to stay afloat. Their breathing echoed oddly, as it had in the tiled rooms of the Pashtin house, and water lapped against walls nearby. It smelled cold, without a hint of growing things or open spaces. The fear that had gripped Malenie in the tunnel still banded her lungs.

"Paza," Malenie whispered. Trailing sibilants answered her.

A man's voice cut across the echo. "Paza."

She shrieked, "I-wish-we-were-in-Raleton-right-now!" clutching Malenie's arm with both hands. They sank.

But the expected magic and wrench of dislocation to another place didn't happen.

Malenie choked and kicked. They bobbed back to the surface. Paza screamed, the words unintelligible with hysteria and spluttering. Malenie didn't wait. She thrust Paza towards where she thought the tunnel was. Paza flailed, pushing them both under. Rough stone bruised Malenie's searching fingers. *Where is it?* Malenie pulled herself deeper, probing the stone until the need to breathe became unbearable and she kicked back up. Malenie wheezed for air. Paza rammed into her again and wrapped around Malenie like a tangle vine.

Steel rasped on flint. Light blossomed behind them, revealing a stranger standing almost within arms' reach in front of them, up to his waist in water with his back to the Wall. Malenie yelped, the sound echoing, and he flexed his fingers, daring her to try to get past him. Paza's weight dragged them down. Malenie tried to unpeel her arms and Paza's grip tightened convulsively.

"Let go," Malenie said in Paza's ear. "We're going to drown. I need you to be brave." The center of Malenie's back itched. She knew he was behind them, watching them. Paza pressed her forehead to Malenie's and then unclamped her hands and started to kick. Malenie wanted to close her eyes as the movement swung them around.

It was he, of course, torch in hand, with two more rough-clad men, armed and menacing. One held a drawn dagger. The other had a hand on his sword's hilt. And *he* was perched to the side on one of the short columns framing the shallow steps leading up from the pool. Behind him, a stone room reflected and multiplied the torchlight. The pool itself was almost a well, encircled by walls that reached a man's height above the water and blocked their view of anything more.

"Paza, my dear, it was so considerate of you to meet me here."

"I—didn't." The words jerked out of her.

Doubt flared in Malenie's mind, again. *This is what he does. I won't let him trick me*, Malenie thought grimly. *We were so stupid to think we could avoid him.* Her legs ached and she was sinking more often, breathing water as often as air. She spit out a mouthful.

"Come on." She kicked harder, towed Paza to the side and hooked her arm over an outthrust rock. Her feet found the ledge the henchman was standing on. Malenie slumped with relief against the cold stones. *It's ridiculous to feel safer just because no one can come up behind us.* But her skin didn't crawl so much, now. The ugly one hadn't moved; clearly he knew exactly where the tunnel was. Malenie squinted through the bewildering light, trying to find the exit. There had to be one; *he* had gotten in after all.

The flames glittered in his eyes. "You're wasting your time." Annoyance edged his voice.

He doesn't like being ignored.

"You'll have to come to me. There's no other way out, and your magic won't work here." The torch flared, shadows billowing over the men below him, creating the illusion of movement, and Paza flinched against Malenie's side. Malenie gripped her hand and squeezed.

"Why not?" Malenie asked. She didn't want to talk to him. But she needed to know. *Without knowledge you can't heal a patient, can't solve the puzzle*, Papa's voice whispered in her memory, and longing made her heart ache.

He handed the torch to one of his men, proving they weren't the statues they were pretending to be, propped his elbow on his raised knee and rested his chin on his fist. "It's a hideaway," he explained conversationally, "made of the same stone as the Wall, which nullifies all magic except its own. Paza should have known, but she never was a good pupil, except for the things she wanted to learn." Paza twitched violently, sending waves racing in all directions to slap against the rocks.

The cruel humor in his voice made Malenie cringe. She didn't like this glimpse past his avuncular pretense. *I'll never be afraid of Rooster Boy again.* He was nothing compared to the man in the blue robe. Surprisingly, thoughts of the bully in Trader Town steadied her. *He* was just another bully. A big, dangerous one.

"If she had been a good pupil, she would remember that it is very dangerous to use magic the way you have, disappearing from one spot and appearing in another. I would hate for something to happen to you both." Malenie tried to exchange a glance with Paza, but Paza was staring at the water. "You're both very important to me. But you asked about the hideaway. Our ancestors built them and cowered in them while the world broke around them. They were fools!" His voice cracked like a whip on the last words. Malenie thought the man with the dagger flinched, but it was hard to tell in the uncertain light. "They debased us, debased our magic. They made us weak." He took a deep breath and recovered his easy tones. "What it means for you, my dear little girls, is that we are all equal here. No magic tricks, no miraculous escapes. I was quite upset you managed to get away last time. I didn't know you could think that fast, Paza.

"You know what I do to those who upset me."

Malenie hung on to Paza, whose long shudders threatened to tip them both off the ledge.

"Of course, we are not equal. I have the superior forces, superior arms, superior wisdom.

"You." He snapped his fingers at the thug guarding the tunnel. "Bring them here."

The thug moved slowly but inexorably along the ledge. Malenie poked Paza in the ribs, bent her knees and tensed, waiting. At the rotten smell of his breath, she shouted "now!" and launched herself and Paza towards the tunnel.

The water smacked the air from her lungs. She had two heartbeats of hope before the thug landed right on top of her, plunging her deep underwater, trapping her below him. *Air. I need air.* She kicked frantically and an elbow cracked across the back of her head. She went limp, stunned. Water rushed up her nose and wormed into her mouth. She hung, suspended. *I have to…* The thought slipped away.

Her collar tightened around her neck, and she was dragged above the water by her tunic. Convulsions wracked her and her lungs heaved for air. She clawed her tunic away from her neck as the thug hauled her out of the pool. He dropped them at his master's feet, planted now on the highest step, and backed up to take a wide-legged position on the lowest riser. She shuddered and gasped, trying to calm her breathing, trying to calm her mind. Paza curled into her side. Pride forced Malenie up, but her trembling arms and legs didn't have the strength to raise her above her knees.

A gentle hand stripped Malenie's tangled hair from her face. She recoiled and tumbled down the stairs, colliding with the thug, who roughly set her upright again. His hard hands and ugly breath were preferable to *his*. There was something on his face as he stared at her and in his hands as he touched her that she did not want to think about. Paza huddled on her knees; her hands worked nervously, squeezing water from her clothes, and her head was bent, hiding her eyes.

"You're like a new-born butterfly," he mused, eyes on Malenie. "Just emerged from your chrysalis, wings weak and crumpled and wet." He laughed at his own joke. "Almost ready to fly." Malenie looked away from his disturbing stare. The room was made of the same massive blocks as the Wall, as tightly fitted together. It stretched into darkness in either direction. There was an arched doorway directly ahead. Heavy shadows cloaked the passage beyond.

"I'm looking forward to learning all about you." The stubborn tilt of her chin seemed to amuse him; his smile widened. His look probed at Malenie's clothing as if he could see past it.

Clenching her fists at her sides, she resisted the urge to pat her sleeves into place. The gesture would give away too much. *I'm tired of people looking at me like a thing, she thought. First the Raleton Patriarch, then the Pashtins and now him. Is that why I'm not terrified?* She was bone-shaking scared, but she was also angry, with a wild, flaring fury that shook her as much as the fear.

He turned away from Malenie and caressed Paza's head. "You made me very annoyed, girl." She jerked under his hand. "First trying to bind me with your friend's magic and then leaving me after I traveled so far to find you. However, you've brought me this prize. And so I'll have to decide which you deserve more: punishment or reward."

"Stop it!" Malenie shouted. Rage swept through her and gave her the energy to jump to her feet. She knocked his hand away and dragged

Paza behind her. Her shout rang off the stones. Stop! Stop! Stop!

She expected blows, anger, insults, and she crouched in a fighter's stance, ready, wanting to fight. The rage was too big for her body, big enough to fight four armed men.

Instead he said quietly to Paza, "You could be a butterfly, my dear girl, if you wanted. Let's go." He flicked a hand at the men. Paza's arms tightened on Malenie's waist and then the thug herded them to the doorway, just like a sheepdog and its sheep, with sharp jabs to the ribs in place of snaps at their heels. *His breath is worse than a dog's*, Malenie thought, each poke ratcheting her anger higher.

The man with the torch went first, through the doorway and up a steeply slanted ramp. The torchlight flickered over rock, rock and more rock, nothing that would help them escape. Malenie's feet slipped and squeaked inside her sandals as she walked, and Paza almost tripped her, still clutching tightly at her waist.

"Do you think there are snakes?" Malenie pinched the inside of Paza's arm, hoping she would guess her meaning and be ready. To do something. No one answered. At the end of the ramp they waited while the first man fumbled at a normal-looking door, and readiness coursed through Malenie. She stuffed her hair down the back of her tunic and shivered at its clammy touch. He obviously thought Paza was too cowed to attempt escape. *I hope he'll try to march us sopping wet through the streets of Suntin.* Someone must notice and interfere. Although he could put slave collars on them and no one would look twice. That was a nasty thought.

The door opened into a small room with a dirt floor and narrow vents that admitted little light. There was no sign it guarded the entry to an ancient hideaway that was impervious to magic. No sign except an overturned chair, a shattered mug and the man trussed tight with rope in a corner. Malenie peered at him covertly, hoping he'd show signs of movement, but he was out cold. Or dead. The first man ground the torch out against the dirt floor and tossed it on a stack of spent torches.

With a touch, the man in the robe detached Paza from Malenie. Paza walked woodenly where he pushed her. Malenie almost hissed in annoyance as he sorted them out, placing two men between her and Paza, then Malenie and the thug last. *He* took the lead. That was bad.

I hope she's not too intimidated by him to act. Malenie's own fear was almost entirely hidden by her anger on Paza's behalf.

As if reading her mind, Paza shuffled out of line slightly so Malenie could see her past the men's backs. *He* opened the door, strode through and hesitated as the bright sun dazzled dark-adapted eyes. The line bunched up around him. Malenie darted forward. *I don't need to see, I just need to touch Paza.*

"Snake!" she shouted, hoping that would confuse them. Let this work.

"You rotter!" Paza shouted, swinging her shiv at him.

Death's ashes. Malenie dodged the men. *What is she doing?* "Paza!" the thug's meaty hand clamped on her arm and Malenie cried out in rage. Her eyes were already adjusting. *We're losing our chance because of this smelly oaf.* Traitorously, she thought, *And because of Paza.* Nes's training took over, as she hadn't truly let it since that awful day she'd gone too far with the bullies. She grabbed his pinkie finger, forcing it back and back towards his wrist. Paza slammed into her as he bellowed in pain like a wounded ox. Bone snapped under her hands.

The world disappeared in blue fire that was pain and noise and light.

And returned, slapping against Malenie's knees as she folded to the ground, retching. Her stomach tried to turn inside out and climb up her throat. Tears and snot slimed her face. Even as the pain of the magic ebbed she relived the crack of bone and her empty stomach heaved again. She curled up on the floor, puking and crying.

After a long time, her stomach finally calmed, and Paza touched her wrist lightly with her fingers. When Malenie sat up, Paza handed her a waterskin. Malenie rinsed and spat and then took small sips to ease her throat. It stayed down, so she took a longer drink and finally looked around. They were in the courtyard of a once-grand house, surrounded on all sides by arcades with bricked-up windows under their sheltering arches. The courtyard itself was bare of everything but dust. Paza hovered at Malenie's elbow, twisting and untwisting the head cloth she had used to cool Malenie's temples and cheeks.

"What's wrong?" Malenie croaked. She corrected herself with a grimace: "What else is wrong?"

"Your nose is bleeding. Did one of them hit you?"

Malenie dabbed at her upper lip; her fingers came away bloody.

Blood and spew caked her tunic. And there was a tickle at the back of her throat that was more than rawness. Malenie pinched her nose and tilted her head back.

"No." Her voice came out muffled. "I don't think we should do that again." Her gesture was vague, arm swinging between herself, Paza and north. "Use the magic like that," she clarified. Each time they traveled long distances with magic it seemed to get worse. At least Malenie thought it was the magic and not…what she had done. "Where are we?" she asked abruptly, unsure if they would have a choice. That set her coughing, which made her dizzy, so she stretched out on her back, careful to keep her feet clear of the mess. Her head throbbed.

"Raleton." Paza's feet scuffed closer and she sat by Malenie's head with the cloth still wound about her hands. "No one knows about this place. I sleep here sometimes. I, uh, here." She thrust a smaller water-skin at Malenie. "You need to eat something."

Malenie took a cautious sip. It was thin grainy yogurt. "Where did this come from?"

"I, uh, took it. From him."

"Really?"

"It was easy. I was mad. Also, I missed when I tried to stab him."

Malenie digested that and decided no response was the best response. She kept drinking. By now she knew she needed to eat after using the magic, but no wonder Paza was so excited about good food. The yogurt tasted like dirt. "Are you hurt?"

Paza followed Malenie's glance to her hands and unwound the cloth. "No. See? He seemed to say—he made it sound like the magic to protect my family didn't work. Do you think he was lying?"

This, I can answer. "I think he lies about everything. I know it did something, or it wouldn't have hurt so much."

Paza fiddled with the cloth. "Yeah. I managed to do the protection, too. He shouldn't be able to find us any more."

"Paza, that's great." Maybe in a little bit feelings of celebration and relief would catch up with her, but right now Malenie felt too awful to appreciate it. She forced herself to say, "That's amazing."

"Um, thanks. Can we—do you mind staying here tonight and going to Trader Town tomorrow? We should still be ahead of your uncle by a day or two." She counted on her fingers. "We went to the night market with Leocarl two nights after Liac left, four more nights with the Pashtins, one night by the Wall, one here—that's eight, exactly how long the matriarch said it would take them. I have another tunic at one of my other hide—hideouts and I could get us food…"

As Paza babbled, Malenie switched hands to clasp Paza's ankle. "It's alright," she interrupted. "I want to rest, too. You did good, in spite of our abysmal plan. Quick as a snake." It hurt to smile, but she did it anyway.

At last Paza's hands relaxed on the rag and she attempted a smile. It was as weak as Malenie's. "An arthritic snake as old as a grandmother."

"A drowning snake."

"An almost dead snake."

"We're not dead," Malenie said seriously.

"No." Paza sighed and rested her chin on her knees. "We need to work on our planning skills though."

15

A rooster crowed as Paza and Malenie stared at the Wall on the edge of Raleton's empty market. The comforting smells of warm cardamom, fried bread and burning dung mingled in the pre-dawn air. They couldn't stand here long; merchants, vendors, peddlers and shoppers would arrive, unlock their stalls, display their wares and fill the square soon. Paza was already tense and nervously scanning doorways and alleyways in all directions. But the Wall had changed shape in Malenie's mind and she needed a moment to ready herself. For the first time she realized it was not a casual thing to cross under the Wall. World divider, magic nullifier, mystery. Who knew what power it used each time and with what effects, even if she couldn't feel it? Something more subtle than vomiting and nose bleeds? But Trader Town was on the other side, and Papa. She didn't know what they'd find. But standing here wouldn't achieve anything and wouldn't change anything.

Malenie rocked back on her heels, struck by a thought. "Paza!" She pounced on the other girl and seized her hands. "Seven hundred gods and goddesses, we never tried to just wish Papa free from here." She ground to a halt as she realized what she was about to do. *I always let Paza choose what to do with the magic. I hate the diamonds because they make me different and I hate the magic because it's linked to the diamonds.* Her hands tightened on Paza's. *But this is for Papa. I'll do anything to get him back, even start using the magic instead of doing what Paza tells me.* She said firmly, "Wish for him to be here with us, right now."

Paza looked a question at her, turning her hands to hold Malenie's tightly. "I didn't think it would work across the Wall…But maybe it will! I wish for Malenie's papa to come here," she said in a rush.

Malenie waited impatiently for the tingle of magic across her skin, or even the gut-wrenching pain she had felt yesterday. Paza's lips parted to tell her it wasn't going to work, but Malenie didn't give her the chance. "No! Say his name, say Serliac."

"I wish for Malenie's papa, Serliac, to be here, free." Paza's eyes and mouth turned down with sympathy in the silence that followed.

"We were in the pool when you sent the three of us across the Wall. That's got to be—that has to be it." Malenie blundered into the pool, frenzied by hope and despair, dragging Paza behind her. "I'm sorry, I'm hurting you," she gasped, forcing her fingers to relax. "Please, I just have to know."

Paza waded deeper into the pool, up to her thighs. "I wish for Malenie's papa, Serliac, to be here, free," she shouted into the sky.

The magic did not come.

Malenie sagged to her knees, up to her chest in water. "Rot you, rot you seven hundred gods and goddesses. I hate you." The words tore out of her, like bone through skin, jagged and cutting and wrong. *I finally use it and it doesn't work.*

Paza let her cry for a few moments before she began to shift uneasily. "Mellie…"

"I know." Malenie wiped her nose on the back of her arm, rubbed the tears away and pushed back her hair. Squaring her shoulders, she stood. "I'm ready. I'm alright. We'll just do it the hard way."

Paza sighed softly. Her shoulder and arm bumped against Malenie's. The water's chill crept into Malenie, numbing her toes, tightening the tendons in her knees, stoking her fight. "We will do it," she whispered to herself. *We will.*

◊◊◊

"Gods and goddesses, what's happened here?" Malenie moaned. A low cloud of smoke hung over Trader Town, holding back the dawn. The air smelled of burning wood and livestock and something else that stung her throat. It was quiet except for the distant crackle of fire. No commands organizing a fire brigade, no shouts as families fought the flames. No cries for help.

The pool was choked with ashes and surrounded with the twisted remains of the market. A brass pot thunked hollowly under her foot and she stumbled. The buildings surrounding the market had cracked open and fallen down. She walked forward, not knowing what she intended. Her ankle twisted as the ground, no—the hand—she had stepped on jerked. The person groaned. Malenie flung herself to her knees and brushed ash away from the small form that she only now recognized as a person, not a charred twist of trash. The person coughed and turned her head.

"Nes," Malenie gasped and bit her knuckles, searching for a patch of skin not burnt or bloody to put her hands to help Nes sit up. Nes's hair was singed away on one side, and her face was raw and red and blistered. Her arm flopped unnaturally when they tipped her upright. She moaned but opened the eye that worked.

"Malenie," she rasped, paused. "All dead. All gone." Tears leaked from one eye.

"Everyone?" Paza whispered.

Malenie's throat clamped shut. She couldn't speak. Nes closed her eye in assent. Papa, Nes's sibs, her ma, all gone? Nooooo! Her chest, her heart, her throat all felt squeezed between two giant palms that were reducing her to nothing but pain. Papa! Malenie felt rooted in place, and at the same time like she would never belong anywhere ever again. She didn't know what to do.

"Malenie," Paza said. Slowly, Malenie realized she had been repeating her name over and over again. She opened her eyes. Paza was clutching both her arms, her fingers digging in. *I'm going to have bruises later.* "Malenie, Nes needs you." The market was still destroyed. Nes still lay broken at their feet.

Funny, I thought a hundred years must have gone by, Malenie thought numbly.

"Rot you!" Paza shook her and Malenie's head snapped back. "Your friend needs you! We have to get her to the Raleton side."

"What?" Malenie's eyes were gummy. Was she crying or was it just the burning tang in the air that made the tears well up?

"You can heal her there."

She didn't understand. And then it hit her. She could keep Nes, save her. "Gods and goddesses, yes." Strength moved back into her limbs and purpose pushed aside all else. The pain was still there, but this relieved the tiniest fraction of it. *Just this. I can do this one thing.*

"Nes, can you walk? We're going to heal you, but you have to move." They levered Nes to her feet. She swayed and Paza lifted Nes's good arm over her shoulders while Malenie hovered, afraid to touch the broken arm. Each step seemed to last a lifetime, each grunt of pain brought tears to Malenie's eyes. "Just a little further," Malenie urged each time Nes faltered. "I promise it will stop hurting soon."

That was a lie, and Malenie knew it. The physical pain would go away, but not the grief. That would go on and on. *Not now*, Malenie insisted to herself and concentrated on clearing rubble out of the way. In the pool, the water supported Nes but made it harder to move her forward. At last they stood on the edge of the drop off. Malenie hesitated, knowing there was no way to do this without hurting her. "Nes, get ready to take a deep breath."

It's got to be done. Malenie pushed away all thoughts but the practical. "I think, if I pull and you get behind her?" Paza nodded, and Malenie stepped into water over her head, holding her breath and opening her burning eyes wide. Nes tumbled down. Malenie reached for her, fingers scraping something that felt hot and pulpy. A burst of bubbles rushed past Malenie's face. *She's screaming*, she realized, cringing at the agony she was causing. She fumbled for Nes's arm and pulled. *Live*, she prayed. *Seven hundred gods and goddesses, don't let me kill my best friend.*

The water seemed to fight her. It pushed her up when she wanted to go down; it slowed her when she wanted to go fast. The narrowness of the tunnel actually helped, and Malenie jammed her feet, knees and elbows against its walls to gain traction to pull Nes forward. *She has to make it. She's the only thing left.* Finally, they tumbled into daylight. Malenie fumbled Nes's face out of the water. She was limp and heavy in their arms.

Paza didn't even wait to get out of the pool to clamp her hand on Malenie's elbow. "I wish for Nes to heal."

Nes's body arced like a bow. She and Malenie screamed as the healing magic crashed through them. Malenie felt the pain of each burn and break in her own body. Her skin fought as it was wrenched together. Her bones fought as they ground together. Her heart labored to move blood around her body. Her lungs shuddered to bring in air.

And then the pain was gone. Nes collapsed, thankfully with her face out of the water. Malenie stayed afoot only because Paza held her up. She shook. Every muscle, every tendon in her body felt stretched to the point of breaking. They didn't seem to quite fit back in place.

"I didn't think of asking to make it not hurt," Paza said shakily. The black of her pupils had swallowed all the brown. "Is she dead?"

"I don't think dead people scream." Surprisingly, her hand worked when she reached for Nes's neck. Her pulse beat rapidly. "We didn't kill her," she said in relief. "Not your fault. We probably should have done that slowly. I didn't think of it either." Nes's scream echoed in her head. "We've been stupid, stupid lucky. I think that could have killed either of us or both." Nes's lips were gray and bloodless in her unscarred face. Her burnt hair still made a ragged half halo to almost match Paza's.

"Can you stand more magic?" Paza asked. "I think we should get out of here."

The frantic barking of dogs and worried shouts penetrated Malenie's awareness. "We... that was loud." Paza nodded. "So much for going unnoticed. Don't...I don't think..."

"No more magic." Paza pulled Nes's arm over her shoulder. Malenie managed to do the same with the other one, and they stumbled out of the pool and the marketplace.

◊◊◊

"I was in Gravin's compound, helping Salla," Nes said, her voice no longer a painful rasp. They were back in the old courtyard, in the shade of the crumbling arcades. Nes was propped against a column. "Suddenly the guards shouted that we were under attack. The gates were open for a delivery and they just rushed in. It wasn't no one I had ever seen before," Nes said, "not that I could tell anyways. It was chaos. They pulled your pa out, still alive, and threw him on a camel. I saw that."

Malenie's knees went weak. "He's alive?" she choked. "You said everyone was dead!"

"I did?" Nes frowned and tugged on her hair. "I don't remember— you thought he was dead?" She rocked forward and grabbed Malenie's hand. That little weight was enough to make Malenie collapse to her knees. "He's alive. I saw them take him. He was walking."

Malenie covered her face with her hands so the others wouldn't see her tears. It was too abrupt. *Papa's not dead?* Her body didn't believe it. Grief lingered in a hard knot in her throat and weighted all her limbs. *I'm not an orphan*, she insisted to herself. *Why am I crying harder now?* Sobs tore at her chest.

After a long time, they seemed to clear away some of the grief. Slowly her heart and head came back into synch and belief seemed to reach down all the way to her toes and scrub out the pain. *Papa is alive! Thank you!*

Guilt followed on the heels of relief. Here was Nes, right in front of her, who had lost her whole family. Most of Trader Town was dead; so many people. *I haven't done anything to deserve this. But neither has Nes.* Especially Nes, who had already lost so much.

"Hey, you going to cry all day or can Nes tell her story?" Paza's harsh words made Malenie scrub her hands over her face and rub her eyes.

"Don't talk to her like that," Nes said sharply. "You don't know what she's going through."

"No, it's alright." Malenie pushed her hair out of her face and looked up. She didn't mind Paza's callousness, knowing what was protected under it, but the other two were glowering at each other. "I want to hear what happened," she said, drawing their attention back to her.

"So they rushed in. There were so many of them, so many more than Gravin's men. There was fighting everywhere, and then it came to us." Her control over her voice was so complete it was almost toneless, oddly flat. "Salla pushed me behind her and she was fighting, swinging her washing paddle. One got past her and broke my arm. Salla killed him. I took his sword, but it wasn't like drilling with Pa. And then they rushed us." Nes's fingers were clutched so hard the knuckles showed yellow, except for the dark lines of the creases. "The third, no the fourth killed her, just like that, and we all three of us went down together. Maybe Salla killed him too as she was dying. I hit my head. When I woke up all I could hear was fire. No one was left alive." Her voice got quieter and quieter. "Everyone was dead. The gates were burning, even the adobe seemed to be burning. I've never been so hot, not even on the hottest day in the desert at mid-day. It felt like my insides were crisping every time I took a breath. I covered my eyes and ran. That's when I got burnt. I made it to my house, but my sibs weren't there." She didn't say anything about her ma.

No one spoke. Malenie thought of all the people in the town: bandits, merchants, the women who spread their blankets in the market, the boys that had tormented her, Salla, who had helped them, her friends Steph and Jak.

"I'm sorry," she said, frustrated that words were so useless. She groped for something else to say.

Paza broke the silence. "How come you were there, by the Wall?" she asked suspiciously. Gone was the glimpse of the girl who had desperately tried to heal another's hurts, hidden again under the hard outer shell. As much as Malenie liked and relied on the tough street urchin, she wished the other, hidden Paza would stick around. She suspected it was the Paza from her life before *he* interfered in it.

Nes of course hadn't seen that side of her, and her voice was sharp again when she answered. "I was waiting for Malenie. I knew she was coming." She lifted her wrist and Malenie saw a narrow bracelet—a braid of her hair.

"How…?"

"There's a connection between you and your hair. It…it knows it belongs with you. So it sort of tugs towards where you are. I started feeling stuff like that last year."

"You're a shaper?"

Nes shrugged uncomfortably. "I guess I am. I don't know what other shapers can do." She cleared her throat. "I haven't asked."

Malenie touched her hair, wondering what else Nes could feel or do with it. She forced her hands down. She had chosen to trust Nes. She still trusted her. Paza's glare said as clear as words that she did not.

"But you took that hair before," Paza pointed out.

"Yeah. With you going off, I thought, I could use it to find you if anything went wrong. And then, all this happened. I don't have to do anything to feel it and you were suddenly close. I didn't find—there was no one else. I didn't know what else to do, so I got as near to where you were and waited, figuring you'd be coming back here."

"So you were there all night?" Paza asked skeptically.

Malenie ignored her, thinking furiously. Nes was a shaper, but she wasn't trained, yet, even if one day it would make her wealthier than her family had ever been. Papa was alive, but even further out of reach. Maybe Nes's sibs had been taken, like so many other children, to the same place they were taking Papa. *If they meant to get me, had always meant to get me, it kind of made sense. Running after them, hoping that luck is on our side doesn't. We tried luck with the man in the blue robe and it got us caught.*

So far I haven't been that clever. I've been reacting. Doing what Papa said. Doing what Emelenie said. Doing what Paza said. Even after this morning, I'm still trying to avoid using the one thing I have that very few people have. Her stomach churned with the thought of not just using the magic, but thinking about it, choosing how to use it, over and over again. *But aren't I just a tool, like I was afraid of, if I don't? Think about Papa. Think about Nes's sibs. Not using the magic would be, would be, well not as wrong as killing people, but like standing by while someone else was killed. I can't do that.*

"Do you think the magic will let us see across the Wall?" Malenie asked, interrupting whatever Nes was saying. She had done it. The words were out there, and there was no way to take them back. She swallowed against the lump in her throat and waited.

Paza sucked in a breath and nodded slowly. "We could try. What do you want me to say?"

"Wish to see where my papa is." She thrust her hands at Paza and glared at Nes, almost daring her to run away or panic.

Nes's throat worked as she swallowed and she blinked rapidly at the flare of blue light along Malenie's limbs but she didn't run away and she didn't panic. Malenie was grateful for her lack of reaction, though she could tell Nes was shocked. A sheet of darkness appeared on the ground, but Malenie couldn't be annoyed at Nes for drawing in her feet to avoid it since she and Paza were doing the same. The darkness stretched until it was a circle the width of Malenie's outstretched arms. Colors seeped across it in swirls and streaks of blue and gold and brown, and then, between one blink and the next, it was an image, like in a bronze mirror, but much clearer. A string of camels stalked across the desert, trailing a ragged line of people on foot in a cloud of dust. Another breath, and the image lurched into motion, and Malenie clutched at the ground in sudden vertigo. The perspective swooped closer and there was Malenie's papa, hands tied in front of him on one of the first camels. Only Paza's grip on her hands kept her from falling over with relief. *He* is *alive*. His turban was dirty and askew. Malenie gagged at the sight of the putrid bruise that had swollen one eye almost shut. "Papa." *What now?*

"Make it go back," Nes said in a strangled voice. Paza muttered and the image rushed to the people on foot: the children from town, in slave collars and roped together. Rooster Boy was there, all his strut reduced to weary plodding. Nes's hand clamped tight on Malenie's arm in the same moment she saw them, all three of Nes's siblings: one boy and two girls. "They're alive." Her grip crushed Malenie's fingers. The image moved even closer, close enough to see the tear-streaked dirt on Del's face and the blood at the corner of Tep's mouth. "I can't stand it! Make it show where they're going," she demanded hoarsely. "Can you do that?"

"We can't," Paza explained almost apologetically. "It only works on live things." Nes dropped her head and covered her eyes. A shudder twisted her shoulders. Paza whispered, "Let's see if it will show us the leader." She made another wish.

"We know his name: Harashan. Papa told us," Malenie said, but the image was already swooping and spinning. It centered on a familiar face with narrow eyes. "That's him," Malenie said grimly. The Parthavian who had chased her in Trader Town. The image blacked out. "What's it doing?"

"I didn't do anything!"

Nes looked up. The blackness pulsed and spread, paused and pulsed. Malenie shifted uneasily. In one burst, color invaded it and fractured into a face, a fall of dark hair, a blue robe, and then cracked into nothingness and was gone. The light under Malenie's clothes faded and disappeared. Malenie and Paza stared at each other. Horror sealed Malenie's throat.

Nes's eyes narrowed. "Who was that? You know him."

"Harashan—"

"And the man in the blue robe—"

"Both sides of the Wall.

"Try it again, Paza—we just assumed, but maybe we can see him after all."

"I wish to see the man in the blue robe." Paza looked a question at Malenie.

"It's not doing anything. Try to do it the same way, Harashan first and then him." The image of Harashan formed quickly enough, but when Paza attempted to direct it to the man in the blue robe, pain lanced through Malenie's head and dark red blood gushed from her nose, over her chin and down her front. She swayed.

"Stop!" Nes wrenched them apart. For a few moments everyone was quiet while Malenie tilted her head back and pinched her nose. The pounding in her head hadn't quite stopped when Nes demanded an explanation.

"You know the one from Trader Town. Harashan." Malenie tried to take a deep breath, choked on blood and looked at Paza, whose lips were tightly pressed together. "The second is the man that kidnapped Paza and, and killed her sister. And he's on this side of the Wall."

"What does it mean?" Nes asked.

"They're working together," Malenie said. "They have to be. Paza said, 'Show us the leader,' and it did, only there were two leaders."

"And you're not trying that again. Look at you." Nes glared at both of them until they nodded. "But I don't understand. You said they're on different sides of the Wall," Nes objected. "I didn't even know there was something here until you told me. How could they be working together?"

"We've been going back and forth," Malenie pointed out. *The Pashtins do, too*, she thought uneasily. "And Harashan saw the Wall, that night, I know he did. What do you think?" she asked Paza, who was scowling ferociously at her feet.

Paza shrugged. "That…"

Nes broke in. "But we can go and rescue them! You healed me, found them; why aren't we leaving now?" She hauled Malenie to her feet, her hands hard in her impatience.

"Wait." *I don't want to have to explain*, Malenie thought. Paza pulled her legs in to her chest and hugged them, still scowling as if she were concentrating on something. Malenie took a deep breath, feeling like she was piling pain on top of pain as she spoke.

Nes's face got stonier and stonier. "You're sure?"

"Of course she's sure," Paza said. "Don't you think we would have gotten her Papa out if it had worked?"

"Does that mean…" Frowning, Nes ran her fingers over the braid.

"It's not gone. But it's not strong either. It's like someone talking just out of hearing, when you can hear them, but not really what they are saying. I wouldn't be able to find you with it like this."

"That's strange," Malenie said. "When we tried to use the, uh, magic to rescue Papa on the other side of the Wall it really, really didn't work. We figured that out before we got to him. It doesn't even exist there."

"There must be some way." Head bent, Nes paced the arcade.

Paza bounced to her feet as if filled with new purpose and stepped right into Nes's path, forcing the other girl to stop. "We can't catch them," she said, head tilted back to meet Nes's eyes. Nes glared obligingly back. "And even if we could, it's the three of us against all of them, without weapons, camels or fighters, which they all have. Or much magic." Paza paused until Nes gave the barest nod of her head in agreement.

"I can do small things, not like…" Nes touched the arm that had been broken.

"And they might have shapers or spell stones or whatever. But here," Paza pointed to the ground, then swept her arm east, "it's three of us against fewer men. And here, Malenie's magic works."

She might have been eavesdropping on Malenie's earlier thoughts. *But…* "It doesn't matter," Malenie said crossly. "We can't find him without his name."

"But we can find someone who can!" She walked away from Nes to look down at Malenie on the ground. Briefly Malenie felt like the audience for a storyteller in the market, but she shook away the thought. She didn't doubt Paza's hatred of the man in blue. "There's a man—the Wise Man of Sarnath—he's a seer, and a magic user. He can tell us the robed man's name and then we can go after him. Stop him here—and maybe stop them there and save your papa and her sisters and brother."

"So let's say we find this wise man—and I'm guessing he's not in Raleton or we would have just gone to him before?" Malenie waited for her nod. "So we find this wise man, somewhere out in the desert, and he tells us the man in the blue robe's name, and then what? What's the plan? Because we said we needed a better plan and I don't see how finding him is any different from just serving ourselves up on a platter. He's come this close," she held up her thumb and index finger with less than a finger's width of space between them, "to catching us three times. The last time he did catch us and we only got away through sheer luck!"

"Why are we even arguing about this?" Nes interrupted, pushing past Paza to face Malenie. "Tell me how to get back so I can go after my sibs!"

"They'll survive," Paza said nastily.

"Paza!"

"I don't want them to just survive! I don't want them to suffer at all."

"Everyone suffers!"

Malenie jumped to her feet, needing the height if the only two people in the world she could depend on right now decided to start brawling. "Paza, stop it! Nes, please let her answer me. No matter what we decide, we need a plan. A good plan. And that means we have to talk to each other."

Paza glowered at Nes, and Malenie was tempted to kick her. She couldn't understand why Paza was acting like this. If anything she should be more sympathetic to Nes's problems since they were so similar to her own. "Because the wise man won't just tell us his name, he'll tell us how to stop him," Paza said.

"So you think this is a teller's tale, and he has some fatal weakness?" Nes ridiculed her. "Like we just have to cut off his hair and he'll fall at our feet and beg our forgiveness?"

Paza's hands flew to her head and then curled into claws as she lunged at Nes. "Shut up you corpse-worshiping maggot!"

Nes pushed her away almost contemptuously.

"Who do you think you are?" Paza swung wildly, spit flying with her curses. Nes backed away, just fending her off, not even bothering to counter the blows or respond to her taunts. Her indifference enraged Paza, but Malenie knew Nes wouldn't fight unless she really meant to hurt someone. Paza didn't fall into the same category as bullies. Unfortunately Paza didn't know, and probably wouldn't care, that this was Nes's version of tact, and was really trying to hurt the older girl.

I should have kicked her. "Stop IT!" Malenie tackled Paza and pinned her arms, half hugging her, half restraining her. Paza bucked and smacked Malenie's head in exactly the spot bruised by the thug's elbow. "Ow! Rot it," Malenie snapped.

As if the blow knocked sense into Paza's head, she went limp in Malenie's arms. The sudden change pulled them both off balance and they fell. "I'm sorry," Paza said sniffling. "Are you hurt?" She probed the bump with her fingers.

"Ow." Malenie batted away Paza's hands. "Are you both done acting like caravan guards on a three-day drunk after a fifty-day journey?" Paza gaped at her. "The seven hundred gods and goddesses wouldn't be enough to keep us safe from each other if you keep going on like this." Her glare took in both her friends. "Why are you making me act like a peacekeeper? You'd better say you're sorry."

They both muttered insincere apologies, and then Paza surprised them both by adding, "I'm sorry I said that about your religion."

"Right. Let's sit down," Malenie said and the two girls settled on either side of her, stiff backed and as wary as two hounds. *No, worse than the hounds*, Malenie thought, remembering Shay's companions. *I hope he's safe.* "I think Paza is right, magic is our only advantage, but it's not worth much without knowledge. What else do you know about this wise man?" Malenie looked at her lap, wondering what it would be like to meet an adult with a similar…affliction as she. From the corner of her eye she saw Paza stick out her tongue and decided to ignore the rude gesture.

She longed for Papa's advice. She needed someone to tell her how to help Paza with her rage and pain. Someone to tell her how to help Nes with her sibs and her grief. Someone to tell her what was right, because Paza had said 'stop him'—and Nes was right, this was not a tale—as if it were as easy and simple as catching a baby's hand before it touched a flame. This man would not stop unless they made him stop. From the very first Paza had wanted to kill him. And Malenie herself didn't know anything else that would make him stop, short of death, because he seemed to be broken, in a way that she didn't think healers had learned to fix. *Could I…? I think it would kill me*, she thought, remembering the pain of healing Nes. And killing him…just breaking the thug's finger had made her sick. It went against everything Papa believed in and taught her. *I don't know how to reconcile that with what he's done to Paza and everyone else. Doesn't protecting them outweigh his right to hurt more people?*

"Um. He lives in the desert borderlands." Paza interrupted the flow of Malenie's thoughts. "You have to pay. He's from a place named

Sarnath, that's where he gets the name, but all I know is that it's east of here. He's very wise." Probably realizing this wasn't a very persuasive, she added, "He doesn't turn anyone away, and he's known for helping people. You know, people who have been robbed or wronged or something. People like us."

I don't know what else to do. Papa was out of reach, and she wouldn't be much use to him or Nes's sibs even if she were standing right next to them. That left this side of the Wall and what they could do here. *Am I just trying to give the responsibility to someone else again? To Paza's wise man this time? I don't think so. This is like Papa trying to help a sick person without medicines or bandages or prayers.* "And seers are real here, not charlatans like they say at home?"

"Malenie, no! You're not really thinking about this!"

"They're real." Paza shifted from foot to foot eagerly. "The Suntin girl told me the Families go to see them especially, all the time. That's where I first heard about him."

"And you think he'll really help us?" At Paza's eager nod, Malenie bit her lip, but she knew she had already decided. "Then I think we should go. It might be as useful as a broken spellstone, but it might also be our best chance. We'll see what he says."

Paza smirked at Nes.

"No," Nes said. Malenie could tell she was angry, and under that hurt. "I'm not going."

"Yes, you are!" Malenie said, doubt and fear making her yell. "Paza's right, there's too few of us. Everyone we know is dead or captured! Isn't that right? Isn't that what you said?"

"Yes," she whispered. "They're dead or captured."

"Then there's no way we can help your sibs alone. You saw how many slavers there are! We need help. I need yours, you need mine, we both need Paza's, and we all need someone else's. This wise man may be it."

"No—no."

"Yes! I won't let you throw yourself away or push me away or whatever you think you're doing. I let you before, and I won't let you again. This is our best chance. My—my uncle is searching for Papa right now. This uncle, I don't know him well, but Papa would never be rescued and not take your sibs with him—all the kids from Trader Town, even the worthless ones."

"Are you sure? Not—about your uncle," Nes hurried to prevent a new explosion. Malenie took a deep breath. Nes had ignored most of what she'd said, but that didn't mean she hadn't heard it. Maybe she would even believe it.

"I'll show you," Malenie said recklessly and grabbed Paza's hand. "Go on, do it. Show her my uncle." The magic whipped out of her with the force of her anger and old and new grief. The image built up rapidly, color and motion at once, Liac at the center, surrounded by guards, the captain at his shoulder, observing Trader Town and issuing orders. He pointed and the guards broke into groups and entered the rubble.

"You see?" Malenie challenged herself and Paza as much as Nes. She wrenched her arm away, unable to bear seeing the destroyed town or whatever else the magic might expose. The image blinked out. Nes twisted locks of her hair and stared at her knees while Malenie bottled her screams of frustration inside.

Finally Nes looked up. "Do you swear this will help them?" She jerked her head west, towards home. "And we'll find some way to save them?"

Unexpectedly Paza answered first. "I swear on my family." She touched her fingers to her lips.

"I swear on my papa's living breath," Malenie said, "and my mama's place with the seven hundred gods and goddesses." Her breath puffed on her fingers as she spoke.

"Then I'll go," Nes said.

16

After another argument they made Nes buy a camel and supplies with more fake coins. With her short, fluffy hair cut to the same length all around she looked like a nomad, but she was still the least conspicuous because she was Thessem. And haggling was haggling no matter which side of the Wall you were on. By dusk, sullen even to the camel, they were ready to start out, equipped with dried meat and fruit, salt for the camel, water, discreetly obtained directions, flint and steel, and extra clothing.

They walked in silence for most of the journey. Nes brooded about her sibs and avoided Paza, who was lost in thoughts she didn't share and spoke only to Malenie, who brooded about Papa and magic. The camel was the most vocal, bawling and balking at being separated from the herd, and Nes was the only one who could get her moving.

The one non-hostile conversation involving all three of them was short. "I could use magic to look for your ma. Do you want me to?"

"No."

Paza looked up, an emotion that was not suspicion or animosity flickering over her face. "Why not?"

"It's not your concern," Nes said sharply and turned her head away. Paza bit her lip, and Malenie didn't ask again.

The rolling hills covered in dry grass and short spindly trees were a two-fold relief for Malenie. First, they gave her something to think about besides the worries looping endlessly in her head. Second, according to the directions, they meant they were close to the wise man's house. By mid-morning of the fourth day they found the well-marked turn-off and trudged down a narrow lane. One moment it was hills all around, and the next they had stumbled into the yard of a tidy house surrounded by orchards and cultivated fields. The fissured cliff behind it gave more shade than the trees.

An old man with a shock of bushy gray hair was squatting in the dirt with a surprised look on his face, up to his elbows in the slick mud and straw mixture he was using to patch the adobe walls of his house. The camel groaned and tossed her head. She was answered by more of the beasts, somewhere out of sight. A man and a woman clad in leathers came at a dead run from behind the house. Their hands were also coated in mud, but they wore swords and the woman had a bow. She had a strongly molded face and the man looked youthful despite flecks of gray in his hair. All three were Thessem.

"Visitors," said the old man, who had to be the Wise Man of Sarnath. He stripped the mud from his skin with long sweeps of his hands and stood easily, his eyes assessing. "And I didn't see you coming." The guards' hands dropped to their sword hilts.

Malenie barely noticed. Her gaze was pinned to the seer's arms and the scrolling vines, vibrantly green, circling his wrists and elbows. They seemed charged with energy and light, ready to writhe off his skin into the air. Her own skin prickled, and she thrust her hands behind her, as if her marks might somehow answer his and betray her. She would have hidden behind her friends if she could, but Paza was practically glued to her usual spot behind Malenie's shoulder and Nes was still struggling to hold the camel in place.

"But not dangerous for all that," the wise man said to his companions and their hands relaxed at their sides. "Jos, will you finish so we don't lose this morning's work? Tal will be sufficient." To the girls, he said, "If you would like to tie up your beast there," pointing to a post with rings, "you can join me for some refreshment."

It was cool inside the thick-walled house. Sunlight from the open door and narrow windows reflected on sand-colored walls and exposed darker patches of recent repairs. Shallow niches held metal cooking pots, clay jars and other homey objects. The wise man removed the scrap of cloth covering the full water pitcher, set the table with mismatched mugs and gestured for them to sit. Tal stood at his side without helping until his hand on her shoulder urged her to a place at the table.

"Please, drink and be welcome," he invited them.

When Nes and Paza didn't say anything, Malenie thanked him and reached for the water. The tangy sweet taste of ginger and honey surprised her and she drank greedily. Water sucked from a leather skin warmed by the sun for days was barely water in comparison to this. She looked up to find the old man watching her closely. Flushing, she put her mug down with a thump. He seemed to look through her, his eyes unfocused. It was eerie and uncomfortable, and Malenie turned to study the woman beside him. She was much younger, with no gray in that black hair, which was twisted into glossy loops. Her skin was very dark, and above a crooked nose her eyes watched and measured. Her clothes couldn't hide the muscled strength of her body. They might hide other things. Like metal to a magnet, Malenie's gaze jerked back to the green marks on his arms.

"It's been a long time since I've had visitors from across the Wall." His face sharpened and he focused as all three girls twitched and Malenie rose. His voice careful, he asked, "What, did you come to the Wise Man of Sarnath and not expect him to be wise?"

"How can you tell?" Nes asked. Malenie blinked; they were her first words in two days that were neither rude nor belligerent.

"I see more parts of you, not just whether you have straight hair or curly, or are tall or short, than most people see."

"Do you know why we've come?" Nes demanded.

"Not yet. That takes more active seeing," he said easily.

"What's your price for answering our questions?" Malenie blurted out.

"That's not something I can tell you before the question is answered." The girls exchanged uneasy glances. Paza had told them—a day and a half into the journey, and did that have something to do with Nes not speaking?—but the vulnerability of it still made her flinch. "It won't be more than you can or want to pay," the wise man added. Malenie pressed her fingertips into the table and hesitated.

"I'll pay it. We came all the way here," Nes said scornfully in response to the protest Malenie hadn't voiced. "We're not going to just leave because we got scared. I'll pay the price."

Tal was as still as a boulder. The wise man inclined his head, accepting the offer.

"We all will," Malenie said, glaring at Nes. She sat down hard. Two days of silence and Nes opened her mouth to show them up. Annoying things, friends. "Because we all agreed." She included the man and the woman across the table in her glare. *If they show the least sign of being amused or condescending…*But their faces were serious. They reminded Malenie of Papa with a new patient.

"What is your question?"

"We need to learn the name of a man," Malenie said. "He's not…a good person and we need to know how we can stop him. Knowing what he wants would help, too." It sounded so vague stated like that, and Malenie braced herself for questions they couldn't answer.

"I will look. I can't promise what I'll see. Who has seen or touched him the most?"

Malenie and Nes looked at Paza. Malenie expected questions and incense, maybe bones or shards of semi-precious stones. Instead he placed his empty hands palm up on the table. "Give me your hand."

Paza shook her head violently, stuffed her hands under her thighs and hunched her shoulders to her ears. Malenie was amazed she stayed at the table. She tried to remember if Paza had voluntarily touched any of the men that had been kind to her, but she had kept even good-humored Leocarl at a distance.

"Does it have to be her?"

"It would be best. The more I can touch through her, the better the chances of learning what you seek." His voice was smooth and hid his thoughts completely, but the woman's hands tightened into fists in response to something she saw in their faces.

Anything Nes said would probably upset Paza more, so it was up to Malenie. She cleared her throat. "Look, we came here because we trusted you, Paza. You know I trust you. Now you have to trust me and, and Nes when I say we won't let anything happen to you." Paza huddled smaller. "I promised, remember? You know firsthand Nes is a pretty good fighter, and you saw me fight Deek's whole gang so you know I'm not a rotter. The seer's not going to do anything to you and it's not going to hurt, right?" she appealed to him.

"Correct."

She was rambling, but a look at Tal had given her an idea. "We both know you can't trust someone based on how they look or what they say." At least Paza nodded at that. "But you trust me." She waited for the nod, not sure it would come. It did, and Malenie took a hidden breath. "And you'd trust a steel dagger." Nod. "So Tal will give Nes her dagger—"

"No," Tal said.

"—because she's better with a knife and we'll be your bodyguard like she's his. I'll guard you." Paza's head came up and she looked from Malenie to Tal to Nes. It wasn't enough. Taking a deep breath, Malenie cupped her hand to her face so only her friends could see and mouthed, "Be ready to use my magic."

Paza's shoulders finally relaxed, her head came up. "Yes," she said. Malenie had seen mirages that were more definite, but it would have to do.

"Agreed," the seer said without prompting. His eyes looked sad, and Malenie wondered if his magic told him something or if he was just perceptive.

"No. You can't mean to agree," Tal said.

"I have agreed. Please give our guest your dagger and remove your sword."

"Sarl, how can I protect you when you do things like this?" Tal didn't point out that even without weapons she could probably easily overcome the three of them. They were taking them seriously, respecting both Paza's fear and the protection Malenie had promised her. "You're mad," Tal said.

"Sometimes that is what is needed in an insane world. Madness, courage, the ability to see clearly. Can you tell the difference?"

She snorted but unsheathed her dagger and laid it on the table, hilt pointing away. "Careful, girl, it's not a toy." Nes had never looked at any weapon as a toy, but they were strangers to Tal, so she barely even bristled in response. Malenie nodded respectfully to show she understood. Glaring at the seer, Tal pulled the baldric with the sword over her head and crossed the room to place it on a carved wooden chest. She took a few steps away, leaned against the wall and folded her arms.

"Now, give me your hand," he said.

Looking slightly away and screwing her face up in anticipation of pain, Paza extended her hand. He clasped it in his two large ones.

Malenie held her breath.

For long moments nothing seemed to happen. Paza's face relaxed, Malenie's hands grew slippery with sweat, and Tal watched. A frown gathered the wise man's brows together. He began to wheeze and his face convulsed in pain and anger, sorrow and regret. Tal started forward and hovered at his elbow, hands reaching but not touching.

Choking, he flung Paza's hand from him and collapsed across the table. His labored breathing sounded loud in the otherwise quiet room. Bit by bit it slowed, and he straightened up, reaching trembling hands for the pitcher. Tal was there before him and guided the cup to his lips. He seemed like an old man, his glamour diminished.

"Wine," he requested after gulping down the water. His breathing eased and healthy color rushed back into his face, although the marks on his arms seemed pale. "Well," he said, and his voice was normal again. Malenie held her breath. "It was a very strong seeing, and like all the strongest visions I saw very little and felt too much." He pressed the heel of his hand over his heart as if it troubled him. "I saw enough to know time is short and that I need to travel with you. We'll leave immediately."

"We're not going anywhere with you," Nes said.

"You haven't answered our questions," Malenie added.

"To answer your questions in reverse: I don't know what he wants, but I fear it very much. We are all needed to stop him, and we must therefore travel together."

"And?" Malenie asked when he stopped.

He drew in a shuddering breath and the lines around his eyes deepened. "I saw the man you seek. I know his name very well, for my wife gave it to him.

"He is my son."

17

Malenie's chair clattered to the floor behind her. Nes was on her feet a heartbeat after, the dagger pointed at the seer. In two swift strides, Tal was at his side, sheathed sword once again in her hand.

"Don't move any further," Nes warned, and no one moved.

I have to think. But the words "He is my son" kept repeating in her head.

"The other one is still outside," Nes said. Paza's grip pinched Malenie's shoulder, and some of her panic subsided at the reminder that she didn't have to handle this all on her own. Her friends were smart and together they were strong, and so far they had escaped everything that had tried to trap them. *And he doesn't know about me,* Malenie thought, *what I can do.*

"Please," he said, his hands open on the table, the palms up and vulnerable looking.

"What do you want?" Malenie asked roughly. Suspicion rode her hard, but his sad eyes—and their need—kept her from bolting.

"To tell you what I saw and answer the questions you brought to me."

"I think we should listen to him," Paza said.

We can hear him out and run afterwards, if he is plain crazy or a threat. "Go on," Malenie said. "We'll listen, but that doesn't mean we'll believe you."

He closed his eyes, and Malenie thought he wasn't going to speak after all. She kept her arms loose at her sides, ready to snatch ahold of Nes and let Paza magic them out of there. After a few breaths he opened his eyes. "He was my son," he said softly. "But no longer. The things he has done… he is no son of mine, and I told him so many years ago, when I gave up hope of the boy I remembered. When he was a child—well, the fault is mine, that I did not try harder. But as an adult…" He rubbed at the lines on his face. "I thought he was dead. My sight has not touched him for…years."

The mix of grief and guilt on his face made him look, not just old but worn-down tired. He ground the heel of his hand into his chest, and Tal gently set the sword on the table. From a hook on the wall she lifted a small leather bag, tipped a dark powder into his mug and added water. With a grimace, he drank. "Seeing him, when I touched you, was a shock. I wouldn't have said what I did otherwise." He looked up from the residue in his mug to their faces. "You don't believe me. Why should you?" He stared at them so intently Malenie wondered if he was doing the seer thing again and what he saw when he did it. *How far—how closely—does he see?*

The corners of his mouth pressed tight in decision. "I'll show you a thing that might make you believe me." He reached for the hem of his tunic.

"No, don't," Tal protested.

Turning, he smiled a real smile at her. "You are too protective of my dignity, my friend. Only my ego will be harmed by doing this." Facing Malenie again, he pulled his tunic off, revealing more green marks on his shoulders and, prominent across his chest, an ugly puckered scar over his heart. It sliced from his left collarbone to halfway down his ribs, and the skin was pulled tight around it, shiny, raised and tinged with red, as if it were still inflamed. Paza's hand tightened on Malenie's shoulder.

"My own son did this to me, using a child's magic." His hands closed into fists and veins stood out in his throat. "What kind of man does that? What kind of man could inflict that kind of pain, not once, but twice, for the child—the child suffered the same pain I did. That is one of the prices the gifted pay."

Malenie shivered, imagining it. She believed him. She couldn't under-stand how a son could attack his father, but she believed the pain in his eyes and his voice, she believed in the friendship she saw between the two adults. She could picture the man in the blue robe's attack on his father, the gray-haired man pleading with his dark-haired son…

"You're lying, rot you!" On either side of her, Paza and Nes startled. "He can't be your son!" Malenie accused him. "You're Thessem and he's Parthavian." It was so obvious, she hadn't seen it. Everyone knew the different peoples couldn't have children together. Too much was happening, too many unexpected emotions clogging her ability to think: fear, nervousness, relief, shock, fear… "It's not possible."

"A seer can't lie," snapped Tal.

"Paza?" Malenie asked uncertainly.

"Maybe… I don't know."

"A seer who lies can't see," Tal insisted.

"Stop," the seer commanded. "I am his father. Would I claim the destroyer of Suntin as kin if I had a choice? Would I share with every stranger my guilt over what he has become? No. No, I didn't father him, but I was married to his mother and I was—" Sucking in a loud breath, he pressed his shaking hands to the table and the veins stood up across their backs, too. "I will share the shameful story, but we have no time to sit. I tell you, I saw fire and destruction surrounding him now, or very soon. I cannot allow what happened to Suntin three years ago to happen again."

Abruptly the growl left his voice and it was all entreaty. "Please. It will take too long, to sit here and explain, while people die. The only way to have enough time is if we talk as we travel. There are people who need us. The six of us together can prevent the destruction he intends, if we can figure out how. I saw that, too." For a long moment he stared at the tunic on the table and then re-dressed, settling it across his shoulders.

Nes spoke first. "Where?" she demanded.

"Where do we need to go?" he clarified, ignoring Nes's hostility. "To Suntin. Will you come?"

Of course. Suntin. It had a strange inevitability to it. *I always seem to go back to places I just left.* But in spite of the arguments clamoring in her head, Malenie had already decided. She couldn't make that decision for her friends, though, and if they decided differently…she didn't know. Both Nes and Paza had many good reasons to not go to Suntin. It was the last place Paza would want, or should, go. And this would take Nes even further away from her sibs without any promise that it would help them.

"I think we should go and hear what he has to say. He claims to want the same thing we want," Malenie said.

"I'm going," Paza said, chin tilted, daring Malenie to what? Contradict her? Argue?

"Are you sure? We just…" *left Suntin,* Malenie finished in her head. Since he hadn't found them again he was probably still there. Waiting. Paza just shrugged in a way that meant she wasn't answering any questions.

New scowled at them all. "Malenie, where is this place?"

"It's far," she admitted reluctantly. She wanted Nes with her. "About the same distance between Trader Town and Pashtin."

"No." She set her jaw.

"Nes—"

"Why don't you ask him," Paza said, jerking her head at their silent audience. "He's a seer. He could tell you the best way to help your sibs—whether you should go back or not." Malenie gaped at her and Paza smirked. *Is she saying this to convince her to stay or to go?*

Nes swung around to face the old man and Tal and even uncrossed her arms. Naked emotion showed on her face, too complicated for Malenie to decode, but it seemed a mix of hope and need and challenge, most of it directed at Tal. That made sense; Tal was a lot like Nes's pa, soldierly, dedicated, a little harsh. *You better not pity her!* Malenie thought. Sarl had that quiet waitingness that meant a grownup was ready to help if you just out and said you needed it. And how many times had Malenie not recognized that implicit offer from an adult?

"Does he do that?" Nes asked Tal.

Taken aback, Tal cast about for an answer and fell back on blunt honesty. "Well, yeah, that's what people come to him for."

Nes thrust her hand at Sarl. "I gotta find my sibs." Her voice cracked, exposing all the grief hidden under her fury. "You tell me what's my best chance of doing that."

"I'm sorry," Malenie said. "For bringing you here, for everything."

"Shut up." Nes took back her hand and punched her lightly in the arm. "It ain't your fault." To the seer, she said, "Well? You going to take it?" She stepped closer to him and held her hand out, palm up.

"Do you understand there is an additional price for this?" He gestured helplessly. "It's not something I control—it's a balance the gift itself seeks. Without this rendering of accounts, the gift would leave me."

"I don't care about all that. Just answer."

"Very well." His hands closed on Nes's, and he went distant and blank. And was back again quickly, without the agonies of the last time. He folded Nes's fingers closed and gave her hand back to her like a present. "If you went after them now—returning to your side of the Wall—they will be safe, but only for a time. If you go with us and do whatever it is we must do, they may be safer for longer."

"Huh." She looked at him hard, stared at Tal, measuring her too, and turned to Malenie. "Do you believe him? Seems to me if they're lying about having to tell the truth, then this is the best way to get us to do what he wants with the least fuss." She ignored Tal's indignant protest and the seer's surprised choke of laughter. "So do you believe him? If you do, I'll go with you. And if not…" She shrugged. "I trust you."

"Oh."

What was the correct response when someone put not only their life but the lives of their brother and sisters in your hands?

You gave them everything they needed and more than they asked for. Papa's warnings lost their force in the face of this. For the first time, Malenie wanted to use the magic. In Trader Town, they had truth stones that changed colors when a person lied. *I could do something like that….* She turned to Paza. "Can—"

"No, that's not what I meant." Nes cut her off. "Just…what you think." She nodded in answer to Malenie's questioning stare.

Magic might have been easy compared to this. She stared at the adults. Tal was like a mule being asked to do something new: steady, strong, but uneasy at her new task and her skin twitching with it. *She doesn't know what to make of this situation. I think she'd like us, if it weren't for what we brought with us.* Sarl was Tal's lodestone. She defended him, maybe even from himself, and gave him her care and, it seemed, her love.

And Sarl? He was like a pool of water at the base of the Wall: deep, mysterious, confusing in its mere existence, but pulling on some profound feeling of peace. You could meditate to him and his silences and learn from his experiences. Just a little, he reminded her of Papa. They both had the same focused intensity while they measured a person. So was she seeing clearly?

"Yes. I believe him."

Nes gave a sharp nod. Malenie guessed Nes's own opinion tallied with hers and she had wanted the confirmation.

Sarl looked bemused and then relieved, but didn't speak.

Tal strapped on her weapons and packed supplies into bags. The seer called softly at the door for Jos, and when they walked out of the house, Jos had their camel and three others, already strapped into harnesses and saddles.

Standing at the camels' heads, Tal commanded them to kneel, and they folded their great stalky legs, settling into still alarmingly tall lumps. The bags were secured first, and then Malenie watched dubiously as Sarl swung up. Even with all the camels—and camel byproducts—in Trader Town, she had never been atop one. "Jos won't be riding, so one of you can ride his or all three of you can ride together. These beasties can carry a lot more weight than that." Affectionately, Tal smacked the long loop of a neck nearest her. Nes took the offer, no doubt thinking some distance between her and Paza would be a good thing, and mounted confidently.

Jos stepped up to give the other girls a helping hand, but Tal waved him back and took his place. Paza ignored or maybe missed the exchange. "Step here." Tal pointed to the camel's neck. "And grab here." The leather and wood saddle seemed small and high. Malenie followed directions and almost flew off the other side when Tal gave her a helping push. Paza followed and perched in front of her, and the world rocked as the camel unfolded its back legs and then the front ones, heaving its great bulk upright. Belatedly, Malenie jammed her fingers under the harness straps and held on. The others were also up. Jos was disappearing down the narrow track. The lead rein for Malenie's camel was clipped to Tal's mount in an accurate evaluation of her skill. That is, none. Nes at least had control of her own mount.

And that easily, they were on their way to Suntin again. Malenie bit back a sigh. The last moon had been spent traveling north and south over essentially the same stretch of desert and lands bordering on desert without achieving much and without freeing Papa. Only the method of travel differed each time, afoot and footsore, by magic and ill with it, on camelback and…motion sick? So far she'd been lucky in most of the people she'd met. Was she still?

"We don't know what to call you," Malenie called to the seer.

"My name will do. Sarl," he added, twisting to look at the girls as he answered. "And yours?" They made their own introductions.

The low hills quickly hid the little house from view. The track forced them into single file and Malenie swallowed her questions, waiting for when they reached the main road and could ride abreast. Jos ranged ahead, mostly out of sight. It was strange being up so high. The new viewpoint allowed Malenie to see over the scrubby brush that closed in on the path, to see more scrubby brush in all directions, all shades of brown and gold and beige. A black snake coiled in on eggs in a nest, the mother bird squawking frantically to decoy it away. Once in a while a wiry tree poked higher in the fold of a hill, its defiant green leaves signaling some hidden tap of water.

Sarl didn't speak and Sarl didn't speak, so Malenie copied the defiance of the trees and asked her questions. "How can he be your son? I didn't know the different peoples intermarried." She had said she believed him, but that didn't mean she was going to be dumb about it. At a sign from Sarl, Tal obligingly hauled on the rein to bring their camel even with hers, and the beast responded eagerly. Really, she seemed much calmer now that she was part of a herd again.

"I was born to the Sarnath Family in a city far to the east—that's Sarnath." So…his family was powerful if the city had the same name. Like the Pashtins. Sarl paused and his silence stretched, unspooling down the road with them. When he spoke again he seemed to try to find another way into his story. "You must know a little of magic, to have crossed the Wall and brought friends from both sides with you."

Malenie's heart thumped. *Does he know about me?*

"I've been told that on the other side of the Wall, all magic is in things. Stones are the most common holders of magic, but thread, cloth, hair, even bone can all hold magic in certain conditions. " Malenie glanced at Nes, who was fingering the braid of hair around her wrist and frowning. "Here all the magic is in people, but can only be wielded by another person."

"That's not really true though is it?" Nes said. "Not everyone on our—my—side can tell what will hold a spell, and not everyone can shape them either. To most people a rock is just a rock, until a shaper makes it into something else. And a rock might be magic in itself, but cloth is one thing made into another. I never heard that the animals or plants are magic, so it's got to be the people working it. And here, if you haven't got those designs, you don't have magic. You could say the designs on your arms are a kind of thing."

"You're quite right, the difference is in how the magic is expressed, but in any case it draws on some strength within an individual. Many scholars have in fact wondered if the designs—we prefer to call them patterns—are something external to our bodies that are somehow passed from mother to infant during pregnancy. Like dye staining cloth or the dyer's hands. Experiments have been assayed, often with gruesome results, attempting to separate… but I digress."

Nes nodded sharply to herself. Malenie wondered, *What is she thinking about? What else has she discovered she can do?*

Sarl cleared his throat. "Legends tell us the world and magic were not always divided thus, that once pattern magic, or glow magic as it is sometimes called, and shaper magic existed side by side. More importantly to those who have or desire power, pattern magic was wielded by the person whose body contained it, without the need of an intermediary. You can see how that idea would appeal to many people. In this far distant past, the world and the magic were separated in two and the Wall was built. Many schemes have been tried to undo what was done."

Tal urged her camel on as it balked at a narrow bridge across a deep ravine. Cooler air wafted across Malenie's face, but when she craned her neck to peer into its depths she couldn't see the water it must hide.

"That none of those schemes has worked has not stopped people from trying others," Sarl said. "The Sarnath Matriarch and the Suntin Matriarch decided to mix Thessem and Parthavian blood in an effort to recapture the old magic. A bit like breeding sheep, but with less scholarship behind it.

"The Sarnath Matriarch sent me to Suntin. The girl they chose—we were both young—was lovely and kind and had a young son."

The buzz of insects was loud in his silence. A hawk keened, its wild cry sounding like grief. From the look on her face, Tal had not heard this story before. Paza passed Malenie a waterskin.

"It wasn't hard to do what our families required of us. We fell in love. Nowadays unions between the different people do not produce children unless a lot of magic is involved, but that was not always the case. Indeed it's not even clear if there were different peoples as we have now. It seems to be a side result of whatever was done to divide the magic, or as the Matriarchs postulated, it was the cause that kept the magic divided. Join the peoples, join the magic."

Jos trotted toward them, beckoning, and Malenie realized with a start that the mauve and rose of the sunset was turning gray and blue. He led them to a clearing in the scrubby bushes and prickly grass and, while they made camp with quick efficiency, the stars came out. Jos roasted quail seasoned with salt and wild sage. They were fatter and better tasting than the game Shay had hunted in the desert.

Sarl ate little before taking up his story. "Neither my ancestors nor her gods and goddesses blessed us with a child. We had only a few short years together. She died alone in a fall, before I or the healers could get to her."

Malenie felt the shock of his words in her stomach, even though she'd been almost expecting it. From the way he spoke of her, Malenie thought his wife would be with him today otherwise. She was glad she couldn't see if his eyes showed the grief his voice hid.

"I did not…behave as a father should. I couldn't look at his face, and I did not see things I should have seen. My mother's house was full of aunts, uncles, siblings and cousins. I thought they were caring for him. I never imagined…Instead he was alone. Not the child the Matriarch desired, with no magic, Parthavian among Thessem. Vulnerable.

"When I finally saw—my own uncle!" His lips drew away from his teeth in a grimace of pain, and each word was forced out past the barrier of his own body. "I took him away. To Suntin. I hoped living with his mother's family would help. The old Matriarch had died, and the new one was kinder. She didn't share her aunt's obsessions.

"It wasn't any better; he was wild. He was so angry. He would not let anyone touch him, not even me. He wouldn't let us use magic or any other means to heal him. Consent is everything for those who have the pattern magic. But I thought the anger was a good thing, that feeling he could express it meant he would eventually heal." His eyes strayed to Paza.

He thinks she's been hurt, just like I do. Seven hundred gods and goddess, he thinks his son hurt her the way he was hurt. Malenie dug her fingers into her thighs. *I don't want to feel bad for the man in the blue robe. He didn't have to hurt anyone else, just because he'd been hurt.*

"I don't know if anyone ever hugged him. I did not either. He looked so like Tessalina…." He took deep breaths. Jos threw his bones, gnawed clean, into the fire, which crackled and curved around them. Tal sat facing away, preserving her night vision for sentry duty, but her rigid back showed she was listening. *This is too private*, Malenie thought. She didn't want to know adults had regrets, had doubts.

"You did the best you could," Tal said. "It's the only thing any of us can do."

"I didn't. I should have done better. Of all people, I should have seen what was happening." Abruptly he stood and strode beyond the reach of the firelight to stand facing the night, a darker shape against the dark.

18

Malenie woke, slipping over the edge between sleep and wakefulness with no transition. An owl hooted softly, and bats flitted soundlessly between her and the stars. The fire had burnt out, and with the smell of smoke gone, the air was full of the tang of creosote and wild sage. Jos was snoring and the others were quiet, sleeping with their feet towards the ashes of the fire. Except for Paza. She was sitting up with her blanket around her hips.

"What is it?" Malenie whispered.

"Nes is gone."

"Gone? Where? What happened?" Malenie untangled herself from the blankets in a rush to crouch at Paza's side. "Which way did she go? What are you waiting for? We have to go after her." Malenie fumbled with her sandals, but Paza's hand on her ankle stopped her from standing.

"Are you sure about her?" Paza whispered harshly.

"Am I—yes, of course."

"It's strange, though, how she was waiting for us."

"She explained all that."

"When we found her, she explained it; but what about the first time? When she was spying on us?"

"Paza, when we find her, I'll ask her, alright? But I'm as sure of her as I am of you, and I'm getting tired of the way you act towards her." She just stopped herself from saying out loud, *And it's making me wonder about you.* She shook off Paza's hand and stood. "She's my friend, has been my friend for a long time." Paza didn't move. "Are you coming with me?"

"I don't see why I should," Paza muttered to the ground. "She's been nothing but trouble."

"Because I want you to."

No answer.

"Fine." Malenie stamped away, fuming. *What is wrong with her?* But a moment later, the rustle of cloth and the scuff of footsteps told her Paza had changed her mind. Malenie paused at the edge of camp with relief. The bowl of the sky seemed impossibly wide and the wilderness around them too empty. A person could get lost out there and never be found.

"Look," Paza said, pointing at a faint track, white against the dark scrub, leading away from the poorly maintained road they had followed during the day. A small form that had to be Nes breached the crest of a hill and disappeared down the far side. She was heading into the mountains that had grown up in the east all during the afternoon. Malenie set out after her and Paza trailed a few paces behind. Bright moonlight lit the chalky path, but no matter how they hurried, they couldn't close the lead Nes's longer legs and head start had given her. The path rose more steeply, and the pungency of pine replaced the wild headiness of creosote as they climbed into the foothills of the mountains. A sudden sharp desire to take the time to see them ached in her chest. *I'm traveling farther than I ever dreamed of and I'm not really seeing any of it.*

A branch snapped behind them and Malenie froze, realizing they might not be the only, or even the biggest, hunters in the night. She slowly turned to look behind them, still clutching the slender trunk of a pine tree and scrabbling for a rock with the other hand.

Jos rounded the bend, sword unsheathed. He seemed larger and fiercer in the moonlight; the glittering arc of his sword, the whites of his eyes, the flash of his teeth bright. "Where are you going?" he asked in a low harsh voice.

The rough edges of the rock bruised her palm; her arm was half cocked to throw while her body tried to decide if Jos was a threat or help. "N-nes," she stuttered.

"We're following Nes," Paza said clearly, and Malenie wondered where her fear of men had gone. She looked down; Paza's sling traced tense half circles, loaded and ready. Maybe that was where.

Jos lowered his sword. "Where is she going?"

Malenie recovered her voice to answer before Paza could fling any of her accusations. "We don't know."

"What do you know about her?" Jos demanded.

"Enough!" Malenie said hotly. She hurled the rock into the night. "Why does everyone keep asking me about her? Why should I trust you more than I trust her? You're the one waving around a sword."

"It could be dangerous here," he said in a more normal voice, but he seemed slightly abashed and sheathed his sword. "And because I came to help, while your friend is running away."

"She is not running away!" Malenie turned on her heel and stomped up the trail before he could ask what Nes was doing. She wished they would both stop asking her such questions. She had known Nes all her life, even if only the edges had overlapped these last years.

Behind her she heard Jos say, "I didn't know you were armed."

"That's the point," Paza said scornfully.

After another turn and a climb straight up a fall of boulders, Malenie teetered on the edge of a cliff. At her feet the ground plunged away, dropping to a roughly circular pit scooped out of the hills. The white rock gleamed against sharp-edged shadows, too regular to be natural. Across the gap, the mountains loomed, blocking the stars in half the sky. Fixated on the panorama before her, she called over her shoulder, "Watch—" Paza bumped into Malenie and they staggered on the edge, rocks rolling under their feet and skittering into the darkness. Malenie threw herself backwards, dragging Paza with her, and slammed into the shelf of rock encircling the pit. "—out," she finished.

Jos hauled himself to the rim and balanced there, hand resting on his sword hilt, but the threat was gone from the gesture, which seemed more a habit than anything. *On second thought, that kind of habit is a threat,* Malenie thought, with a shiver not entirely from the cold. *What would Papa think if he saw me now?* "It's the Forgotten Quarry," he said, his voice awed.

"Why do they call it that?" Paza asked. "It can't be forgotten, the trail was easy to follow."

"But they say you can only find it on certain nights, nights with a full moon."

Malenie looked over her shoulder to the moon. It was low in the sky.

Moonset was near, and sunrise would quickly follow. She shook off the feeling of mystery in favor of practicality. And maybe some sleep, eventually. "Where's Nes?"

"There she is," Jos said, just as Malenie spotted her, about a quarter of the way around the rim, kneeling on a small promontory jutting above the pit, her hands pressed to the ground. There was no sign she had noticed their arrival.

"What is she doing?" Malenie muttered. A path hugged the edge of the cliff, smooth enough to run along. Malenie skidded to a stop in a cloud of dust next to Nes. Her eyes were closed and she didn't react to the sound of their footsteps. Her hands were splayed flat, the tips of her fingers digging into the bare rock, as if she were afraid of falling. Only her chest moved as she breathed.

"This is spooky," Paza said.

"Nes?" Malenie asked tentatively and then repeated herself a little more loudly.

"What's wrong with her?" Paza asked. There was almost a note of relish in her voice, as if she delighted in the setback of a… rival? Malenie snapped a quick look at Paza. Was she jealous over Malenie's friendship?

"Have you ever seen her sleepwalk before?" Jos asked.

"No—you think she's asleep?" Malenie poked Nes's shoulder. "Hey! Wake up!" Nes wobbled as Malenie shook her hard, but her hands stayed firmly planted and her eyes remained closed. She didn't even twitch.

"We'll just have to leave her," Paza said.

"Stop it!" Malenie hissed, struggling to hold her temper. "Would you want someone to say the same thing about you?"

"We're not leaving anyone. Sarl said all six of us are needed, and I wouldn't leave an enemy to the mercy of the wild dogs and two-legged animals in these hills," Jos said.

Paza drew back as if slapped, and Malenie didn't know if she should hug her or shake her. Jos crouched in front of Nes and called her name. When she didn't respond, he gently pulled her hands off the rock. Some of the rigidity left her, but she didn't wake. "Do you have a sling too?" he asked Malenie.

"No." It was in her bag, back at the camp, so it wasn't a lie.

"Here, grab her hands and keep them away from the ground."

"You think this place is doing something to her?" Malenie asked, clasping Nes's dusty hands.

"I'm not taking the chance." Jos unbuckled the dagger sheath from his baldric. "That's for you since you seem to like knives. You," he said to Paza, "keep your sling ready, but for enemies only, not your friends." He knelt beside Malenie and took Nes's wrists. The warmth of him sent a shudder through Malenie, reminding her she was cold and tired and awake at the deepest part of the night. He pulled Nes across his shoulders, face down, head on one side, feet to the other. His left hand held an arm and a leg, while the other was free to draw his sword.

The dagger both a reassuring and worrisome weight in her hands, Malenie watched anxiously as Jos navigated the steep parts of the trail. He didn't look like he needed her concern, while she was so tired her feet felt like boulders at the end of her legs. The dagger dragged at her arms, no matter how often she switched hands, and the return trip seemed endless.

After they descended the hardest section, Malenie looked back to check on Nes. Jos hitched her higher on his shoulders, and her head bobbed out of rhythm with his steps. She was awake.

As Malenie shouted, "No!" Nes elbowed Jos in the nose and twisted, clawing at his eyes. Jos pinned her hand and heaved, flipping her over his head to the ground. She rolled, coming up in a defensive crouch, hands in front of her chest, facing him.

"No!" Malenie rushed to fill the space between them.

Grumbling a curse, Jos stepped back. "You three are the most vicious group of girls. Tal will be pleased." Considering his bleeding nose and the long scratch at the corner of one eye, he didn't seem very upset. He might even be as pleased as he claimed Tal would be.

But Nes wasn't listening. She turned frightened eyes on Malenie. "Where are my sibs? Where did they go?"

"Nes—"

"They were right here! Where did they go?" Hysteria pulled her voice into a shriek.

Malenie wanted to shriek too, but she said softly and firmly, "It had to be a dream. They were never here."

"I saw them. They were falling into a huge hole in the ground, screaming for help." She finally looked around and faltered. "Where are we?" She straightened and scanned their surroundings, confusion mixing with fear on her face.

"You don't remember walking up to the quarry?" Jos asked.

"No. What are—a quarry? That's where they are. I have to go." She tried to bolt up the path. Jos blocked her and she ran straight into him. He grabbed her arms. Malenie lunged forward and seized a fistful of Nes's tunic for good measure. "Let go! What are you doing?" Nes shouted.

Paza sat on a nearby boulder with a disgusted grunt.

"They weren't there," Malenie said as calmly as she could. Nes squirmed in Jos's hold and clutched Malenie's hands.

"I have to see!"

"No one was—"

Nes shook her, and Malenie bit her lip hard as her head rocked forward. "No, I have to see them. You can use—"

"Shut up!" screamed Paza, launching herself at Nes. She slammed into them. Jos danced back a step to keep his balance. Malenie fell on her butt. Nes landed flat on her back, Paza on top of her hips. Paza pummeled Nes's head and chest, shouting incoherently.

Jos stepped forward. It would be easy for him to pick Paza up and restrain her, but it would not be good for Paza. Malenie found her feet, leaped and swept Paza off Nes. The ground smacked the air out of both of them. Paza's cries cut off. Malenie skidded through the shale at the edge of the path, scraping the whole right side of her body and chin.

"Ugh." Malenie spit out gravel and blood. She sat up and probed the cut on her face. The worn fabric of her sleeve flopped open, exposing an elbow and a smear of blood along her forearm. And blue-tinged diamonds. She pulled the edges together.

Paza wheezed as she stared up at the sky. She didn't react as Nes padded up to them and crouched. "I'm sorry." The panic was gone, but so was all other emotion, clamped down so tightly her voice was expressionless. "I need to know they're safe."

Paza hissed at Nes, voice vibrating with fear and anger. "They're not safe—but Malenie was, before you started telling all her secrets, and now she won't be."

"At least…alive," Nes said. "And you said trust him, trust the wise man—did you only mean with my sibs, who you don't know and don't care about?" Fury was creeping back into her voice.

Malenie spoke up quickly. "Nes, I understand." She understood her friends were more similar than they thought and protective. And she could no more ignore Nes than her papa could ignore an ill or injured person. Jos's back was to the moon and his face hidden, but he was so still Malenie felt it, like an extra person in a room. *He must have an idea of what this is about.* She felt even colder than before. *He'll tell Sarl and Tal.* She put that thought away. It couldn't matter right now. *I'm sorry, Papa. I can't it keep it a secret anymore.*

"I won't help," Paza said, seeming to sense Malenie's decision.

"Fine. I won't ask you to."

The other girl sucked in a loud breath. "You're choosing her!"

"I'm not choosing anyone! You just said you wouldn't help." Malenie offered her right hand to Nes, releasing the tattered scraps of her sleeve.

"You can't do that!"

"Will you help?"

"No!"

"Then I have to." Resolutely she turned away from Paza's horrified face. "You know how to do it. It's easy," she said to Nes. Her eyes drifted to Jos, who was watching them. With one last reflex of secrecy she thought, *I can't believe I'm doing this where he can see.* Nes closed uncertain fingers on her wrist. Jos's shoulders stiffened at the brief flare of blue light. Malenie closed her eyes in surprise. The magic felt different as it swirled over her skin and through her blood, almost as if she could taste—although it had nothing to do with her mouth—Nes's stubbornness, her worry for her family and even her wonder at what they were doing.

When Malenie opened her eyes, Jos squatted next to her, and even Paza had sat up to peer at the dark smudge at their feet. Malenie didn't know what else to call it. Not a billow of dust, but a darker slice of the night hanging in the air, obvious to her eyes, as if the moonlight here didn't touch the night there. A bend in the air. Then, as her eyes adjusted, she saw children sleeping, all tumbled together for warmth on the bare ground. Nes bit back a cry, a distorted sound of mixed relief and anguish, just as Malenie spotted them, the oldest girl with her arms around as much of her sibs as possible. After a breathless moment, Nes raised a tentative hand to touch—but there was nothing to touch. Her hand fell heavily to her lap.

"I want to see Papa," Malenie whispered, almost afraid her voice would wake the sleepers. This time Nes's words were more confident, and the air quickly wavered and then steadied, showing Papa on his back, staring up into the sky. Moonlight glittered on the moisture at the corners of his eyes. Nes caught her breath. Malenie felt like pieces of her heart, of her very place in the world, were being flayed off. She wanted to hide her face—she had to hide his face. "Seven hundred gods and goddesses." No one should have seen this. "Change it! Show my uncle. He's got to catch them!"

The image rippled and Nes cursed as she tried to force it to respond. The magic coiled in Malenie's belly with nowhere to go, giving her something else to think about, and she welcomed the ache. Gorging herself on milk pastries had given her this same feeling of all her insides pulled tight. With the pastries—with the sight of Papa crying—she had had to endure. This she could control. "You have to say his name: Liac Pashtin!" The cut on her lip broke open and stung.

Nes repeated the name and Malenie's stomachache eased. The ripple in the air showed guards readying to ride, while Liac and the captain walked among them, saying something to each one or just gripping their shoulders. They were surrounded by desert and bare tumbled rock that could be anywhere within ten days ride of Malenie's home, but she had to believe they were pursuing the slavers.

"That's enough." As if Jos's words were a knife cutting the connection between Nes and Malenie, the image folded in on itself and disappeared. The exhilaration of using the magic, of defying years of secrecy, drained away like sand slipping through her fingers. Exhaustion hit Malenie like a body blow, and she slumped under its weight.

"Ancestors," Nes said and Malenie flinched. What if that sight of her sibs changed Nes's mind about Suntin? *Has seeing Papa changed my mind?…No, I know it's right. I think.* "It tingled," Nes said, and it was awe in her voice, not regret or goodbye. Just awe. "It felt like my blood lit up inside me. Like the excitement before a fight, but more."

Malenie's mouth and eyes felt round in surprise. "That's not…" *Why doesn't it feel like that for me? I feel like I had a three-day fever.* Confused, she turned to Paza but stopped short at the set expression on her face. Malenie's resentment at Paza's stubbornness disappeared and she reached out to her. "Wait." Malenie wasn't sure what she was going to explain, but Jos didn't give her a chance to find out.

He heaved himself to his feet. "It's time to go," he said, very, very neutrally.

Malenie twisted to look up at him. For the first time tonight he moved clumsily and looked tired—and worried. She couldn't meet his eyes. *Gods and goddesses, did I really do…what I did?*

The sky was gray behind him, the whole night spent. Malenie groaned, unable to organize her limbs enough to stand, glad the aches and bruises gave her something else to focus on. Years of secrecy, gone. And Papa, staring at the sky in despair. *No. I'm not thinking about that.*

"I can carry you," Jos offered, immediately galvanizing her upright. Her knees shook, and she clutched at a handy boulder, but she was up.

"I can walk."

"Good. Sarl will—" He broke off, spinning to face the opposite direction and drawing his sword in one smooth motion. His other hand reached for his dagger, but it was still at Malenie's feet, seemingly a long ways away. *How can he be that alert?* Malenie was too tired to muster up fear of a new danger. She slumped against a craggy boulder, distantly noting it was cold, much colder than she. Her breath puffed white in the air. Just as quickly, Jos sheathed his sword.

Tal appeared on the path below them, hands held wide and empty. "You found them," she said when she was close enough not to shout. Her bland survey made Malenie feel even blearier and set every bruise and scrape throbbing as she remembered them anew. "Sarl wants to hurry on our way and hear where you went, in that order. What do you have to tell him?"

"Lots." He bent to retrieve his dagger—sparing Malenie the embarrassment of toppling over—and Tal's eyes widened in surprise. "But I only want to say it once. Let's go."

19

Jos led the way down the trail, and Tal motioned the three girls to follow so she could take the rear. Malenie wobbled for a few steps, until Nes hooked Malenie's arm over her shoulder. When their strides matched, Nes whispered in her ear, "I'm sorry. It seems stupid now, but I just knew my sibs were in trouble—more trouble. Thank you for helping."

"Of course I was going to help."

"There's no 'of course' about it. I can kind of guess that wasn't the easiest thing for you. And I wasn't a good…I'm sorry for everything else, too. For not stopping the bullies in Trader Town, for not talking to you, for not teaching you to—"

"That was not your fault, and don't you dare think it was. I broke Rooster Boy's arm all on my own." A long shudder ran through Malenie as she felt the crunch of the bully's bone under her hands again, now mixed with the feeling of the thug's finger bones snapping.

"I should have—"

"I should have stopped. But for a moment, I wasn't scared, I was in control, he couldn't hurt me, and it felt wonderful. But then I heard—felt it break. And it felt awful, and it's felt awful since. But I did it, so don't make excuses for me."

"Yeah, I know. Mellie…I'm sorry I threw rocks at you that time," she said in a rush, referring to a time just after her aunt and uncle went looking for Nes's sibs.

The expression on her face bothered Malenie. She had seen Nes sullen, angry, determined, gleeful, delighted and awed, but not ashamed.

It didn't suit her. Malenie had wallowed in enough shame in the last nine moons over being bullied to know she didn't want Nes to keep feeling ashamed. "You know, I knew you weren't throwing the rocks at me, just near me."

"You did?"

"Yeah, because you never actually hit me." Malenie didn't care anymore about what Nes had done. Yeah, it had been one of the worst moments of her life, but it was one of the worst moments of Nes's life, too. And now she was back, ready to be her friend again.

Giddy with happiness, Malenie elbowed Nes in the ribs. "I rather you beat me up than look so ashamed." Just as suddenly the giddiness changed to worry she'd gone too far. Malenie bit her lip, right on the cut, wishing she could call the words back. *I am really tired.*

But Nes grinned. "So you're saying me apologizing is worse than me mad at you? And I thought I was so fierce."

"You are!" Malenie bumped into her and tripped. Nes's arm tightened like a clamp around her wrist and she hitched Malenie's arm higher around her shoulders.

They walked a few more steps and Malenie's gait evened out a bit before Nes spoke again. "I needed to be angry back then, after Pa, after everyone…they were gone—like they never existed. It was be angry or lie down and never get up again. Ma really lit into me. She wouldn't let me lie down. So instead I was angry all the time, even, especially, with the people who didn't deserve it. And maybe I was a little worried they would disappear, too, if I cared. That you would disappear. So I tried not to care." She frowned at their feet, obviously not seeing the dust and grit they walked over.

"Ashes, Nes."

"Don't you feel sorry for me," Nes said.

"But we're good, right?" Malenie asked.

"Ancestors, yeah." The frown slid into a real smile. "You're my only hope of getting home. I'm not so dumb as that," Nes joked. "Friends, for real," she added solemnly,

Malenie felt lighter. Nes's rejection had been like a blister, chafing at every step, sometimes better, sometimes worse. Now it was like she had taken the sandal off—no, better, like all that was left of the blister was a scar.

Nes slowed and Malenie looked up. Paza turned her back abruptly, but not before Malenie saw the hurt on her face. *I have to fix that, too,* Malenie thought, not sure if she could, and then saw they had arrived back at camp. Sarl stood up with a rush that startled the camels. There was no time to speak to Paza in the flurry of orders Sarl barked out ."Let's go. It's already light. We can't waste a minute of it."

Once Tal gentled the camels and got them to sit, Jos mounted and said, "I'll report as we ride."

Malenie said "No," but Sarl was talking to Jos and didn't hear. "No," Malenie repeated loudly and tugged herself free from Nes's support.

"What?" Sarl took a long step closer and loomed over her.

All three adults pinned her with their stares as if she were a rock that had started speaking. Her exhaustion flared into stubborn anger.

"I said, 'No.'" Her voice squeaked, but what she had to say was too important to back down just because they didn't want to listen. She just wished her head didn't feel so thick. "We had an agreement," she said more firmly. "You'd tell us your story and we'd decide if we were going with you. We're halfway to Suntin—"

"We're not even close—"

"—and you haven't even told us his name."

"Ah." That brought Sarl up short. He bowed his head and Malenie gulped to see all the authority drain out of him. "I don't like to say it. I don't like to say any of it. But a secret, hidden, gathers shame and regret and anguish to it." He lifted his head and straightened his shoulders. "A secret let out into the light may become easier to bear."

Malenie's breath hissed between her teeth and Nes grabbed her elbow as she swayed. He was speaking to himself, not even looking at her, but his words showed her the shape of a cage she hadn't known surrounded her.

"His name is Colvin." He opened his hands as if letting something go. "Tessalina always used it with such love." He sighed and covered Tal's hand on his shoulder with his own. His gaze went to the sun, judging the hour, and then inward, judging whatever he found there, too.

"I've labored too long at this confession. I only hope my ancestors and the gods and goddesses of Tessalina's faith forgive me. Quickly now. And then you must decide.

"Colvin. I told you about his childhood and my failures. When he was a little older than you," he nodded at Nes, "he ran away. I found him of course, and I brought him back. I tried to be a better father, but he ran away again and again. Each time I brought him back. The last time, I was in Sarnath for a family emergency. Before I returned, he sent a note saying he had found work as a caravan guard. Just that. I let him go. I don't know if that's what he wanted," Sarl said in anguish. "Maybe he needed me to go after him. Maybe he needed me to prove I loved him."

"You are not all knowing, in spite of your sight," Tal said roughly.

"If I had protected him…"

"We all make mistakes, terrible ones." Tal paused and rubbed the bump on her nose. "We are not—cannot—be responsible for the mistakes of others."

He sighed and frowned at the green scrolls etched on and under his skin.

"It's easy to make mistakes. It's harder to do something about them," Nes said.

He barked a sharp laugh, but the lines on his face eased. "The wisdom of children." Nes bristled, squinting at him hostilely. He patted the air and added, "At my age even Tal and Jos seem like children." Jos rolled his eyes, and the lines on Sarl's face eased. When he continued, the anguish in his voice had dulled. "Yes, and I should avoid making another mistake now.

"So—eventually he returned to the city, although he lived apart from us. I thought we made progress when he agreed to start coming to the house. But then…I discovered he was harming children. I confronted him—and I repudiated him. I took his family name back—and he gave me the wound I showed you.

"After that, for years I didn't know anything about him. I should have…" He grimaced. "Then I had a vision so strong it stopped my heart. Tal was with me, and she brought me back with the last magic flickering over my skin before I truly died." Sarl thumped her shoulder. "In it, I saw him and the one they now call the Suntin girl—" Paza looked up, her mouth open in surprise, "—and fire and destruction. I went looking for him. What I had seen hadn't yet happened, but it was close. Too close. When we reached Suntin, the earth was swallowing a quarter of the city and another quarter was burning. That was when I had my last vision of him, consumed by that poor girl's fire. Ancestors hold her. Her screams went on and on, long after she was dead. I can still hear them….And so I thought he was dead. My sight never touched him after.

"And that is all the story."

"Until we make an ending of it," Jos said, knuckles shiny around his sword hilt.

I didn't know I was so lucky to have Papa, Malenie thought, shaken. "But, can you really take all the guilt for yourself?" she asked, trying to figure out what she wanted to say as she said it. "When he was a child, yeah, you didn't protect him." Like Papa hadn't protected her; but she'd never asked, not understanding he wouldn't just know. It was confusing to think about, but she pressed on, saying something she'd been realizing about herself. "But he grew up, and it became his responsibility to choose the kind of person he wanted to be. Didn't it? So that shame is his, not yours. Like Tal said."

Sarl rocked back, touching his heart again.

She fumbled for words. "You made another family and it looks like this one works." She pointed at Tal and Jos with her chin. "You decided who you wanted to be."

"Ah." Sarl tilted his head back and blinked rapidly. He choked out, "That was not the response I anticipated, but it will do. It will do very well."

◊◊◊

Malenie struggled out of a sticky doze and opened heavy eyelids. The camel rocked beneath them and the ground blurred past beneath its feet. Nes was a hot weight against her back. It took a moment to work out why she hadn't simply fallen off when sleep overcame her, but they were securely roped in to the saddle. Paza was…Paza was on another camel. Sarl had asked if they were going on together and, once the girls agreed, hustled them a-camelback. Paza had ignored Malenie and Nes and mounted the beast they were not on.

Malenie sighed and looked around. Sere hills and scrubby trees still surrounded them. Not much had changed. Tal was out of sight on foot. Sarl and Jos rode side by side, their heads bent close, and she knew—with the same awareness that warned of someone's gaze on the back of her head—that they were discussing her. Sarl's gray head lifted, and his eyes met hers. With a sure hand, he guided his camel towards her.

"Wha'? Wuz happening?" Nes jolted awake as Malenie stiffened.

Jos told him, and now he wants…what? Panic crawled through her guts and she tried to push it down. *I put all our lives in his hands when I decided to trust him. This is no different.* The panic cried back, *It is different, he knows your secret.*

Malenie forced herself to say calmly, "We're not in danger. It's just Sarl."

The air felt almost cool against her sweat-dampened back as Nes straightened up. "Alright," Nes mumbled, soothed, and, "Right," in a completely different tone of voice. If she'd had weapons, Malenie imagined she'd be checking them. For Nes, even more than Malenie, deciding to trust someone was not the same as trusting him.

"Malenie," Sarl said. Daringly, she examined the patterns on his arms openly. They were vibrantly green and graceful, and they still made her uncomfortable. "I have been thinking and thinking about what we shall have to do once we find Colvin, to no avail, I'm afraid. I even tried a seeing while you were gone this morning. Also to no avail. Paza has agreed to another attempt later." He nodded at Paza, who scowled at them all impartially and twisted her fingers together.

Malenie cleared her throat and peeled her sweaty tunic away from her skin, uncomfortable in several ways. "And you want me to… what?"

"To tell me your impressions of him. Your viewpoint might well be different from Paza's."

"Um, he seemed like anyone else at first, except for his hair." She touched her own and saw Paza do the same from the corner of her eye. "Do you know why he doesn't, um, cover it? Is it because he was raised…um."

"I suspect he's giving us all the back of his hand." Sarl sighed, and Nes snorted a repressed laugh at his reference to the insult she used. A lot. It was a stretch of the imagination to picture Sarl—dignified even riding a camel—using it. "He was raised to respect his ancestors and the seven hundred Parthavian deities. Perhaps theological confusion…"

"Sarl," Jos warned.

"Correct. No digressions." He nodded at Malenie to continue.

"Right. But then…" If he wasn't going to mention her magic, Malenie wasn't either. But when Paza wished to protect her family, it was as if his intent to cause harm had been so deep and wide all the magic it had sucked in had not been enough to fill it up, until Malenie had been drained almost dry. "He seemed damaged." Sarl watched her steadily, demanding honesty. "Broken. Mean, cruel, obsessed—he's obsessed with Paza. I was more afraid for her than for me." Was Paza listening? Did she hear what Malenie was saying? "He was like—like a drunk, teetering on his feet and he was grabbing her to hold him steady, but it just made him tip more."

"Ah. And did you—" His words cut off at Tal's sudden silent appearance out of the brush.

"Stop," she said hoarsely, jogging to intercept them. "Trouble. At least ten fighters, waiting in ambush near the trail." Nes's fingers dug hard into Malenie's hips. With a chill Malenie looked around, expecting…what? No vultures circled overhead, no outward signs of danger appeared except for the slight tenseness around Tal's eyes and mouth. It was the same hot day it had been a moment ago, only her perception of it had changed. Traveling in a group had made her feel safer, though she hadn't felt really safe in a long time, even before Papa was taken away. Tal continued, "The trail narrows to a bottleneck at a bridge. It's the perfect place for an ambush."

"Can the two of us sneak up on them and take them out?" Jos asked.

"Too many in good defensive positions." She glanced at the girls. "We should go around."

"And leave them at our backs?" Jos argued.

"Not a prospect I like, either," Sarl said. "What I want to know is what they want and what they know."

"And how they found us," Malenie muttered. Walking and riding through the desert and its borderlands had given her an appreciation of its vastness she hadn't had before she left Trader Town.

"I need to check behind us. There wasn't time before I stopped you." Tal shaded her eyes to look back the way they'd come while Jos kept a sharp eye on the way they had to go. Nothing in the landscape communicated the pressure of hidden watchers to Malenie, but Tal and Jos seemed to read some answer there.

"We'll both go," Jos said. "If they have watchers on us, they'll already be suspicious of us stopping like this. Wait there," he nodded to a gnarled tree a few paces away that threw shade over half the trail, "and eat something. But don't get off your camels. That might confuse them a bit."

"Let me put some protections on you," Sarl said.

"No," Tal and Jos said and grinned at each other, a brief flash of teeth.

They want to fight. They seemed to relish the readiness running through their blood. Malenie felt it too, but though it made it possible for her to fight, she didn't like the feeling.

"It won't last long enough anyway," Jos said. "We'll be moving slowly."

"And you need to be ready when you're truly needed, not spending your strength on little things. What if Colvin is there?" Tal said to Sarl quietly. "We're trained for this. This is what we do."

20

Tal and Jos stepped into the brush, and by the time the rest of the group had crowded into the shade, they had disappeared from sight. Nes picked apart the knots in the rope tying them in place and stowed it in one of the carrysacks. Malenie unwrapped her head scarf—the worn scrap Shay had given her—and tunneled her fingers through her hair, lifting it away from her scalp. No one said much. She forced herself to gnaw a strip of meat but refused the water, afraid she'd have to pee if there was a fight. A breeze tossed the green leaves and dropped its burden of dust on her.

Paza swung off her camel's neck to the ground.

"Paza," Sarl said.

"I'll be fast." She crouched at the rough edge of the road, filled her bag with fist-sized rocks and remounted.

How much time had passed? An eternity and not very long at all before Tal and Jos reappeared under the camels' noses. Tal had a smudge across one flat cheekbone and Jos's face was streaked with sweat and dirt. A long, shallow slice across his upper arm leaked blood and there was a darker stain on his dark leathers. Malenie averted her eyes, tucked her hair and the trailing edge of her headscarf into the back of her tunic, and drew out her sling. Her breath came fast and she clenched and unclenched her fingers around her rock.

Tal reclaimed her bow and arrows from her saddle. "I'm going ahead. Colvin isn't there." She blended into the brush between one step and another.

Sarl cleared his throat. "If I may have your permission, Jos and I will put a protection on all of us to stop their weapons from hurting us. It's for a short time only, or it interferes with the body's natural processes, and it won't protect your eyes or ears."

When they agreed, Sarl and Jos clasped hands and called the magic. It tickled Malenie's skin briefly, and Nes squirmed behind her, and that was all.

"Let's go," Jos said.

Nes whispered in her ear, "Courage." She smelled of sweat, hair oil—where did she get that?—and adult.

"You too," Malenie answered awkwardly.

"Right," Nes said, and she sounded like Tal. Malenie felt an irrational spurt of jealousy and sudden sympathy for Paza. "Don't hit me in the head with that thing," Nes added. She knuckled Malenie in the ribs, and Malenie whispered a brief prayer for all of them.

Their camel lurched after Paza's, still tied together. Malenie strained her ears and eyes for signs of the ambush. It felt like they were galloping headlong in spite of the camels' easy jog. They rounded a sharp bend. Ahead, the trail squeezed between the shoulders of two folded hills and dipped to a wood and rope bridge spanning a dark canyon wider than a man was tall.

Malenie ducked, only afterwards realizing she had reacted to the buzz of Tal's arrow. A man cried out in pain, hidden in the thick undergrowth to Malenie's right, and a bearded man in leathers with an arrow in his shoulder tumbled down the hill and lay still. Arrows burst wildly from the ambushers' side.

Malenie's hand trembled as she whirled her sling, its whine a reassuring sound in her ear. She wanted a target, something to do.

An arrow sped directly for Sarl's heart and bounced off. Just bounced off, dropped to the ground and was trampled by Sarl's camel. Malenie gaped. Tal's bowstring twanged again and again. An arrow lightly hit Malenie in the calf and spun away. She flinched, though it felt more like a flick of a finger than a weapon.

"Ancestors," Nes said, amazed.

Only a few arrows flew at them now, as the attackers realized they weren't hitting their targets.

"You can't harm us," Jos cried. "Surrender. Come down—all of you, come down."

A man stood up behind an enormous smooth boulder. Another

man, where a low bush twisted back upon itself in a tangle of bare black branches. Another, and two women across the trail. They were just people, like any on the streets of Trader Town, dusty with the desert and armed for it. The one nearest her was only a little older than Nes, and he shook, maybe even with the same shock of emotions that shook Malenie but in some other combination: confusion, terror, rage, triumph.

They stepped awkwardly around rocks and cacti and on to the sandy road. Six of them. Already they seemed too close. The musky scent of their sweat invaded Malenie's nose, stronger than the green smell of broken branches and the tang of a small yellow flower among the rocks. The young man was lagging behind; the man now closest to her had a scar across his cheek that pulled his right eye down.

"Stop!" shouted Jos. "I wish for your joints to fuse." Sarl's magic flashed green, but the attackers still closed in on them. In a rush they closed up their trap. Malenie had time to think *Why isn't the magic working?* before the woman on the left raised her dagger to throw—but Jos's was already buried in her throat before she completed the motion. Her hand spasmed and her dagger fell. She staggered one more step, blood leaking around the blade, shock blossoming on her face, before she collapsed.

Malenie gagged and swallowed hard. The camels lurched uneasily in place, tangling the lead rope shorter. Paza and Malenie cracked kneecaps.

And then the scarred man was on them, reaching for Paza's leg. Nes backed the camels and he missed, swearing. Intent and menace masked his face. He was too close for the sling. When he reached again, Paza stabbed down with the shiv in her fist. He screamed but seized her leg.

Nes kicked him in the face, her foot glancing off his cheekbone as he twisted to the side. She urged the camels further back. Paza's swung around and stepped on his foot. His eyes bulged and the tendons in his neck stood out. A thin shriek escaped his lips and he beat at the camel's shoulder with both fists, leaving smears of blood on its hide. Finally it shifted again and he collapsed, curling around his foot.

About fifteen paces away, the others were fighting hand to hand. Nes kept backing the camels. The scar-faced man moaned from the ground and the young man stepped around him. Malenie's throat and gut cramped in fear. Her palms sweated and she wished she could wipe them on her thighs.

"I'm not going to hurt you," he said, holding his empty hands out.

"Ha," derided Nes.

From behind them Jos shouted unintelligibly and Sarl's magic flared strongly again, but without any effect Malenie could see. But Malenie had been fighting without magic for a long time. "Stop right there," she ordered with as much authority as she could muster, and he wavered, foot raised mid-step. "Your friends are hurting mine. Try again."

He swallowed nervously, close enough for Malenie to see the fine scars over his collarbones like stitchery, marking him as a desert nomad. "Your friends are tricking you," he said earnestly. "They're dangerous. We're here to save you."

Paza hissed in outrage, and Malenie reached across and poked her in the ribs, choking off whatever she meant to say. "Why should we believe you? They've never attacked us—you have."

Another shout from behind the other camels and the beat of sword on sword paused and then took up again, different somehow. Malenie didn't dare look away from his intent brown eyes. The others would have to warn her of any new threat.

For the moment her questions had stumped him; he rocked back on his heels and even scratched his head like she had asked him the distance between Trader Town and Pashtin and he couldn't remember. Malenie licked her lips and forced herself to breathe; cat-footed, Tal crept up behind him.

"You've been lied to," Malenie said loudly to distract him.

Tal wrapped one arm around his throat and wrenched his arm behind his back. He gasped in shock and pain and glared at Malenie. "You have," Malenie insisted and finally looked around to see Jos drop one of the swords he had been beating with his own to fake the sounds of fighting. The other attackers were slumped on the road. Malenie drew in a shuddering breath. If she hadn't been pinned between Nes and Paza's camel she might have fallen down, grinning in relief.

Tal surveyed them above her captive's head. Her face was calm in spite of the blood smeared across half of it. "Good work." The bandit rolled his eyes, unable to move because of her grip, but desperately trying to see who held him.

"Don't knock that one out," Sarl shouted across the width of the road-turned-battlefield,

"You don't have to shout." The bandit writhed and abruptly stopped as Tal twisted his arm higher. He hung there panting. "We don't kill captives, even the ones that attack unarmed children." She shook him lightly.

"We weren't unarmed," Paza pointed out.

"He didn't know that." Tal grinned up at them.

Sarl fastidiously picked a path around fallen bandits to Tal's side. "Were you harmed?"

Malenie shook her head. A little more of her breathlessness eased at his concern. The bandit had reawakened…not doubts, but second thoughts she didn't want to look at too closely.

"What kind of man attacks children? Young girls," Sarl amended at Paza's mutter.

"We—we weren't," he stuttered. Sarl merely glanced around pointedly with raised eyebrows and waited.

"We weren't to, to h-hurt them!"

"That's not what it looked like to me."

He stared back furiously and strained forward in spite of Tal's armlock. "We were just to bring them to—" He bit his lip and wrenched his head down.

Unexpectedly, Malenie felt sympathy for him and his misguided efforts to save them. At least, she supposed, that's how he saw it. "He was just talking," she offered and surprised him into looking at her. His eyes were round with fear, the whites showing all around. Nes pinched her arm.

"Where did you come from?" Sarl asked.

He shook his head and fought against Tal's hold. "Stay still," she warned him. When he ignored her, she yanked on his arm, her lips folded down with distaste. He yelped and slumped limply in her hands.

"We don't have time for you," Sarl said. "As much as I want to know what Colvin is up to—" The bandit choked. "—Yes, I know who hired you. I don't believe you can tell me much more that's useful that I can't figure out for myself. Jos?" he called.

"They didn't get here too long before we did, and there may be more out there, covering different roads." Jos finished straightening the tangled limbs of the corpses and pressed their eyelids closed. He whispered too quietly for Malenie to hear, then began to search corpses and unconscious bodies without seeming to care which was which.

Malenie slid down from the camel and leaned against its comforting bulk in the shadow it cast. The sun seemed barely to have moved. Her legs were shaky. She had seen dead people before. She had even seen them get dead, violently, at others' hands, but she had been a distant witness, not involved. She didn't like it, and she didn't like that it made her feel sick, especially when everyone else seemed to take it in stride.

Jos finished and sat back on his heels. "Apart from a large number of coins, just the usual you'd expect: water, food, whetstones. They had camels somewhere. One man had an extra set of hobbles." He held up a twist of rope. "But no family names or markings, no tattoos, no jewelry, not even any makers' marks on their weapons, though I'd guess this dagger was made in Raleton. Which means next to nothing since half the blades this far south are forged there." He cocked his head and squinted at Sarl. "Do you want to wake the others and ask them?"

"I can't. They are completely impervious to magic, and I don't know how Colvin did it. It's not like what I did, which was specific and short lasting. Do you recognize any of them?" Tal and Jos shook their heads no.

"I do," Paza said. She had dismounted and was stabbing her shiv into loose sand to clean it of blood. "He sent them. I seen him before." Her eyes flicked to and away from the line of corpses and she pressed her lips together, but her chin wobbled.

Tal jerked her head at Jos and handed over her captive. "Which one did you see before?"

"This one." Paza marched over and kicked the corpse on the end in the head. Malenie flinched. So did the bandit. "I seen—saw him in Raleton, with *him*."

"And what were they doing?"

"Nothin'." She looked away.

"Paza!" Malenie burst out.

Paza bit her lip. Finally she answered slowly. "He was cutting one of the boys. He was just a little one—could fit places us bigger ones couldn't." Malenie eyed Paza's skinny, short body. How much littler could he have been? "Wouldn't tell us his name—just shook his head—

so we called him Toad on account of his eyes. They were buggy like a toad's when you squeeze it.

"This one," two more kicks showed she meant the dead man, "cut him while *he* watched and didn't do anything. But then he kilt him and *he* was mad, but it wasn't any use to Toad, he was already dead." One sob tore out of her before she clamped her jaw closed.

The young bandit choked and gagged, and Jos pushed him as far away as possible without loosening his grip, like he thought the younger man was going to vomit on his boots. "I didn't know," the bandit whispered. "The man who hired us just said she belonged with him and you had taken her. We were just supposed to bring her to Suntin with us."

One step brought Sarl close enough to grab the man's face and haul his head up. Voice grating, Sarl asked, "Who—who were you supposed to bring to him?"

The bandit cringed and pointed at Paza with his chin. He couldn't meet anyone's eyes. Jos said a word Malenie hadn't even heard before. Sarl's arm dropped as if the nerves had been cut. Hoarsely he said, "Tie him up, but leave his weaker hand free. Listen to me. If you're smart, you'll get yourself free before any more of your friends show up. And then you'll run far away and never have anything to do with Colvin or slavers or banditry again." He stepped back and turned away, his hand reaching for his heart.

While he was talking, Malenie sidled up to Paza and then stood there helplessly, wondering what to say. She was relieved when Tal knelt in front of Paza and said, "It is not your fault. Not Toad's death or any of the terrible things he did to you or the other children. It is his fault and his shame, and you should be very proud you are brave enough to help make sure he can't hurt anyone else again." Tal held out a hand, palm up. Paza stared at it as if she didn't know what it was for. Moving slowly, Tal took one of Paza's hands and enfolded it in both of hers.

Paza trembled, but didn't pull free. Her chest rose and fell quickly as if she couldn't get enough air.

"Always remember, it is not your fault," Tal said.

Jos strode up. "We're ready to go."

Tal's hands parted like the wings of a butterfly opening to the sun and Paza stared at her hand as if it had transformed in Tal's grasp.

21

Jos tied the young bandit to a slender tree at the edge of the road. Tal and Sarl trussed up the unconscious ones and stripped them of their weapons, which they dumped into the ravine. The corpses were laid out straightly opposite them and the wind teased their clothes.

"Can you get the camels down?" Sarl asked Tal. His throat worked and he managed to produce a somewhat gentler voice for Paza. "You'll have to ride with someone." She slid behind Malenie, hand still half raised as if to avoid touching any other part of her body and diluting Tal's touch.

The camels knelt at Tal's command, the one Nes had bought last, shaking her head in protest.

"Check them," Sarl said. The three adults tested straps and buckles, the position of the saddles and the hang of supply bags. Beckoning Jos with a hard wave of his hand, Sarl placed both palms flat on the camel's neck. Jos hastened to stand behind him and grasp his shoulder. "Speed and endurance," Sarl ordered sharply.

"I wish endurance for you, camel, and speed to match a swift flying bird." Jos said. Light and magic crackled, the deep green color of tree leaves at a rich waterhole. Sarl rose, shrugging off Jos's helping hand and they repeated it a second time and a third. Sarl's breath grew harsh in his throat, and he stopped evading Jos's hand, which had shifted from shoulder to elbow. Malenie shuffled her feet and looked up as a shadow flitted over her. The carrion birds had found them and circled overhead, their great wings hardly needing to flap.

After the fourth camel, Sarl's head hung and his chest moved like a bellows. When he stopped gulping for air, Tal handed out pies with onions and raisins baked inside. They made Malenie's mouth water in spite of the dead men lined up across the road and Sarl's heavy silence. Water dribbled down her chin as she sucked on a waterskin, and she wiped her face with the back of her hand. Reluctantly she handed it to Nes when Nes poked her in the shoulder.

"Everyone up," Sarl directed. "Jos, lead them until we cross the bridge. Then you're riding, too."

"You need me to scout," he protested. "This attack proved that."

"We'll be going too fast for anyone to ambush us."

"But—"

"You're riding," Sarl said flatly. "Now help me up." It took the two of them to get him on the camel, and his skin was gray again by the time he was seated.

Jos waited for Tal and Paza to mount, and then gathered up the lead lines and coaxed the unhappy camels towards the rope and plank bridge across the ravine. Malenie glanced back at the young bandit. He was staring after them, the skin around his eyes pinched and tight.

On impulse, Malenie called for everyone to wait. She slung the waterskin over her shoulder, grabbed the edge of the saddle and let the weight of her body pull her down. For a moment she hung, slapping against the still-moving camel and then she let go. The sand cushioned her landing. She brandished the waterskin before setting it to his mouth. He gulped eagerly, steadying it awkwardly with his left hand. The other was tied behind his back and to the tree. It would be a hard job undoing knots he couldn't see, but not impossible. Most of the water went into his mouth and the spillover dampening his throat wouldn't hurt him.

Finally he pulled back with a gasp. "Why?"

"Because we don't mean for you to die." They stared at each other. Then Nes's call snapped the moment and Malenie scampered back to the camels, which were stopped before the narrow bridge.

Tal boosted her up, saying only, "That'll be another incentive to getting untied soon." Malenie choked on a laugh, surprised she could, and settled into place. Jos stepped onto the bridge.

"Wait!" The bandit's voice cracked. "The bridge, it's sabotaged."

Jos let go of the lead lines and froze. Tal's camel jostled his shoulder and the bridge creaked. Cold sweat sprang up between Malenie's shoulder blades.

"Jos," Tal said, and her voice sounded as fragile as the bridge suddenly looked. She gathered up her rein in steady hands. Malenie never knew what she planned to do because a gust of wind whipped through the ravine. With a ping, a strand of one of the support ropes frayed apart. The bridge shook and the rope unraveled, ping, ping, ping, faster and faster. Jos flung himself backwards as the boards jerked out from under his feet. Sarl and Tal were too far apart to use his magic in time.

Jos fell.

Malenie's hand clamped on Nes's thigh. "Now! Save him!"

"I wish he wouldn't fall!" Nes shouted. Malenie felt the familiar rasp and burn of magic. A rope of light thickened in the air between Malenie and Jos, ghostly blue, bristly and as thick as both her legs together. She braced herself. The other end opened out like a net and cradled him. Malenie almost fell backwards off the camel when the expected tug of his weight didn't come. Not the physical weight anyway. Her chest ached. It felt like the magic was prying the knitted layers of muscle and tissue apart deep inside.

"Do something," she gasped. If she started to unravel, would it just be the magic or her very flesh and bones too?

"But what?" Nes was rigid behind her, flustered, staring at Jos hanging immobile like a strange bug caught in a large spider's web. His head was flung back and his arms spread wide.

"Bring him up!"

Sarl said, "Keep it simple."

"Ah. I wish, um, Jos to come up here slowly and stop next to us. On the ground."

Ow. Malenie bit her lip, right on the cut again. She could barely breathe. *Now I know how the bridge felt as the ropes pulled in both directions.*

Jos rose slowly through the air. His thighs came into sight, then his knees, until he stood on air, rigid as a plank. For a moment he dangled, feet vaguely pointing down, and then they scraped the canyon rim. The magic thinned and dissolved, and he stumbled and dropped, pressing his face and hands into the dirt. Half falling, Tal sat next to him and touched his back.

The magic loosed its grip on Malenie and she pressed her hands to her chest, trying, too late, to hold everything in place. Except for the hard thump of her heart, everything felt normal to the touch.

Finally, Jos sat back on his heels and caught Tal's hand. Damp brown dirt streaked his cheeks and forehead. "Thank…" He coughed and cleared his throat. "Thank you." He stared at Malenie until she realized she had to say something.

"Ah…you're welcome." Her own voice sounded hoarse and inadequate. But it seemed to be enough, because he nodded and pushed to his feet with Tal's help. The line he walked to the camels was not straight. He fumbled with a pack and pulled out a sheathed dagger and a small package wrapped in oilskin. Deliberately, he turned and paced towards the bandit, who pushed as far back as possible into the tree. Malenie grabbed Nes's hand. Everyone seemed to hold their breath.

Jos stared down at him before bending to place the knife and package at the furthest reach of the rope. "Run far," Jos rasped. "I don't know whether to thank you or kill you. If I never see you again, I won't have to decide." The bandit swallowed convulsively and drew his legs to his chest. "Go home." Jos straightened and turned on his heel. He didn't falter until he mounted his camel, and then he sagged, and wiped at the dirt on his face.

"I have a question," Tal said to the bandit, "you said you didn't want to kill the girls."

"Um." He waited to see if she would say more, and then said to the ground, "The leader, he said you wouldn't send the girls first because we might have more people on that side. Which we don't."

Malenie thought Tal might take the knife away from him again, but instead Tal asked, "Do you have more people waiting for us?"

"He does, not me," he said, panicked. "I don't know how many, maybe ten. I don't know anything. Please…"

"I'm ready," Jos said, in an almost normal voice. Tal turned to look at him, and he held her gaze. A deep breath lifted her shoulders and she nodded at him, a slight tilt of her head. "Which way are we going?" he asked.

"That's a…very good question," Sarl said, staring into the canyon that had almost been Jos's death. "Does anyone have a suggestion? Tal?"

"That we move away from that boy before we make any decisions."

They took her suggestion and followed the edge of the ravine until the bandit was out of earshot. "We passed a crossroads about midday," Tal continued. "If we go east there, it'll be another day before we meet the next road heading north. We'll lose two days. If we cut across country...I just don't know. It could take us half a day to hit that road, it could take us four." Idly she ran her fingers over a new scratch in her leather jerkin, souvenir of a close call with something pointy. "That's the best I can guess."

"What do you think? Did Colvin hire people to follow us north or are they coming south to intercept us?"

"They're following us," Tal answered. "For all that they got ahead of us, they didn't bother hiding the trail they broke through the brush. They're coming up north, too."

"So if we turn south, we might run right into more of them."

"Doesn't mean there aren't any north of us," Jos said. "Breaking through the brush will slow us down and leave a trail as clear as they did."

"Sarl, why don't we just wish ourselves across the bridge, or even all the way to Suntin?" Paza blurted out.

Malenie's stomach cramped. She wanted to curse. Everyone had been doing a nice job of pretending she hadn't just horribly exposed herself until Paza brought all their attention back to her. Malenie glared at the back of Paza's head and hoped Paza could feel it. Sadly, she wasn't clutching her head in agony so she probably didn't. It was very quiet and very still. Even the breeze had died again.

"Malenie." Sarl's voice exploded into the silence, startling her into looking at him. "Is that what you've been doing?" he asked.

Donkey balls. She nodded.

"You must never—" His voice cracked, but he was speaking really loudly, shouting actually, so it wasn't a surprise his voice would show the strain.

She let her eyes go unfocused. *Who is he to yell at me?* she thought resentfully. *He can't tell me what to do.*

His camel crowded up against hers and his fingers wrapped around her wrist. Paza squeaked and grabbed Tal's tunic. Behind her, Nes tensed, and Malenie wished Sarl had seen Nes kick that bandit in the face so he'd know he shouldn't mess with them.

But he merely said quietly, "I thought to wait until you trusted me enough to talk about what you obviously wanted to keep secret. But that is a very dangerous way to travel; a very dangerous magic. Too many things can go wrong."

She remembered the man in the blue robe saying the same thing and met Sarl's gaze. A muscle ticced near his eye, and Malenie wondered how she had thought him serene when they met. He looked haggard, as if he were aging in front of her. He said, "If you don't know where you are going as well as you think you do, and most people don't, you may never arrive. Or your strength may give out and you'll never arrive. Anything could happen and you'd never arrive, and we'd never know why." He paused and his eyes crumpled at the corners. "My cousin was lost that way, we believe.

"Promise me, all of you," he pinned them each with his gaze, "you will never do that again, never. Unless it is the only way to survive."

"I promise," Malenie swore and Nes copied her. His fingers finally loosened on her wrist but she didn't rub it, not wanting to show it hurt.

Paza said, "I promise, sir."

"Paza, you don't need to call me sir." She jerked a nod, and Sarl finally nudged his camel away. Malenie slumped as his attention left her.

Nes whispered in Malenie's ear, "Notice he told her that after he got her promise." Malenie snorted. She didn't hear any accusation in Nes's voice, just acceptance of using whatever advantage he had.

He turned back. "At least I know the price of your seeing: instructing you in magic to keep you from hurting yourselves or others."

"How is that a price?" Nes asked. "It seems like you're paying it, not us."

"That's one way of looking at it. The other way is that you'll be spending a lot of time with me until your instruction is done. All three of you."

"If we're talking about magic now, I want to know what the rules are," Nes said.

"There are really only two rules. Pattern magic only works here, on this side of the Wall, and you can't use more energy than you have. That's it."

"But shouldn't there be more? What you said, and that it only works on things that are alive, that the shaper's sense works on my side of the

Wall and it only works on things that aren't alive?"

"The shaper's sense and its effects do exist here, or the Wall would not stand and possibly several other things I'm not aware of. But it's not a living magic here. It is static, and not even the smallest magics a shaper could work can be done.

"But it's human to feel that's too broad, too limitless, so we make up rules to guide us and we say, it takes two people—except when the magic bearer has gone mad. Or we say, it will only work on live things, except it will work on things that were once alive, but aren't any longer. Like bone or hair or blood or plant fibers. But shapers, on your side of the Wall, will tell you that they can only work with things that are not alive, like rock and metal, but they also work with cloth and bone, saying they are not alive."

"That doesn't make sense."

"It's magic, not mathematics." Nes looked at him with the same incomprehension Malenie felt. Sarl sighed. "Think of it like healing. The basic structure is there but each body is different in its influences and experiences. Look. You," he pointed with his chin to Malenie, "may get heart palpitations if you use numb-root too many days in a row, while you," he indicated Nes, "might have no other effects, aside from the desired one of numbness, and you," this time Paza, "might need twice the usual dose to get any effect at all. Do you understand? Magic is the same."

"But—"

"Rules are an imperfect way to explain the world.

"But—"

"Ask me your questions later. We must go. Tal, you lead. Across country."

"Ha," called Tal, spurring the camels into their usual shambling walk. "Ha." From a walk to a jog. "Ha!" Malenie grabbed Nes's leg as the camels lurched into an unnaturally fast run.

The ground sped by in a blur that made Malenie feel sick. She raised her eyes. It was no better looking at the sides of the trail—every time her eyes focused on a tree or boulder, it seemed to slide back and disappear behind them. She gulped and raised her eyes to the horizon. That at least stayed in place, although it bucked with the camel's gait.

"I didn't know camels could go so fast," Paza shouted.

"They can't," Nes shouted back.

"Ha!" Tal shouted. Impossibly, the camels' speed increased. The wind stung Malenie's eyes to tears.

"This is his magic. 'Speed to match a swift flying bird.' Look!" Nes wasn't reckless enough to let go to point, but it was easy to spot what had caught her attention: little brown birds startled out of hiding and taking flight. They darted in all directions alongside the trail.

And were outdistanced, left behind.

22

Malenie fought free from a nightmare of being dragged across a battlefield by her feet. The dream had been a confused brown muddle of places and people that changed from breath to breath. Her eyes snapped open and were dazzled by the moon. Everything was gray in its light. But she was still being dragged by her foot.

Another jerk of the rope—yes, rope, she remembered now, one end tied around her ankle and the other around Nes's—towed her forward about half a step. It hurt. Malenie gritted her teeth, sat up and twisted the rope around both hands. Nes was halfway across the campsite, heading south with the determination of the sleepwalker.

"We should have tied it around both her ankles," Malenie said, not caring if she woke anyone else. She heaved on the rope. Nes staggered, still straining forward. *No marching off into the night for you.* Tonight she was tethered and the hobble was going to fight back. As Nes lifted her foot, Malenie yanked the rope and jerked Nes off balance. Malenie pulled herself hand over hand along its length, not letting it go slack. *Good thing Nes isn't as smart asleep as she is awake.* Malenie had to win this tug of war. Just one more step, one more, one more.

"Nes!" Malenie shouted. *Is everyone sleeping?* "Wake up!" *All of you.* It wasn't a long rope, but Nes had hauled them almost to the edge of camp, and Malenie's arms were shaking by the time she reached her. *Now what?* Malenie wound the extra rope around her arm and tried to pull Nes around to face her, but the older girl outweighed her by a good measure and didn't budge. "Will someone help me!"

Without waiting for an answer, Malenie darted around Nes and braced her arms against Nes's shoulders. Her eyes were open wide, staring straight through Malenie. Nes bulled forward another few steps. Malenie leaned all her weight against Nes, until she was almost parallel to the ground, and dug her bare feet into the cold dirt. *This was a mistake*, she thought and then lost her balance as Tal appeared behind Nes and wrapped her arms across Nes's chest. Malenie snatched her hands out of the way and dropped to her knees. "What took you so long?" she said without any real heat.

Nes jerked in Tal's arms, still trying to walk. Her fists were clenched. Jos dropped a blanket over Malenie's shoulders. Sarl stood close by, rubbing his chin, and Paza was a lump wrapped in blankets. Moonlight glinted off her eyes, proving she was watching.

"Actually seeing the phenomenon does not provide me with much more information than your description, Jos," Sarl said. "I don't believe it is dangerous, to her or to us. If I weren't so exhausted, I would attempt to see further."

"But what are we going to do about this—her?" Tal asked. She at least sounded worried for Nes, not like she was some kind of interesting puzzle.

"I don't know."

"Throw water on her?" Jos suggested.

"Argh." Malenie dropped the blanket and stalked forward. She yanked on Nes's hand, expecting resistance, and almost fell over when it came up easily. Muttering an apology, Malenie jammed her fingers under Nes's and pried them open. A dusty pale rock sat on the center of her palm. Malenie tipped Nes's hand and the rock fell with a dull clunk to the ground. There was no change to Nes's face, though. Malenie worked quickly at the other hand. Another pale rock. She dumped it and looked up into Nes's face, still holding onto her.

Nes blinked. She closed her eyes and didn't move. By the time Nes's eyelids fluttered open again Malenie realized holding her breath wasn't helping.

"What?" Nes croaked and touched Tal's arms banding her chest. "Was I...?"

"Sleepwalking," Malenie confirmed.

Tal loosened her grip and tried to hand Nes a waterskin, which she ignored. "So the rope worked?"

"Yeah, but I'm not going to be your hitching post again. Someone else—someone heavier—can tomorrow, or better yet, a tree."

"But Malenie, how did you know?" Sarl asked.

"Just a guess." She shrugged and winced at the pain in her back. More bruises and scrapes. She was not going to tell them what she suspected about those stones and why Nes kept trying to, to, commune or whatever with them. If Nes wanted everyone to know she was a shaper, she would tell them herself. She had always been very private. "I could tell she had something in her hands, and getting her away from the quarry stone worked before."

"What?" Nes sounded crabby. Malenie pointed with her chin to their feet. The pale rocks were obvious against the dark ground. "Ancestors," Nes said under her breath and rubbed her forehead.

Sarl said, "Well…"

"We should all go to sleep," Tal said briskly. Malenie stared at her grubby toes, waiting for them to leave.

"Yes, of course. Malenie, you should heal yourself."

Her head snapped up. "No!"

"I can't do it and still have enough magic left to use on the camels tomorrow. You can't be in good shape after being dragged around like that."

"No, I'm not—not going to."

Nes looked at the furrow ending at her feet. "I'll help you. It's because of me."

"No." Malenie avoided looking at anyone, but she saw Tal touch Sarl's arm and mutter something before they went back to their blankets. Jos strode without a word into the brush around the camp.

"Are you going to leave them there?" Malenie asked once they were alone.

"Nnno."

"I didn't think so." She scooped up the rocks and offered them to Nes, who took them hesitantly. When she didn't snap into another trance, her shoulders relaxed.

"My whole pouch is full of them," Nes confided. "But I don't remember putting them there."

"Not surprising. You were probably asleep at the time," Malenie said, deliberately offhand about it. "They remind me of the Wall."

"Me, too."

They stared at the rocks for a long moment. "I don't want to get rid of them," Nes said.

Malenie shrugged. "I didn't think you would." She wiggled her toes and finally looked up. Nes looked as unhappy as she'd expected. "Tell you what, though. I'm not letting you sleep with them anymore. How about you give them to me at night?"

"Yeah, that's a good idea." She dropped the two rocks into her belt pouch, tied it closed and handed it to Malenie. "Do you think there's something wrong with me?" Her tone demanded honesty. Not that Malenie would give her best friend anything but.

"Not any more than the rest of us," Malenie said glumly.

Nes's face brightened. "Hey, if we're abnormal in an abnormal world, that makes us normal, doesn't it?"

"I hadn't thought of it like that before." The thought was kind of cheering. "I'm glad you're here," Malenie said. Nes grinned at her and tried to sling her arm across Malenie's shoulders, and Malenie added, "Just don't touch me and all my bruises."

◇◇◇

The saddles needed to be adjusted in the morning. The poor camels' humps were noticeably smaller and floppier, and the camels were more bad-tempered than usual, making it harder to get them ready. Malenie was so stiff and sore she wanted to bite someone, too.

Before mid-day they found Tal's road, and they rode long after dark. As Malenie fell into her blankets, she thought, *At least we made it through the day without any surprises.*

It wasn't enough sleep. In the morning—and she knew it was morning only because Tal told her so when she woke her in the dark—Malenie stared blankly at her bent knees, unable to move. *Seven hundred gods and goddesses, don't make me do this again.*

"Here." Tal pressed a packet of trail rations into her hand. The real food had run out the day before. Trail rations weren't so bad: a mix of dried dates, almonds, honey, salt and something that kept it all stuck together, but they had already eaten it three times in a row and would probably eat it at least that many more times again before they reached

Suntin.

"Come on." A hand appeared before her nose, and Tal hauled Malenie to her feet. "I'll get it." With quick efficiency Tal bundled Malenie's blankets into a tight roll. "I can see how stiff you are."

"I don't want to—to—to—" Malenie stuttered to a halt, unwilling to say 'magic' or 'heal myself' for reasons she couldn't explain even to herself. Too much had happened, too fast. She wanted to pretend she hadn't—well, no, she couldn't wish she hadn't helped Nes or Jos—but she didn't have to do anything just because they wanted her to…or just because she could.

"I didn't say you should," Tal pointed out mildly and handed her the bundle. "But I've been with Sarl for six years, and if you want to talk about it…"

"Sorry. No," Malenie muttered. She clutched the blankets and stood there feeling stupid and rude.

Tal sighed. She sounded tired, too. Perversely, that made Malenie feel a little better. "Just remember that it's easy to see everything in the worst possible light when you're exhausted. Come on, Sarl's just about finished with the camels. Paza," she called after the younger girl, who was trudging into the shoulder-high bushes, "don't go too far, even if you need some privacy."

Trailing after her, Malenie turned Tal's words over in her head. *Will I feel differently after I've slept in a real bed?* She both dreaded and wanted to reach Suntin. It meant a confrontation with *him*, but it also meant an end to the rotten running. *And hopefully I will be closer to rescuing Papa, somehow. That's the point of all this.*

Ahead, Sarl levered himself to his feet by hanging onto the saddle. Jos impatiently knocked the camel's head away when it snaked around to look.

"Malenie!" Paza shrieked behind her.

"Bandits," Tal shouted.

Malenie spun around, her heart thundering at the terror in Paza's voice. At the far edge of the clearing a strange man tucked Paza under his arm and took off awkwardly, trying to ignore her writhing, kicking and biting. "Paza!" Malenie ran. He was already among the scrubby trees and would disappear from sight in a moment.

Nes jumped out of the bushes and launched herself at his back, grappling for a choke hold. With a twist he threw her off and kept going. Paza didn't make it easy for him. She thrashed and squirmed, and he lurched from side to side.

"Someone help!" Malenie cried. *Where is everyone?*

Nes picked herself up and threw herself at him again. She caught his elbow and dug her fingers into the pressure point there. His arm jerked like a spring and Paza fell heavily to the ground. For three breaths, four, she lay stunned, and then she half crawled, half ran out from under Nes's and the stranger's feet as they circled each other. One of his arms hung down, useless, but with his other hand he drew a long, wicked-looking dagger. He twisted it, showing her the edge and the flat, and it winked in the moonlight. It intimidated Malenie, but Nes's face was blank. She crouched, waiting.

"You motherless mongrel," he taunted her. "You're going to die and I'm going to take your friend." He stepped in, knife swinging wide, almost careless in his assurance that he could kill her easily. Nes stepped in to meet him. Her right hand helped the knife move past her and to the side. A step in on her left foot, angling her body. He stepped back, not quickly enough. Nes's left hand, flat and stiff, crushed his throat. He crumpled. Tried to breathe. Died.

Nes met Malenie's eyes across his body. Her lips moved and her face wasn't blank anymore.

"No!" Paza's shout was a mixture of rage and fear. Another stranger menaced her, arms spread wide to catch her as she darted to one side. He caught her tunic and it ripped apart as she spun away. He threw it down with an oath and captured one of her arms, his hand easily spanning its thinness. With her free hand Paza grabbed his pinkie finger and forced it back, but he trapped that arm, too. Paza shrieked and battered his shins with her bare feet.

Rage surged up inside Malenie. She jumped over the corpse, almost not noticing his hand under her foot, and gripped Nes's forearm. "Make him burn," she ordered hoarsely.

Nes's eyes widened, but she whispered, "I wish his hands and clothes would burn."

He released Paza as if she were the one on fire and stared at his hands. His shrill shriek, worse than any of Paza's, satisfied Malenie. And then the magic and the agony boomeranged back into her and she doubled up over her hands, unable to even scream at the pain. Blackness crept over her vision, closing in on all sides, and she fell to her knees.

Suddenly the pain was gone. Its absence was the most rapturous feeling she'd ever had. Her vision snapped back and she looked at her hands. They were whole, with no sign of the agony she had inflicted on herself. She sniffed and gagged. The air smelled of burning meat and linen. The rapture faded and she realized what she had done, what she had wanted to do.

Nes knelt beside her. "I'm sorry, I shouldn't have done what you said. I didn't think it would work, like with the other bandits."

"You—" Malenie coughed, said more clearly, "you didn't kill us and you stopped him. That's good enough. Where…?"

"Paza hit him in the head with a rock while he was screaming."

"Um, good?"

"Not really."

Malenie looked beyond the comfort of Nes's face and noticed that they were crouching next to the man Nes had killed. Ugh. Then she saw the reason none of the adults had come to help: they were fighting for their lives. Sarl and Jos each faced one attacker, while Tal faced two. More bodies on the ground showed that they'd been fighting and winning for a while.

"If magic worked on one of them, maybe it will work on all of them? Make them go to sleep," Malenie said.

Paza had crept up to them and now she asked hesitantly, "Can I do it?"

"Yes." Just in time Malenie bit back 'of course,' realizing this was important to Paza. "That would be good," she said instead and braced herself against the expected pain. There wasn't any, just the mild tingle of the magic under her skin and the familiar feel of Paza in the magic. It wasn't even enough to make her bones thrum. Malenie relaxed a little and sat down cross-legged as one by one the attackers passed out. It got very quiet. And then she just sat there while a whole bunch of mixed emotions roared through her: anger, shock, shame, relief.

Tal limped up. She checked the bandit Paza had knocked out and tied him up with his own belt and strips of his tunic. Then she settled on her heels next to them. A quick glance at the corpse told her she didn't have to tie him up.

"A bit grim, isn't it, including him in your conference?" She tilted her head at the dead man.

"I wasn't sure I could move," Malenie confessed. Her voice sounded startlingly normal.

"Did you…?"

"I did." Nes's voice did not sound normal. It was too high, too stressed.

"And how are you doing?" Tal asked calmly.

"I didn't feel anything when I did it." She swallowed heavily. "It was just like training, so easy." Her voice pitched higher and higher. Abruptly she turned away and vomited. Malenie bit her knuckles to keep from joining her. When Nes's heaves subsided, Tal handed her a scrap of fabric to wipe away the snot, tears and puke from her face. "Now, I don't feel too good," Nes said with a half laugh.

"Your first, right?" At Nes's nod Tal continued, "For people like us, who respect life, it's never easy, not your first and not any of the ones after. You do what you're trained to do and what you have to." She paused. "I bury them proper when I can. And I offer prayers for them. But those are just patches we put over it. It's a part of you now, like the shape of your nose."

Nes nodded, less shakily. Paza touched the back of her hand, just two fingers, as quick as a bird alighting and departing, but it surprised a lopsided smile out of Nes.

Malenie stared at her hands. They didn't look any different, they held no trace of what she'd done, what she'd felt… "Tal."

"Hmm?"

"It…" If they could talk about killing, she could talk about this. "I wanted to hurt him—it made me happy or satisfied or something to hurt him."

Tal was quiet and Malenie's heart twisted up inside her. She wished she could take the words back. She was a monster, and Nes was wrong about abnormal being normal in an abnormal world. She was so far inside her own thoughts, Tal's voice shocked her when she spoke. "You've been in fights before, right?"

"Not like—yeah."

"And did you ever hurt someone like that before or feel like that?"

"Yes." Her voice came out as small as she felt.

"He deserved it!" Nes said. "You don't know, Tal, how they followed her and taunted her and beat her up! She was just doing what I taught her."

"Alright. Did you do it again, on purpose, when you had a chance? Did you hurt someone more than you needed to to get away?"

Malenie remembered the Parthavian girl in Deek's gang and how she'd had the chance to crush her nose but didn't. "I guess not."

"And this time they were hurting your friend, who you know has been hurt before, very badly, and you wanted to protect her, right?"

Malenie couldn't look at Paza, sitting there as still as a rock. "Yeah." *We really should have moved*, she thought, staring at the dead man's hand instead.

"How long had it been since Nes taught you how to protect yourself that you hurt this person who'd been hurting you?"

"Not long."

"And how long have you known you had pattern magic?"

"The same, not long."

"Here's what I think." Malenie jerked her eyes back to Tal's face. "Knowing how to fight or having magic is a big responsibility. You can do things other people can't, in both cases. Fighters spend a lot of time learning how to kill people, but we also spend time learning how not to kill people, like if a kid jumps out at me on a street or my granny surprises me in the dark. You haven't had that training, not for fighting or magic."

Malenie nodded reluctantly, not feeling much better.

"I'm not done. I think you don't really like fighting. You were terrified for your friend and you have a gift you haven't explored very much or learned how to control. You've also spent a lot of time with your da, who's a healer. I think you needed to feel those emotions to be able to hurt him. Burning him was maybe not the wisest, but that's what training and experience are for. You accomplished what you set out to do."

Malenie bit her lip. That might all be true but she had also wanted to compete. Nes had killed, Malenie wanted to do something worse. To prove she was just as tough as Nes, to prove to Paza she cared as much, to make Nes feel better… She didn't really know and she wasn't going to try explaining that.

"Trust that you're the same person now with your gift as before you knew you had it. It's just a tool that you need to learn how to use. Like how to fight. We all feel and think ugly things. It's what you do with them that matters." Tal pushed herself to her feet and stood looking down at them. "Ask Sarl. He's a lot like you, aside from the obvious reasons." She left, dragging the corpse away by its heels.

Paza coughed. Was she getting sick? It was cold and she was half naked under a ripped blanket. Glad to have something to do, Malenie popped up, bundled the rest of their blankets together and gave them to Paza.

"Thank you," Paza said in a thin voice. Sitting up very straight, she wrapped one around her shoulders and handed the rest to Nes and Malenie. "You rescued me, both of you." She looked at Nes directly for the first time in days. "Even after I was horrible to you and jealous."

Astounded, Malenie blurted out, "You sound like you think we didn't care because of it—you do think that! You're still my friend! I wouldn't let, let kidnappers carry you away." Nes nodded vehemently.

"I forgot what friends are like," Paza admitted.

Again Malenie felt a fierce urge to protect her. She was so little, all skinny arms and legs, like a much younger girl, but old in how much she'd been through. *That's what I was feeling when I told Nes to burn the bandit. So maybe that was alright.*

"That's what friends do," Nes said gravely.

Paza stared at her and then darted away, leaving the blanket in a crumpled heap.

"What did I say?"

Before Malenie could guess, Paza returned with one of their carrysacks. She turned it upside down and shook it. Malenie choked on hysterical laughter, even though it wasn't funny at all. The camp couldn't get much more disordered; bags, blankets and the ashes from their fire were all mixed together and trampled. Out dropped a bag of salt tied up tight, an extra set of clothes, the gold bracelet Paza had stolen, a coil of rope, packets of dried goat meat and the extra sling Harris had given them in the night market. Before they had a third friend to give it to. Malenie sobered instantly and nodded when Paza looked questioningly at her.

"You should have this." Paza plopped the tangle of leather and hemp in front of Nes, who carefully teased the cords straight and test-ed them.

"It matches yours."

"Yeah. I think you were meant to have it. Friends?" Paza asked hesitantly as if she still wasn't sure or the word felt strange in her mouth.

"Friends," Nes said immediately. She spit in her palm and looked a question at the others.

"For water," Paza said.

"For life," Malenie said.

They spit, too, and the three of them shook on it. Malenie felt shaky, but this was a good shakiness. She had friends again, friends who cared about each other, who accepted each other. They weren't alone in the world.

For a while after, they watched the adults reorganize their belongings. Malenie's eyelids were beginning to droop and the sun shone redly through them, enough to hold at bay memories of the kidnapper's face, surprised in agony, the terror on Paza's face and the crunch of the bandit's throat when Nes killed him. She was dozing off when Nes asked tentatively, "Do you—can we look for my sibs?"

"No!" Everyone jumped. Jos's hand flew to his sword and Tal pulled an arrow from her quiver and set it to her bow. Malenie waved reassuringly. "Sorry, it's nothing." The adults relaxed from ready for action to merely extremely alert. "I mean, I just don't—I'm too tired right now."

"You'd see your pa."

"No." Malenie crossed her arms tightly.

Nes really looked at her. "You're not scared, are you? Tal's right, it's just a tool."

"I can't right now. And I don't want to talk about it."

Nes would have said more but Sarl interrupted. "Colvin is using magic to find us and send men after us. I want to hide you from him with my magic, if you will let me."

"But we already did that," Paza said. "I said 'I wish for me and Malenie to be invisible to anyone looking for us with magic.'"

Sarl rubbed his chin. "That's almost exactly what I would have said. But if it worked, how is he finding you? Paza, do you remember anything, anything you saw, anything he said that might explain it?"

Paza folded and unfolded the hem of her replacement tunic while she thought. Finally she shook her head.

Sarl sighed. "It was worth a try. I can't see him, either. I need to hide the rest of us anyway. I'd like to include you, too. It's the only thing I can think of to do." He ran his hands over his hair, caught the cut on the crown of his head and winced. When they nodded he said, "After we eat. Jos decided we needed more than trail rations and trapped some rock lizards. He's cooking them now."

Malenie sniffed. As if on cue, she smelled meat roasting and her stomach growled.

"We're staying on the road. Suntin is close enough that we should be safer on the road than off it. We should be there by mid-day."

23

They had to abandon the road after all when they could no longer make headway against the refugees from Suntin. At first, there were only a few families in wagons with their belongings and children piled in and orange ribbons tied around every arm. As they passed, the refugees shouted warnings, but wouldn't stop to talk. Jos pulled his camel around and rode south with them, and when he returned his face was grim.

"A woman told me another girl has been stolen from the Suntin Family and is being held hostage. Someone sent the Suntins a lock of her hair and said body parts would be next if he doesn't get what he wants."

Paza gasped and smoothed her hand over her head, again and again. Gently, Malenie pulled her hand down. Paza's fingers were cold. She was surprised when Paza let her hold them.

Sarl slumped in the saddle and rubbed at his chest. "Colvin."

Jos nodded. "It has to be. And that's not all. The woman was at the Suntin's house when the news came and decided right then she was getting her family out. By the time she did, parts of the city near the Wall were burning. The others I spoke to didn't know as much, but they told me it was poor Ananaletta back from the dead to finish what she started."

"The Suntin girl is dead," Sarl muttered. Paza stiffened and squeezed the bones in Malenie's hand together.

They passed a family on a camel. The two girls, an older boy and their mother were crowded in the saddle while the father held the lead rein. Malenie turned to watch them and met the scared eyes of the youngest girl, who stared after them until they were out of sight. The trickle of refugees became a stream, and then a flood of people on foot with thin bags and their children on their bowed backs. Malenie's group moved more and more slowly.

It was strangely quiet until a Parthavian man shouted, "The city's no place for those girls!" It sounded like a warning, but the shouts that followed turned angry.

"What are you doing with those girls?"

"Are they even yours?"

"You don't have to go with them! Come with us."

Sarl turned them off the road then, and Malenie called over her shoulder, "It's alright. We're fine." A couple more people shouted and a dog ran after them barking, but no one followed.

◇◇◇

Malenie saw the dark tree of smoke before she saw the city. Nes choked and pressed herself more tightly against Malenie's back. "It smells like Trader Town did." Paza hunched her shoulders up and wrapped her arms around herself. She didn't respond to anything Malenie said. *She shouldn't be here. But she doesn't have anyone else.*

They entered Suntin the same way Malenie and Paza had entered Pashtin: on a side street that started out as a bare patch beyond the last buildings. By the time they got up between them, the dirt was packed hard into a proper street. The city passed by in blurred glimpses of painted houses and hurrying people with orange ribbons on their arms, fountains and stone. Smoke burned Malenie's throat and stung her nose and tinged everything gray.

They entered an area with large houses behind walls and stopped in front of big iron gates that reminded Malenie of the Pashtin gates. She wondered where Papa was and if Liac were any closer to rescuing him. *I've been too exhausted to look for him with magic,* she told herself. It was mostly true. *As soon as we're inside, I'll ask Paza or Nes to help me look for him.*

On top of the red and cream-colored wall a guard trained a loaded crossbow on them. Paza whined deep in her throat like a sick dog.

"He's not going to hurt us," Malenie tried to reassure her. Paza didn't respond.

"Sarl, from the Sarnath Family, also known as the wise man of Sarnath, kin by marriage to the Suntin Family," Tal announced and Sarl spread his arms to show off the green designs on them.

"Your pardon," the guard said, lowering the crossbow. "But because of recent…events, I must send for a family member who can identify you."

"We understand," Sarl answered. "We will wait." He looked over his shoulder. His eyes seemed to linger on Paza and then he jerked his head at Tal, asking her to guard their backs against anything coming up the street.

It wasn't long before someone new peered over the wall. A moment later the gates swung open and then closed noiselessly behind them. Malenie had expected them to clang shut like the jaws of a trap. Paza's nerves were contagious. As they rode through, the adults bunched together ahead of them, blocking Malenie's view of the house and grounds. Paza dismounted, keeping the camel between her and everyone else. Malenie followed gratefully. Her legs refused to hold her up and she bumped into the camel. The poor thing was so exhausted she barely noticed. Paza darted looks in every direction. Her teeth were chattering.

Nes dismounted and watched her warily. "Are you sick?"

Paza shook her head.

"We've come to help," Sarl said, out of sight. "As soon as I learned something was wrong and who was behind it." No hint of his personal pain touched his words; he was once again the serene and knowledgeable wise man of Sarnath.

"Sarl, you are welcome," a woman's voice answered and Paza's knees buckled. Malenie and Nes caught her, all her weight suspended from their arms.

"Do you want to leave? It's something about here, isn't it?" Malenie asked in belated understanding. A pit opened up in her stomach. This was bad. Paza shook her head no. "No, you don't want to leave or—"

The woman was speaking again. "Please come into the house. You look like you need some rest."

"Jessanna," Sarl said softly, "I can't come into your house without letting you know who is with me."

"Don't be so formal." A boy led the camels away and Malenie finally saw the woman who had greeted Sarl. She was about Papa's age and familiar looking. Her hair was pulled back simply, and her eyes were red and hollowed. Paza jerked in Malenie's arms like the start of convulsions.

"Sarl, she's…" the woman said. Her eyes widened and she stumbled forward. The guard barked a question, raised his crossbow and wavered, uncertain where the threat came from.

Malenie looked between Paza and the woman and sick certainty welled up in her throat. The family resemblance was obvious. Lies. So many lies. She couldn't move, not even to free her hands from the girl she had thought was her friend.

Jessanna croaked, "Paza. What has he done to you?" She wrapped Paza in her arms, trapping Malenie and Nes in place. Tears burned behind Malenie's eyes in unwanted sympathy.

Paza stood stiff and unyielding and then it was as if the earth heaved and everything came down in a different place and she wrapped her arms around the woman and sobbed.

Relief, desperate worry and love cracked Jessanna's voice as she spoke. "My daughter, you're safe, you're alive. Thank the seven hundred gods and goddesses."

The word slid into place with a click in Malenie's head and she broke out of the embrace. Nes turned away. *Do I look as envious as she does?* Sarl watched with a slightly smug look, as if he had correctly guessed the answer to a difficult puzzle. Of course, Paza was a daughter of Suntin. It all made sense: her knowledge about magic, the Suntin girl and the disaster, the reason *he* had taken her… and Paza had lied about it the whole time.

Guards ran into the garden, trampling the flowers and vaulting over scattered boulders, and were waved back by an older woman with dark hair streaked with gray. The woman nudged Jessanna's shoulder and managed to herd everyone into the house.

It was cool inside and dim, and more austere than the Pashtin's house, but still unmistakably wealthy. Malenie scuffed her feet on the tiles, so completely unlike the feel of packed earth underfoot. *I've been pitying her all this time, and she grew up with this. What did I have?* As soon as she thought it, she hated herself for it.

She was glad when they stepped into a big room, glad to drop into a comfortable chair and eat the food they gave her, glad to concentrate on Sarl's explanation. She was less glad to see Paza's family seek her out and hug her and kiss her and worse, touch her covered head, never noticing that she sank lower and lower in her chair to avoid them. *I should tell them to stop. But what right do I have? She's not my friend, she was just using me. She didn't tell me anything. She never trusted me. I told her everything and she lied to me, over and over.* Malenie knew she was being unfair, but she couldn't stop the ugly thoughts.

The older woman paced as she listened to Sarl. When she came near, Tal whispered, "Lissetta" and something more in her ear. Lissetta's eyes jerked to Paza. "Everybody, sit down please," Lissetta said. "Let your daughter eat, Jessanna." Malenie's stomach curdled with guilt that she hadn't been the one to speak up.

Lissetta didn't wait for everyone to settle before turning back to Sarl. "I don't see how what you've told me fits with what's been happening here. Colvin arrived in Suntin two days ago and came to the Council building before the day's meetings started. He found Anandan, Paza's father, and told him to move everyone in the city into the hideaways—you know about those? He said he was going to heal the world, repair the crack and bring back the old magic. 'The way magic was meant to be,' he said. And that it was going to be dangerous and he didn't want us harmed. Those same old legends the past generation of matriarchs believed." Her mouth twisted as she met Sarl's eyes. "Anandan pretended he was listening and waited for help to arrive. He didn't know Colvin's hire swords were keeping everyone out, and Colvin was able to walk away. Yesterday, he destroyed the Council building with some kind of flammable oil that explodes and burns everything it touches, even adobe and stone. Everything except the Wall."

Paza, huddled in her chair, asked, "And Papa?"

"He's fine. He's out in the city now and will be home soon. I sent him a message that you're here."

"That explosion sounds just like what happened in Trader Town," Nes murmured so only Malenie could hear.

"The building was empty, but people on the street and in near-by buildings were hurt," Lissetta said. "People started fleeing the city, and we encouraged them. Whatever he said about not wanting to hurt people, his past actions have shown that he is callous in the extreme. We—the Family, I mean—were arguing whether we should send the children to one of the hideaways or out of the city when a package arrived." She hesitated and suddenly none of the Suntins were looking at Paza.

Malenie locked her hands around each other so she would not touch her sleeves, Mama's necklace or her hair, but the words burst out of her anyway. "Just say it. She's—we're—going to imagine something really bad anyway."

Lissetta rubbed the center of her forehead and after a moment nodded. "It was a finger. He said it was Paza's and he would kill her if we didn't order everyone into the hideaways. And if we didn't surrender the Gate in the Wall to him."

"But it's not hers," Sarl said. Paza spread her fingers without looking up.

"It's someone's," Nes muttered, not very quietly.

"I've made a terrible mistake," Sarl said. He crouched in front of Paza. "I should never have brought you here. I thought you would be safest with your family. But he must need you somehow for his plans and I brought you right to him."

Paza's chin went up like she'd been hit in the face. "You didn't. I decided. We all did. And there's something else you should know." She looked right at Malenie. "I knew all along that he was working with someone on the other side of the Wall, I just didn't know…until later that it was the man who had chased you and taken your father."

Malenie couldn't even be grateful Paza avoided mentioning Malenie's magic because her stomach felt like it was trying to fold in on itself. She started to shake her head.

"He used kids as messengers to the other side of the Wall," Paza said.

Malenie shook her head harder and the trembling spread to her whole body. "No."

"But not me," Paza insisted. "It wasn't never me, and I didn't know about you. I didn't figure it out right away."

"Why should I believe you? He took my father. He still has him. You lied to me, lied and lied and lied." Malenie's voice rose in a shriek. It felt good to get it out and make Paza feel as bad as she did—*wait, that's not right*—but the words kept coming out of her mouth. "I don't believe you and I don't want to talk to you—you're a liar and a thief." Paza's face stiffened but her chin wobbled. *No, I didn't—*

The Suntins closed in around Paza, shielding her from Malenie. Their glares made the huge lump in Malenie's stomach grow even bigger, as if all her meanness and pain were mixing up with guilt and too much food. Lissetta rubbed her forehead again. Not even Tal would meet her eyes.

Nes did though. "That was bad, Malenie," she said, "about as bad as anything I've done. You'd—"

"Rot it." Malenie bolted out of the room, wishing she could leave herself behind.

◊◊◊

Malenie pressed her hot cheek to the cool tile wall and sniffled. She had cried a burst of tears in this lonely corner of the big house, but had quickly gotten impatient with herself. Plus a sense of fairness had gained on the feelings of anger and betrayal. There were a lot of things Paza didn't lie about. She pushed herself up and rubbed the wetness from her face. *I shouldn't have acted like that. And they're probably deciding things, important things I'll want to know about.* Unfortunately she had no idea how to get back to the big room.

Most of the doorways were draped with simple curtains, but at the end of the hallway there was a wooden door that looked like it led outside. Reasoning that it would be easier to go around the outside of the house and back in the front door, Malenie decided to try it. It opened on a small, secluded garden with pretty little stone paths that led to a fountain half hidden by vines and trellised trees. Malenie plopped down on the rim and splashed water on her face, trying to think about Paza and what it meant that she was a Suntin.

The Suntin girl Paza had told her about and the sister he killed were the same person. Paza had watched her be tortured, go insane, kill part of a city and die. The blue diamonds seemed to burn on Malenie's skin. *And that's how Paza knew exactly how to help me. Even after he threatened Paza's family if she ever disobeyed him. Even though he might have rewarded Paza for bringing him another girl with magic. And—wait, what if some of those messages were about me? What if Harashan was after me for Colvin?* It made sense. *It's even the same strategy: threaten Paza's family or Papa, so we'd cooperate. And not tell anyone anything. Would I have asked for help, if it were Papa who was threatened? Probably not.*

Of course Paza never told Malenie her secrets. At first she couldn't have trusted anyone that much and later there was no time. *And the longer you keep a secret the harder it is to tell. I know that if anyone does.* Malenie heaved a deep sigh. *I'm an idiot. I have to—*

"What a sad sound for such a young child," a voice observed. Malenie's head snapped up. She had missed the two slight forms seated in the deepest shade of the tallest tree. His henchmen, here? But the voice didn't sound threatening. It sounded old, and curious.

"Oh dear, she thought she was alone," said a second voice. Malenie sidled along the fountain so the sun wasn't in her eyes. Two ancients sat on a cushioned bench, a man and a woman, so old the blue swirls around their exposed wrists almost disappeared into wrinkles. "Everyone forgets about us," confided the man. "One night they forgot to bring us in. We waited and waited until we waited too long and the cold was in our joints with the pain and the creakiness and we couldn't get up. I thought we might die of the cold."

"I didn't!" said the woman. "We piled the cushions around us. If it hadn't been quite so cold, it would have been lovely. No one takes us out to see the stars anymore."

"Who are you?" Malenie moved closer. The blurred marks were mirror images of each other. Two sets of curious eyes stared at her from faces so alike that if the man hadn't worn a turban, Malenie wouldn't have been able to tell them apart.

"Lara and Thëo," said the woman.

"Thëollon and Larella," said the man at the same time, peering at her. "Who are you?"

"Malenie."

"Are you a Suntin?" Lara examined her from head to toe. "A great-niece or fourth cousin twice removed that I can't remember? I didn't think we were getting senile," she said to Thëollon.

"N-no, just Malenie. I'm not a Suntin."

"Ah-ha! I knew it wasn't senility," Lara declared. "You're a guest.

Although you could be a Suntin. Do we know your father or mother, dear?"

"I don't think so. But why are you out here?"

"We're old," Thëollon told her. "And our spouses and children and even some of our grand-children have died—"

"Don't boast, Thëo."

"—so it's just the two of us again. We're twins, you see."

"Um," Malenie said.

"And the young ones don't let us help with the Family magic or the Family business—"

"They think we're too doddery," Thëollon interjected, tapping his temple with a finger.

"—so we sit here in the shade and every once in a while someone has a question to ask us or the children want a story," Lara finished.

"That's um…" It sounded boring to Malenie.

"Frightfully boring," Lara confided and Malenie's ears burnt as if the old lady had read her mind. "We may be old, but we're not dead. So tell us why you're so sad," Lara wheedled.

"Um."

"Don't pressure her, Lara. She doesn't want to tell us," Thëollon said sorrowfully.

"But I do!" And she did. She liked them; they were like no one else she had known before. As curious as magpies. No one else was around and they had to know most of Paza's story already. Maybe they would tell her she wasn't an idiot, and she could put off apologizing in front of everyone just for a little while.

"Goody," crowed Lara. "Take a seat."

Malenie settled at their feet and Thëollon offered her a pillow embroidered in red and gold. They watched her expectantly with bright eyes. Malenie fumbled for the beginning and started with the end instead. "I did something bad."

"Did you break your mother's favorite vase, brought all the way from—"

"Did you put frogs in all the soup bowls when there were important guests to dinner?" asked Thëollon over Lara.

"No. No. I was mean to a friend," Malenie said. "Really mean."

"Is she dead?"

"Did you scratch her eyes out?"

"No! I found out something she hadn't told me, and, instead of thinking about how much it must have been hurting her, I called her a liar."

"That was mean," Thëollon said.

"But not unforgivable," scolded Lara. "Why haven't you apologized? It's not too late if she's not dead and still has her eyes."

"Because I just realized how stupid I was and now I feel… I feel stupid."

"You do use that word a lot," Lara observed tartly.

"But you can't be that stupid, or you wouldn't have figured it out so quickly," Thëollon said. "And a smart girl would go ask her friend's pardon right away. Waiting only makes it harder."

"Yes, and then run back and tell us all about it. And bring her with you. Is she—"

A terrible percussive boom filled the air, vibrating Malenie's chest and toppling one of the urns from its base beside the bench. It cracked from top to bottom. Dirt trickled out, exposing pale roots. Malenie and the twins stared at each other in confusion and then a woman's heartbroken wail ruptured the stunned silence.

"I have to—" Malenie scrambled to her feet, her throat tight.

"Go!" The twins urged in unison.

24

Inside, the chaos centered on a room upstairs. Jessanna held a man with a grim face and tears leaking from the corners of his eyes. Blue ovals were visible on one of his wrists. Children watched from the safety of adults' arms; the youngest hid his face and hiccuped exhausted cries. One girl with her hair chopped raggedly short and an angry tilt to her chin made Malenie's heart jump, but even as she was thinking, *Paza*, she knew it wasn't. Broken glass crunched under her feet as she slipped along the corridor looking for—Nes. She stood with her back to a mosaic of a young woman at a spring. The stone woman's face was serene; Nes's looked stormy and dangerous, like a brooding dust cloud swelling on the horizon.

"It's Paza, isn't it?" Malenie choked out. It had to be. She forced herself to ask the next question. "Is she…" She couldn't say it, but Nes understood.

"Ancestors, no!" Malenie's knees buckled and Nes grabbed her, half hug, half support. "Her pa came in and hugged her and she just disappeared in front of his eyes." She lowered her voice even more and pointed with her chin. "That's him with Paza's ma. He said Colvin must have done something to him when they were alone together talking and when he touched her the trap went off. Her pa don't know how Colvin did it. Sarl and one of the Suntin men—an uncle—are trying to get her back now."

"Oh, Paza," Malenie whispered, the horror of it rolling over her with Nes's matter-of-fact report. Paza was back in that monster's hands. Malenie had promised to keep her safe and she had failed. "Death's ashes, Nes, we used the magic to protect her family but not her! We didn't include her. He'll hurt her. This is all my fault. If I had just told her to include herself—he wouldn't be able to hurt her now. And she thinks I hate her!"

"Shut up!" Nes said, her breath hot on Malenie's cheek. The clean smell of mint and the desert clung to her. "I'm going to slap you if you don't."

"I'd like to see you try!" Malenie flared back.

"It's not your fault," Nes said in a too reasonable tone. "Paza needs you to think. You know her and Colvin better than I do."

"Right. You're right." There was no time to feel ashamed. Several crashes and the crack of breaking furniture sounded inside the room. Jos cursed. Malenie and Nes wormed their way to the door and peered in. Sarl was lying amid the wreckage of what had been a delicate table, Jos crouched over him, preventing him from sitting up. On the floor on the opposite side of the room, a man with hexagon patterns on his wrists held a handkerchief to his head. It was rapidly turning red. A woman knelt at his side.

There was no sign of Paza.

"I almost had her," Sarl said to Jos, dragging him down to the floor. "It was as if something were pulling against us."

In the hallway behind Malenie, Lissetta gently but insistently shooed family members away. "As soon as I know anything, I'll tell you," she repeated again and again.

Malenie grabbed for her courage. "Nes, I'm sorry for the way I was acting," she whispered.

"I know." Nes squeezed her shoulder.

One mistake accounted for.

Jos and Tal levered Sarl to his feet. "We'll get 'er, Malenie," Sarl slurred as they walked him to a chair.

"Is he going to be alright?" Malenie asked Tal.

"We'll take care of him," answered Tal. "Lissetta, do you—"

"I sent for our healers. Are you sure you should move him?"

"'S fine," Sarl said.

"No, it's not," Jos snapped. "The Matriarch is right. Stay still."

Sarl's eyelids drooped and his eyes rolled back until just the whites were showing. Tal hurriedly pressed her fingers to the pulse in his neck.

"He just passed out," she said, her shoulders rising and lowering with her breath of relief.

Across the room, Paza's uncle lifted the blood-soaked handkerchief from his head. "Don't do that, Fidadan, you're still bleeding," the woman with him exclaimed. "Here, use this." She reached for a familiar-looking scrap of fabric on the floor.

"No!" Malenie shouted. She snatched it up and pressed it to her chest with her palm. "I mean, it's Paza's," she choked out. "I'd rather you didn't…it seems like…"

The uncle's face softened in the first sympathetic expression Malenie had seen on a Suntin since she'd yelled at Paza. "Of course I can't use it."

Malenie tucked it into her sleeve as another young woman and a man squeezed into the room, their arms loaded with hot water, astringent smelling soap, cloths and a sewing kit. They looked tired. Had they been healing people injured in the fires? Malenie knew how it felt to heal one person. Healing many people…that would be hard.

"Come on." Nes led Malenie out of the crowded room and into the next empty one.

Malenie wanted to watch them use their magic, but she also wanted to do something.

"Why does he want her, specifically?" Malenie asked, clenching her fists. "If we knew that…"

Nes twisted a lock of her hair, scowling. "But we don't," she said. "And there's no time to figure it out. We could go and look for her."

"We don't know the city. Even if we used, um, magic to track her, if it worked, we'd be face to face with him. That should be our last option. If we can't go to her, we should bring her to us. But Sarl tried and couldn't. What would we do differently? I feel like…" Her pacing brought her past a west-facing window. The sun was gone, a thin line of gold and grey-blue on the horizon the only sign of it. "It's so late," she said, and thought of Thëollon and Larella's story of being left out in the cold. Surely in this confusion no one had remembered. She explained rapidly to Nes. "They'll have forgotten all about them."

"Malenie, focus. Someone else will bring them in."

"No, listen, I am. Sarl said his wife was a Suntin. He lived here." She followed that logic to an unexpected, disturbing conclusion. "Seven hundred gods and goddesses. He's—Colvin is related to Paza," she whispered. Nes scrunched up her face in distaste. "That's—that's—that's—I don't know why it would be better to do the things he's done to a stranger but it's so much worse—he's her cousin or uncle or something!"

"It's disgusting."

Malenie wrenched her mind back to what she had originally planned to say. "Larella and Thëollon. They've been here forever. They're ancient. They probably remember Colvin. Maybe they can help, tell us something useful. Everyone here is doing the obvious thing, but maybe we need to do something different."

When Malenie and Nes reached the garden, the twins were gone, only the bright cushions proof that Malenie hadn't imagined the odd conversation. She bent to pick up the pillow she had sat on, irritably pushing back her hair. Stupid gods and goddesses, to care if she tied back her hair before she was a woman. Hair…Paza's shorn head, the hesitation before she said she'd sold it…

"Hair!" she yelled at Nes. She pulled her to the door and opened it. Light spilled into the garden and Malenie pushed up Nes's sleeve to expose the braid wrapped around her wrist. "He has her hair! 'Something pulling against us,' Sarl said. Don't you think?"

"No, that doesn't make sense. You're forgetting that we're on the other side of the Wall. Magic doesn't work like that here. Or something."

"But remember what Sarl said about there being only two rules. Shaper's magic does exist here, but in most circumstances it doesn't work. What if hair isn't most circumstances? What if he's using her hair and pattern magic together? You said you could feel something from my hair, even on this side of the Wall. And, you know why I'm not allowed to cut my hair—the seven hundred gods and goddesses forbid it because it's 'an intrinsic part of me.' And when it falls out, we burn it so it can't be used against us."

"You don't know it's the same here. Just because they swear by the same gods doesn't mean the religion is the same. It could just be because shapers can use your hair against you on our side of the Wall."

Malenie ignored that. "But it makes sense and it doesn't matter if it's shaper's magic or pattern magic. It's still a part of her," she said rapidly, "and there is so much we don't know about magic. Why else would he have cut her hair?"

"To shame her."

"That only works if they have the same religion here," Malenie argued.

"Not really. But let's say it is true, that Colvin is using her hair to anchor her, like tying down cargo on a camel. Alright, I don't see how it could hurt us to try to get it. And if it is true and we had it instead…"

"It'll help us, instead of working against us!" Malenie finished. "Let's do it right now."

They clutched each other's hands and Malenie closed her eyes, picturing what Paza's hair must look like, very like her own; dark, fine, long, but severed. She tensed as Nes whispered, and the magic rushed over her skin like spider webs, like fine thread, like the string Nes used in her hair, like coarse cords, like heavy rope, tickling, cutting, abrading her skin. She held tighter and tighter, setting her teeth. *I won't let go. I won't let go. I WON'T let go.* Blue light glowed through her eyelids.

With a wicked snap like the sound of a whip, air rushed between them and hurtled them apart. Malenie skidded across the pathway on her butt and Nes tumbled through the open door and sprawled on the floor of the hallway.

"Ow." Nes shook out her wrist. "Did it work?"

"I don't know." Malenie crawled forward, too impatient to even take a moment to stand.

Something lay curled on the pavers.

Malenie reached out, hesitated and said, "You're blocking the light." Nes moved and Malenie recoiled. "Ew!" Almost under her hand was a bristly tangle nothing like the clean, neat hair she had been picturing. It was menacing. It almost seemed to pulse, but that was probably from the flickering flame lanterns.

"That's it?" Nes asked doubtfully, crouching next to her.

"It has to be. So he's done something to it." Under the bristle of broken hairs, it was twisted into a double loop, the beginning and end tucked away somehow so it looked seamless.

"I don't think we should touch it," Nes said. Malenie broke off the end of a curling vine and poked it through one of the loops. "I'm not sure we should use it. I don't like the look of it."

"I still think Thëollon and Larella can help." Malenie shoved the vine handle into Nes's hands. "Don't let anyone see it."

A shadow moved between them and the light, and Malenie shied back, but it was just a woman in the doorway. "What are you doing out here?" She peered at their faces. "It's you." She frowned. "You'd better come in."

Malenie flushed with the reminder of how terrible she'd been to Paza in front of her family. "Where can I find Larella and Thëollon, please?"

"Why?"

"Um..."

"Sarl thought they might be able to help," Nes lied.

"Fine. That door with the swirly designs above it." She stood there watching, but Nes shielded the mutilated hair from view with her body.

At the curtain, Malenie cleared her throat, pushed it aside without waiting and pulled Nes in behind her, relieved to get away from that disapproving stare. Inside, the elders sat on a soft-looking bench with a high back. "Thëollon, Larella, this is my friend Nes."

"Oh good, dear, you apologized." Lara crowed happily. "Finally, some good news on this grim day."

"No—I didn't. I—this is different friend. We need your help."

"No excuses, girl," Thëollon scolded.

"It's not. You see—you probably heard—my friend is the one who's...missing." Larella looked sad and Thëollon pulled the blanket higher on his lap.

"I'm so sorry," Larella began.

"No," Malenie interrupted. "I mean, we're going to get her back and we were coming to you because you've lived here so long that you might remember him—you know, Sarl and uh, Tessalina's son—but we thought of something and tried it and it worked, but not in the way we expected. Nes, show them."

Nes plunked the tangle down on the floor. The twins leaned forward and then drew back involuntarily. Was that understanding on their faces or just curiosity?

"Ah," Thëollon breathed.

"That's nasty. What has Colvin been doing and studying?" Larella muttered. "You." Her gaze stabbed into Malenie, who wondered how anyone thought these two were doddery. "Come here and give me your hands."

Malenie obeyed. She closed her eyes, opened them again. Larella's fingers were cool and light against her skin as she pushed Malenie's sleeves up as far as they would go. They all stared at the diamonds on her skin, especially Nes, who had never gotten a good look at them. After a moment, Larella looked up and smiled at Malenie comfortingly.

I must be getting used to them. They didn't look so strange anymore.

"Hm." Larella pursed her lips and exchanged a look with Thëollon. She tugged Malenie's sleeves into place and gave her hands a quick pat. "That's how you got her hair?" At Malenie's nod, she said, "One mystery solved."

"And another one staring us in the face." Thëollon waved her back and they all stared at the ugly thing.

"The question is, should we take the time to clean it up before these youngsters bring Paza back, or should we hurry forward?" Larella asked.

A little silence followed her words. Malenie stared at the hair until she went cross-eyed. She bit her lip to keep from urging them to hurry. Anything could be happening to Paza right now. Anything.

"I've seen something like it before. We have, Lara. It was a long time ago." Thëollon stared into the air. "When Betella was Matriarch. I know." He refocused on the present. "It was that mess with Lashan. His cousin tried to curse him. He mixed in magic, religion and super-stition until it was an almost impossible tangle."

"I remember! Lashan did get sick, and Betella decided it was best to assume the magic had some effect and that it should be treated seri-ously."

"His cousin cut off his hair?" Malenie asked, appalled.

"Yes, it was—"

"But how does that help us now?" Nes interrupted.

"And does that mean Paza's been cursed? What does that even mean?"

"Ah." Lara and Thëollon looked at each other. Malenie wanted to shake hurry into them. At last, hesitantly, Lara answered. "Probably not. That part is superstition." *Probably!* "But the magic part, that's real. It's—well, you don't want all the theoretical stuff—it represents his hold over her. Cleaning it will symbolically weaken that connection, strengthen its natural connection to Paza and make it easier to retrieve her."

"What do we do?" Malenie asked impatiently. They talked as much as Sarl.

Lara threw off the blanket. "Help me up—no, you go, it's quicker." She handed Malenie a tiny key she took from a chain around her neck and directed her to a long wooden chest under the window. The smell of cedar and frankincense wafted out when Malenie opened it. At Larella's directions Nes and Malenie set aside miniature portraits, heavy books and soft wrapped packages until they found a bronze brazier in the shape of a panther, a small blanket and thin kidskin gloves.

"Sage and cedar," Thëollon reminded Lara.

"I know, I know. There should be a bag of kindling and another of sage leaves. And a comb."

Nes lit a fire in the low-slung belly of the panther. Smoke curled out of its mouth, filling the room with a fresh burning smell. If they had replaced the cover, smoke would have escaped through the pattern of holes that formed the panther's markings.

"The leaves too," Lara said. "Put on the gloves and hold the hair in the smoke." Malenie obeyed.

"Should we say anything?" Thëollon whispered loudly. "I'm sure the priest did."

"Shush. I think a short prayer—in our heads."

Thëollon snapped his mouth shut and sulked at her. The only prayer Malenie could think of was: *Please, let this work.* Did that even count? Her arm was getting tired by the time Thëollon spoke again.

"That should be enough," he said. "Put it on the blanket." Nes flipped open the tan and cream blanket. Was that the Pashtin emblem? Malenie squinted at it. "No, wait, do you have anything belonging to Paza?" he asked.

Malenie pulled the headcloth from her sleeve. It looked worn and thin in contrast to the blanket.

"Perfect. Put that on the blanket and the hair on the cloth."

Larella and Thëollon pushed up their sleeves and grasped each other's wrists, right to right and left to left so their hands crossed. "I'll do it," Larella told him.

"Don't you need someone to make the magic work?" Nes asked.

"What have you been spending your days doing? Of course we can act as a caller for each other."

"There hasn't been time to learn everything," Malenie protested.

"Or opportunity," Nes said neutrally and Malenie's ears got hot because she knew Nes meant Malenie hadn't been willing.

"Those of us with the magic inside of us," it made Malenie's back itch to be included so casually in that 'us,' "are named sources. And the companion without whom the magic will not work is a caller. Anyone can be a caller, but usually a source and caller form a lifelong partnership. Our callers are long gone, so we've become accustomed to using each other. It's such a personal thing, you know, and some of the caller's strength goes into the magic, too."

Larella whispered, too quietly for Malenie to overhear. On Thëollon's wrists, the swirly designs seemed to gain depth, until it was like looking into the night sky, and a blue glow rose to the surface of his skin. Blue light leaked through his clothes at his elbows, knees and ankles.

With a hiss, an oily spiral of smoke sputtered up from the hair and the flat, dark color leached away, revealing naturally black hair that shone with glints of brown and red.

"Nasty, indeed," Lara said, looking well pleased with herself. "More sage leaves." The dirty smoke was swallowed up in the fragrant billows from the brazier.

"Ah, that was fun," Thëollon sighed. "Excuse me. I know it's not the proper time, but we rarely get to do anything anymore."

"No apologies, Thëo, it's one of the perks of being old."

"It's not safe to touch until we undo the knots," he warned, looking at Larella for confirmation. "You put on the other gloves." As Nes followed Thëollon's order, the slender bracelet of hair on her wrist was exposed. He pushed her sleeve up further. "Now what's this?"

"Malenie's. It helped me find her, on the other side of the Wall."

"So you're a shaper?" She nodded and he tapped his chin while he thought. "Do you feel anything from it, here? You do. That's good. While your gift doesn't work, exactly, it gives you…weight. A new plan?" He consulted Larella with a glance.

They never told us the first plan, Malenie thought.

"How do you feel about another?" Larella nodded to the hair on the floor. "We need to anchor her here. I want the two of you to unknot Paza's hair and comb it, but then Nes should make the braid." When they were finished, she said, "Put the rest on the brazier and take off your gloves."

The hair flared up in a stink and Larella sneezed. Nes wrapped Paza's braid around her wrist, over and under Malenie's braid, and paused with the ends pinched between her thumb and index finger.

"Well done!" Thëollon said.

"You have good instincts," Lara agreed. "I'll sew it up for you." She pulled needle and thread from a basket at her elbow and stitched the loop closed. "An excellent anchor." She patted Nes's wrist.

"Now," Thëollon said, sitting up straighter. "Before you get our Paza back—yes, you." Malenie's heart thumped. "You'll do a much better job, the strength of youth and all that—go to the chest and get that bottle, yes, that one, and the matching glasses." The bottle was heavy glass with a fat, faceted belly of smoky green.

Larella poured two fingers worth into each glass and raised hers in a toast. "For strength. To success, Paza's safe return and family." She sipped delicately. Thëollon knocked his back in one gulp. Malenie sipped cautiously and choked. The liquor burnt her throat, the inside of her nose, all the way to her stomach and sent heat racing over her skin. It didn't taste like anything she had tried before, but she hadn't tasted much liquor, just a little palm wine with Papa.

"Quickly, now—the alcohol will help until it gets you too muddled," Thëollon urged. "Concentrate on Paza, what she's like and how she acts…and be as precise as you can be."

Malenie knelt on the blanket, remembering Sarl's warning that moving someone with magic was dangerous. *But it is life and death.* She clasped Nes's arms above the elbow. Sweat stood out along Nes's hairline. She looked a bit unsteady, but determined.

"Ready?" Nes asked and Malenie nodded. "I wish for Paza to come home, to us, Malenie and Nes, here in this room."

Fire ran up Malenie's arms and down her legs, so hot it felt cold, followed by blue-colored lightning. Her teeth chattered. She tightened her grip and felt Nes's fingers clench in return. Nes's eyes widened and Malenie looked down. Her clothes were smoldering everywhere they touched her diamonds.

Help! Malenie thought right before the pain socked into her, taking away breath and vision in a sheet of blue flame, like fainting into light instead of dark. It hurt, but distantly. Was that the liquor? She couldn't feel Nes's hands or arms under her own hands; she had to trust they were there, that this would work. *Paza!* she shouted in her mind. Her bones and her blood seemed to vibrate. Pressure squeezed her eyeballs, ears, her forehead, her cheekbones.

A booming clap of sound rattled the walls. The sudden weight of a living body bowed the cradle of their arms. Paza, her face shocked, her mouth open mid-shout, the sound catching up to them as Malenie and Nes were thrown apart with the force of her arrival. Malenie's head hit the hard tile floor with a thunk and she stared at the dark beams of the twins' ceiling. The cold tiles were soothing on her hot skin. She was too tired to move.

Paza bent over her. One eye was swollen almost shut and she was crying, dripping on Malenie. Malenie licked the salty taste of Paza's tears from her lips. "Shorry," Malenie slurred. Her tongue felt too big for her mouth. Was that the liquor or the effects of too much magic? "Shorry fur b'fur."

Paza half laughed, half cried. "I forgive you. There's nothing to forgive. You saved me, you and Nes. What's wrong with her?" she said to someone behind her. Nes's face joined Paza's and blocked out the light. Her hair looked like a lopsided halo of dark fire around her head.

"Nuh—not drinkin' wif th'twins 'gain," Malenie said as chills pulled her muscles tight. Pain seared her. Not the liquor after all; magic. Malenie gave up fighting her pounding head and all the rest and let her eyes drift closed.

<h1 style="text-align:center">25</h1>

The first thing Malenie saw when she woke up was Paza's face hanging over her again, framed by a similar dark-timbered ceiling. Only instead of cold tile, there was a soft mattress beneath her and a light sheet over her.

"She's awake!" Paza shouted over her shoulder and Malenie blinked again, trying to focus her eyes.

"Is your hair longer?" she asked incredulously.

"Do you think so too?" Paza crowed, touching her hair with hesitant fingertips. "I did, but I didn't want to ask. How are you?"

"Hungry!"

"The Matriarch was here, waiting for you to wake up. She knew you'd want to eat and had food prepared. I'll be back in a snap."

Malenie pulled herself up, surprised at how weak she felt. The sleeping gown exposed her arms and—she lifted the sheet—her legs to the knees. She frowned at the dark blue diamonds inscribed on—under— her skin. They looked strange and exposed. She had always avoided looking at them before. Now she traced the points of the diamonds and wondered if her unknown mother had worn these same shapes on her skin. She rubbed her fingers over the patterns, pressing hard, knowing they wouldn't just go away. *Do I still even want them to?* They had been the cause of a lot of bad things, people chasing her and wanting to own her, and a whole life spent feeling like a misfit, but they had made a lot of good things happen: healing Nes, saving Paza, twice really, bringing the three of them together. She would never have met Paza otherwise.

"Look what we brought!" Paza exclaimed as she came in with a tray. A maid carried a pitcher and Nes had three cups. Malenie twitched with the impulse to cover her arms with the sheet, but then what? She couldn't eat like that. The tray went across her lap so Malenie could feast in bed.

"Nes, are you alright?" Malenie asked as the three of them bustled around her.

The maid didn't stare and didn't stare 'til it was worse than if she had. Finally she left.

"More right than you. Just a bit of a headache from drinking the twins' alcohol. Matriarch fixed my head while the healers worked on you and scolded them for giving it to us. I guess they knew the magic could hurt you an awful lot. It was firewater."

"No!" Malenie paused with a roll halfway to her mouth. Firewater was almost pure alcohol and drunk only by the truly rich or desperately ostentatious; ounce for ounce, it cost as much as a horse or a truly fine spell stone. It was normally drunk in sips alternating with juice.

"But you were a mess, Malenie," Nes continued soberly. "Burnt to a crisp, in stripes everywhere you have diamonds. I didn't know you had so many. You were like a piece of bacon left too long. You kind of smelled like it too, a kind of rancid overcooked meat."

"Nes!" Paza protested.

"She has to know. The Matriarch was furious at Thëollon and Larella for letting us, or making us—she couldn't decide which—do such a dangerous piece of magic. They told her something about resonances and you being more powerful than them…I wasn't really listening because by that time they were picking threads from your clothes out of your skin one by one. Though the Matriarch made sure I heard that you're not supposed to do any magic for a while. When the healers said you were going to recover fine she finally said the twins were right and she wouldn't have them horsewhipped on account of it and them being so old."

"I'd do it again," Malenie said firmly, "though I'm glad I missed all the pain of being roasted. We couldn't leave you there," she said to Paza. She hesitated. *Should I ask?* Awkwardly she said, "Was it bad?" Behind Paza, Nes shook her head and mouthed 'no!' Too late.

Paza wouldn't meet her eyes. The bruise on her face wasn't puffy any more, just an ugly purple and yellow. "Yes." She paused and moistened her lips. "But most of the time he left me alone, too busy working magic with another…and yelling at all these fighters. I told Matriarch." She looked up, fervent. "I knew you and Nes would get me out. After the last time—I knew."

"Uh." Malenie didn't know what to say under the weight of Paza's confidence. She couldn't say, 'We almost didn't.' Instead she asked, "Why isn't your eye all healed?"

"Everyone was too exhausted from trying to get me back to do it properly. The healers said they'd finish it today after they recovered from you, but they haven't come looking for me yet."

"That's…" *strange*, she was going to say, but the expression on Nes's face stopped her. "What do you know?" she demanded.

"I'm not supposed to tell." Nes looked like she'd bitten into a lemon.

"Donkey dung! Tell us."

It didn't take much forcing, Nes wanted to anyway. "The reason they didn't come is because they're not here. The healers, a lot of the Suntins and almost half the Family guards. The rest are on high alert. Sarl said it was something to do with the Gate in the Wall and Colvin. The Matriarch's the one who said not to bother you."

"He's attacking the Gate?" Malenie knocked over a cup of pomegranate seeds and they spilled redly across her tray. "Did Sarl stay?"

"He went. Tal and Jos, too." Nes fished a seed out of the sheets and ate it.

Leaving Paza here. Not unprotected, but…Malenie wiped her fingers, the rest of the food forgotten. "I don't like it," she said slowly.

Nes's eyes flicked to Paza and back. "Me neither," she said. "But Sarl said he felt like he had to go."

While Malenie watched, Paza shredded the flat bread into smaller and smaller pieces and then trailed her fingers through the crumbs. *She knows what this means and she's afraid. Is asking again really going to make that worse?* Malenie took her courage in both hands and said, "Paza, it's you Colvin has always been after." Paza's head jerked and her shoulders hunched, but she stayed sitting on the edge of the bed. "Did he say anything this time?"

Paza touched the edge of her black eye. "No," she said huskily.

"It's alright. It's not like I expected him to tell you his plans." Malenie set the tray aside, dropping it the last little bit when Paza spoke again.

"I don't know what was him just being mean and what was for a reason. He liked to hit us and hurt us. He also made me eat rocks and sleep next to the latrine."

"Paza…" Malenie searched for words. She wished again that Paza would let her hug her.

"We don't know enough," Nes said, frustrated. She slammed her fist on the bed and the plates and cups shook on the tray. And kept shaking as an explosion boomed in some part of the house. The bed rocked and Malenie clutched the bed covers. Nes tumbled to the floor and crouched defensively, ready to attack something. The walls groaned and dust sifted over their heads, powdering their hair gray as the plaster between the beams cracked. Finally the shaking stopped, but the house continued to groan and creak as it tried to settle back into place.

"He's here," Paza whispered, trembling.

Nes tilted her head back, watching a crack zigzag across the ceiling. "We have to get out of the house."

"That's got to be his plan," Malenie said, fumbling out of bed and testing her legs. "But we have to know what's going on. I feel fine," she said in response to the concern on Nes's face. "Paza?"

The younger girl stared back blankly without moving, the sheet bunched in her fists. Malenie touched her shoulder and then shook her gently when she didn't respond. *Gods and goddesses, has it been too much? How much can one person stand?* Remembering Paza's rage when they had almost been caught, Malenie made her voice hard. "Paza. We're going to fight him, but we need you. We're going to stop him from hurting anyone else. Are you going to help us?" she rapped the last words out.

Paza blinked and nodded, slowly at first and then faster and faster. "Yes." She tumbled off the bed and rushed to the door.

"Wait. Where are my clothes? My shoes? I can't go out in a sleeping gown," Malenie cried.

Another percussion rocked the walls and a chunk of ceiling plaster fell on the bed. Nes threw Malenie's sandals at her. "No more time." Malenie shoved her feet into them and let Nes drag her out of the room. They sped through the house, Malenie's sleeping gown flapping against her legs, the diamonds below its hem distracting her with each step. When Nes hesitated at a turning, Paza pushed into the lead.

Outside the closed doors to the dining hall, Paza skidded to a stop. A blue tile pinged and popped off the wall mosaic, and then another, revealing rough plaster patches like scars. "What's that?" Paza sniffed the air.

"Something's burning." Malenie touched the door. It felt hot under her hand. "I don't think we should—"

Paza wrenched the door open and thick heavy smoke billowed out, smelling sharp and strange. Flames roared up as the air from the hallway was sucked into the room. As they watched, the wall hangings caught fire and the flames raced to the ceiling and curled over the doorframe. Nes pulled Paza out of the way and slammed the door shut.

"Which way do we go?" Malenie asked.

"He's waiting for us," Paza gasped.

"And we're going to give him exactly what he wants and shove it down his throat." Somehow. But Paza drew herself up straight, backtracked down the hall and opened a door to a sick room with pallets along one side and scrubbed tables on the other.

"We can't—"

"Your brain is pickled. We can go out the window."

Malenie slapped her forehead. All the windows had low sills and were as big as doors, just like at the Pashtin house. Paza swung open the screen and got ready to jump the short distance to the ground.

"Wait." Nes grabbed the back of Paza's tunic and leaned out cautiously. "Ancestors' bones, that's not good."

Malenie squeezed in next to them. The garden was full of people fighting. Men and women struggled together and grunted and cut each other with swords and punched with bare fists. Brown dust from the garden covered everyone and the spiky green plants had been trampled. Her heart thumped uneasily as she realized some of the dark brown smears were blood. She didn't recognize anyone.

One side of the gate hung askew and the other was lying in the opening. More fighters entered the yard, almost hiding the gate under their feet. "Those aren't Suntin guards," Nes said.

"I don't—" But Malenie finally recognized someone: the guard who had let Malenie and her friends into Suntin house. One of the newcomers clubbed him in the head as he passed, and a woman kicked him in the ribs as he fell. Malenie clenched Paza's hand so tightly the bones ground together, but she couldn't force herself to let go.

"Look, it's over," Nes said.

More fighters exited the house, roughly pushing children, older people and servants in front of them and into the rocky garden. The older Suntins pulled the children into the middle for all the protection the unarmed adults could give. Half of the hire swords stayed to guard them and the other half moved around the yard, checking bodies. A few they left where they were; a few they tied up and a few they dragged to the Suntins, where they were accepted with a flurry of cries and demands for healing supplies that were not answered. Ash sifted down on their heads and a billow of smoke shredded around them. She didn't see the twins.

Malenie glanced behind her into the room, checking for fire, and when she turned back, Colvin was striding into the yard. For once he was wearing a turban and had had the audacity to pin a shiny pilgrim's medallion to it. He looked ugly to her, now, though only her perception of him had changed. A small Thessem boy and an older Parthavian boy and girl scudded behind him. Colvin stopped halfway between the gate and the house, and the children whirled around him like a lost dust devil. Paza sucked in a harsh-sounding breath. The hire swords who had been checking bodies gathered next to Colvin. They exuded menace, with their bloodstained leather armor and bare swords.

"There's almost fifty of them," Nes said softly. "But—"

"Are you happy to see me, beloved family?" Colvin asked. "You should be. I'm here to save you all by mending the cracks in the world."

A few of the Suntins shifted and grabbed hands. Blue light flickered around them. Colvin watched them calmly, and Malenie bit her lip, knowing he must have a reason to be so confident. One woman in the fancy clothes that showed her patterns strained forward, fists clenched as if she wanted to fling herself in the wake of her magic and physically pound on Colvin. Her patterns flashed blue. He met her glare and shrugged exaggeratedly. The woman looked puzzled and turned to her caller, who summoned the magic again. One of the hire swords collapsed. His fellows passed him to the back of the group and laid him on the ground.

Colvin laughed at the woman. "I'm immune to your magic. I've been immune for years. You can't touch me. And you can't touch my fighters. Most of them, anyway. Go on, keep trying." Blue light flickered from three different people, without any effect Malenie could see. "But don't even attempt to harm me physically." He raised a hand and gestured.

The thug from the hideaway stepped forward, a small child clasped in one arm. The fingers Malenie had broken were splinted. In his other hand he held a dagger against the boy's neck. A hire sword with a slightly older girl and another dagger took up a position next to him.

"If you harm or kill me, my fighters will kill these children. And then they will kill your children." He paused to let that sink in. Malenie swallowed heavily and Nes cursed. The Suntins huddled together. A child's sob was quickly muffled. The blue light died. "I see we understand each other. Paza, where are you?" he asked, his voice turning coaxing. "Come back where you belong, with me, and I won't let anything hurt you, ever again."

Paza jerked and slammed her elbow into the wooden screen. They froze, waiting for Colvin's reaction. When he didn't turn in their direction, Malenie put her hand on Paza's shoulder and Paza let her. It seemed Paza didn't breathe, she was so still, but her pulse galloped in her neck.

"We need to get her out of here," Nes whispered. She pushed them back into the room, blocking Colvin from view, for all the good that would do, but at least it was something.

"I didn't see the twins. We can—"

"No," Paza said. "Did you hear him? He said magic hasn't affected him in years. That means the magic we did in Raleton doesn't mean anything. He can hurt my family." Her voice started rising. "He's hurting my family."

"Shh. He's going to hear—"

"Paza, I know you're here," Colvin said, all coaxing stripped away. "Your sister knows you're here." Paza lunged for the window and gripped the sill. Malenie wrapped her arms around her, holding her in place and trying to offer comfort at the same time.

"You care about her, don't you, Paza?" Colvin said. "I remember how you hung on your older sister before she died. You don't want your little sister to think you don't care about her, do you?" Over Paza's shoulder, Malenie saw the little Thessem boy huddle into himself as Colvin squeezed his neck. "Nathania, I want you to come here. And you'll die if anyone tries to undo my command." Green light flared under the boy's tunic. His face clenched with pain.

From within the protective huddle of Paza's family, a young girl cried out. A woman staggered free of the crowd as if she'd been pushed, and the rest tightened around its center as if to keep someone in. "Nathania, no!" a woman shouted.

"It hurts!" Nathania sobbed. "Let me go. I have to go."

Over her sobs, Colvin said, "If you don't let her come to me, eventually she'll die. But first she'll experience a lot of pain. I know none of you want that. I don't give a camel's teat, just as none of you did about me. If you let her die, Paza has more sisters after this one."

Paza flinched, and Malenie tightened her arms, expecting Paza to run. Towards Colvin. "Wait," Malenie urged. "The adults, they've got to do something. Let them." *Please let them.*

Nathania screamed again. Paza's father Anandan roared in anguish and burst out of the group, Nathania squirming and shouting in his arms. It was the girl with the cropped hair Malenie had seen upstairs. The hire swords around the Suntins stepped aside to let him pass. Colvin gestured the men with the child hostages back and two fighters stepped closer to Colvin, their hands near their weapons. Anandan didn't seem to notice. He charged at Colvin. Malenie held her breath.

At the last moment Anandan bundled Nathania under one arm and drew a dagger. He stabbed savagely but inexpertly towards Colvin's gut. A hire sword slammed Anandan's arm wide, spinning him around, then punched him twice in the lower back. Anandan arched in pain. Nathania screamed. He collapsed, twisting, Nathania still in his arms, and managed to fall on his side and not on top of her.

She wriggled free, crawled to Colvin and clutched his feet. Her screams stopped. She hid her face, but her shoulders shook with her sobs. A self-satisfied smile curved the corners of Colvin's lips.

"Nathania!" Paza screamed. She smashed her elbow into Malenie's chest and wrenched away. Malenie staggered back, gasping. Nes grabbed for Paza and missed as she jumped out the window. She raced across the yard, and Colvin's smile curled wider as he watched her. One of the Suntin women screamed and a man shouted desperately, "Paza, no!"

Paza threw herself on top of Nathania, hiding her.

"Ah, Paza, you've returned to me." He laughed, his horrible, normal laugh and used his foot to flip her onto her back. He planted his heel on her chest and pressed her down.

Paza stared at him, the mouse before the snake, and then bucked wildly, trying to dislodge his foot. "Let us go!"

"Be quiet, girl," he said, shaking the little boy again. Paza obeyed, going unnaturally still. "You've made a nuisance of yourself, running away and trying to use magic on me. Did you really think that would work, that anything you could do would affect me? You're nothing. All your attempts are nothing. You're back where I want you."

Malenie clenched her fists so tightly the nails bit into her palms. Not knowing what to do locked her muscles into place. It was like facing the bullies all over again, before Nes had taught her to fight. She shook with fear and frustrated rage. A quick glance at Nes showed that she felt as helpless. *Why doesn't anyone do anything?* She realized it was the same thought she'd had at home. *I never asked Papa for help. I just kept waiting for him to see because he was the grown-up and he must have known every-thing. But they don't.* It was a scary thought. "Nes." *I'm not going to make the same mistake again.*

"Since Anadan is such a poor fighter and I am not a monster, I won't order my men to kill the children," Colvin said. "This time. Don't try my patience." He shook the boy and pointed at the woman who had confronted him. "Put all her magic into Paza."

A glittering stream of blue light rose from the woman, wavered in the air like a heat mirage and then snapped to Paza and pulled tight like a rope. The woman collapsed to her knees with a mewl of pain. Twin-ing faintly through the blue was a hint of gold, like bright sunbeams in an otherwise dark room, that came from her caller. He stayed upright a few breaths longer and then folded with a little more control. Colvin grinned wider with satisfaction and tilted his head as if admiring his work.

"Nes," Malenie whispered frantically. "Use my magic to call Sarl. Tell him we need him. That Colvin is here, that he's stealing magic from the Suntins, and that Colvin and his hire swords are immune to mag-ic." Nes's fingers were cold on Malenie's hand. The magic whispered so easily into place that only the faint thrum under her skin and the light showed they had done anything at all. It was strange seeing the diamonds themselves glow; they had always been hidden underneath her clothes before. Malenie twisted her hand to hold Nes's when it was done.

"Did it work?"

"I don't know. Keep thinking about what we can do."

One of the older Suntin boys shouted wordlessly in anger. Colvin stabbed his finger at him and a second stream of magic twisted towards Paza. The ropes of colored light were strangely beautiful, like liquid glass, like captured rays of sunset. With a flourish, Colvin pointed at several adults in a row, and they staggered and collapsed as their magic swept into Paza.

A woman with green ribbons in her hair threw herself at one of the hire swords, triggering a rush from the rest of the Suntins. They beat at the hire swords with their bare hands, and were clubbed and punched and knocked to the ground. Malenie lost sight of the first woman, but not one person fought free.

26

Nes threw one leg over the low windowsill and tugged on Malenie's hand. "We got to get out of here while they're all fighting. Sarl and the others aren't going to get here in time. If we go now, they might not see us."

"We can't run away."

"We're retreating, not running away. Colvin's going to look for you next. He'll take your magic and use you as another hostage and we won't be able to fight. If we leave now, we can figure out another way to fight him later."

"I don't—"

The boy Colvin was using as a caller started to shake. All the strength seemed to go out of him and his head lolled to the side. Colvin dropped him like a broken toy, seized the Parthavian girl and turned towards the street. She was stiff with terror but made no effort to escape. For the first time, he shouted, almost chanting as if it were a ritual he had practiced many times. "Come here, shaper magic, primed by blood by Harashan. Come here. Cross the Wall. Come home. Live in Paza until I release you." He grabbed the other boy and repeated it.

"What the rotting Ancestors is he doing?" Nes's voice shook. "What does he think he's doing?"

"Gods rot him—the Wall, the rocks; Nes, hit the children!" Malenie wrenched open Nes's belt pouch, pulled out her sling and the rocks from the Forgotten Quarry and pressed them into Nes's hands.

"What? No!" Nes let them drop.

A hot wind blew over them, like the beginning of a sandstorm. A wind that didn't lift and tangle Malenie's hair, that didn't stir anything but her sense of dread. It seemed to press her harder into the floor. Paza whimpered and began to toss and turn. The air thickened as if a pall of dust hung around her.

"Do you feel that?" Malenie picked up the rocks. They glittered with mica in the sunlight. "Something really bad is going to happen. But I think we can stop it. I think the Wall was made with stone from the Forgotten Quarry and that's why you kept having that strange reaction to those rocks. Because they're some kind of natural spell stone, even here. The hideaway where Colvin found us was made of the same stone and my magic didn't work there so maybe these rocks will stop the kids' magic or make it weaker or something. But they have to touch them. I know it's awful. But it's the only thing I can think to do. He's hurting Paza and going to destroy everything and everyone. Please. Hit them somewhere it won't hurt too much. I'd do it, but my aim is not as good as yours. I might hurt them more."

Nes stared at her for what seemed like forever. Then she clenched her teeth and jumped out the window. She took the rocks and planted her feet, whipping her sling through the air. Once, twice. On the third rotation, she hopped forward, arm reaching out, sling cracking at the release.

The stone flew, almost invisible against the washed-out blue of the sky. Malenie held her breath. *It won't work*, she thought, praying the opposite.

Impact.

The caller girl staggered, clutching her stomach. Colvin almost lost his grip on her. The heaviness of the air lightened.

"It's working!"

Nes's sling whined and cracked again, and the older boy jerked on the ground. The heat lessened, and it felt like there was more air to breathe. Colvin spun around and Malenie went cold at the rage on his face. "You. What are—Stop them," he ordered his fighters.

Nes cursed and hit both the callers again. The girl howled and Nes cringed. But the dust fizzed away, a real breeze teased Malenie's hair, and the heavy hotness to the air broke apart and slid away. Cooler air curled into the cracks.

Colvin recovered his grip on the girl and shook her, making her head flop back and forth.

"Ancestors-cursed baby stealer," Nes shouted. She bent, pried up an ornamental rock and reloaded her sling just in time to hit one of the hire swords racing towards them. He fell but the others kept coming, blocking Malenie's view of Colvin. The others ran faster.

"Ashes." Malenie tumbled out of the window and grabbed more rocks. Her hands shook as she passed the first one to Nes. She threw the second, but it flew wide and slammed into the dirt. Nes hit a hire sword in the shoulder. It knocked him off balance but didn't stop him. Malenie's hands shook even more as she backed up and aimed again. *I can do this.* She took a deep breath. They were so close it was hard to miss. Unfortunately, her rock didn't seem to damage the hire sword when it struck. "Nes."

"I know," Nes growled. She took a deep breath and said more calmly, "Get ready to—"

An arrowhead sprouted below the collarbone of the hire sword on the left. His mouth opened wide in shock and pain, and spit and blood flew out of it. He staggered forward a few more steps. His hands opened and closed like he was reaching for something. Malenie couldn't tear her eyes away, but she was aware of the other men falling and of shouting.

"Look." Nes shook her. Malenie followed her pointing chin. Archers lined the top of the Suntin's wall. Tal knelt at one end, Paza's uncle Fidadan and Jos at her side. A flicker of blue light told Malenie they were using Fidadan's magic, but not how. He frowned and rubbed his forehead. Half a heartbeat after, the child hostages knocked the daggers away from their throats at the same instant, eerie mirror images of each other. Tal shot one of the hostage takers in his back. The archer next to her copied her. The men slumped, seeming to fall in slow motion. Malenie's muscles twitched in useless reaction as the children tumbled from their hands, but Anadan and another man rolled, caught them and backed away.

"Surrender," Tal barked, her voice booming through the yard, amplified through a speaking horn. It cut through all the other shouting.

"You surrender," Colvin said, his voice sounding thin after Tal's. He held the caller girl in front of him with a knife at her throat. Paza was still crumpled motionless at his feet.

Sarl stepped through the open gateway. "It's over, Colvin. Put her down. Let her go."

Father and son stared at each other across the width of the garden, across the width of pain that separated them, across the chasm of their broken family.

"It's not over," Colvin said.

"Put the knife down and let her go."

"Don't come any closer," Colvin warned. "It's you who've lost, again." He sounded so sure of himself, in spite of the archers and the Suntin guards and Sarl's calm voice, that Malenie looked around, wondering what he knew that they didn't. "How does it feel to be powerless? How do you like it?" Colvin asked.

"I'm sorry. I'm sorry I didn't protect you when you were a child. I'm sorry I didn't know." Sarl took a deep breath. "But look around you. How is what you're doing different from what was done to you? Look at the pain you're causing."

"It's not the same. I am protecting them. I'm going to give them back the world as it should be, a better world."

"Son—"

"I'm not your son," Colvin said flatly, betrayal like a hidden knife in each word. "You said so yourself."

"I was wrong," Sarl said hoarsely. "You are always my son."

"I am not your son."

Sarl pressed the heel of his hand to his chest, his face gray.

"Does it hurt?" Colvin asked savagely, the smug smile finally falling away, revealing old pain and new anger welling up fresh. "Does it hurt like I did? It's your turn, now." He chopped the air with his hand, using the caller girl's magic. Sarl choked and clutched his throat.

Paza, forgotten at his feet, reared up, her shiv glinting silver in her hand, and stabbed Colvin in the thigh. Shouting in pain, he backhanded her and slammed her into the ground. The caller girl squirmed and ducked out of his hold, knocking the dagger out of his hands. Paza kicked it away, curled around and kicked at his ankles and shins. She shrieked, "Kill him!"

Malenie started running. She didn't know what she was going to do, but by the seven hundred gods and goddesses, she was going to do something. "Leave her alone!" she screamed.

Colvin howled and stomped on Paza's foot. She scrabbled away from him on her elbows and heels, her face twisted with pain and fear. He screamed incoherently, stomping after her, not noticing Jos racing towards him, not hearing the murmurs among his hire swords, not seeing anything but the little girl in front of him.

Jos, grimly silent, tackled Colvin. They skidded through the gravel. Colvin struggled ineffectually, no match for Jos, who pinned Colvin's arms and legs with a quick motion. After one vindictive glance, Paza crawled to her sister and wrapped herself around her. Malenie threw herself to her knees next to them but was too worried about how Paza would react to touch her. She wiped her hands uselessly on her legs.

Sarl knelt next to his son and began to tie him up.

"Surrender," Tal ordered the hire swords, pulling back on her bow. "You may be immune to magic, but you're not immune to weapons. And if you even think about using any of the Suntins as shields I will kill you." A few lowered their weapons and shuffled away from those that didn't. "Don't think your fellows at the Wall are going to save you. They were defeated and captured." Malenie looked up, caught by an odd note in Tal's voice. The fighters didn't seem to notice, but they hadn't spent every waking moment with Tal for days. Grumbles passed from hire sword to hire sword. "Your leader can't help you." Tal pointed to where Colvin, tied, gagged and blindfolded, was being carried away by Suntin guards. The rest of Colvin's hire swords glanced at their fellows and put their weapons down and their hands up.

Just as Nes finished checking Colvin's three callers for injuries, Paza pushed away from Nathania. She spasmed and curled in on herself. The shiv was still clenched in her hand. Light seemed to flicker over her exposed skin—her collarbone, her forearms, her forehead. Malenie rubbed her eyes, but it wasn't a mirage.

Paza started to shake. Her body arched up in a bow and her heels drummed the ground. Blood smeared her chin. Her teeth shredded her bottom lip.

"Nes, I need you," Malenie yelled. More blood ran down Paza's neck. Nathania stuck her fist in her mouth, muffling her sobs.

Gravel sprayed up as Nes skidded to a stop next to Paza. A piece flew up and stung Malenie's cheek. "What's happening to her?"

"The magic Colvin did. It's still affecting her. What did he say?"

Malenie demanded. "About the shaper magic? We have to get it out of her. Send it back where it came from. Now." Obeying, Nes clutched Malenie and a cloud of diffuse gold and rose light wavered around Paza. It steadied, and Malenie pressed her palms to the dirt. *Please, seven hundred gods and goddesses, let this work.* The light frayed around the edges like smoke in a brisk breeze and then curled away and dissipated.

The tension drained out of Paza and she collapsed. Malenie pressed her hand to Paza's chest and under her nose. For a long moment she didn't feel anything, and then a puff of air sighed across Malenie's fingers. "She's breathing!" She shouted, feeling like she was just remembering to breathe herself. "She's not dead." She used the bottom of her sleeping gown to wipe the blood away. "We need a healer!"

"My daughters!" Jessanna tore across the garden, her hair draggling out of its braids. She reached Nathania first and scooped her up. Nathania clung to her, sucking her thumb, her face dirty and smudged with tears. The child's weight barely slowed Jessanna down, but the sight of Paza brought her to a full stop.

Malenie stood up and realized everyone was looking at her.

And she was half naked.

And everyone could see the diamonds on her skin.

Heat flushed her entire body and her face burned. "Rot it," she whispered and pushed her shoulders back. *We saved Paza, and we used my magic to do it.* She straightened even more. *And half the people here have the marks. I'm not a freak. I wasn't ever a freak.* Maybe she was even…a little proud to have them. She was proud of what she'd done.

Paza moaned and her eyes fluttered open. She looked right at Malenie and there was sense in her eyes. Suddenly Malenie didn't care if everyone was looking at her.

"We're alive," Paza whispered. "Is he…?"

"Tied up and," a quick glance confirmed it, "taken away. And we're all alive." A sob caught in Malenie's throat and she forced it down.

Jessanna took another step and Paza's eyes flickered to her. "Mama," Paza said, the word almost lost in the gasping sobs that shook her. Somehow there was still room for Paza in her mama's hug. Paza fell against her, crying out years of pain and fear. The shiv finally fell from her hand. Furtively, Nes plucked it up and two of the stones from the Forgotten Quarry. She rolled them around in her hand and hesitated, then with a shrug dropped everything in her bag.

Malenie felt lost. Tal and Jos were herding the hire swords out of the yard. Some of the Suntins were helping their magic-drained or injured family members and others had run to fight the fire that still sent up dark streamers of smoke from four places in the back of the house. Sarl was nowhere in sight. Malenie was wondering if Jessanna would hug her, too, when Lissetta strode up. Her eyes missed nothing, but the fine lines around them were deep with stress. Amazingly, she held a tunic, which she passed to Malenie. No one seemed to be missing their clothes, and Malenie decided not to question matriarchs bearing gifts. She struggled into it, briefly feeling more exposed and then much better. Her head had barely popped out when strong arms wrapped around her and Nes and gathered them in. "Tal!"

She smelled of sweat and blood and, underneath that, like Tal, a familiar smell even after such a short time. Malenie hugged her back. Much better than a stranger's hug.

"You three." Tal didn't let go even when she started talking. "You were amazing. You saved the day."

Malenie rested her head against Tal's shoulder and let the other woman hold her up. Tal was broad and steady, her praise and the feeling of security sweet and heady, and Malenie's knees trembled with reaction and the aftereffects of terror. Nes muttered something.

Tal's embrace tightened. "It's alright. It's over. You did good." She murmured reassuringly until Malenie didn't have to hold on quite so tightly. "Colvin had no idea what he was up against," Tal said. "So tell me, how did you know what to do?"

Malenie turned her head so her words wouldn't be muffled. Nes's eyes were closed but she was practically floating at Tal's praise. "I guessed the rocks Nes took from the Forgotten Quarry were like the Wall and the hideaways," Malenie said. "They look exactly the same. But—"

"And she used her magic," Nes said pointedly, opening her eyes to stare at Malenie.

"Yes. Yes, I did. A lot. Because I had to, and because I wanted to. And I didn't hurt anyone, and even though everyone stared at me it was alright." It was alright. It was more than alright for the first time in a long time.

"They were staring because you saved Paza," Nes said.

"We saved her." Malenie looked up at Tal. "But what about you? Did you get our message?" Tal finally pulled back and looked them over. Malenie tried not to blush again.

Nes pushed upright as if she could pretend she never needed to lean on anyone. "What happened? You were fighting."

"We heard you. Colvin's hire swords blasted open the Gate in the Wall and were guarding it, but they didn't realize how enraged the people in the city were. We were still fighting when we heard you calling us. The archers are going—"

Jos jogged up. "Are you injured?" He seized Nes's and Malenie's arms and held them out wide, examining them closely. He looked like he was just restraining himself from patting them down like a camel. Assured they were in one piece, Jos reluctantly dropped their arms. "Just as I said once before: vicious. You two and Paza could found a whole new family of clever, vicious fighters. I would run rather than fight you. Well done."

"You're all right?" Sarl came up from the other side and touched Nes and Malenie on their shoulders. He stiffened, and Malenie looked around wildly for a new threat. Nes did, too. But then Malenie saw the expression on Sarl's face and realized he was having a vision. They all waited, a little anxiously. Sarl blinked and looked down at them. A grin lit up his face. "Malenie's papa and Nes's sibs are on the way here."

"What?" Malenie didn't understand at first. It was too much, all at once. And then a bubble of laughter expanded her chest.

Nes fell back a step and her hands flew to her mouth. "Say that again?"

"Your brother and sisters and Malenie's Papa are on the way. They'll be here soon. They're well." Nes's mouth opened and closed and the laughter burst out of Malenie. She pulled Sarl's head down and smacked a loud kiss on his check before flinging herself at Nes and dancing her in a circle.

"We did it!" Malene told Nes, until Nes shouted it too, and they meant everything: Papa, Nes's sibs, Paza, Colvin, desert journeys and magic.

27

The next afternoon Malenie was sitting alone in the twins' garden, kicking the bench with her heels. Sarl hadn't been able to be more specific about Papa's arrival than 'soon' and had forbidden her to use magic to look for him—something about her body's reserves being drained. That wouldn't have stopped her, but the healers wouldn't let Paza out of their sight and Nes had said 'no' when Malenie asked. She was taking her caretaking role seriously, and had gone off with Tal to practice drills to avoid temptation. If sheer determination could keep Nes's family safe from now on, they'd be very safe.

"Hey," Paza said softly and Malenie sat up straight.

"They let you out of bed! Or did you escape? Here, um, sit down." Malenie patted the bench and Paza balanced on the edge of it. Malenie checked her sleeves nervously, remembered she wasn't doing that anymore and folded her hands in her lap. "So…"

"Are you mad at me?"

"What?" Malenie hiked one leg over the bench to face her. "No, I'm—you mean what I said to you? I shouldn't have done that. I was going to apologize before—and then you were gone and I hated thinking—I'm sorry." Malenie stopped talking and bit her lip.

Paza tilted her chin up and met her eyes. "Because I never lied, you know. I didn't know his name. I was really little the last time he was here. Anyway, there were just things I didn't tell you. At first because it didn't matter and then because it hurt too much. And maybe I thought you should—that it shouldn't have made a difference."

Malenie nodded rapidly, feeling guilty but relieved Paza was talking to her.

"People feel like they have a right to know everything," Paza said, hugging her arms across her chest, "but they're wrong. Sometimes the need not to say some things is bigger."

"You mean like Emelenie in her parlor, demanding you take off your headscarf. Rot it, I did the same thing about your family. Paza, I'm so sorry. I wasn't thinking about you at all. Do you…do you hate me?"

"Never." Paza rubbed the cuff of Malenie's sleeve between her fingers. Their hands brushed together, but Paza didn't flinch away. "Friends?"

"Yes. Always." Malenie beamed at her, feeling the knot of guilt finally melt away.

"That's what I like to see," Larella cried, leaning on Nes and taking slow careful steps. Next to her the Matriarch supported Thëo. She levered him onto his bench with an 'oof.' Thëo wriggled to settle himself and then clasped his knees and surveyed them all. Sarl, Jos and Tal rounded the corner of the house and joined them.

"If you don't look at the house, you'd hardly be able to tell there'd been a battle here," Thëo proclaimed. It was true, this corner of the garden was as shady and inviting as before, but Malenie didn't have to look at the charred, crumbling screens in the windows to know it had happened. She felt different inside, relieved and anxious, triumphant and sad, all at the same time, and she thought Nes and Paza did, too. They could tell, even without seeing the damage.

"The things my brother says." Lara rolled her eyes and let Sarl spread an orange blanket on her lap. "This is a perfect place for a conversation, though." Paza tensed and Nes moved to stand next to her.

"Don't tease," Lissetta said. "We just wanted to talk to you."

"Or feed you," Lara added. "You look hungry." She pulled a bag out of her sleeve and beckoned to Jos. "Young man, pass these out." The bag held pistachios covered in honey and cumin. Paza relaxed a little as she crunched them between her teeth.

"Speaking of food, did Colvin give you a lot of yogurt to eat?" Sarl asked, watching her.

Malenie said, "Because you think he…Colvin was putting dust from the Wall in it and giving it to Paza. And to himself. That's why he was immune to magic, isn't it? But I don't understand why he was giving it to Paza."

"You knew, Paza?"

Paza shook her head.

"I guessed," Malenie said. "When I had that idea about using the rocks against the, against the children he was using as callers, I kind of guessed that, too. I'd had some of his yogurt once and it was awful and gritty."

Tal laughed at Sarl's gobsmacked expression. "You forgot she's a healer's daughter, used to mixing medicines into liquids and getting people to drink them."

Malenie grinned at Tal.

"I should have asked you, Malenie," Sarl said. "I spent a lot of time talking to the little boy—"

"His name is Thom," Nes said.

"Yes. Nes, you did a great job convincing all three they were safe, and they started telling us all sorts of things. Thom told us it was his job to go to the Wall, scrape rock dust, measure what he collected and mix it into yogurt."

"Colvin ingested much, much more than you did. Once Thom opened up, the girl told us she collected rock dust, too, although she didn't know what happened to it. We think Colvin was giving it to his hire swords, too, and that's how he made himself and his fighters immune to magic."

"But I'm not immune to magic," Paza protested.

"Good thing, too, or you'd be feeling a lot worse," Lissetta said calmly. "You haven't been with him for more than a moon and that might have something to do with it. But we're still trying to figure out why he did it."

Malenie stared at her hard, sure she was leaving something out. She opened her mouth, but Paza straightened up and asked, "What's going to happen to him?" She still had ahold of Malenie's sleeve.

"We'll send Colvin to the Raleton Patriarch. It's too dangerous to keep him here. But no one has pattern magic among the Raletons, and he will be kept away from all children. He won't have the freedom to make trouble again. They'll make sure he can't harm anyone and they'll put him to work. They'll—I don't know if you want to hear this—try to help him. Not everyone who is hurt as a child grows up to hurt others, and if someone does, they can change, can decide to live their lives differently." She watched Paza carefully, who looked uncertain.

"That's it? You're not going to punish him or, or kill him or something?" Nes asked.

"His life will be very restricted. He'll be living among strangers, and he won't be in control of much, just himself. We also want to know if the immunity will eventually wear off and to learn what exactly he thought he was doing. He'll be watched closely.

"Some of the Suntins demanded his execution. I decided against it. Sarl also asked for mercy." She paused for Sarl to speak, but he deliberately ate another pistachio. "Colvin was badly hurt as a child, and part of the responsibility lies with the former Matriarchs and our two Families. Executing him would falsely let us believe that that responsibility has ended. But I'm also thinking of Paza and the other children he's hurt. Someday, when you have had time to recover and the years have passed, you may want to face him. To see him with adult eyes. It might help you heal. If he's dead, you'll never have that chance."

"And he'll remind all of us that we have the power to choose what kind of people we will be," Tal said.

"We will also talk to the Raleton Patriarch about you, Malenie. They should have treated you better, not locked you up and scared you. They could have done something drastic. We'll have to make sure there's no possibility of that happening again, and one of the ways to do that is to talk to them more."

"What about Thom and the two other kids?" Nes asked. "Did you recognize their family names? What's going to happen to them?"

"I hope you'll help us. They can stay with—"

"Paza?" Jessanna interrupted from the edge of the group. "The healers want to look at you again."

"Tell me everything," Paza whispered in Malenie's ear. She sighed exaggeratedly, but willingly tucked her hand in her mother's and let herself be led away.

As soon as she was out of earshot, Malenie, trying not to sound accusing, said, "You know something about Paza and the Wall and Colvin that you didn't tell us."

Lissetta leaned on the bench next to Thëo and rubbed the bridge of her nose. Thëo took her other hand and squeezed it in both of his. "I didn't want to say it in front of Paza," she admitted. "She's brave and strong, but I don't want to put any more burdens on her right now. When she feels safe here again and some of her wounds have become scars, then we'll tell her."

"We think he was trying to create a connection to the shaper's magic," Thëo said. "He destroyed the Gate in the Wall and somehow called someone's shaper magic through and told it to live in her."

"You need a stronger word than connection," Lara said. "She was his stand-in. She represented the Wall. In a way, she was the Wall, because it was inside her."

"And he wanted to destroy the Wall," Malenie said. The Matriarch nodded, waiting for her to figure it out. "But the Wall is immense, too big to destroy. And the—our magic here won't work on it and I don't know for sure, but I don't think the shaper magic could do it. So he made Paza a symbol, by giving her the dust to eat….And he was going to…destroy…her?"

Thëo pursed his lips. "Kill her."

"And I think he chose Paza to get back at us, the Suntins, for our failures," Lara said. "Paza and her sister Ananaletta were the old Matriarch's first grandchildren. We had better let the Sarnaths know in case he set something up there too."

Malenie put her foot down to steady herself. Her stomach squeezed tight at how close they'd been to losing Paza and everything. He really would have killed her. All morning she'd swung between anticipation at seeing Papa and the thought that once they were back together, they'd leave and she'd lose all these people she'd met and come to care about. *But they'll be alive*, she tried to comfort herself.

She ignored the adults arguing about proxies and sympathy and what exactly Harashan could have done on the other side of the Wall until Lara slung a pistachio at Thëo and hit him in the middle of the forehead. "Pistachios for your theory! It's ridiculous!"

Thëo's mouth dropped open in faked offense and then his face turned sly. He made a big show of popping the offending nut in his mouth and chewing. "Seasoned with just the right amount of nonsense," he pronounced.

"You're worse than the youngest children," Sarl said, and both Lara and Thëo turned on him with raised arms and pistachio missiles.

"You'd better take it back," Jos told him. "I don't think even Tal and

I can save you."

"I wouldn't even try," Tal said.

Whatever Sarl was going to answer disappeared under the sound of unfamiliar voices shouting and camels bawling in the front. Lissetta ran around the side of the house and Malenie followed with a horrible feeling of déjà vu. *Colvin was defeated*, she reminded herself. *I saw him tied up and taken away myself. The Matriarch promised.*

Men, women, horses and camels filled the yard, milling around and throwing up dust. Three children tumbled off a tall black camel, pulling a wordless cry of excitement and relief out of Nes. She sprinted past Malenie, gathered them in her arms and tumbled to the ground, crushing the few yellow flowers that had survived yesterday's battle unscathed. A lump rose in Malenie's throat. She spun back to the confusion of people, searching. A man with a ragged blue turban pulled himself free of the crowd.

"Papa!" She was running and he was running and then they were hugging and laughing and crying.

"Papa, you're so skinny," she said, finally pulling back to look at him. He was thinner than she had ever seen him and there was dirt under his ragged fingernails and his turban might once have been someone's pants, but he was here and whole and it was such a relief that Malenie felt dizzy.

"My kidnappers didn't feed me very well," he said, "and then Liac and his captain had us ride hard to reach Emelenie. We stopped only long enough to learn you weren't there and for Emelenie to let me know how angry she was with me. Then we came straight here. Luckily I didn't have to depend on her to open the Gate in the Wall. Lissetta's messenger had waited." He pulled her into another hard hug and said something into her hair.

"What?" she demanded.

"You're taller," he said. "Saving the world agrees with you."

"Finding you agrees with me. What happened? How did you get away? Why did Harashan kidnap you?"

"Lissetta," Papa said, turning as the Matriarch approached them.

"Hello, Serliac," the Matriarch said. She gestured for him to go on. Malenie was surprised they knew each other but too impatient for Papa's story to interrupt. She would ask later. She would ask many things later.

"I think Harashan wanted you, Malenie. Though I don't know how he found out about us."

"Colvin." Lissetta's lips pressed into a thin line. "He must have wanted to give Malenie to Colvin because of her magic. He thought it would be easy to kidnap you, Malenie, because you didn't have the protection of your father's family. Excuse me, Serliac, for saying it."

Papa sighed. "There's truth in that. I thought I was doing the right thing at the time. But, Lissetta, don't blame yourself for Colvin's actions." Obviously someone had filled Papa in on recent events.

"Who else will I blame?"

"Colvin," Papa said. "Being an adult is choosing how you react to the experiences that shape you. You can hurt children or help them. He wasn't doomed to his actions."

"But what would he have been if we had loved him as we should have? Looking back, I can see how grief-stricken we were when Tessalina died. Sarl was devastated by her death and we were all oblivious to how much worse it must have been for Colvin to lose his mother."

"We can't answer what ifs," Papa said softly. "We can only remember the past as we look forward and try to do better."

"I know—and no more meddling in bloodlines trying to bring back former glories," she said firmly.

Papa looked ready to say something sharp but stroked Malenie's hair instead.

"So Colvin sent a messenger under the Wall to Harashan," Malenie said, picking up the thread of the conversation, "and Harashan chased me right to the other side of the Wall. This side, I mean, since I was over there. If Paza hadn't decided to rob me, Colvin would probably have found me and neither of us would have gotten away from him."

"I should have protected you more," Papa said bitterly.

"If I can't blame myself for Colvin, you can't either," Lissetta scolded.

"Just so." Papa's face eased a little. "And Mellie escaped him. So Harashan changed his plans when he couldn't get you, Malenie, or went ahead with his plans for all we know, and his men attacked Trader Town. They practically destroyed it with a fire weapon I'd never heard of before. It shook apart the houses, and what didn't fall was burnt."

"And k-killed everyone, except the kids."

"No, they didn't!" His hands tightened on her shoulders. "What made you think—"

"Nes said—"

"Jak, Steph," Papa called. "Nes, come here. There's something you need to see."

A couple of the armed men strode up, except they weren't both men and they weren't from Pashtin. "Jak?" Malenie got out before her friend from Trader Town swept her up in a crushing embrace that lifted her feet off the ground.

He put her down and tweaked her nose. "My wee red chick, I'm glad to see you safe. But I told you to stay out of trouble. Why didn't you come to me?"

"I didn't think, I just I ran. I ran so far I got to the other side of the Wall. After we found Nes, we thought everyone was dead." Steph hugged her, too, strange and hard in leather armor, but somehow the same as when selling meat pies in the market.

Nes stumbled when she saw Jak and Steph, and her older sibs straightened up under her arms, proud to prop her up and be of use. Even the youngest stopped tugging at the off-white bandage around her neck and put a hand on Nes's back to steady her. There were no slave collars on their necks, but the memory was there in their eyes, which were sunken, like they had been sick for a long time and were just now starting to recover.

"Not everyone died?" Nes choked out.

"Most of Trader Town survived," Jak said. "And your sibs were brave, all of them. We're glad to get you lot back together. You take care of each other now, you hear?"

Papa swept Nes into his arms and she pressed her face into his shoulder. "I'm so sorry," he murmured. "Your ma…"

She clung to him for a few breaths more. When she pushed away, her eyes were wet, but her voice was firm. "But how? I don't understand."

"Gravin's complex was hit the hardest, but almost everyone in the town got away, except for a few, though to look at Trader Town you wouldn't guess," Jak explained. "We're too canny to the way of bandits to stay and fight. Run away and live another day. Or so we thought, until they ambushed us one night and got about half the kids. We didn't expect it. Thought they were marauding, not slaving. Then it was us chasing them and arguing the whole time about how to do it because they had so many more fighters."

"Then the Pashtin Family guards caught up to us," Steph said. "Once we sorted out that we all wanted the same thing, we joined together and slammed into the bandits. We got our Trader Town kids back, and Serliac."

"Except Harashan got away," Papa said, his brows crinkled in concern for their reaction, but too much had happened for Malenie to be worried, not now. Maybe later, when they were on their own again.

"We'll find him," Jak promised. "Gravin's dead, so I have all the time in the world to hunt bandits."

"And Pashtin's support," Papa said.

"And Suntin's," Lissetta said.

"And maybe you'll have time to look for someone?" Malenie asked, thinking about Shay. "I can explain later."

"I thought Gravin and Harashan were working together?" Nes asked.

"They were, until they weren't. I think—"

"Malenie, are you going to stay?" Paza shouted, pelting up to them. On the front steps, her mother shaded her eyes to watch her. "Mama said grandmother is going to ask you!"

"I haven't asked yet, Pazaletta," the Matriarch said dryly and Malenie snorted. *What an awful name.* Paza crossed her eyes, and Malenie smirked back, glad Paza was acting so normal. "What do you think, Malenie? If I asked you to stay, if I asked you as my granddaughter to stay, would you?" There was nothing distant about her now; she let Malenie see how much she cared about her answer.

Malenie couldn't understand what she had said. "What?"

"Your mama was my daughter."

Thoughts tumbled through Malenie's mind and she remembered wondering if her unknown mother had had diamonds or maybe squares or hexagons. *And then I never thought about the squares and hexagons and circles I've been seeing since I came to Suntin.* "You're my grandmother? And Paza's my cousin?" she blurted out. They couldn't break that kind of bond: friend, caller, cousin. And then another question burst from her lips. "So Sarl is also my cousin by marriage?" *If I have to be related to Colvin, at least that means I get Sarl, too.* She was a little ashamed of the thought since almost everyone here was related to Colvin, had lived with him and known him, and was probably deeply upset about what he had done.

"Yes, although his wife, my first cousin, died a long time ago. He is kin."

She sounded amused, but Malenie barely noticed. Her heart was pounding and her palms were sweaty, just like the times she had been in a fight. She didn't know what she was feeling, it was too much, a whole house full of relatives who didn't judge Paza for her hair and accepted Nes and knew about Malenie's marks and had their own, where she wasn't a freak—and then all her feelings and emotions splintered on one certainty. "I have to go with Papa," Malenie said, and realized she would like to stay and learn her cousins' names, get to know the Matriarch, find out about Mama and see what it was like to have a big family.

"Of course I'm asking Serliac to stay, too." Lissetta turned to Papa. "Malenie needs to be tutored. Her magic is strong and she needs to know its limits and how to use it. She won't learn that with the Pashtins."

"Um. Learn about magic?" At first Malenie didn't know what she felt, but then she realized the expansive feeling in her chest was hope and relief and a little bit of anticipation. Everyone here accepted magic. The healers had used magic to help people, without hurting them as she had accidentally hurt Nes. "I think I'd like that," she said, her voice getting firmer as she spoke. "But, Papa, don't you want to go back to Trader Town?"

"Not with Harashan still out there. He may be searching for you for his own reasons. I can't take that chance. But I do want to know something. Why," he asked sternly, "did you flee Emelenie in the middle of the night? She was frantic and convinced you'd been kidnapped out of your beds until Lissetta's message reached her."

Malenie gaped at Papa. Now that she knew Paza was a Suntin, the conversation they had overheard between Emelenie and Yasmin had an entirely new meaning. "Paza, you must have guessed Emelenie wanted to send you here, and not to Colvin. Why did we run away?" But if they had come directly to Suntin without first returning to Trader Town, they wouldn't have found Nes and saved her life, or met Sarl.

Nes wouldn't have picked up the rocks from the Forgotten Quarry. They wouldn't have defeated Colvin.

Paza glared at her, her chin high. "You didn't trust Emelenie, so how could I know what she really meant to do with me? And she wouldn't have sent you, just me." Malenie's heart pinched and she tried to interrupt, but Paza curled her shoulders in and kept talking. "Besides, I didn't know if they still wanted me," she whispered. Malenie's eyes stung with tears.

The Matriarch lifted Paza's chin gently. "We will always want you."

Like Sarl wanted Colvin back, in spite of everything. "Papa," Malenie asked hesitantly, winding her fingers in her mama's necklace, "why didn't we live with your—our—family?"

"We did live here after you were born, but I didn't get along with the former Suntin Matriarch. She believed we could breed for magic, like the Sarnath Matriarch." He met Lissetta's eyes and her mouth pursed in reluctant agreement. Malenie understood with a little jolt that she must be the result of those beliefs. Pashtin and Suntin across the Wall. Two great families. What else could it be?

"That was Lissetta's aunt," Papa said. "Next we lived with my family, in Pashtin. But Emelenie thought we should live with the Suntins because of the marks on your arms and we argued. It seemed like the only way to stop the arguments was to leave. Once I did, we were both too proud to apologize, and Trader Town needed a healer." He pulled mama's wedding necklace free of her tunic and rubbed the links between his long fingers. "Yasmin came with us to the Gate. She hopes you'll come back to see her, and she told me it's time I talked to you about your mama."

Malenie searched his eyes. They were clear, without the sadness that had prevented Malenie from asking questions in the past. "I'd like that very much."

"Are you ever going to say what you're going to do?" Paza demanded.

Malenie looked at Nes and her sibs. Nes met her gaze, her face a mask. *She doesn't know how much we love her and need her. Just like Paza couldn't tell how much her family loved and needed her. Or me, not able to ask Papa for help. She thinks she'll be out on the streets.* "Only if Nes and her sibs can stay—if they want?" she faltered.

"Nes is a hero, just like you and Paza. She's also one of your callers. She and her brother and sisters are very welcome to stay here. Or we will help her wherever she wishes to go," said Lissetta. "Tal was asking me about Nes's plans, and Sarl has said he'll stay with us for a time. I intend to put him to work, teaching, and Nes and Paza will be an essential part of those lessons."

"Are Tal and Jos staying?" Malenie asked because she knew Nes wanted to and wouldn't.

"Absolutely."

Nes looked at her sibs, their hands held tightly in hers once again, and swallowed heavily. "Then we want to stay."

Everyone turned to look at Papa.

"How could I say no?"

Paza bit her lip and smiled at Malenie almost shyly. "I'm glad," she said quietly.

Malenie beamed up at all the people surrounding her: old family and new; old friends and new, all together, all safe. More of them were alive than she had ever thought possible. She had found Papa, two whole families, Nes had found her sibs and Paza had regained her family. They had saved the world, but...

Malenie sighed. "Papa, I feel like I traveled all over the known world to rescue you and in the end you found me instead!"

"Well, that's true," he said, "but if you hadn't told Emelenie and her guards what had happened, Harashan would still have me and all the kids. That's as much a rescue as if you freed me with your own hands."

"I should say so!" Paza scolded. "Right, Nes?"

"Paza's right. We all helped each other."

"And now we're together again," Malenie said. *I don't have to run anywhere any more.* She took a deep breath and leaned against Papa. The sun shone hot and brilliant on the big stone house and the people around her, but was no match for the joy expanding inside her chest. Her family and friends were her shelter, her home. She had found where she belonged. With them she was safe, and with her magic she could protect them while they protected her in turn. She didn't have to hide any longer. With that thought she turned up the cuffs of her sleeves to show her diamonds to the world, and Papa smiled down at her with approval.

Free short story

Get *The Gift*, a short story about what happens when Malenie and Nes go shopping for a gift for Paza. The story takes place after the events of *The Desert Wall* and is only available to members of my mailing list.

If you sign up, I'll keep you updated about the next book in the series, *The Red Fortress*. I also talk about books I love and will send information about exclusive giveaways and other fun things. My newsletter comes out about once a month. Building a relationship with my readers is one of the best things about being a published author. I'd love to hear from you!

Sign up at www.subscribepage.com/m2h1r6_copy.

Did you enjoy this book?
You can make a big difference.

Leaving a review is one of the most powerful thing a reader can do for a book they enjoyed. Honest reviews help bring a book to the attention of other readers and to retailers' algorithms that decide which books to show people. And that means I can keep writing new books for you to enjoy.

Please consider leaving a quick review (it doesn't have to be long) on the review page where you purchased this book.

Thanks so much!

Raf Morgan

About Raf Morgan

I've been preparing all my life to be a writer, though I didn't know it. Like that time I volunteered to protect sea turtles on a beach in Costa Rica and wound up with half my body in her nest at 3 am with a blue plastic bag under her butt to catch her eggs to relocate them so poachers couldn't find them. Or living in Bangkok, Thailand, which is where I am now for my day job. (I'm from the USA, but I've lived in Mexico, Costa Rica and Nicaragua.) You never know what's going to happen here and every day is an adventure. Once we hired a driver to take us to the beach and he removed the steering wheel from the dashboard. While we were driving!

Mostly I've worked as a technical editor and a Spanish to English translator in the US, Mexico City, Lima, Moscow and Surabaya, but I've also worked as a dog walker (sometimes taking 11 dogs to the park at once, but usually only two or three), on bilingual websites in Bogotá and Montevideo, and in district court (criminal) and family court in the US as an advocate. I've been asked to interpret from Portuguese even though I don't speak Portuguese (it was an emergency) and gotten up at 4 am to edit a meeting report and ended my day at the Bolshoi Theater watching Russian ballet.

My favorite things are long rambling walks, preferably under trees, but a city will do, the smell of rain and a good book. My favorite poetry anthology is *Americans' Favorite Poems*, edited by Robert Pinsky and Maggie Dietz, and don't even ask me to pick a favorite book. I have too many.

Acknowledgements

I wrote this book in 2008, rewrote it in 2012, and decided to publish it in 2018. A lot of people have touched it over the last 10 years, and I'm not going to remember everyone. If I miss your name, that doesn't mean I haven't appreciated your help, support, comments, feedback, reads and re-reads!

In vaguely chronological order: Jill Molloy, Katie Lisa, Joanne H., Teri Duerr and Dania Rajendra read very early versions. Alison Cherry, TJ Volonis and Renée Lasher read it after that. Marcy Collier, Suzi Ryan, Suzy I., Christine H. and Gayle K. gave me feedback on the first chapter at the NJ SCBWI conference in 2011. Melissa Walker might not even remember she helped me with my first query letter! SCBWI friends Ryan Shirilan-Howlett, Axie Oh, Shawn Anderson, Eson Kim and Pam Mayer, and Viable Paradise XVI friends Erik Gern, Theresa, Tam MacNeil, Alison M. and Camille G. all read the almost final version.

Thanks to John Pantuso for formatting the print version and to Sara Lisa for suggesting it.

Jill Molloy and Christian Torres Roje helped me believe I could write again.

Suzanne Grossman, Katina Paron, Will Turnage, Katie, Alison C., Teri, TJ and Dania and many more kept me going.

My Mom and Dad gave me books and love, read to me, made me a reader by example and always had books in our house.

Joanna Penn's The Creative Penn podcast gave me the courage and the tools to plunge into this self-publishing adventure.

Without the encouragement, support and feedback of all these people, I wouldn't be putting this book out into the world now. You all helped me figure out what I was doing with this writing thing.